Books by Irene Hannon

Heroes of Quantico

Against All Odds

An Eye for an Eye

In Harm's Way

Guardians of Justice

Fatal Judgment

Deadly Pursuit

Lethal Legacy

Private Justice

Vanished

Trapped

Deceived

Men of Valor

Buried Secrets

Thin Ice

Tangled Webs

Code of Honor

Dangerous Illusions

Hidden Peril

Dark Ambitions

Triple Threat

Point of Danger

Labyrinth of Lies

Standalone Novels

That Certain Summer

One Perfect Spring

Hope Harbor Novels

Hope Harbor

Sea Rose Lane

Sandpiper Cove

Pelican Point

Driftwood Bay

Starfish Pier

Blackberry Beach

TRIPLE THREAT 2

LABYRINTH OF LIES

IRENE HANNON

Revell

a division of Baker Publishing Group
Grand Rapids, Michigan

© 2021 by Irene Hannon

Published by Revell
a division of Baker Publishing Group
PO Box 6287, Grand Rapids, MI 49516-6287
www.revellbooks.com

Printed in the United States of America

Library of Congress Cataloging-in-Publication Data
Names: Hannon, Irene, author.
Title: Labyrinth of lies / Irene Hannon.
Description: Grand Rapids, Michigan : Revell, a division of Baker Publishing
    Group, [2021] | Series: Triple threat ; #2
Identifiers: LCCN 2021004378 | ISBN 9780800736187 (paperback) | ISBN
    9780800740504 (cloth) | ISBN 9781493431779 (ebook)
Subjects: GSAFD: Romantic suspense fiction.
Classification: LCC PS3558.A4793 L33 2021 | DDC 813/.54—dc23
LC record available at https://lccn.loc.gov/2021004378

21 22 23 24 25 26 27   7 6 5 4 3 2 1

To Tom—
my one and only.

Happy milestone birthday!

May the years ahead be filled with
health, happiness, love . . .
and wondrous new adventures together.

For as Robert Browning said:
The best is yet to be!

1

THEY WANTED HER to take on another undercover gig? No way.

Not happening.

But if both her boss and the head of the Crimes Against Persons unit were ganging up on her, getting out of the assignment would require finesse.

Brain firing on all cylinders, St. Louis County detective Cate Reilly crossed her legs, clenched her hands together in her lap, and surveyed the sergeant behind the desk—and the lieutenant seated beside her. Five seconds. That was all she needed to formulate a diplomatic, persuasive refusal.

Sarge didn't give them to her.

"We're aware you prefer not to do more undercover work, Cate. It's not for everyone, and we appreciate you giving it a try this year." He rested his forearms on his desk and linked his fingers. "But this is a . . . unique . . . situation, so I'd ask you to hear us out. Lieutenant?"

The commander of the unit picked up the cue. "It goes without saying that what we discuss here stays here, no matter how this meeting ends." He locked gazes with her.

"Of course." After ten years with the St. Louis County PD, she knew when to zip her lips.

He gave a curt nod. "Two months ago, Gabe Laurent's seventeen-year-old daughter, Stephanie, disappeared from a private girls' boarding school in the far western portion of our jurisdiction, along the Missouri River. You know who Laurent is, I assume."

"Yes." In an era when badge holders were often painted as the bad guys, every County PD employee was aware of the software executive's staunch—and vocal—commitment to law enforcement. "Why haven't I heard about the girl's disappearance?"

"We were keeping it under wraps until we determined whether it was the runaway situation it appeared to be. Only the detectives assigned to the case were privy to the details."

"*Was* it a runaway?"

The lieutenant shifted in his seat. "That was our conclusion. All the pieces fit. Her backpack was gone. Her boyfriend also went missing—as did *his* backpack and car. Everyone our people spoke with agreed she was troubled and unhappy. That's why her father sent her to Ivy Hill Academy. He didn't like the crowd she was running with—or her boyfriend, slipping grades, and attitude. In addition to being a prestigious all-girl college-prep school with high academic standards, Ivy Hill is known for its rigid discipline."

"Is the investigation still active?"

Sarge leaned back in his chair. "We've been keeping an eye out for her, but it hasn't been our highest priority."

No, it wouldn't be.

Teen runaways were disturbing, but the County's heavy homicide caseload and other serious crime investigations took precedence. The detectives were already stretched thin, and the long hours couldn't expand much more without significant fallout—like a major decline in morale or a mass exodus.

"So why are we talking about it now?"

The lieutenant rejoined the conversation. "We've been asked to dig deeper."

"By whom?"

He held up a hand. "Let me back up first. Gabe Laurent wasn't satisfied with our conclusion or our promise to continue our efforts to locate his daughter as resources allowed. He ended up hiring a PI who turned up one piece of information that suggests there may be more to the story than a mere runaway situation."

Ouch.

That put County in an awkward position.

"What did the PI find?"

"Two days before he disappeared, the boyfriend had been in touch with a counselor at one of the community colleges about registering for the spring term."

O-kay.

That put a whole different spin on the case.

"In other words, he may have taken the backpack for a weekend getaway with his girlfriend, but he wasn't planning to disappear." Cate exhaled.

"That was Gabe Laurent's conclusion."

"This is starting to smell like foul play."

"I agree."

She furrowed her brow. "How did our people miss that nugget?"

"The boyfriend—Alex Johnson—lived with a grandmother who's in poor health and a father who comes and goes . . . mostly to the local bar. The PI happened to be at the apartment talking with the grandmother when a financial assistance application from the school arrived in the mail."

"She knew about his plans?"

"No—nor did the father. Based on what the PI gleaned from the counselor, Alex decided the laborer job he'd taken with a roofing company after high school graduation wasn't going to lead anywhere and intended to continue his education."

Uncovering that key piece of intel may have been a fluke—

and a huge piece of good luck for the PI—but it was distressing nonetheless.

And Sarge and the lieutenant weren't the type to enjoy having egg on their face, deserved or not.

Still . . . an undercover operation? Those kinds of resources were usually reserved for larger-scale operations, like the human trafficking setup she'd helped investigate for her first—and she'd hoped, last—undercover assignment.

"So we're going back to take another look at the case. I get that." She kept her inflection neutral. "What I don't get is the undercover component."

The lieutenant stood and walked over to the window. After a few moments, he pivoted back. "Pressure is being exerted to use every available tool to expedite the investigation. Gabe Laurent wants answers." The man clasped his hands behind his back, his expression neutral save for a flare of . . . annoyance? . . . that tightened his features for a fleeting instant. "He also happens to be a big contributor to the campaigns of his state representative and the County Executive."

Ah.

The man had called in favors. Talked to friends in high places, who'd contacted County—not with demands, but to drop a few strong hints that the case might deserve renewed focus.

Yet it didn't explain the undercover angle.

"Why not just assign more personnel?"

The lieutenant scanned his watch and crossed to the door. "I'll let Sarge explain the particulars to you. I'm already late for another meeting." He swung back to her. "I hope we can count on your help with this."

Without giving her the opportunity to respond, he exited, closing the door behind him.

In the ensuing quiet, her pulse accelerated.

That hadn't been a request.

He wanted her on this job.

Why?

She laced her fingers more tightly together and redirected her attention to Sarge. "You know how I feel about undercover work." One taste had been more than sufficient to dim any allure it may have had. Who knew why it had held such appeal for—

Mashing her lips together, she severed that line of thought. It was pointless to revisit history. Her attempt to figure out what motivated a person to live a life of deception and shadows had been a bust, and it was time to move on.

Past time.

"I know, Cate—but we need you on this one."

She waved his comment aside. "There are plenty of detectives at County who like undercover work. Why not tap one of them?"

"Because you're the only one who can pass for a seventeen-year-old."

Her jaw dropped as she processed that bombshell. "You want me to go in as a *student*?"

"Yes."

"Sarge." She gaped at him. "Let's be serious here. I'm thirty-three. Seventeen is a distant speck in the rearview mirror."

"Not that distant—and age is nothing more than a number. With appropriate hairstyle and clothes, you won't have any difficulty convincing people you're seventeen."

She shook her head. "This is crazy. I could be a seventeen-year-old's *mother*."

"Cate." Sarge leaned forward again. "When were you last carded?"

Dang.

He would bring that up.

She cleared her throat and flicked a speck of lint off her slacks. "I don't drink."

11

"You're avoiding the question."

Okay.

Fine.

She did buy wine on occasion as a gift for party hosts—as Sarge knew, since she'd not only brought a bottle to the retirement barbecue he'd thrown last summer for one of the detectives but joked about having to produce her driver's license for the clerk.

"So I get carded now and then." Like always if she went makeup-free off duty and pulled her hair back into her usual ponytail. "So what?"

He looked at her in silence.

As seconds ticked by, sweat beaded on her upper lip. The moisture in her mouth evaporated. A wave of nausea rolled through her.

Huh.

Who knew that being backed into a corner would have the same effect on her as being trapped in a small space?

Not the best time for her latent claustrophobia to rear its head.

Chest tight, she rose and began to pace. "Maybe the school has nothing to do with this. Stephanie and Alex could have run into trouble away from the campus."

"That's possible—and we'll continue to work that angle with a conventional investigation. But given the high-level interest in this case, we want to cover all the bases—and you know firsthand how much more you can learn from the inside."

Yeah. She did.

If she hadn't befriended the key people in the trafficking case, convinced them she was on their side, the ring would still be operating.

Instead, thanks to the evidence she'd been able to amass, the operation had been shuttered and the leaders rounded up and charged.

"Look at it this way, Cate." Sarge leaned forward, using his most persuasive tone. "If Stephanie told another student where she and her boyfriend planned to go for the weekend—and you can get that girl to confide in you—we can realign our resources. As soon as we have a trail that leads off campus, we'll cut you loose. That could be as fast as a week or two."

She narrowed her eyes. "The trafficking job wasn't supposed to last long, either."

"It didn't—not for an investigation like that."

That might be true . . . but it had felt like forever.

Another reason to write off undercover work.

Hardened as she'd become to violence and gore and man's inhumanity to man during her decade in law enforcement, it was a whole different ball game to live that seaminess every day from the inside.

But the lieutenant and Sarge had presented a compelling case.

She *was* the best candidate in the department to pass for a seventeen-year-old.

And if foul play *was* involved in the girl's disappearance, as the new evidence suggested, they should use every tool at their disposal to track down the truth whether there was political pressure being brought to bear or not.

She let out a long, slow breath. "You're not giving me much choice here."

"Yes, I am. We won't force you to take an undercover assignment. If this isn't a role you think you can pull off, we'll try to come up with an alternative plan. For the record, we did check to see if the school has any open staff or faculty positions. It doesn't. But even if it did, the ideal is to place someone who can talk to the girls—especially Stephanie's roommate—as a peer. A student is the best candidate for that."

His rationale was difficult to refute.

She was stuck.

Much as she disliked undercover work, her passion for justice wasn't going to let her walk away from an opportunity to help solve what appeared to be a crime.

"When would I go in?"

"You'd move into the dorm January 4."

That gave her eight days to psych herself up for the assignment and get up to speed on the players—and her cover story.

"Won't it seem odd for a new student to arrive with one week's notice?" She was stalling, delaying her commitment as long as possible.

But Sarge played along, giving her a minute to adjust to the reality and accept the inevitable. "We've got it covered. Your father's been transferred here, and while he wraps up loose ends on the East Coast and makes arrangements to relocate, he's sending you ahead rather than have you join the spring semester in progress."

"From what I've heard about Ivy Hill's price tag, this operation will require significant up-front money for tuition—unless you're clueing in the administration to our presence."

"We're not—and we'll tap the reserve fund for the tuition."

She did a double take. "We have a reserve fund?"

"So says the lieutenant, and I'm not asking any questions. Finances are his problem. I just go after bad guys. So what's the verdict?"

Her brief reprieve was up.

She exhaled . . . and gave up the fight. "I'll do it."

"Great!" Sarge pushed a bulging file folder across the desk. "Case notes to date. Bone up. And this"—he slid a much slimmer file in her direction—"is your cover. The minute you walk out the door, we'll begin setting this up. We wanted to be certain you were on board first."

She picked up the latter and flipped through the material.

"A lot of work has been put into this." She looked at him. "You knew I'd say yes, didn't you?"

"I thought the odds were in our favor. You like challenges—and you *don't* like puzzles with missing pieces. That's why you're an exceptional detective. I assumed this case would pique your interest enough to overcome your aversion to undercover work—and convince you you're the right person for the job."

"I'm the *only* person."

"You're also the right person. We want someone on this who will dig deep and ferret out the truth, and—pardon the cliché—you're like a dog with a bone when you're on a case."

"I appreciate the compliment if not the analogy." She gathered up the files.

"There is a bright side to this, you know. Going undercover at a cushy girls' school will be a cakewalk compared to the trafficking gig."

"That depends on what I find."

"*If* there's anything to be found. Our team on the street may end up solving this before you do."

"Hold that thought." She transferred the files to the crook of her arm and stood. "I'll let you know if I have any questions after I get up to speed on all this. Any special instructions?"

"Just keep your ear to the ground—and keep this gig under wraps. We're sharing details on a need-to-know basis. The fewer fingers in this, the less risk of leaks." His phone began to ring, and he picked it up. "And do something fun this weekend."

"Already on the books."

Thank goodness.

Maybe the relaxing get-together she'd planned with her two sisters would help her shake the sense of foreboding—and dread—seeping into her pores, so pervasive it seemed almost like a premonition . . . or warning.

Which was ridiculous.

Huffing out a breath, she shifted the weight of the files in her arm and left Sarge's office.

Her nerves were kicking in, that was all. Being a bit spooked was normal in light of her aversion to the mere thought of plunging back into undercover mode.

Yet a caution sign continued to strobe in her mind—as if warning her to beware of sinister secrets lurking in the shadows at the exclusive school slated to become her temporary home.

She shook off a shudder as she entered the office she shared with a fellow detective. Dropped the files onto her desk with a thud.

Too bad she couldn't toss off this assignment as easily.

But she'd agreed to take it on, and backing out wasn't an option. If that young woman had, indeed, gone missing—and the school had played a role in her disappearance—someone posing as a student would be in an ideal position to find the truth.

As for the unnerving vibes coursing through her?

She'd control them as best she could . . . but she'd also listen to her gut.

So just in case the challenges waiting for her ended up being far more formidable than simply convincing everyone she was seventeen, she'd go into this assignment on high alert . . . and she wouldn't let her guard down until she left Ivy Hill—and her student persona—behind forever.

2

"HAT WRAPS UP THE TOUR." Richard Tucker opened the door that led from the school's main corridor to the Ivy Hill administrative offices. "I'm sorry more staff members weren't around for you to meet, but this place is a ghost town over Christmas break."

"Understandable." Zeke Sloan followed the president into the office suite, giving it another discreet perusal. The place was functional, but the original artwork, mahogany furniture, and custom rugs on the polished hardwood floor spoke of a solid financial base.

Not a luxury many private schools had these days.

"I'll introduce you to the rest of the faculty at our staff meeting next Friday and—" A door to the right opened, and Richard swung toward it. "Will! I thought you'd left for the day."

A uniformed, fiftyish balding man who could use a few extra trips to the gym paused. "I decided to make one more circuit."

Richard smiled. "I've been raving to our new Spanish teacher here about the dedication of our faculty and staff. Thank you for giving witness to that. Zeke, meet Will Fischer,

Ivy Hill's director of security. Will, this is Zeke Martinez, who'll be filling in for Teresa while she recovers."

Zeke took the hand the other man extended as Richard introduced him with his new name, returning the security chief's lukewarm squeeze as they exchanged conventional pleasantries.

"How's Teresa doing?" Will directed the question to Richard.

"The infection is finally under control, but it set her rehab back by weeks." Richard shook his head. "A car accident, broken bones, surgery, and then an infection. Not her best Christmas. We're lucky to have found someone with Zeke's credentials on such short notice."

Not to mention his pedigree—essential for a school like this.

Richard was too discreet to put that into words, but they both knew Zeke had been a perfect fit on many levels for the position.

"I consider myself the fortunate one." Zeke slipped his hands into the Brioni trousers that spelled class—and breeding.

For all he knew, his clothes alone had landed him this job.

But his credentials were also impeccable.

At this stage, though, whatever qualification—or combination of qualifications—had secured the position was irrelevant.

He was in.

That was all that mattered.

"How did you hear about the job, anyway?" Will squinted at him, a hint of wariness in his demeanor.

Hmm.

Perhaps not everyone was as convinced as the school president that the new Spanish teacher was here through a lucky coincidence—nor as happy about his presence.

Then again, security types tended to be suspicious.

"A combination of circumstances and connections." He maintained an easy, conversational tone. "My mother has a friend in St. Louis who knows the injured teacher, and she mentioned the accident—and Ivy Hill—to her in a phone conversation a couple of weeks ago while I was visiting. It seemed like a good fit during my own recovery from a messy Jeep crash."

"You're not from this area?"

"No. Nor from the States these days. I grew up in Denver, but my father returned to Spain after my parents divorced. I joined his extreme adventure firm nine years ago—but the accident has temporarily sidelined me."

The man's eyes narrowed. "Taking people kayaking or hang gliding is a far cry from teaching."

"My undergraduate degree is in secondary education. I taught for a few years in Spain at a private boys' school before joining my father's firm. It will be a pleasant change of pace to return to my roots for a few weeks—or however long Ivy Hill requires my services."

Richard flashed him a silent apology. "I've thoroughly vetted Zeke's credentials, Will, and the board is delighted he accepted the interim position. Finding a qualified Spanish teacher on such short notice was a godsend."

"Sorry." A faint flush tinted the other man's cheeks. "I didn't mean to overstep or give offense."

"None taken." Zeke called up another smile. "I think it's admirable for staff members to be concerned about the quality of the faculty." He checked his watch. "Richard, if we're finished for the day, I do have an engagement this evening."

"Of course. This is still the holiday season, after all. Let me show you out." He retrieved Zeke's Brooks Brothers wool topcoat from a rack near the door. "Will, are you staying for a while?"

"No. I'm almost finished with my circuit."

"I'll swing by before I go to turn off lights."

"Okay. Welcome to Ivy Hill, Zeke." With a clipped nod, the security director exited into the main hall, closing the door behind him.

Richard waited while Zeke slid his arms into the coat and retrieved the folder of information the man had passed on earlier. "Will's a bit on the worrywart side, with a tendency to be overly suspicious—but those are admirable qualities for a director of security. And he's also been a little high-strung since he separated from his wife a few months back. I hope you'll cut him some slack."

"No worries." Zeke followed the president into the corridor and toward the main door. "I doubt our paths will cross much."

"True. Have you found a place to live yet?"

"Yes. A corporate housing firm arranged a short-term lease for me on a condo at the western end of Chesterfield."

"Perfect. That won't be a long commute." Richard pushed open the main door. "Enjoy your evening, and I'll see you here next Friday at the staff meeting."

"In the meantime, my work is cut out for me—bone up on lesson plans and school information." He lifted the bulging folder.

"I suspect you'll be a fast study."

Yeah, he would—in terms of staff and faculty backgrounds. He was already fully briefed on the players.

The lesson plans, however, would require total focus for the next week or he was going to tank at this job.

And after all the work that had gone into securing this position, he wasn't going to flunk out before he'd gotten what he'd come for.

"What do you mean, you're going back undercover?" Eve froze, mug of coffee poised an inch from her lips.

Ignoring her, Cate picked up another piece of the world-class baklava her youngest sibling had brought to the Reilly sisters' gathering and meticulously gathered up the crumbs. "This is spectacular as usual, Grace. I wish you made it more than once a year."

"It's too time-consuming—and don't change the subject. I thought you said never again?" Grace set her fork down beside her plate, the moussaka Eve had contributed forgotten.

"It was a special circumstance."

"What does that mean?" Eve shifted the mug away from her mouth and leaned forward.

"Down, girl. This is not a media interview." Cate tried for a teasing tone. "And before you jump in"—she turned to Grace—"save that forensic pathologist curiosity of yours for people who can't talk back. I'm not at liberty to discuss the case. I only told you about it to keep you from worrying when I don't respond to your calls and texts."

Eve and Grace exchanged glances.

"I don't like this." Eve took a sip of coffee and skewered her with one of the probing, razor-sharp looks she usually reserved for unsuspecting guests on her drive-time talk radio show. "Did they strong-arm you into this?"

Sort of.

But she *was* the logical choice for the job.

"The term strong-arming may be too . . . strong." She shrugged, as if the assignment was no big deal. "I fit the criteria for this particular investigation."

"Do you *want* to do this?" Grace joined the inquisition.

"I want lawbreakers to pay for their crimes. If going undercover is what it takes to get justice in this case—so be it."

Her conviction sounded so convincing she almost fooled *herself* into believing she was fine with her decision.

Almost.

Her sisters, however, seemed to buy her assurance.

"How long is this going to last?" Grace jabbed her fork into the last bite of her cooling moussaka.

"As long as it takes."

"Will you be here for my birthday next month? The big three-oh only comes around once."

"And we can't celebrate properly without you," Eve added.

"I'll do my best. You know I try to make every family gathering."

But her sisters weren't concerned about her missing the landmark birthday.

They were concerned about *her*.

Her vision blurred, and she swallowed past the lump that formed in her throat.

What would she do without Eve and Grace? With Mom gone all these years, and Dad doing a stint as a visiting professor at Cambridge, the three of them were tighter than ever. Siblings, yes, but also best friends.

So of course they'd worry about their big sister—especially after her negative comments about her previous undercover assignment.

Yet much as she dreaded this job, she could handle it. While the trafficking case had soured her on undercover work, it had also boosted her confidence that she had the acting chops to handle whatever was thrown at her.

And she had to convince her sisters of that. Vanquish the sudden pall that had fallen over their holiday get-together.

"Hey." She waited until she had their full attention. "Stop worrying. I have the skills for the job, and the environment is much nicer than my previous gig. You could almost say cushy. I'll be fine. And I'll be back in the ranks of regular detectives very soon."

"Until the next undercover job comes along." Eve wrapped her fingers around her mug, mouth flat.

"Sarge knows this is a one-off."

"You said that after the last undercover job."

"This time I mean it. I was very clear about that. The stars just aligned for this one in a way that made me the right person to handle it. If I said no, there's a reasonable possibility the truth would never be found—and that doesn't sit well with the truth-seeking gene we all share. Look at the careers we chose."

"At least my clients don't carry guns or knives or other lethal weapons." Grace skewered a piece of baklava and transferred it to her plate.

"Of course not. They're dead." Eve shuddered. "I couldn't do what you do every day if they paid me a million bucks a year."

"I *wish* it was that lucrative."

"It should be. There isn't enough money in the world to compensate people who are willing to cut up dead bodies."

"I don't do it for the money."

"Lucky thing. And as for Cate"—Eve pointed to her—"they don't pay her enough either to hang out with the dregs of society."

"I'll pass that on to Sarge." Cate took a swig of her Diet Sprite. "You guys up for a game of Scrabble?" If a cutthroat round of their favorite board game didn't distract her sisters, nothing would.

"I'm in." Grace washed down a bite of baklava with the last of the high-end mango iced tea she favored.

"Me too." Eve gathered up their empty plates and stood. "You want these in the dishwasher?"

"Yeah. Thanks. I'll go get the game." Cate rose and headed for the hall.

"Wait. When does this undercover job start?"

At Grace's question, Cate pivoted. Over the counter that separated the small kitchen from the eating area, Eve had angled toward her to hear the answer too.

"Next Friday."

"You're coming over on New Year's Eve, aren't you?" Eve propped a shoulder against the wall, the determined set of her jaw brooking no argument.

"I don't know. I feel funny about barging in on a newly engaged couple."

"The Reillys always get together on New Year's Eve."

"Things change—as that four-day-old ring on your finger demonstrates."

Eve lifted her left hand, lips curving as she examined the sparkling solitaire. "Some change is positive." She lowered her hand, smile vanishing. "But it doesn't have to alter a family tradition. What excuse will you use next year? That we're newlyweds, and you don't want to barge in then either?"

"You're getting married in May. You won't be newlyweds next New Year's Eve."

"Actually . . . according to everything I've read on the internet, a husband and wife are considered newlyweds for one year after their marriage," Grace offered.

"You read about wedding stuff online?" Cate stared at her.

"I can hope, can't I? Don't you want to find a hot guy like Eve did and be blissfully happy? Have a real home with a yard and porch swing instead of this one-bedroom, bare-bones apartment?"

"For as much time as I spend here, this place suffices. And I can be blissfully happy without a hot guy. You can too."

"True—but maybe I can be even happier *with* one."

"You should go read a few books about female empowerment."

"Hey—I'm empowered. How many women cut up dead bodies for a living, as our middle sibling so elegantly put it?"

Eve wrinkled her nose. "I'm not sure that's empowerment. It's kind of ghoulish if you ask me."

"I'm blazing a trail. *That's* empowerment." Grace stuck out her tongue at Eve.

"Whatever." Eve waved a dismissive hand at their youngest sister. "Back to the subject at hand. You're both coming for dinner, right?"

"I am." Grace brushed a few crumbs from the table into a neat pile.

"Are you certain Brent is on board with the plan?" Cate crossed her arms. "I mean, he's a great guy and all, but I bet he'd rather have you to himself on New Year's Eve."

"He's fine with the plan. Better than fine, to tell you the truth. He hasn't had many family traditions in his life, so he's looking forward to being part of one—and I have the document to prove it." She pulled a folded sheet of paper from the pocket of her jeans and passed it across the counter to Grace with a smug look.

Grace gave it a quick scan, grinned, and held it out.

Cate returned to the table, took the paper, and read the handwritten message.

Cate and Grace—

Eve tells me you're concerned about intruding on our New Year's Eve celebration. Don't be. I'm all for family gatherings. And remember—Eve and I will have the whole next day all to ourselves to welcome the new year privately.

Brent

"Satisfied?" Eve smirked at her.

Leave it to the host of a controversial radio show to anticipate and prepare for every counterargument—and secure documented proof for her position.

"Fine. I'll come." She handed the paper back to her sister.

Eve slid the note in her pocket. "So how are we supposed to keep in touch with you while you're on this undercover job?"

They were back to that.

"I'll have a handler again. As soon as I get contact information, I'll pass it on. And FYI, my gig is being shared on a strict need-to-know basis, so keep it under wraps."

Eve picked up the dishcloth and swiped the counter. "Is Brent in the loop?"

Logical question, since he was also a County detective.

"He may know I'm undercover, but I doubt he'll be up to speed on the details, if that's what you're asking."

"So much for my inside source." Heaving an exaggerated sigh, Eve went back to stacking dishes.

"If there are no further questions"—Cate continued down the hall to discourage any—"I'll get the game."

But as she rummaged through the closet in her bedroom, the muted conversation between her sisters drifted toward her.

". . . not telling us?" The tail end of Grace's comment registered, and Cate tiptoed back to the door. Cocked her ear.

". . . much as she can. But it doesn't . . . as dangerous as the . . . earlier this year."

It was hard to hear Eve, who was farther away, in the kitchen.

"I hope not—but she hated that other assignment. I can't believe they talked her into doing this again."

"I don't know why . . . first time. She ever open up to you about . . . to do that?"

"No."

"I think . . . complicated . . . ever shared with us."

"That's possible—but you know Cate. She can play her cards close to her vest."

"Yeah, and despite her . . . I'm worried."

"Me too. I don't have a warm and fuzzy feeling about this whole thing."

The murmured conversation continued, but Cate retreated, guilt nipping at her conscience. Eavesdropping was wrong, even if she was only trying to figure out how to spare her sisters further worry.

But that was going to be difficult to do, in view of Grace's last comment.

Besides, how was she supposed to dispel her sisters' bad feelings about this assignment when she had the same negative vibes?

Think positive, Cate. Banish pessimistic thoughts.

Excellent advice.

She reached up to the shelf in the closet for the Scrabble game and tried to look at the bright side.

It was possible they were all fretting unnecessarily.

Maybe there was nothing ominous at all going on at Ivy Hill.

Maybe whatever trouble Stephanie and her boyfriend had run into had happened off campus.

Maybe the concurrent traditional investigation would solve this case fast and she could return to her normal life.

However this played out, she'd be fine, just as she'd assured her sisters.

But her confidence wavered when she lost her grip on the Scrabble game and it fell to the floor, contents scattering all directions.

For as she dropped to her knees and began gathering up the wayward tiles, the cause of her clumsiness became apparent.

Her hands were shaking.

She closed her eyes.

This was not good.

She had to get a grip, corral the apprehension swirling through her.

Tracking down criminals was what she did, and if there were secrets in the bowels of Ivy Hill, she'd unearth them. That was her mandate, and she wouldn't fail.

Clamping her teeth together, she tightened her ponytail and captured the last wayward tile. Threw it in the box.

In six days, when she walked into that exclusive school as a student, she'd be ready to tackle the challenge—no matter how many pep talks she had to give herself or how many psychological games she had to play between now and then.

Because two missing teens deserved her best effort—and she was *not* going to let them down.

———

Selling his soul to the devil had been the biggest mistake of his life.

And that was saying a lot, considering his track record.

"Will? Did you hear me? I need another favor."

Will knocked back another gin and tonic, set the empty glass on the counter, and pressed the cell tighter against his ear. "I thought you said after our last arrangement we'd be done."

"The location is working out well." The voice had a strange timbre to it, as it had during previous calls. The person on the other end must be using a voice-changing device to disguise his—or her—identity.

"Is it? What about the student who went missing in October on one of the nights you used the facility? I'm guessing there's a connection."

"She ran away."

"How do you know?"

"That's what the police concluded."

"Is it true?"

"Does it matter?"

Will began to sweat. "Yeah. It does."

"It's not your problem."

"I don't like being in the dark—or being used."

"Being in the dark is safer . . . and you were happy to use my money when you were desperate for cash. Call this payback."

More like extortion.

He balled the fingers of his free hand. "I should have come clean instead."

"And lost your job? Perhaps gone to prison?"

"In hindsight, that may have been preferable."

"A moot point at this stage. Are our January 2 and 3 target dates still workable?"

"Yes."

"Some personal reconnaissance in advance to ensure the area is clear would be advisable."

So there *was* a connection between Stephanie Laurent's disappearance and whatever illegal activity was taking place on Ivy Hill property.

His heart stuttered, and fear congealed in his belly. "I don't make a habit of tramping around the grounds. It would look suspicious."

"You have a perfect excuse. In light of the disappearance in October, you think it makes sense to have physical eyes on all parts of the property rather than rely on a few security cameras. Add a day and evening circuit of the grounds to the routine— and schedule yourself for the night shift on certain dates."

Stomach churning, Will slid onto a stool at the counter and dropped his head into his hand.

Leaving a duplicate key under a rock for the lock on the gate to the remote dirt access road and dealing with the security camera for that entrance were one thing.

A physical patrol in that area, however, put him too close to the scene of whatever was taking place.

If only he could rewind the clock, refuse the lifeline that had been offered.

But desperation could short-circuit brain cells.

Logic should have told him that once his so-called savior had blackmail material, the persecution could go on forever. That he could be forced to continue aiding and abetting whatever illegal activity was taking place.

Making the lifeline he'd welcomed an ever-tightening noose.

"Will? You with me?"

He filled his lungs. "Yeah."

"I can count on you?"

What choice did he have? He was in too deep to backtrack.

"Yeah."

"Good."

The line went dead.

After a moment, Will stabbed the end button.

What was he going to do?

If Suz ever got wind of how he'd managed to meet her ultimatum, she'd never come back to him.

And he couldn't handle that. After twenty-six years of marriage, life without her was empty. Living in this cramped apartment, eating frozen dinners, going to bed alone night after night—it stunk.

Their six-month trial separation would be up in five weeks, and he couldn't risk exposure at this stage or he'd lose her forever.

Meaning he had to do what his anonymous rescuer demanded.

And really, even with an added patrol, his part in whatever was going on was minuscule. How accountable could he be for the nefarious activity taking place? He knew nothing.

Except that a girl—and her boyfriend—were missing.

A tremor snaked through him, and he reached for the bottle of gin again.

Hesitated.

That might not be the best idea. It would be too easy to start relying on booze to smooth out the rough edges in his life.

And he sure didn't need to add another vice to the one that had plunged him deep into the murky waters of deception—where he was sinking fast.

3

WHAT IN BLAZES was Cate Reilly doing at Ivy Hill Academy?

Sucking in a breath, Zeke took a quick step backward, around the corner in the hall. Dropped to one knee on the pretense of tying a shoelace. Leaned forward slightly until the woman with long auburn hair and her middle-aged male companion standing near the reception desk in the distance were visible.

Could his eyes be deceiving him?

Was that Cate?

He squinted at her profile, tracing the aquiline nose, strong chin, graceful neck.

She wasn't wearing her usual ponytail—but yeah. It was Cate.

Eight years may have passed since he'd last seen her, but a man didn't forget the only woman who'd ever managed to infiltrate his defenses and make him second-guess his choices.

But why had he run into her here, of all places?

And how was he supposed to play this?

"Everything okay, Zeke?" Richard clapped a hand on his shoulder as the other faculty members spilling out of the conference room detoured around them.

"Yes." He finished retying his shoe and stood, shifting into wing-it mode. "Lace came undone. I wouldn't want to trip in front of my new colleagues and lose face the first day." He called up a grin.

Richard chuckled. "I hear you—but they're a forgiving bunch. Are you joining us for lunch?"

That had been the plan. If he wanted to get to know his coworkers, begin laying the groundwork for relationships that could produce useful information, he should take advantage of every opportunity for social interaction.

Except a more urgent priority had arisen.

"I hope so, but I have to deal with an issue my new landlord texted me about during the meeting." The lie tripped off his tongue, deception second nature to him after all these years. "May I join you in progress if I can resolve this quickly?"

"Of course. I'll be delayed myself. I have to do a meet-and-greet with a new student. No one will mark you tardy if you're late." With a wink and a grin, he continued around the corner, out of sight.

After a few moments, Zeke checked on his progress.

He was heading toward Cate and her companion.

As he watched, Richard shook hands with the man, then with Cate, and motioned them down the hall, toward his office.

Toward him.

Zeke backtracked to the deserted conference room, slipped inside, and shut the door behind him, replaying Richard's words.

A meet-and-greet with a new student.

Not computing.

Unless Cate had a daughter she'd never bothered to mention, that story didn't add up.

He needed answers.

Keeping tabs on the closed door, he pulled out his cell and keyed in the contact number reserved for emergencies.

Like this one.

Because unless he could find out what was going on and take proactive measures to protect himself, Cate Reilly could ruin everything.

———————

She did *not* want to be here.

Heaving a sigh, Cate plopped onto the twin bed she'd been assigned in a dorm room, scooted back against the wall, and wrapped her arms around her knees.

At least the meeting with the president yesterday had gone well. He'd seemed to buy the story the fellow detective posing as her father had told him.

Now all she had to do was figure out what had happened to Stephanie.

Piece of cake, right?

Ha.

Despite Sarge's reassurance, this could end up being a long gig.

And until there was a break in this case that would let her get back to her normal routine of homicide and murder investigations, she was stuck here.

So what could she do to expedite the process?

Unfortunately, not much today other than wander around and get the lay of the land. Classes didn't start until Monday, and most of the students wouldn't arrive until tomorrow.

She wiggled into a more comfortable position, tension thrumming through her nerve endings.

Strange to be at loose ends on a Saturday. If she was home, she'd either be working or catching up on all the personal errands that got relegated to the weekends. Sitting around felt wasteful. Unproductive. Frustrating.

She drummed her finger against her knee and surveyed the leaden sky through the window.

A hike around the grounds could be useful—but braving the biting wind and the hint of ice in the air held zero appeal. Mom's fault. The Athens-born matriarch of the Reilly family had passed on her preference for warm, sunny Mediterranean weather to her firstborn.

So why not save the outdoor activity for tomorrow? Give the textbooks for the classes she'd be taking another pass?

Especially trigonometry.

Math may have been a breeze back in high school, but cosines and secants felt like a foreign language at this stage of her life. Putting in a few hours over the weekend on—

The door opened, and a slender teen with cornrows and guarded brown eyes entered, toting a bulging duffel bag.

Her roommate.

Last she'd heard, though, the girl wasn't expected until tomorrow.

But having an extra day to get acquainted before classes began was a bonus.

"Hey." The girl stopped inside the door, lowered the duffel to the floor, and gave her a cautious once-over.

"Hey." She stayed where she was. "You must be Kayla."

No question about it.

Her "father's" request that she be paired with a diverse roommate to broaden her exposure to other demographics and enhance her ethnic sensitivity had almost guaranteed she'd be assigned to bunk with Kayla Harris, given the limited minority population in the student body.

The very same Kayla who'd been Stephanie's roommate

during the other girl's short tenure—and who now had an empty bed in her room.

"Yeah. You're Cate, right?"

"Uh-huh."

"They told me your name at check-in. When did you get here?"

"Yesterday. Dad dumped me and took off back to the East Coast."

Kayla lifted her duffel again. "It's not a bad place to get dumped."

A predictable response, based on the information in the girl's background file.

The seventeen-year-old junior from the impoverished north side of St. Louis was here on one of the few grants offered to promising students from lower-income families, established at the urging of Reverend Tyrone Wilson, a longtime member of the school's board of trustees and the prominent pastor of a church on the north side.

Thanks to her strong standardized test scores—and Reverend Wilson's recommendation—Kayla had been offered the opportunity to profit from the excellent education Ivy Hill offered. An opportunity her parents had encouraged her to pursue.

But while her record here was impeccable and her grades high, she wasn't a joiner. Her name was nowhere to be found in the school's roster of clubs or sports teams.

In other words, she kept to herself—and kept her nose clean.

If any student had been privy to inside info on Stephanie, however, she could be the one—even if she *had* been away on a retreat the weekend of the disappearance and wouldn't be able to offer any insight about that.

Kayla hauled the duffel to her side of the room and heaved it onto the bed in silence.

After debating her next move, Cate leaned over and pulled a pack of cigarettes from her purse.

Kayla glanced toward her as the cellophane wrapper crinkled, twin furrows creasing her brow. "You can't smoke here."

"Who'll know?" She shook one out.

The girl faced her. "I don't want trouble."

"So don't smoke." Cate shrugged and fished around for a lighter.

"Listen . . ." The teen took a step closer, panic flaring in her eyes. "I don't wanna get busted, okay? The class mom can smell smoke like an elephant smells water."

That would be Marian Howard, the pleasant, sixtyish widow who'd shown her to her room yesterday. The quiet, wouldn't-hurt-a-flea type.

"I met her yesterday. She seemed pretty laid-back."

"Not about smoking. Her husband died of lung cancer and she hates cigarettes. If you want to smoke, go out in the woods like my other roommate did."

Ah.

Two useful pieces of information.

Kayla stayed on the straight and narrow—and she followed the rules.

Stephanie didn't—and she disappeared into the woods to break them.

"She get caught? Is that why she's gone?" Cate shoved the cigarette she didn't want back into her purse, where it would stay. The prop had served its purpose.

"No." Kayla turned back to her bed. "She ran away."

"Yeah? How come her parents didn't haul her back here?"

"She's still gone."

"You mean she, like, disappeared?"

"Yeah." Kayla zipped open her duffel bag. "With her boyfriend."

"That is so lit." According to her research, *lit* was a common teen expression for amazing—but in view of the odd vernacular high schoolers used these days, she'd have to dispense her slang sparingly. Enough to sell her role, but not enough to make an inadvertent mistake.

"No. It's stupid." Kayla began yanking out clothes with more force than necessary. "She shoulda talked to Reverend Wilson instead of Mr. Evans if she had issues."

"Who are they?"

But she already knew.

In addition to being a trustee, the reverend was also the school's chaplain. Noah Evans was one of two guidance/career counselors.

"Chaplain and counselor."

"Why shouldn't she have gone to Evans?"

Kayla continued unpacking, keeping her back turned.

Several seconds ticked by.

"Kayla?"

"Just stay away from Evans."

"Why?"

Silence.

"Fine. I'd rather listen to music than talk anyway." Cate retrieved her earbuds, plugged them into her phone, and called up a tune from the latest teen heartthrob.

But she lowered the volume as she planned her strategy.

If Stephanie had gone into the woods to smoke, a hike around the property would have to move up on her priority list, cold weather or not.

And despite Kayla's warning, she wasn't going to avoid Noah Evans. Just the opposite, after her roommate's loaded comment.

As soon as school started, she'd find an excuse to seek him out and see what he knew about a missing student who'd gone to him for guidance—but perhaps had gotten something else entirely.

"What do you mean, that's it?" Phone to ear, Zeke began to pace in the living room of the high-end condo where he'd be spending his free hours until he finished the Ivy Hill job.

"I mean, that's it. Confirmation of employment with the County PD. Period."

Translation? Cate was at the school on official business. In an undercover role, from what he'd observed.

But why would she do that? She'd never had any interest in clandestine work.

He raked his fingers through his hair. "What happened to interagency cooperation? Can't someone pull strings? Go higher? Find out what she's doing there?"

"If I push too hard, they'll want to know why we want to know. You want us to spill *our* operation?"

Checkmate.

Too much effort had been invested in this setup to risk any leaks.

"Fine. I'll get my own answers."

"Whatever she's doing there, she won't want to jeopardize her position either."

"I'm aware of that." He paused at the window as ice pellets began pinging against the glass.

Wonderful.

The commute tomorrow morning for the first day of school was going to be a bear.

"I'll work some other contacts discreetly on my end, but you may get answers faster from the source."

"Yeah." Zeke rubbed his temple, where a headache was beginning to throb. "Thanks."

"Good luck—and keep us in the loop."

"That's the plan."

Zeke ended the call, slid the cell back into his pocket, and retrieved a soda from the fridge. Popping the tab, he wandered through the rooms filled with upscale furnishings.

Quite an improvement over most of the places he'd set up camp in during the past eight years.

He could get used to this sort of environment, though, now that the shadowy, dangerous existence he'd once embraced was beginning to wear on him—as veterans had warned him it would.

Like it or not, and despite his commitment to his job, burnout was setting in.

He stopped at the window again, shifting his weight off his bum leg.

It would be easy to blame his current mental state on the injury that had sidelined him, but that would be a lie. The truth was, he'd begun to consider changing course months ago. This assignment should have been the perfect chance to think through next steps in his career without the distraction of having to watch his back constantly.

In fact, his boss had billed the job as a cakewalk compared to his previous roles.

But that was before Cate had entered the picture.

Cate.

He sipped his soda and stared into the darkness.

How many times had he thought of her through the years? Pictured that glorious, dark auburn hair . . . those intense eyes that could burn with passion . . . the firm mouth that had yielded so appealingly beneath his?

How many times, as he lay awake in a grungy, sweltering fleabag motel, his pistol inches from his fingers, tensing at every squeak in the hall, had he calmed his jitters by calling up memories of her soft skin, the silkiness of her hair, the gentle touch of her fingers against his face?

Too many to count.

More than he wanted to admit.

Because after they'd parted on that long-ago day in the park beneath a blaze of autumn color, he'd vowed to put her out of his mind. To focus only on the priority which, at that stage of his life, had superseded everything else.

He took another swig of the sweet beverage—but the fizzy soft drink left a sour taste in his mouth.

Maybe, if he'd been able to explain to her about the demons that drove him, she'd have understood why he'd chosen to take an unexpected opportunity to switch career paths over their relationship.

Maybe.

But the hurt inside him had run too deep.

The *guilt* ran too deep.

And dredging up the courage to expose his shame to a woman like Cate, who was all about honor and integrity and principles, had eluded him.

So he'd broken her heart instead.

Another source of guilt.

Headlights arced across his window, and he jerked back, every muscle stiffening.

Overkill, Sloan.

Right.

The reflexive self-defense moves that were force of habit after all his years in law enforcement shouldn't be necessary on this job.

He rotated his shoulders until the rigid line softened.

As long as he maintained his cover at Ivy Hill, no one should come gunning for him.

Which brought him back to Cate.

Tomorrow they were going to meet face-to-face.

He was forewarned and ready.

She wasn't.

A plan to get her alone so they could hash out what was

40

going on was already forming in his mind—but it all hinged on her reaction when she saw him.

If she was well trained . . . if her acting skills were strong . . . if she was able to think fast and mask her surprise . . . they could pull this off.

If she wasn't?

They could both be hosed.

4

WHAT IN THE WORLD . . . ?!
From her slouched position in a seat near the back of the classroom, Cate stifled a gasp as the tall, dark-haired man who'd once been the center of her universe entered and strode to the desk in front.

Zeke Sloan was the Spanish teacher at Ivy Hill Academy?

No.

Impossible.

Teresa Medina taught Spanish here—and Zeke's name was nowhere in the dossier of school personnel the department had prepared for her.

Heart banging against her rib cage, Cate sank lower in her seat.

What was going on?

In light of the murmur that rippled through the students as Zeke faced them, she wasn't the only one surprised by his presence.

"Good morning, ladies." He gave the room a commanding sweep and displayed one of those half-hitch smiles that used to turn her to mush. "As you can see, I'm not Ms. Medina. Complications from the injuries she suffered in her car accident have delayed her return. I'm Zeke Martinez, her temporary replacement."

As he finished the explanation and introduced himself with an unfamiliar surname, his gaze lingered on hers.

There was no flicker of recognition or acknowledgment in his eyes.

But he knew who she was, despite the blood-red streak she'd added to her hair and the dark eye makeup that wasn't part of her usual beauty routine.

You didn't give a man your heart without learning to read his every nuance.

Yet he wasn't surprised by her presence.

Why not?

Who had tipped him off she was here?

Why was he using a fake name?

What had caused the barely detectable limp in his authoritative gait?

Was he at Ivy Hill on an undercover assignment for the DEA job that had sabotaged their relationship?

If so, how much did he know about *her* case?

As questions raced through her mind, she dipped her chin and fiddled with the cap on her pen.

She had to calm down. Play this cool. Zeke obviously didn't intend to expose her. She owed him the same courtesy.

At least until she had a handle on what was going on.

Somehow she managed to function during the class, introducing herself when it was her turn, calling up the rudimentary Spanish Zeke himself had taught her, which had proven useful on a number of investigations.

But getting through the test he passed out—designed to assess the competence level of the class, he said—was a challenge. Speaking Spanish was one thing. Writing it, another.

As the students worked on the quiz in silence, Zeke circled the room, pausing here and there to look over a girl's shoulder. Sometimes he asked a question or offered a suggestion in the husky-timbre voice that used to set her nerve endings aflutter.

Used to being the operative term.

She tightened her grip on her pen, focused on the sheet in front of her, and willed her pulse to behave as he started up her aisle from the rear.

Zeke Sloan was history.

This intersection of their lives was nothing more than a piece of bad luck—for both of them.

He may have been alerted to her presence in advance of this class, but he couldn't be any happier than she was about the freaky combination of circumstances that had put them in the same orbit.

She kept writing on the paper in front of her, but she knew the instant he stopped behind her. The sense of his nearness was so acute she had to forcibly regulate her respiration to keep from hyperventilating.

"You may want to rethink that word, Ms. Sheppard." His long, lean finger entered her field of vision as he pointed to one of her scribbles.

And when he leaned down to offer a few suggestions in Spanish, the warmth of his breath caressed her cheek.

Or was that wishful thinking?

Cate clamped her teeth together and banished that errant thought.

She did *not* wish to be close to Zeke ever again.

They were over.

Done.

Even if the man's close proximity was awakening unruly, traitorous hormones.

He moved on, but she kept her head down. Until she regrouped and got her emotions under control, focusing on his broad shoulders, muscled torso, and those impressive biceps straining against the fabric of his dress shirt could be dangerous.

Somehow she made it through the interminable class—but the minute it was over she sped toward the door.

Someone in the department needed to research this new development ASAP.

Hefting her book-filled backpack into a more comfortable position, she half jogged toward the cafeteria, detouring toward the door that led to the courtyard where students congregated in warm weather. It ought to be deserted in January—the perfect place to call her handler . . . aka father.

Even if someone did venture out, there was no rule against calling family—and the cell number was registered in his name. In fact, if anyone happened to check her phone log, all the calls would appear legit.

She dropped her backpack beside the door . . . waited until the hall cleared . . . and exited.

A shiver rolled through her.

Mercy, it was cold out here!

She tucked herself into a small alcove that offered a modicum of protection from the biting wind and leaned against the frigid stone wall.

Her handler answered on the second ring, and she gave him a quick briefing.

"I remember Zeke from his County days, before the DEA recruited him. Let me see what I can find out. I'll text you once I have information, and you can call me back."

"Thanks." She ended the call, slipped back inside, and picked up her backpack.

As she stowed her phone in a side pocket, the edge of a piece of paper tucked in another compartment caught her eye.

She pulled it out, hoisted the backpack into position, and opened the folded sheet.

Library. 4:30. Bring Spanish textbook.

No signature—but the cryptic note didn't require one.

Zeke had pulled an impressive sleight-of-hand trick to get this in her backpack without anyone noticing.

So much for the after-school hike she'd planned around the property.

She continued toward the cafeteria, appetite vanishing as the looming meeting with the man she'd once expected to marry sent a shaft of tension spiraling through her.

Whatever his story—personal or professional—it was imperative she remember why she was here and do nothing to threaten her cover. If she let Zeke's presence distract her, she could make mistakes. Assuming there were links to foul play within these walls, a slip of any kind could put both her investigation—and herself—at risk.

Ivy Hill might be cushier than her last gig, but she couldn't discount the possibility of danger.

Because the more time that passed, the less chance the two missing teens would surface unscathed. More likely, they'd come to a bad end.

And if someone was willing to kill two innocent young people for motives yet to be determined, that same someone wouldn't hesitate to kill an undercover detective who got in the way—or got too close to the truth.

So no matter what Zeke had to say, she'd keep her emotions to herself and make it clear that as far as she was concerned, the teacher/student role play that had allowed them to infiltrate this institution was the only thing they had in common.

He could do his job, she would do hers—and they'd steer clear of each other as much as possible in the process.

End of story.

———————

Wolf ducked into a doorway, pulled out his latest burner phone, and turned up the collar of his coat against the icy wind.

The day he could leave this kind of weather behind forever couldn't come too soon.

And with his nest egg growing rapidly, he didn't have long to wait. The minute he hit his target number he was heading for sun, sand, and surf.

Until then, however, he had a business to manage.

He tapped in Razor's number, scanning the trash-littered alleys, empty storefronts, broken-out windows.

As neighborhoods went, this one ranked high on the most-dangerous list. No wonder the patrol officers were SWAT team members.

But no one would bother him. He was well known here, and even the few who might risk doing him harm if he was wandering around at night would leave him alone in the middle of the day.

Fear of retribution was a powerful safety net—and he had many allies.

"What's crackin', man?"

He swallowed his disgust. Slang was for losers. "Save the street talk for your lower-level contacts. You're above that."

"Thanks to you—but the lingo comes in handy during deals. What's up?"

"I'm past due for a status report on the last shipment."

"It's still in distribution. I was gonna call you once the inventory was gone."

"Transactions are slower than usual. You sure there wasn't any trouble at the pickup point?"

"Nope. It was smooth. Not a soul in sight. But everybody's on different schedules during the holidays. Getting the word out that we have merchandise has been slower."

"The holidays are over." A homeless man across the street wove down the slippery sidewalk, and Wolf grimaced in disgust.

Another druggie who'd lost the battle to get clean—if he'd ever bothered to enter the fray.

What a wasted life.

"What's that supposed to mean?" Razor sounded miffed.

Wolf refocused.

Maybe his comment—and inherent insinuation—*were* out of line. There was no reason to doubt the trusted lieutenant who was his face on the streets. Razor owed him—and the man knew it. Without his intervention, Razor would be just another hash mark on the OD list, one more nameless statistic.

Instead, he was positioned to take over an operation that would bring him wealth beyond his wildest dreams—as long as he stuck with the program.

Continued cooperation was the key to both their futures.

Better backtrack.

"Nothing. Sorry. It's been a busy holiday season. I'm overdue for a vacation."

"You're headin' toward a permanent vacation. Hang in and keep your eye on the prize."

Wolf arched an eyebrow.

Once upon a time, he'd been the one offering pep talks.

Another sign he should hand over the reins soon and fade out of the picture.

"You're right. A few more months, and my kingdom will be yours."

"Don't rush on my account. I don't know if our contacts are ready for new management."

"They will be. I've been laying the groundwork. You should start grooming your own second-in-command."

"I'm workin' on that."

The wind picked up, and Wolf set off down the street at a brisk pace. "I'll be in touch when the next delivery is scheduled."

"Same pickup place?"

"Yes. It's easier than changing locations with every shipment."

"I don't like it out there—especially alone. I'm not a country boy."

"After what happened in October, solo is safer. You ever have any hassle about your grunt guy going missing?"

"Nah. Going missing is a way of life here. I'm more worried about the other missing persons."

Wolf frowned as he crossed a street, detouring around a discarded syringe. "Why?"

"I hear the cops are still poking around."

"I assume they won't find anything." Razor was quick-thinking and thorough, and if the man said the problem had been handled, there was no need to entertain doubts . . . or ask for details.

Leaving the messy tasks to others was a perk of management.

"No—and a chop shop took care of the car."

"Then let's not dwell on it. The situation was unfortunate, but the fault was partly theirs. And the odds of anything like that happening again are too small to be of concern. I also have inside help to ensure the area is clear."

"Good."

"Call me after the inventory's depleted." Wolf checked his prepaid minutes. "On second thought, this phone is history. I'll be back in touch with a new number."

"Got it."

The line went dead.

Wolf pocketed the cell that was destined for the same fate as all the others—a fling into the river—and continued toward his destination.

When a police cruiser rounded the corner ahead, however, his step faltered.

But that was suspicious behavior.

He picked up his pace.

As he'd learned, if you acted innocent, most people gave you the benefit of the doubt.

The patrol car slowed, and the officer behind the wheel leaned forward. Peered at him.

Wolf called up a smile and lifted a hand in greeting, giving him a clear view of his face. As if he had nothing in the world to hide.

The officer's forehead smoothed out. He returned the wave, picked up speed, and rolled on down the street.

Wolf's lips flattened, and he inhaled a lungful of the cold air. Blew out a puff of vapor that quickly dissipated.

Living a lie was getting old.

Worse since October.

Hard as he'd tried to justify what had transpired on that autumn night, guilt continued to haunt him.

Profiting from people's weaknesses was fine. They were the ones making bad decisions, after all. If their flaws padded his bank account, so what? The problem began with their choices, not with him.

On the other hand, the three people who'd found themselves in the line of fire in October were a different matter.

The grunt guy—he was no great loss. Collateral damage. Risking exposure would have been foolish. What if, while in a drug-induced haze, he'd let slip what had happened that night?

However, despite what he'd told Razor about that young couple being partly at fault for what had happened, the truth was they'd simply been a victim of bad timing. They hadn't deserved their fate.

Yet what other choice had there been?

Sighing, he turned in to his destination.

Perhaps those two wouldn't have told a soul about what

they'd seen, since their own purpose for being in the woods at that hour of the night was suspect.

But they might have shared what they'd witnessed with someone they trusted . . . who could have passed the information on to the wrong people.

With his goal in sight, taking that gamble had been unacceptable—as Razor knew.

He pushed through the door, raised a hand in greeting to the familiar crew, but continued without stopping to chat. In his present mood, small talk would require too much effort.

Besides, he had an important meeting this afternoon, and that's where his energy had to be directed. Not toward socializing—or rehashing a regrettable October night.

Odd how guilt over two innocent lives could take such a toll, considering the business that was providing him with the funds to live in comfort for the rest of his days.

Then again . . . in light of his history . . . maybe it wasn't that odd after all.

"He has to leave, Margarita. The risk is too high if he stays." As he delivered the ultimatum to his wife, putting as much bravado as possible into his inflection, Eduardo Garcia curled his fingers into a tight ball and pressed the phone harder against his ear.

Please let her see the light.

"But how can we send him away? Where will he go? He is my only brother, Eduardo—and he needs us."

Her tear-laced entreaty jabbed at his gut.

Except Miguel Hernandez didn't need them. He just needed a place to crash. A safe base where he could come and go as he pleased that didn't cost him a dime.

Shoulders slumping, Eduardo leaned against a tree in the

woods that rimmed the sweeping Ivy Hill lawn, the grass now dried and brown from the winter chill.

Causing Margarita grief was dangerous. After two miscarriages, she could still lose this baby at six months—and stress didn't improve the odds of a full-term pregnancy.

Yet giving in—and getting in any deeper with her brother—could bring ruin on them all.

"Margarita, we have to think of ourselves too." A pleading note entered his voice—but if begging was what it took to win her support, so be it. "You know how important the income and health benefits from my job are. Our future is at stake here. If your brother gets in trouble with the law, there will be guilt by association. I could be back doing seasonal work without benefits . . . or worse."

"I know. But couldn't we give him one more chance?"

"We've done that already."

"He promised last night he'd clean up his act."

Another lie.

Miguel knew how to charm his sister into acquiescence—but he was more talk than action when it came to honoring his word.

Eduardo hardened his tone. "He has given us no reason to believe that."

"Please, Eduardo."

The front door opened, and the new Spanish teacher emerged.

Eduardo straightened up. Lounging around, making personal phone calls during working hours, could suggest he was shirking his duties—especially with a dozen maintenance items clamoring for attention.

Zeke Martinez raised a hand in greeting, and Eduardo returned the gesture as he walked toward the building. "I have to get back to work."

"I do believe he's trying to stop, Eduardo."

Not if the man's tiny pupils and frequent inability to follow a conversation—all classic symptoms of heroin use—were any indication.

Bad as using was, though, Miguel's illegal status and the funding source for his drugs were more worrisome. The odd jobs he'd picked up after slipping into the US last year didn't pay for a heroin habit.

But he was getting money somewhere . . . and since he used drugs himself, dealing could be a distinct possibility.

Eduardo's stomach knotted.

A *mojado* with a heroin habit who could be involved in the drug trade living under his roof.

It was a nightmare.

"We'll discuss this more tonight." He picked up his pace.

"Does that mean you'll reconsider?"

"I can't talk anymore. I'll see you tonight." He pressed the end button and slid the phone into his pocket.

"*Buenas tardes.*" The Spanish teacher smiled as he approached.

He returned the greeting while ascending the steps to the front door.

"It's too cold to be working outside. I hope you have indoor chores on your schedule for the afternoon."

The man's Spanish was impeccable, as if it was his first language.

No need to switch back to English for conversations with Zeke Martinez, as he did with most of the other faculty members, whose grasp of Spanish was rudimentary.

He continued in his native tongue. "Yes, I'll be inside for the rest of the day."

"This is quite a large property to maintain." The man swept a hand over the landscape.

"The crew is only responsible for the buildings and grounds we use. Most of the acreage is wooded. The school likes to keep the setting natural so it feels secluded and remote, even though civilization is nearby."

"Any trails on the property? I like to walk between classes to clear my head."

"Nothing formal, but the students have worn a few paths. If you go straight out the back door to the woods, you'll spot them."

"Anything I should be cautious about if I go walking?"

"No. There's no wildlife to speak of, ticks and poison ivy aren't a concern in winter, and the one well on the property is boarded up. You'll come across a few abandoned outbuildings, but they're locked as a safety precaution."

"Thanks for the tips. I heard a student went missing here in the fall, and I didn't want to wander anywhere risky."

"The police said she and her boyfriend ran away." Eduardo eased toward the door. It was always best to avoid gossip—or topics that were touchy. There were enough rumors floating around about the disappearance already. "I have to tackle those inside chores."

Turning his back on the man, he took a deep breath of the cold air.

Too bad he didn't have time to indulge in the luxury of a long walk to clear his own head—and strengthen his resolve to do what had to be done.

Hurting Margarita would be painful, but he had to keep his priorities straight for both their sakes.

And his top priority was avoiding trouble.

Except the trouble that had come calling at their doorstep showed no signs of leaving.

5

AS CATE PUSHED THROUGH the library door precisely at four-thirty, a tiny smile flitted across Zeke's lips.

Punctuality was still one of her virtues.

From his half-hidden position in the stacks, he gave her a quick sweep.

Worn jeans, one knee artistically shredded, hugged her killer legs. An oversized black sweater hit her midthigh—a smart choice to mask the soft curves beneath, which were more woman than teen. Her lustrous auburn hair was parted in the middle, one long swath dyed red in the style some trendy young people favored. Purple glitter nail polish screamed youth.

No one would ever guess she was thirty-three.

She had the adolescent mannerisms down too. Her bored perusal of the room and I'd-rather-be-anywhere-than-here slouch were typical of a disgruntled teen.

Despite her veneer of indifference, however, waves of tension radiated off her—though only someone who knew her well would detect them.

Someone like him.

Perhaps *only* him, aside from her sisters.

Because Cate was adept at hiding her feelings. Cautious about opening her heart. Miserly with her trust.

Yet she'd trusted him with . . . everything.

An honor no other man could claim, Cate had confided days before their breakup—making his decision to end their relationship even more gut-wrenching.

So yeah, he knew her well.

Or he had.

But much could change in eight years.

One thing, though, had remained the same.

Her effect on him was potent as ever.

Just looking at her jump-started his libido and—

Clenching his teeth, he cut off that inappropriate line of thought—but her roving gaze stopped on him a scant moment too soon.

Fast as he chilled the heat in his eyes, it wasn't fast enough. The slight catch in her breath, magnified in the silence of the deserted library, was telling.

He'd have to be more careful in the future.

Slipping his hands into his pockets, he strolled toward her. "Ms. Sheppard." It took every ounce of his acting skills to pull off a smooth, impersonal greeting.

"Mr. Martinez." Cate matched his inflection.

Impressive, given the shock she'd had difficulty controlling after seeing him in the classroom this morning.

"I've reviewed your Spanish quiz. It may be wise to discuss your comfort level with the material in my class."

She propped a hand on her hip and tossed her mane of hair, playing the part of a snotty teen to the hilt for the benefit of the librarian at the desk—the only other occupant on this first day of school. "I never liked Spanish."

Her ability to stay in character was a positive sign.

"That may be true, but you *are* taking my class. We can talk in the group study room." He indicated the glassed-in cube with a table for six he'd scoped out earlier. To anyone passing by, their exchange would appear to be a work session.

"Whatever." She flipped a hand at him.

He took the lead, waited for her to precede him in, and closed the door. "Let's sit there." He motioned to two chairs facing the window. Offering a clear view of their conversation would add to the aura of innocence.

She scanned the chairs that backed up to the window . . . hesitated while she no doubt processed his strategy . . . then flounced over and sat in one of the seats he'd indicated. Crossing her arms over her chest, she gave him a defiant look that fit her rebellious teen character—but might not be all acting.

After taking the adjacent chair, he set his cell between them, activated a white noise app, and folded his hands on the table. "I doubt the room is bugged, but precautions can't hurt. This will mask our conversation." He kept his volume low. "Put your Spanish book on the table."

In silence, she pulled out the text and placed it in front of her.

He reached over and flipped to the first chapter. "Keep your attention mostly on the book as we talk." He pointed to a word on the page. "What are you doing here?"

Playing along, she leaned forward and peered at the word. "Working a case. What are *you* doing here?"

"The same. I didn't think you had any interest in undercover work."

"I was a fit for this job. Are you still DEA?"

"Yes."

"What are you working on?"

He moved his finger down the page. "Breaking up the St. Louis portion of a Mexican drug cartel pipeline."

Silence.

He glanced over to find her frowning at him.

Instantly she refocused on the textbook. "At Ivy Hill?"

"It's become a drop point for the St. Louis operation. Trucks with merchandise destined for Chicago detour here, leave the drugs for pickup, and continue on. We discovered the location by chance in November after one of our agents on another surveillance gig spotted the truck turning into a back entrance, thought it looked suspicious, and did a little poking around after it pulled out."

The creases on her brow deepened. "Is someone here involved?"

"TBD—but likely. A key is used for entrance. We've got a handful of the St. Louis players under surveillance, but we haven't identified the brains behind the operation. We could grab the secondary people and shut down this location, but unless we get the head of the ring who has the connections to the cartel in Mexico, the pipeline will adapt and continue to flow."

"So you came in as a Spanish teacher. Lucky timing—for you."

"I was prepared to play a number of roles, depending on what worked best and was most plausible, but the Spanish teacher gig is a strong fit without any finagling on our end. We jumped on it as soon as we got wind of the opening. It was a scramble to assemble the fake credentials."

"Which were . . . ?"

He filled her in on his backstory.

"Extreme adventure firm in Spain. Clever. Is the limp fake too?"

"No."

"What happened?"

"Raid gone bad." His cryptic response didn't come close to capturing the chaos that had erupted in the Sonoran desert when the Mexican Feds had shown up too early during a negotiation with a major cartel operative and blown his cover—but why share all the gory details?

"Recent?"

"A year ago. I've been doing desk duty for the past few months while I recover. I'm not quite ready to return to my usual type of assignments, but more than capable of handling this job. Since I'm familiar with this area but have been gone long enough to reduce the odds of anyone at Ivy Hill recognizing me, it was an excellent fit. I intended to lay low—and I didn't expect to run into anyone I knew."

"Surprise."

"On both sides, I expect. Why are you here?"

She gave him a topline of her assignment and her backstory, turning the page of the book as she concluded. "Where's the drop spot?"

"An abandoned barn near the western end of the property." He indicated another word on the page, keeping his attention on the text.

"I wonder if Stephanie and her boyfriend met up there and ran into trouble with the drug crew?"

"It's possible. We don't know how long that pickup point was in use prior to November, or if other drops occurred here. I heard about the disappearance, but it's a peripheral angle that probably has little bearing on the outcome of my investigation."

She glared at him. "That disappearance is *my* main focus— and your investigation is secondary to *me*." A hard edge crept into her voice. "Like I was secondary to your career."

The moment the words spilled from her mouth, her eyes widened, a flush rose on her cheeks, and she jerked her chin down, feigning interest in the book.

In the sudden, oppressive silence, Zeke stopped breathing as shock reverberated through him.

After all these years, her anger hadn't dissipated. Her hurt hadn't healed.

Did that mean . . . ?

"Cate—you did meet someone new. Get married. Right?"

She swallowed. "Not that it's any of your business—but no."

The selfish wave of relief that swept over him was all wrong.

She *should* have married. She deserved a happily-ever-after.

Hard as their breakup had been—on both of them—Cate was a strong person. A survivor. How could she not be over him? How could she not have moved on? Found someone else to love?

For the same reason, it appeared, that he hadn't done any of those things either.

His feelings were too strong—and no one had ever lived up to the only person who'd stolen his heart.

He may have thought he'd buried his feelings, locked them away forever—but they'd been lying dormant, waiting to surge to the surface at the first opportunity.

Like an unplanned reunion at a girls' boarding school.

"Are *you* married?" Cate's cheeks remained flushed, her knuckles white as she gripped her pen.

"No."

A few beats ticked by.

"Let's talk about our jobs." She cleared her throat and tried for a businesslike tone—but the tiny tremor in her voice betrayed her unsettled emotions. "I propose we conduct our investigations independently. If either of us comes across information that may be useful to the other party, we arrange another meeting here. Agreed?"

A practical plan workwise—but it came nowhere close to dealing with the electricity zipping between them.

Yet given the taut line of her shoulders and firm set of her jaw, any suggestion that they also discuss personal issues would shut her down.

The wise course was to approach that loaded subject gradually—and with caution.

"I have a counterproposal."

"What is it?" Her inflection was wary.

"Let's meet here twice a week for a short tutoring session. I'll reserve the room. If there are developments that require an immediate conversation, we can schedule an extra session." He jotted down his cell number on a slip of paper and set it on the table in front of her. "You can text me with times that work for you—preferably during the day or right after school."

After a brief hesitation, she picked it up. "Unless our two investigations happen to intertwine, we aren't going to have much to discuss at these regular sessions."

"We'll find something to chat about."

The look she lasered at him would have intimidated a lesser man. "We have nothing else to chat about."

"Maybe we do."

"No, we don't." She closed the textbook and shoved it into her backpack.

"A regular schedule of meetings will call less attention to itself."

"Fine." She yanked one strap over her shoulder. "Do you need anything else today?"

Yeah.

A lot.

Like forgiveness . . . and understanding . . . and perhaps a chance to see if the relationship he'd shredded on that beautiful autumn day could be repaired.

But he didn't say any of that.

"No. I'll wait to hear from you."

She rose, hefted the backpack into position, and pushed through the door.

He watched until she disappeared through the stacks, then killed the app on his phone and stood.

Wobbled.

What the . . . ?

He grabbed the edge of the table . . . and sucked in a breath as the cause of his unsteadiness registered.

His legs were shaky—both of them, not just the one that had taken two bone-shattering bullets.

Staring into the eyes of cold-blooded killers, facing torture and death if his cover was blown, had never rattled him as much as the past fifteen minutes had.

More proof he wasn't over Cate.

But much as he'd like to have a heart-to-heart with her about personal matters, that would have to wait. She wasn't receptive—and they both had a job to do.

Before he left St. Louis, though, the two of them *would* hash this out.

In the interim, he had a ton of thinking to do—about evolving career aspirations, an unforgettable woman . . . and how to make amends for what may have been the second biggest mistake of his life.

———————

Cate rounded the corner of the hallway that led away from the library . . . verified she was alone . . . and slumped against the wall.

Stupid, stupid, stupid.

There was no other way to describe her loss of control—and the accusation she'd flung at Zeke.

Of course he'd read between the lines, realized she still had feelings for him.

Even worse, the lapse had forced *her* to acknowledge the hard truth that she wasn't over him.

Not by a long shot.

And his simple question about her marital status had exposed the other lie she'd always told herself—that her single state had nothing to do with Zeke. That she'd simply never found the right man.

Hogwash.

She'd never married—or even dated much after he dumped her—because every other man she'd met had paled in comparison.

Stifling a groan, she closed her eyes.

What a mess.

No undercover job was easy, and there was always a degree of danger—but who could have predicted that this case would include danger that put her *heart* at risk?

High risk, judging by her erratic pulse, the tingle in her fingertips, and her balking lungs.

Crud.

One short encounter with Zeke, and she was reduced to a fraying mass of emotions.

Not acceptable.

Even if the man's almost tangible virility was more powerful today than it had been eight years ago—when it had been seriously potent.

Even if the high voltage between them continued to buzz—on both sides, unless her instincts were off.

Even if the regret deep in his dark irises suggested he could be sorry their relationship had been sacrificed on the altar of ambition and adrenaline-pumping assignments.

But talking about the past wouldn't change it—so why stir up old hurts?

She'd have to—

"Is everything okay?"

As the male voice spoke, Cate jerked her eyes open.

Noah Evans stood two feet away.

The very man she'd wanted to see—just not at this particular moment.

But despite the bad timing, she had to suck it up. Switch gears. Take advantage of this encounter with one of the people in her sights.

Fortunately, it didn't require much acting to portray an unhappy teen whose world was shifting around her.

She sniffed and fished out a tissue. "Yeah. I'm kind of . . . I'm new here, and getting used to this place is . . . it's hard, you know?"

"I understand." Compassion softened his features, and he stuck out his hand. "Noah Evans. I'm one of the guidance counselors."

As she slid her fingers into his, she called up his stats from the background sheet the department had prepared. Age forty-one, recent divorce, no children, master's degree, eighteen-month tenure at Ivy Hill after working in a similar job on the East Coast.

"Cate Sheppard."

"Nice to meet you, Cate." He gave her a megawatt smile that was a tad too intense . . . and held on to her hand a fraction too long. "I noticed you in the cafeteria today, and I saw your name on the roster of new students. Anytime you want to talk, my door is open."

Her brain clicked into analytical mode.

How would a troubled teenage girl who felt as if she'd been dumped in a reform school by her parents—someone like Cate Sheppard . . . or Stephanie Laurent—react to this guy's attention and über empathy?

Maybe not in a healthy—or safe—way. Needy people often sought affection and understanding wherever they could find it.

This guy was definitely worth getting to know.

"Thanks. I may stop by."

"Should we set up an appointment? That way, I'll be available when you come and can give you my full attention." He pulled out his cell and opened his calendar.

Perfect.

"I guess."

"Tomorrow after classes? I'm here until four-thirty."

"Sure."

"Great." While he tapped a few keys, Zeke rounded the corner—and almost ran into them.

"Sorry." He pulled up short. "I didn't mean to run you over."

"No harm done. See you tomorrow, Cate." Noah smiled at her and continued down the hall.

Ignoring Zeke, she strode toward the door that led to her dorm.

He didn't follow or try to walk with her.

Thank you, God, for small favors!

At the exit, she took a quick peek over her shoulder—and found him standing where she'd left him, hands in pockets . . . watching her.

His perusal made her as uncomfortable as Evans's had—for entirely different reasons.

She knew Zeke. They had a history. And while her relationship with the former detective turned DEA undercover agent hadn't ended happily, he was otherwise an honorable man.

Evans was a stranger who'd given her an intimate smile and whose honor was unproven. He was also in a unique position to take advantage of vulnerable young women. Those facts, combined with Kayla's warning, solidified his position on her suspicious list.

Hugging her coat close, she pushed outside and followed the walkway, past the lengthening shadows of Ivy Hill, head dipped against the frigid wind.

She shivered . . . but the icy gusts pummeling her didn't bear the bulk of the blame. That belonged to the ominous goings-on at this high-priced girls' school.

Ties to a Mexican drug cartel. Missing teenagers. A guidance counselor with questionable intentions.

Were all those seemingly disparate pieces related?

If so, what was the link?

And what other secrets—and connections—were waiting to be discovered?

So many questions, so few answers.

Yet.

But she'd find them. If Stephanie and her boyfriend had met an untimely end, they *would* get justice. She'd see to it.

And no one—including the handsome DEA agent who'd disrupted her investigative strategy—was going to distract her from that goal.

No one.

––––––

Will downed the last bite of his nuked dinner, swigged his beer . . . and glanced at the laptop on the other end of the table, fingers itching.

He ought to shut it down for the night. Watch a movie, read a book, go to the gym. Those would be the safest pastimes on this Monday evening.

Except none of them were appealing—especially the gym. Despite the new physical patrol policy he'd instituted at Ivy Hill, exercise stunk.

And he'd had his fill of it for today.

What he needed was an activity to help him relax.

If Suz was here, there would be several possibilities—but until the six-month separation she'd mandated was over, his wife was keeping her distance.

So he'd have to entertain himself.

He rose and wandered over to the trash can, dinner container in hand. Tossed it in the bin. Retrieved another beer. Wiped down the counter.

Eyed the computer again.

Swigging the beer, he ambled over.

What could it hurt to browse through a few sites? No one

would find out. It wasn't as if anyone other than Suz—and his anonymous benefactor—knew about his issue. And Suz wasn't around.

He sat at the table, muting the red alert that began beeping in his mind.

Yeah, yeah, he was venturing into dangerous territory. Exposing himself to temptation. But he wouldn't succumb. He'd learned his lesson.

Digging himself into another hole would be stupid.

A man deserved a little fun, though—as long as he had the funds to pay for it and the self-discipline to maintain control. Hadn't he earned a reward for all his months of self-restraint?

His finger hovered over the keyboard.

He had a new credit card since the separation. One that bore his name alone. Nobody but him would see the statement—but even if they did, the sites he used had discreet billing appellations.

Maybe one quick transaction to entertain himself?

Of course he'd be careful. No way would he let it get out of hand again. Too much was at stake—his job, his marriage . . . his blood pressure. Sweating bullets did a number on the body.

But ten minutes of fun wouldn't break the bank—or undermine his resolve to stick with the program.

He could control this.

Will took another sip of beer.

Tuned out the alarms bells that began clanging with renewed vigor in his mind.

And pressed the forbidden link.

6

EDUARDO PEERED THROUGH a tiny crack in the blinds, stomach flipping like a hooked catfish on the banks of the Mississippi that flowed through his adopted city.

Miguel and the man who'd become a frequent nocturnal visitor were having another conversation in the back alley of the south city rental flat he and Margarita had called home for five years.

This did not bode well.

"What are you doing in the dark, *mi amor*?" Margarita entered the room, wrapped her arms around his waist from behind, and rested her cheek against his shoulder.

Two soft kicks prodded his lower back as she hugged him.

His son or daughter, making their presence known.

Throat tightening, he braced for the discussion they had to have. He could not—*would* not—put his child's future at risk. They had to get rid of Miguel.

"Watching your brother."

Her embrace slackened. "Where is he?"

He shifted aside and indicated the slit in the blinds.

After a brief hesitation, she took his place and squinted into the darkness. "Who is he talking to?"

"I don't know." As usual, it was impossible to identify the

age, race, or build of the clandestine caller, who always wore a bulky coat and a brimmed hat pulled low on his forehead. "But it's the same man who's been coming around for the past few months."

She backed away from the window, furrows scoring her brow. "It could be a friend."

Wishful thinking.

"Friends are welcomed into a home, not met in cold, dark alleys where no one can see them." He leaned close to the window again.

A small package was handed off, which his brother-in-law tucked into his oversized jacket. The other man slipped into the night as Miguel strolled back toward the flat.

"It could be innocent, Eduardo."

The note of desperation in her voice suggested she didn't believe that any more than he did.

He pivoted toward his wife. "No, it isn't. We have to confront him—for the sake of our unborn child, if not for ourselves." He placed his hand against her rounded stomach. "You want our son or daughter to grow up in a safe, happy home with both parents, don't you?"

Using their child to press his case was the trump card he'd been saving. A last resort if family loyalty continued to blind Margarita to the risk her brother represented.

"Yes. Of course." A tear brimmed on her lower lid. "But Miguel is a good man at heart. In Mexico, he always protected me. You know it wasn't safe where we lived. And after Papá died, he brought food home for Mamá and me. We would have starved if he hadn't. I owe him so much."

It was the same rationale and defense she always used.

"You repaid that debt long ago. It's past time for your brother to find his own way—especially now that we're starting a family. The room he uses is supposed to be the nursery."

"I'll talk to him."

"You've done that. He's not listening. I think we *both* should talk to him." He extended his hand . . . and held his breath. "Will you stand by me, for the sake of our child?"

She searched his face, lower lip trembling . . . but in the end, she slipped her fingers into his.

Sending a silent thank-you heavenward, he gave them a squeeze and led her to the kitchen.

As they entered, Miguel opened the back door, bringing a gust of cold air with him.

His gaze dropped to their entwined hands . . . and his eyes narrowed. "What's up?"

"We have to talk." Eduardo held tight to Margarita's cold fingers and led her farther into the room.

"Tomorrow. It's late, and I'm tired." He closed the door and headed toward the hall.

Eduardo released Margarita's hand and stepped in front of him. "Tonight."

Miguel scrutinized him, then turned to his sister and called up the smile and endearment he reserved for her whenever he wanted a favor. "Can't this wait until tomorrow, *chiquita*?"

"No. It can't." Eduardo ignored Margarita's silent entreaty.

"Chiquita?" Miguel kept his attention on his sister.

At her pained expression, Eduardo's stomach clenched. She was going to break ranks, succumb to her brother's charm once again, leave him to—

"We have to talk tonight, Miguel." Her statement was shaky, but the line of her mouth was firm.

Thank you, Lord.

Eduardo held out his hand.

Edging around her brother, Margarita joined him at the door and twined her fingers with his.

"Fine." Miguel dropped any pretense of charm now that it was clear he'd lost his ally. "Say what you have to say."

"You need to find a new place to live."

"I plan to. Eventually."

"Now."

"What's the hurry?"

"You've been here almost a year—and we don't want drugs in the house."

Miguel lifted one shoulder. "Who says there are drugs in the house?"

"I'm not stupid, Miguel. I can see the signs. You're using."

"No, I'm not. Not anymore."

"Then you're dealing. Show me what's in the package inside your coat."

His brother-in-law's eyebrows drew together, and a muscle ticced in his jaw. "You've been spying on me?"

"I watch what happens on my property. If you're not involved with drugs, you shouldn't mind showing me the package."

"It's private."

"You have to leave, Miguel."

His nostrils flared, and his features hardened. "Tonight? You would throw a family member out in this cold to wander the streets in search of shelter? I could freeze to death."

"Eduardo." Margarita angled toward him. "We can give him a few days to find a new place to live, can't we?"

That wasn't his preference. The sooner the man was gone, the better.

But ejecting someone without warning in the dead of winter wasn't right, either.

Perhaps he could offer a small concession.

"I'll give you three days. Until Thursday night."

"That's generous of you." Sarcasm sullied his words.

"I think so. More than."

Miguel muttered an oath that made Margarita cringe as he swung toward her. "I can't believe my own sister is turning her back on me. I won't forget this." He shoved past them, toward the hall. Stomped to the room he'd claimed as his own. Slammed the door.

A quiver rippled through Margarita, and Eduardo pulled her close. "I'm sorry to upset you, mi amor. But we had to do this for the sake of our little one."

"I know. You're right. It's dangerous to have drugs in the house. Do you think he'll be able to find somewhere to stay in three days?"

"If not, he can mooch off an acquaintance until he does. That guy who gave him the drugs tonight shouldn't care if he brings an illegal substance into his place. Come. Let's go to bed."

He led her down the hall, past the door to the room destined to be a nursery, the knot that had been in his stomach for months at last loosening.

They'd delivered their ultimatum, and in three days Miguel would be gone. Their life would calm down, and they could begin thinking about their future without a dark cloud hanging over it.

Too bad his brother-in-law hadn't stormed out tonight, feigning insult. That would have given him a window to change all the locks before Miguel came back in a day or two to try more sweet talk on Margarita. If he'd refused to leave, they could have threatened to call the police, charge him with trespassing—and Miguel wouldn't have wanted to risk an encounter with law enforcement. He'd have slunk away and left them in peace.

But the end was in sight. In seventy-two hours he'd walk out the door forever and their worries would be over.

After all, he'd been under their roof already for close to twelve months. What could it hurt to delay a few more days?

"I'm glad you stopped by today, Cate. I like to get to know the new students. And remember—my door is always open if you want to chat." Noah checked his watch. "But I do have another appointment this afternoon. Is there anything else you'd like to talk about before you leave?"

Cate kept her demeanor neutral, hiding her frustration.

The past thirty minutes had been a total waste.

Noah had been cordial, warm, and caring. He'd listened, encouraged, and offered a few suggestions.

The man had done nothing improper.

Nor had he provided any insights on Stephanie Laurent's disappearance, despite the opening she'd given him by mentioning the stories she'd heard about the girl running away . . . and how that notion held a certain appeal.

Noah had discouraged such thoughts, urged her to seek him out anytime she had such inclinations, and talked up the importance of hanging in and getting a quality education.

If he knew anything about the girl's vanishing act beyond the official runaway story, he'd done a masterful job masking it.

Cate tugged her backpack into position. "Nothing else is on my mind today. But I appreciate you reaching out to me in the hall yesterday." She stood.

He rose too and joined her at the door. "That's what I'm here for. Call or text me—night or day." Instead of opening the door, he rested a hand on her shoulder, encroaching on her personal space a tad.

Her antennas went up.

"I don't want to bother you if you're off work." She leaned in ever so slightly.

He didn't back away.

"This is a 24/7 job for me. I care about all the girls here—especially the ones who could use a friend." He gave her a squeeze. "And I try to help however I can. If you—" At a knock on the door, he removed his hand. Retreated a step as he grasped the knob. "My next appointment." He pulled the door open.

Another girl waited on the other side.

"I'm sorry . . . am I early?" The student looked between the two of them.

"No. We were finished. Come on in. Cate, I'll see you around."

She eased past the other student, retrieved her coat from her locker, and set out for the dorm, a sense of unease tingling through her.

It might behoove County to dig deeper on Evans, beef up the cursory intel they had. The man may not have done anything overtly offensive in either of their encounters, but he exuded a definite creep factor.

And her roommate knew more about that than she was telling.

She pulled out her access card and held it up to the scanner. The door to the dorm clicked open, and she entered.

The challenge was getting the reticent girl to talk. Up to this point they'd barely exchanged a dozen sentences—and not for lack of trying on her part.

Kayla was at her desk when Cate entered their room, head bent over a book. She didn't greet her or even acknowledge her presence.

Initiating a productive conversation was going to require finesse.

Cate passed behind her, mulling over possible approaches as she dumped her backpack on the bench under the window that separated their domains . . . and chipped her nail polish in the process.

Well, shoot.

She examined the damaged polish.

It had taken forever to do this unaccustomed glitter job. Now she'd have to—

Wait.

Nail polish.

Could that be her entrée?

Kayla had admired her nails on Sunday—one of the few unsolicited comments she'd offered.

It was worth a try.

Cate pulled a storage container from under her bed, dug through it for the nail supplies she'd stocked up on in preparation for her role, and retrieved the small kit she'd assembled.

"I hate it when nail polish chips, don't you?"

Kayla's gaze flicked to her . . . then to her own unvarnished nails. "I don't use polish."

"Why not?"

"My nails are too short."

"Mine used to be too—but they get longer if you use polish." Cate extracted the bottle of clear topcoat, the glitter polish, and a makeup sponge from the kit for her repair job and set them on her bed. "You want to try mine?"

Silence.

She looked over at Kayla.

The girl was watching her, expression guarded.

"What?" Cate lifted her hands, palms up.

"You'd let me use your nail polish?"

"Sure. Why not?"

Kayla studied her. "You're different than my other roommates."

"Yeah? How?"

"Slumming with a Black girl was beneath them. They didn't want to breathe the same air I did, let alone allow me to touch anything of theirs."

Cate's heart contracted.

Hard as Kayla tried to affect indifference, there was a world of hurt—and resentment—in her eyes.

But it hadn't yet congealed into hate, the way it had with

too many of the people she ran into on the street every day in the course of doing her job.

For Kayla, there was hope.

"Their loss." She shrugged. "So you want to try this or not?"

Kayla bit her lower lip as she regarded the bottle of polish. After several silent beats ticked by, she exhaled. "I guess."

Yes!

Her last-minute role-play decision to have Cate Sheppard make a statement with her nails was about to pay dividends.

Cate pulled out a bottle of liquid latex and a base coat, gathered up the rest of her supplies, and deposited them on Kayla's desk. "Clear a bigger space."

While her roommate did so, Cate dragged her desk chair over and sat beside the other girl.

"What is all that?" Kayla indicated the paraphernalia on the desk.

Cate recited the glitter application routine she'd memorized from the internet and tapped the desk. "Set your hands flat here."

Kayla complied, and Cate began painting a latex protective barrier around her cuticles.

"You were late getting back from classes." Kayla scooted closer to the desk.

The perfect opening.

"I ran into Mr. Evans in the hall yesterday when I was feeling kinda down, and he invited me to stop in and see him today."

Though she kept her attention on her task, she sensed Kayla tighten beside her.

But the other girl didn't say a word.

"I know you said to avoid him, but he seems nice." She maintained a chatty tone. "Did your other roommate like him? You said she used to talk to him."

"Yeah—but not for the right reasons."

Cate glanced at her. "What does that mean?"

"The kind of help he offered wasn't what she needed."

"How do you know what she needed? I thought you two didn't get along."

"She didn't have to—" Kayla's mouth tightened. "Just be careful with him. If you're really down, go see Reverend Wilson. He's here every week." Her roommate examined the small cross on the wall above her desk, and her features softened. "The help he offers heals the soul. He's all about the long term, not quick fixes."

"What sort of quick fixes does Mr. Evans offer?" Cate capped the latex and opened the base coat. "I mean, talking helps. That's all we did."

Kayla shifted in her chair. "Did he get . . . like . . . kind of close?"

So the other girl had experienced the same thing she had.

"Maybe a little. But he acts like he really cares. Did he get too close to you? Like—touch you?"

"Nothing bad, but it made me kind of . . . nervous. I never talked to him in his office again after that. I feel safer with Reverend Wilson."

"You think Mr. Evans got too close to your other roommate?" Cate kept her inflection casual, but digging up additional background on Noah Evans was zooming to the top of her priority list.

"I don't know. Like I said, we weren't BFFs. But she had a boyfriend, and I got the feeling they were pretty tight. I think she went to Mr. Evans for . . . other things."

"Like what?" Cate capped the bottle of base coat and gave Kayla her full attention.

The other girl fiddled with a pen on her desk, keeping her chin down. "I don't know."

But she did.

After the ten years she'd spent dealing with the underbelly of society, it was easy to recognize evasive maneuvers.

Pushing, however, might backfire. If Kayla closed down, all the groundwork she was laying for a friendship that could lead to confidence-sharing would crumble.

"Whatever. I don't have any plans to go see him again anyway." She checked the nails on Kayla's other hand. "These are dry enough to apply the glitter coat." She cut off a corner of the sponge, opened the glitter bottle, and tipped it onto the absorbent surface. "So were you surprised your roommate ran away with her boyfriend?"

"I never knew what she was going to do—and she didn't share her plans with me. I wasn't even here the weekend she left. I was at a teen retreat Reverend Wilson was leading at a camp not far from here."

So much for any hope that Stephanie could have dropped a hint or two that Kayla had picked up on.

"You ever meet her boyfriend?"

"No."

"He never came to visit?"

"I didn't say that."

Cate continued tipping the polish onto the sponge and dabbing it on Kayla's nails. "You mean they met somewhere on campus?"

"They could have."

"Wouldn't somebody have seen them?"

"Not if they hooked up in the woods."

"You think they did?"

"Maybe. Sometimes on Friday or Saturday night she'd disappear after dark and wouldn't come back until one or two. Usually the next day I'd find bits of leaves and stuff on the floor. Once she woke up with a twig in her hair."

Confirmation that Stephanie *had* met up with her boyfriend on school property—increasing the likelihood they could have run smack into the middle of the operation Zeke was investigating . . . and decreasing the likelihood a lead would surface that led off campus.

The prospects of an early reprieve from this assignment dimmed.

"You have a boyfriend?"

At Kayla's question, she refocused. "No. I did once, but he moved away." That much of her cover was true, anyway. "And I doubt I'll meet anyone out here."

"True. Ivy Hill social life isn't the best. But I kinda like that there isn't any guy pressure either, you know?" The corners of her lips rose. "We can always look at the hot new Spanish teacher if we want a man fix."

Cate almost lost her grip on the sponge. "You think Mr. Martinez is hot?"

"Yeah. For an old guy. Don't you?"

She masked a chuckle with a cough. Only a seventeen-year-old would deem thirty-three old.

"I don't know." She tossed the sponge in the trash. Busied herself opening the topcoat. "I'm not his biggest fan. He's making me meet him in the library for tutoring sessions." No point in keeping that a secret. The more out-in-the-open they treated those get-togethers, the less anyone would pay attention to them.

"Seriously?"

"Uh-huh. I bombed the pop quiz he gave yesterday."

"You could be holed up with worse people. I don't get any bad vibes from Mr. Martinez."

Like she did from Evans.

Kayla didn't have to say that for the message to come through loud and clear.

"I suppose."

"If you want any help with Spanish homework, let me know. I do okay in that subject."

Another opportunity to interact with the girl.

"Thanks."

The conversation shifted to more general school-related topics while she finished the manicure and repaired her own nail, but as Kayla went back to studying, Cate's mind was already processing next steps.

While her roommate hadn't been privy to Stephanie's plans the night she disappeared, she was a fount of other helpful information about Evans and her former roommate's nocturnal wanderings.

A phone call to her handler to request additional research on Evans's background and a hike around the property moved to the top of her priority list. Assuming Stephanie and her boyfriend had used the barn as a rendezvous site, it was possible they'd left a piece of evidence behind.

Cate slipped the polish into the kit and zipped it closed.

If that was the case . . . and if someone at Ivy Hill was involved in the drug pipeline, as Zeke suspected . . . he or she could also have played a part in the disappearance of the teen couple.

She tucked her manicure supplies into the storage bin and slid the container under her bed.

While Zeke considered the missing student peripheral to his case, it was possible her efforts to track down the person responsible for Stephanie's vanishing act could also lead to a link to the mastermind behind the St. Louis cartel pipeline operation.

She sat on her bed and pulled out her cell. Ignoring Zeke's request to give him a list of potential meeting times for their twice-a-week tutoring sessions was silly. She might not want to see him alone on a regular basis, but the premise was plausible and it would give them an opportunity to exchange information without raising eyebrows.

And if their two investigations did begin to intertwine, as it now appeared they might, they did have to talk.

About business only.

She'd be firm on that rule if he brought up anything of a personal nature. Set clear boundaries.

Because whether he was hot or not—and despite the tickle of adrenaline that licked at her nerve endings every time she caught sight of him in the hall—she wasn't going down another dead-end romantic road with Zeke.

7

"YOU READY FOR ME?"

As Cate spoke from the doorway of the study room, Zeke tamped down the sudden uptick in his pulse and looked up from the paper he was grading. "Yes." In more ways than one—but he left that unsaid. "Come in."

She entered, clicking the door shut behind her as he activated the white noise app on his phone and rose.

"I thought you'd be lurking in the stacks again, watching for me. Wondering if I'd blow you off." She sauntered over to the table. Her loose tunic top downplayed her womanly curves, but her snug leggings left little to the imagination.

"You said you'd show on Tuesdays and Thursdays. I've never known you to break your word. Have a seat." He pulled out the chair beside him.

She slid into it, avoiding eye contact, and extracted her Spanish book from the bulky backpack while he positioned the cell between them.

"Any news?" He flipped the book open.

"Some."

In a clipped, no-nonsense style, she briefed him on her encounter with Noah Evans and the information she'd gleaned from her roommate.

"We did background checks on the entire staff." He doodled on the paper in front of him. "Nobody earned a red flag."

"We did the same. But I have County digging deeper on Evans."

"You think he's hitting on the girls?"

"Maybe. Since Stephanie appeared to have had significant contact with him, he's on my list of suspects—though Kayla doesn't think there was anything romantic going on."

"I don't see how whatever sort of relationship they had could be connected to my investigation."

"I don't, either—but it may be relevant to mine. Do *you* have any news?"

"I'm still getting to know the players. Eduardo Garcia interests me."

She raised an eyebrow. "Our background check indicates he's clean. Besides, I don't think the kingpin of the type of operation you're investigating would be working as a maintenance supervisor. Not with the sort of money he'd be pulling in. Targeting the one Mexican employee on campus reeks of profiling to me."

"I'm not saying Garcia is running the show." He flipped ahead in the book, keeping his attention on the pages. "And his ethnic background isn't the main reason he caught my attention . . . though that may be relevant. I've spoken with him and observed him on several occasions, and my gut tells me he's troubled."

"Instinct, helpful as it can be, doesn't take the place of hard evidence. People can be troubled for many reasons."

"True. I'm just letting you know he's in my sights. If you happen to observe any suspicious behavior on his part, I'd appreciate a heads-up."

"I'd ask the same favor in terms of Evans. What's next for you?"

He pointed to a word on the page. "Continue to observe,

build rapport, probe where I can. We have people watching the property at night, and we'll follow the pickup vehicle after the next delivery, whenever that occurs. But so far the couriers haven't led us to anyone higher up. Whoever is running this is deep under the radar. What's next for you?"

"Keep my ear to the ground—and continue to hike around the property, explore the woods. Students are encouraged to get fresh air and exercise—and who knows what I'll find? People do drop items . . . especially if it's dark and they're in a rush—or panicked."

He frowned at her. "You've been wandering around the property?"

"I took my first walk yesterday after school, following the perimeter of the main campus. I want people to get used to seeing me rambling around."

"Are you going to hike into the woods alone?"

She slanted him a get-real look. "Is that a serious question?"

Zeke recalibrated.

Of course she was going alone. She couldn't poke around with another student in tow.

And going all protective on her wouldn't earn him any brownie points. She'd called him on that tendency eight years ago, and after all the additional work experience she'd logged—not to mention the fact they were no longer a couple—she'd be less tolerant about it than ever.

Totally understandable.

Detective Cate Reilly was more than capable of handling dicey situations and defending herself against attack.

Except undercover work required a different skill set . . . particularly in cases where you couldn't carry.

Like this one.

A weapon wouldn't be part of the gear for a student role play.

He chose his next words with care. "Isolated areas being used for illegal purposes can be dangerous."

"I'm going in daylight. From what you've said, deliveries and pickups are at night. Also, a student taking a hike around the property shouldn't raise suspicions, and I intend to establish a pattern. Unless my cover gets compromised, no one should pay any attention to my comings and goings."

He couldn't argue with her rationale.

But that didn't mean he had to like her traipsing through the woods alone.

"Be careful anyway."

"Goes with the territory." She indicated the book. "Are we finished?"

They were—but he wasn't ready to let her leave.

Too bad he couldn't come up with a credible excuse to keep her here for a few more minutes.

"Yes." He closed the book.

"Nice duds." She flicked a finger against the cuff of his Brunello Cucinelli dress shirt.

"Perk of the job. I assume you were given a similar carte blanche at Saks—or wherever rich teens shop."

"Yes. Not that I'll ever wear any of this stuff again."

"The leggings are keepers."

She stiffened and shot him a withering look but let the remark pass. "I doubt you'll have much use for *your* wardrobe in your next assignment—assuming you're still doing gritty jobs in far-flung places."

The perfect opening to alert her to his shifting career plan.

"My traveling days may be coming to an end."

She shoved the Spanish text into her backpack. "What does that mean?"

"I'm considering leaving undercover work. Going to regular agent duty."

For one infinitesimal second, she froze.

Then she jerked her hand out of the backpack and secured the clasp with more force than necessary.

She didn't have to speak for him to know what was running through her mind.

You gave up a whole lifetime with me to do a measly eight years of undercover work?

He couldn't let her walk out of here thinking that was the trade-off he'd expected.

"Cate."

She continued to secure her backpack, waves of hurt radiating off her.

"Cate. Please." It took every ounce of his willpower to restrain the urge to reach out, grasp her hand.

Yet some nuance in his entreaty must have infiltrated her defenses, because she paused. Turned her head.

"When I took the DEA job, I expected to stay undercover for my entire career—like I told you at the time. I wanted to address the drug problem at the source. Help stem the tide of narcotics flowing over the border and flooding our streets. Killing people. Especially young people." His voice rasped, and he picked up his cell, staying in character as he pretended to check his schedule—but the tremor in his fingers was telling.

He slanted a look toward her.

Cate's gaze was riveted on his hands.

So much for hiding his feelings—with her, anyway.

He cleared his throat and stared at the screen. "But I've come to realize that no matter how hard I work, no matter how many risks I take, no matter how many operations I bust, my efforts put only a small dent in the problem. The truth is, I can do as much good working here in the States, at the street level, disrupting gang operations and diverting the pipeline—like I'm doing on this job. I've put my life on the line in nightmare situations for eight years, and . . ." He breathed in. Exhaled. "And I think . . . I hope . . . the debt is paid."

"What debt?"

He kept his attention fixed on the phone, but he could hear her puzzlement.

That was the secret he'd never shared with her. The one he'd guarded close to his heart—out of shame and sorrow and fear of rejection—for almost two decades.

This wasn't the place to reveal it, but at least he'd laid the groundwork should he find the courage to dig deep and bare his soul.

"Long story." He gathered up the papers he'd been grading and tapped them into a neat pile. "If you have anything to discuss that can't wait until Tuesday, send me a text with the word *homework* in it. I'll do likewise. We'll set up an extra study session." He stood, leaving her no choice but to follow.

Brow pinched, she rose and hefted the bulky backpack over her shoulder, questions filling her eyes.

But she didn't voice them.

Thank goodness.

"Fine. See you." She rounded the table and escaped without a backward look.

As she disappeared from view, Zeke released a ragged breath and turned off the white noise app on his cell. Pocketed the phone.

Cate had never been a woman who liked to be rushed, and she'd be less receptive than ever to any overtures he made in light of their history.

He had to decelerate or he was going to scare her off.

Slow and easy wasn't a bad plan in terms of his own well-being, either. After all, Cate had reentered his life a mere six days ago. Getting carried away by possibilities could lead to heartache.

Yes, he'd already been contemplating a career shift when their paths crossed. Yes, his lonely existence had begun to wear on him, making him yearn for a life lived in sunshine rather than shadows, where loving someone wouldn't put that person at risk. And yes, the convergence of their lives seemed somehow providential.

But perhaps meeting Cate again was nothing more than a fluke. A mere coincidence.

Yet as he walked toward the door, bits and pieces of an old quote ran through his mind. Something about coincidences being nothing more than small miracles in which God chooses to remain anonymous.

Was God's hand in this?

Probably a stretch.

In the world he'd occupied for close to a decade, there had been little evidence of the Almighty's presence—or even of the existence of a loving God. Bad people dominated the revolving cast in his dramas, and examples of goodness were few and far between.

But there *was* goodness in the world.

He had only to look at Cate to have his faith in virtue reaffirmed. She radiated integrity and honor and a commitment to justice and duty.

So whatever the impetus for their meeting, it was an opportunity only a fool would let pass without giving course changes—and second chances—a great deal of thought.

And while he'd been called many names in his life, fool had never been one of them.

Even if, in hindsight, walking away from Cate years ago more than qualified him for that title.

———

Miguel's rattletrap car was parked in front of the flat.

Not a positive sign.

Eduardo swung into the alley that led to the back of the unit. Parked. Set the brake.

After a day dealing with a never-ending list of maintenance items, plus the long drive home from Ivy Hill in the dark on icy roads with sleet pinging off the windshield, another taut confrontation with his brother-in-law held no appeal.

But if it had to be done, he'd do it. It was Thursday night, and Miguel's deadline had arrived.

Psyching himself up for an argument, he locked the car and crossed to the back door.

The scene through the canted blinds on the kitchen window wasn't encouraging.

Margarita was working at the stove, her movements quick and jerky. Like they always were if she was under stress.

An unopened six-pack of beer—the brand Miguel favored—was on the counter.

And three places were set at the dinner table.

Eduardo fisted his hands. Took a deep breath. Pushed through the door.

Margarita swung around as he entered, lines of distress scoring her face as she darted a quick glance toward the hall.

"He's still here?" Eduardo joined her at the stove, keeping his volume low.

"Yes." She pressed her hands against her stomach. "In his room."

"You mean in our *baby's* room. Did he say anything about leaving?"

"No. When he came in half an hour ago, he asked what we were having for dinner."

Eduardo gritted his teeth. "Has he packed?"

"I don't know." Her irises began to shimmer. "There's a lock on his door."

"What?" His pulse vaulted into overdrive.

She nodded. "He must have put it on while we were both gone."

Translation? Their unwelcome guest wasn't planning to leave.

Heat surged over his cheeks. "He is *not* going to—"

"Buenas tardes, Eduardo." Miguel ambled into the kitchen,

the curve of his lips more sneer than smile. "Dinner smells good, chiquita."

He started to pull out a chair, but Eduardo yanked it from his grasp.

His brother-in-law regarded him calmly, his pupils normal-sized and alert tonight.

Maybe he *had* stopped using.

Didn't matter.

If he wasn't using, the package he'd taken on Monday night in the alley meant he was dealing—and that was even worse in the eyes of the law.

"Why aren't you gone yet?"

Miguel gave an indifferent shrug. "You said three days. That's seventy-two hours. It isn't nine o'clock yet."

"Does that mean you're leaving in two hours?" A vain hope, in view of the man's attitude.

"You know"—Miguel sauntered over to the counter, fished a spoon out of a drawer, and dipped it into the pot of pozole on the stove—"I've gotten to like it here. And Margarita is an excellent cook." He slid the spoon into his mouth. "Delicioso, chiquita."

Eduardo stalked over to him, snatched the spoon from his hand, and threw it in the sink. "I told you once to leave. I'm telling you again."

"And what will you do if I don't?" Miguel folded his arms across his chest, more amused than angry.

Apprehension spiraled through Eduardo.

What was Margarita's brother up to?

"I'll call the police. Tell them you're trespassing."

That threat would have had more punch if the man had already left and the locks had been changed—but what other ammunition did he have?

"Hmm." Miguel cocked his head, triumph lurking in his eyes. "That may not be a smart idea."

"Why not?" Eduardo braced. Whatever Miguel was about to say was going to change this game. He could feel it.

His brother-in-law wandered over to the six-pack of beer, picked it up, and stowed it in the fridge. "They might find illegal substances hidden in the house while they're here. Well hidden."

Eduardo stared at him. "What are you talking about?"

Miguel closed the refrigerator door and turned to him. "Illegal substances like heroin. Cocaine. Not in my room, you understand. I would never be involved in anything like that." He affected a look of mock horror. "But if the cops show up, it would be my duty to tell them what I've observed my brother-in-law doing in the dark of the night. Making deals, hiding dangerous drugs. The consequences could be bad. Very bad."

A dark, ominous silence hung in the room as the implications of Miguel's threat sank in.

The man was using extortion to force them to fall in line with his plans.

Eduardo's lungs froze.

"Miguel!" Margarita crossed to her brother, the color leaching from her complexion. "How can you do this? Eduardo would never be involved in anything like that. And you're hurting me and your niece or nephew too." She splayed her fingers on her stomach.

"My dear sister." He put a hand on her shoulder, his tone condescending. "In this world, you have to take care of number one. I promised you I would leave your home—and I will . . . when I'm ready. For now, staying here suits my purposes. So let's live and let live. You don't bother me, I won't bother you. Are we in agreement?"

Eduardo tried to gather his scattered thoughts. To think of a way around the cunning trap Miguel had laid for him.

But his mind wasn't programmed to circumvent deceit, nor had experience equipped him to deal with treachery. No one in his circle of acquaintances came close to matching Miguel's evil nature.

If the man had hidden drugs all over the house, it was possible he and Margarita would never find them all, no matter how hard they searched. Should the police ever come, and should Miguel follow through on his threat, it was likely drugs would remain in crevices they'd missed.

It would be his word against his brother-in-law's.

Unless . . .

"You're forgetting one thing." Eduardo swiped the sweat off his upper lip.

"What's that?"

"You're illegal. The immigration people could send you back to Mexico." That was the one possible glitch in the man's plan.

"That won't happen. I have papers now."

"From where?"

His grin was triumphant. "Friends in the right places."

In other words, they were forged.

Eduardo's spirits nose-dived.

He and Margarita were at the man's mercy.

The life they'd built, the job he'd secured, the future of their child—all were in jeopardy because they'd been kind enough to offer a relative in difficult straits temporary shelter.

Apparently the old saying was true.

No good deed went unpunished.

But bad as their present predicament was, a more terrifying question suddenly strobed across his mind.

Now that Miguel had the upper hand, what would he and Margarita do if the man decided to make other demands and entangle them further in the dangerous web he'd created?

8

THIS GIG WAS GETTING OLD.

Grimacing, Noah steered clear of a pile of garbage in the middle of the pothole-filled street, swung into the parking lot behind the rehab center, and parked in clear view of one of the security cameras.

Spending two Saturday mornings a month with druggies was one thing. Putting his car at risk was another.

After sliding out from behind the wheel, he locked the door and trudged toward the rear entrance of the facility Reverend Wilson had established ten years ago with seed money from a few companies with deep pockets and a do-gooder bent.

Hard to believe he'd turned the place into a model program that was touted nationwide and had garnered countless awards.

But a man with vision could accomplish much.

He rang the bell and angled toward the security camera beside the door. A moment later the lock clicked open.

The usual antiseptic scent mingled with the smell of burnt toast assailed him as he entered.

But it was less repugnant than the noxious odors on the street—and it was far safer inside than out in this area of town.

"Morning, Noah." Reverend Wilson waved and approached from down the hall, offering one of his trademark sunny smiles. "Thank you for coming."

"Happy to help." He took the hand the minister extended and returned his firm clasp. The silver flecks in the reverend's dark hair hinted at his age, but his trim physique, lively step, and strong grip were that of a much younger man.

"I see you came prepared to paint." The man's eyes twinkled.

Noah surveyed the tattered jeans he'd retrieved from a dark corner of the bedroom closet. "You did say to wear old clothes."

"They're perfect. The volunteers are assembling in the rec room, but help yourself to coffee first if you like."

"Thanks. I already had my allotment for the day." The Americano from Starbucks with extra shots of espresso would fortify him for the unpleasant hours ahead far better than the weak, no-name brew the center provided.

Besides, buying his own coffee gave him an excuse not to mingle with the lowlife residents.

People who got addicted to drugs were losers.

"I hear you." The minister chuckled. "I should limit my own intake. I'll stop in later in the morning to see how the project is progressing and lead you all in prayer."

"Amen to that."

Reverend Wilson grinned and clapped him on the back. "Brother, you're sounding more like my congregation every day. Any Sunday you want to visit my church for services, you're more than welcome to amen with us."

Noah forced up the corners of his mouth. "I may do that one of these days."

Like when the Mississippi River froze over.

"I'll put you in the front row." Residents began to wander out of the dining room, and the reverend waved at them. "I have to get to the chapel, start everyone's day with a prayer. I'll talk to you later."

Noah unzipped his jacket and slowly shrugged it off, waiting for the small group outside the dining room to move into the chapel before he strode down the hall toward the rec room.

Not that he was in a hurry to paint.

He'd much rather be at the gym, working out—or at Ivy Hill, meeting with a girl who craved a caring ear. Either of those activities would be more enjoyable and gratifying than this.

However, volunteering at the rehab center gave him a legitimate excuse to be in this area.

One he wouldn't have to use for much longer, thank heaven.

The end was in sight.

Until then, though, sticking with the program was smart. It averted any suspicion his trips to this war zone could arouse and earned him a gold star at Ivy Hill, where volunteering for worthy causes was encouraged and lauded.

And if he took care of other business while he was here, who would be the wiser?

No more bad weather excuses. Today was the day for her delayed foray into the woods.

Cate shoved her arms into the sleeves of the high-end, down-filled parka and picked up her Sealskinz extreme cold weather gloves.

Being as frugal as possible with the bulk of her clothing purchases for this role play had been no problem—but if County expected her to tramp around in the woods in freezing temperatures, top-of-the-line cold-weather gear was a necessity, not a luxury.

"Are you for real going to walk around outside in this deep freeze?" Kayla looked over from her desk.

That girl did more studying than a law student prepping for the bar exam.

"Yeah. I'm tired of trig and sick of Spanish. I'm ready for a break. Want to come?"

Fat chance.

No one in their right mind would be out walking on a day like this—unless that was part of their normal routine.

And after wimping out in the sleet Thursday and the sub-zero temperatures yesterday afternoon, letting any more time pass between walks wasn't going to establish any sort of exercise pattern.

"No thanks. You're gonna freeze your butt off."

"Not in this coat."

She hoped.

"I don't know." Kayla gave the parka a skeptical perusal. "No matter how much it cost, I bet you'll still freeze."

"Guess I'll find out."

"Better you than me." Kayla picked up her mug of hot chocolate and went back to studying.

A far preferable activity on this Saturday afternoon than traipsing around in the arctic chill.

But acing tests wasn't why she was here.

Resigned, Cate left the room, pulled on her gloves, and followed the hall toward the exit.

Two steps outside the door, she jolted to a stop as a gust of glacial air smacked her in the face.

Sweet heaven!

They weren't paying her enough to brave this kind of cold.

Then again, she wasn't in this business for the money. It was all about justice—and justice wasn't going to be served if she hibernated in her warm, cozy dorm room.

Pulling up her hood, she plunged into her walk.

After one brisk circuit of the main campus, she struck off down the path at the rear of the property, following the fork that led west—toward the barn.

Fifteen minutes later, as her nose was beginning to grow

numb, her destination came into view through the denuded trees.

It wasn't much to look at—and considering the weathered boards and the rotting siding near the top of the structure, it had been abandoned for a long while.

Not an ideal place for a tryst—but teenage hormones were a force to be reckoned with, so any port in a storm and all that.

She trekked through the underbrush and circled the building. Curious.

From a distance, it had appeared decrepit, but the two windows were sturdy—though scratches on the one with an old crate under it suggested the lock could have been jimmied in the recent past. The main door was also secured with a shiny padlock that seemed to be of recent vintage.

Cate fished out a tissue and wiped her nose.

Man, the cold was playing havoc with her sinuses.

After doing a second circuit of the barn, she eyed the narrow dirt road nearby and conjured up an image of the summertime aerial view of the property that had been in her County briefing packet. If her memory was correct, part of the land abutted the state highway.

This must be the back entrance to school property Zeke had referenced.

She set off down the rutted one-lane drive, and within three minutes caught a glimpse of blacktop.

Yep. State highway.

She followed the track until the entrance came into view. A sturdy gate blocked access—and a security camera mounted in the tree adjacent to it and aimed toward the road would record any visitors.

Zeke had said the drug ring people had a key—but how were they getting past the camera undetected?

She retraced her steps to the barn and bent to examine the padlock on the door.

It was fastened tight, and there was no sign it had ever been picked—adding credence to Zeke's contention that someone on the inside was facilitating the drops and pickups.

Someone who could be in contact with the mastermind. Know their identity.

Given the magnitude of drugs involved in a Mexican cartel pipeline, it was no wonder the DEA had decided an undercover operation was worth a try to find the head honcho.

Zeke's case was a big deal.

But she had her own investigation to worry about—and *it* was a big deal for the two missing teens and their families.

Time to refocus on her purpose for braving the cold today.

Although more trips would be required to complete a rough grid search, a cursory inspection of the area around the barn was doable.

She straightened up from the lock, brushed the dust off her coat, and headed back toward the window that may have been pried open.

If Stephanie and her boyfriend *had* met here for romantic rendezvous, odds were they'd have preferred to find an indoor spot to get cozy, away from nocturnal prowlers of a four-legged nature.

The barn could have served that purpose.

Since only the road was blocked off, it was possible the boyfriend had pulled into a nearby drive on the other side of the rural highway, tucked his car into the woods, and hiked up to the barn out of sight of the camera.

Had County reviewed and kept a copy of all of Ivy Hill's security footage from the night of the disappearance?

Likely, but nevertheless a question worth asking.

If they hadn't, however, it was no doubt long gone. Most homes and businesses recorded until their storage was full, then overwrote the oldest footage. Thirty days was often the maximum retention for businesses, a few days for home systems. After more than two months, any video recorded on the night Stephanie went missing would be—

Whoa!

Cate shrieked and jerked back as she rounded the corner of the barn and came face-to-face with a guy in a ski mask.

Adrenaline spiking, she did what she always did in threatening situations at work.

She reached for her Sig Sauer.

Of course it wasn't there.

She was a student, not a detective.

Stay in your role play, Cate. It's the middle of the day. This person is not part of Zeke's drug ring. React the way a student would who isn't expecting to run into drug runners.

Right.

Besides, the guy didn't seem threatening. He too had stumbled back a few paces.

"Sorry." She pressed a hand to her chest. "You scared me."

After a moment, the man slowly reached up and removed his mask.

Will Fischer. Ivy Hill's security chief.

Why was he hiking the grounds on such a cold day?

"You're the new student, aren't you?"

She feigned innocence. "Yes. Who are you?"

"Mr. Fischer. Head of security."

"Oh . . . right. I saw you last weekend at check-in. Ms. Howard, the house mom, pointed you out."

"What are you doing here?"

She shrugged. "Taking a walk. At home, I walked every day. That's okay, isn't it? One of the girls told me about the trails through the woods."

"It's fine—but it's always safer to walk with a friend. And only in daylight."

She affected a shiver. "I make sure to be back in the dorm

before dark. Trust me, I wouldn't be caught dead in these woods at night."

A flicker of emotion passed across his face, too fast for her to identify. "Ivy Hill is safe, but it pays to be cautious."

"Yeah. That's what my dad always says."

"Listen to him."

She tucked her chilling fingers under her armpits to add another layer of insulation to the Sealskinz gloves. "Is that why you're out here? Keeping the place safe?"

He tugged his ski mask back down, hiding his features. "Yes. We added a day and night grounds patrol first of the year. The safety of our students is our primary concern."

"That's good to know. I heard about the girl who disappeared from here last fall."

"By choice. She ran off with her boyfriend." His tone was flat. Emotionless.

Like everyone else, Fischer was sticking with the original police verdict.

Except someone knew it wasn't true.

Who?

Could Will Fischer be involved?

Did he know if the disappearance was connected to the drug ring?

Yet why would a man who'd spent his life protecting people go over to the dark side?

Still . . . who would be in a more perfect position to provide access to the barn for the drug ring than the man with keys?

Other than Eduardo, obviously. The maintenance supervisor had the run of the place too.

How deep had the DEA dug into the two men's backgrounds?

One more question for Zeke.

Meanwhile, County was about to get a request to take a second look at them.

"Yeah. I heard that." Cate swiped at her dripping nose and glanced around at the lengthening shadows. "I should get back. It'll be dark soon."

"Smart plan."

He stayed where he was as she started down the path through the woods that led to the school.

When she sneaked a peek back before she rounded a bend that would hide the barn from view, he was still there.

Watching her.

Did he want to make certain she was safe—or was he worried about another girl wandering into an area best circumvented?

No answer came as she trekked back to the dorm, frozen leaves crunching under her boots, a mournful wind whistling through the treetops.

Perhaps Fischer's appearance today was innocent. After all, taking into account the secluded acreage and the fact a student had disappeared, any conscientious security chief would be pursuing opportunities to beef up protection for everyone on the property. The addition of patrols around the grounds wasn't at all suspicious.

So why was she picking up a false note in the man's story?

And if he did have inside information about what had happened that night, did that mean he was involved in Zeke's drug ring?

Not necessarily, if the two events ended up being unrelated.

As for Noah Evans and Eduardo Garcia—how did they fit into the picture . . . or did they?

Was anyone else at the school involved in either of the cases under investigation?

So many questions, too few answers.

Yet.

A cracking noise from above her echoed through the quiet woods, and she looked up—just in time to dodge a dead branch that dropped to the ground where she'd been standing.

She stared at the bulky limb blocking the path behind her that led to the barn. Swallowed.

How weird.

It was almost like an omen. A warning to curtail her walks in the woods—and stay away from the barn.

Shaking her head, she huffed out a breath.

That was stupid.

She was just spooked by the unexpected encounter with Fischer and her solo jaunt into the forest. While hiking her favorite trails at Cuivre River State Park and camping under the stars alone when she was off duty was refreshing and relaxing, poking around in the woods by herself with murder afoot was neither.

Picking up her pace, she broke into a half jog.

Truth be told, this whole setting was giving her the willies. A crime scene with scores of County people milling about, or teaming up with another detective to interrogate a suspect who rained threats on her, were far preferable to this.

Without her Sig on her hip, the authority and buffer of her badge, and backup only a phone call away, the sense of vulnerability was unnerving.

Not that she'd ever admit such a thing to Zeke, with his overdeveloped protective instincts.

Nevertheless . . . she wouldn't mind having his company on future excursions like this.

Another confession that would remain unspoken.

She shoved a branch out of her path and scowled.

What was wrong with her, anyway? As she'd told Grace two weeks ago, she did *not* need a man in her life.

She especially did not need a DEA agent who'd led her to believe he loved her, then walked away the instant an appealing job opportunity was dangled in front of him.

How could he do that, after she'd—

Pressure built behind her eyes, and she blinked to clear her vision.

Enough of this pity party.

Zeke was history. His nebulous reference to a debt may have piqued her interest, but it didn't change the past.

It could have a bearing on your future, though.

An image of her mom appeared in her mind on the heels of that thought.

Yeah, that sounded like Mom. If she were here, she'd no doubt view the unexpected meeting as divine intervention. A prod to revisit what had happened, an opportunity to bind up wounds and offer forgiveness.

But how did you forgive someone for shredding your dreams and taking your—

A squirrel skittered away from her as she hurried through the decaying leaves, and she pulled up short.

The critter resorted to zigzag evasive maneuvers and took cover as fast as he could.

An example she'd be wise to follow with Zeke.

For as the anger and hurt she thought she'd buried long ago swept over her again, fresh as the day Zeke had walked out, her world tilted.

And until she regained her balance, being around him could be as dangerous as walking alone in a shadowy forest where murder lurked.

9

"**M**AY I JOIN YOU?**"** Posing the question in Spanish, Zeke stopped beside the table where Eduardo was eating lunch in the student cafeteria—an Ivy Hill egalitarian policy that played right into his plan to get to know the non-faculty players.

The maintenance supervisor looked up from his phone. "Um—most of the teachers eat over there." He motioned across the room, where several of Zeke's colleagues had congregated.

"I know. But I've met all of them. Now I'm trying to get to know the rest of the staff." He lowered his tray to the table and sat without waiting for an invitation.

The other man pocketed his phone and picked up his half-eaten burger. "I'm sure their conversation would be more interesting. I lead a quiet, simple life."

"Quiet simplicity has much to recommend it." Zeke flashed a smile and started in on his soup, keeping his tone casual. "So tell me about yourself. I take it you're from Mexico?"

"Yes." A defensive note crept into his voice. "But I'm here legally."

"I assumed as much. I doubt Ivy Hill would have hired you

otherwise." Zeke continued to sip his soup, staying in chitchat mode. "How did you end up in St. Louis?"

"My wife had a cousin who lived here. He's moved on now."

That matched the DEA's research.

"Makes sense. Family connections are always helpful, especially if you're in a new place."

A shadow darkened the man's eyes, and he averted his gaze. "Yeah."

Curious.

"Any other relatives here?"

"No." His reply came out fast. Too fast. Then he changed the subject. "You speak Spanish very well. Do you have family in Mexico?"

The man didn't want to talk about his history.

Why?

Was he sensitive because of all the attention being directed toward immigration by government and media—or did he have a more personal motive for wanting to shift the focus of the conversation?

Zeke played along as he continued to eat his soup. "No. My father's from Spain, but I've visited Mexico. It's a beautiful country."

"You speak Spanish like a Mexican. Teresa, the teacher you replaced, is from Spain and her Spanish is a little different than yours."

Uh-oh.

While coming across as a Mexican national had been critical for his DEA work, his role here was different. He was supposed to be Spanish, not Mexican.

He'd have to work on adapting the voseo Spanish he'd learned from his Argentine mother to suit this assignment as he had for his previous jobs in Mexico. In the Ivy Hill environment, only a native Mexican would likely pick up on the differences in dialects. . . but perhaps it would be safer to speak English with Eduardo in future conversations.

"I have friends in Mexico." He kept his tone light and scooped up more soup. "I suppose through the years my Spanish has become a blend of different styles."

The other man finished off his burger. "I can see how that would happen. I've heard many variations of Spanish since my wife and I came to the United States." He patted his pocket and pulled out his cell. "Excuse me a moment."

"Of course."

He put the phone to his ear and switched to English. "Yes?" As he listened, his skin lost a few shades of color. "I'll be right there." He ended the call but maintained a tight grip on the cell. "I'm sorry. I have a . . . visitor."

Also curious.

Who would visit Eduardo at work—and why would that person's presence distress him?

Zeke scooped up the last couple spoonsful of soup, wiped his lips, and set his napkin on the tray. "I'll walk with you. I have to stop at the teachers' lounge before my next class." A perfect excuse to accompany the man, as that route took him past the reception desk at the main entrance.

Eduardo hesitated for a moment . . . then stood and picked up his tray in silence.

As the two of them wove through the cafeteria to deposit their trays near the kitchen, they passed the table Cate was sharing with Kayla Harris.

She didn't acknowledge his presence—but she was cognizant of it. Sparks of awareness radiated off her as he brushed by.

The woman who'd once given him her heart might not *want* to have anything to do with him, but her body was sending other signals.

A positive sign for down the road, after they were done

with their undercover assignments and could reassume their real identities.

As they left the cafeteria behind, Zeke attempted to initiate small talk with Eduardo, but the man responded in monosyllables and quickened his pace.

More evidence he was spooked by whoever had come calling.

Will was at the front desk when they approached, and both he and the visitor glanced their direction.

Zeke studied the dark-haired, dark-complected man who was carrying a small parcel. Mexican, no question about it. A friend—or relative—of Eduardo's?

He appraised his lunch companion.

No friend, judging by Eduardo's grim expression.

At the desk, Eduardo took the man's arm. "Thank you, Will. Excuse me, Zeke." He led the visitor toward an empty classroom down the hall without offering any introductions. As soon as they disappeared inside, the door closed behind them.

Zeke turned to Will to find the security officer squinting at the duo.

"Everything okay?" As he asked the question, Zeke skimmed the visitor sign-in log on the reception desk. Miguel something. The chicken scratching was difficult to decipher.

"I hope so." Will regarded the closed door. "In this business, you learn to pay attention to vibes—and I didn't get positive ones from that guy."

"A friend of Eduardo's?"

"His brother-in-law. Says he lives with him."

If that was true, Eduardo had lied about not having other relatives in the area.

"I didn't think he had any family here." He pulled out his cell and pretended to check messages, as if the conversation was inconsequential.

"He's never mentioned any." Will scanned the monitor

behind the desk, which displayed the feed from various security cameras around the property. "I'll talk to Eduardo after he leaves. I didn't get the impression he was happy to see him—and we can put him on the no-admit list if that's his preference."

"Sounds like a plan. In this day and age, you can't be too careful."

"Yeah." Will busied himself straightening the papers on the desk.

The conversation was over.

Zeke continued down the hall, once again playing with his phone as he strolled past the closed classroom door.

The low rumble of conversation on the other side was in Spanish, but hard as he tried, he could pick up no more than a few words.

Yet the ones he heard set off a red alert.

Riesgo. Policía. Peligroso.

Risk. Police. Dangerous.

He also detected two distinct emotions in the inflections—fury . . . and fear.

Cate had suggested his singling out of Eduardo amounted to profiling.

Maybe it was, to a certain degree.

But from all indications, his suspicions were paying off.

Perhaps Eduardo didn't have any involvement in the cartel pipeline under investigation, but it was looking more and more as if he had information that could be useful to law enforcement.

Yet every instinct in Zeke's body told him there *was* a connection between the maintenance supervisor and the illegal activity taking place on the far end of Ivy Hill property.

Instead of continuing to the lounge, he detoured into another empty classroom. A background check on Miguel could turn up helpful information—if there was any to be found.

And therein lay a problem.

While Eduardo's background check had indicated he was a legitimate immigrant with the proper papers who was trying to make a new life for himself, his wife, and his unborn child, his brother-in-law—if that was, indeed, the visitor's connection to him—could be one of the many who came across the border illegally.

Some for nefarious purposes.

If that was the case, there likely wasn't much information to be had—and hauling him in for questioning could be a mistake. If he was somehow connected to the pipeline, such a move could tip off the main man that law enforcement was onto the operation. Tents would fold, the players they'd already identified would melt into the night . . . and all the work they'd done would be in vain.

Best case was to convince Eduardo to talk.

But family loyalties were strong in Mexico—perhaps stronger than loyalties to an adopted country.

So for now, he'd keep watching, listening, probing—and hope either he or Cate came across a solid lead that would put them on track to solving a missing persons case . . . and blowing up a drug cartel pipeline.

"I have a tentative time frame for you."

Will closed his eyes. Clenched his teeth. Slumped against the wall in his tiny kitchen.

The nightmare never ended.

These calls had become so routine, in fact, that his contact didn't even bother with a greeting anymore. Just got straight to business.

"Already?"

"Business is booming. What can I say? And we're planning a bit ahead. The target is around February 1. I'll give you definite dates as soon as I have them. Same procedure. You've added physical patrols to the routine?"

"Yes."

"Excellent. A circuit in the appropriate areas around midnight on certain nights would be advisable to avoid any . . . complications."

More confirmation that Stephanie Laurent and her boyfriend had tangled with the wrong people—as if he'd had any doubt.

The permanent knot in his stomach tightened.

"I can't keep doing this. Someone's going to catch on. And I can't stop people from wandering the grounds. That would be suspicious. I found another student out there yesterday. She said she walks every day."

"You'll have to control that."

"How?"

Several beats of silence ticked by.

"We'll see if we can give you an excuse to suggest to the administration that it would be best if students and staff confine their wanderings to the main campus around the buildings and stay away from the woods."

A muscle beside Will's eye twitched. "What sort of excuse?"

"That isn't your concern. When does she walk?"

An ache began to throb in his temples. "After school on weekdays, I guess. She said she's always back in the dorm by dark. I don't—"

"Text me the student's name and photo."

His pulse surged, and he pushed off from the wall. Began to pace. "Look—I don't want anyone else to get hurt."

"And we don't want our arrangement exposed. I'll be in touch with dates soon for delivery and pickup. While we wait for that information, I suggest you take advantage of any convenient excuse that arises to restrict access to the far reaches of the property."

The line went dead.

Will stabbed the end button and muttered a string of words he would never use on campus.

This was out of control.

If the person who'd bailed him out of his troubles was willing to target another innocent person to create a safe zone for illegal activities, nothing was off-limits.

His only hope was that a glitch would develop and render the Ivy Hill location less desirable.

But *he* couldn't create that glitch. Not without risking his life. The methods these people used to get rid of problems were lethal.

Nor could he go to law enforcement with the information he had. He was too complicit—and he couldn't even bargain for leniency by offering to identify his contact. The brains behind this had gone to great lengths to remain anonymous, as evidenced by the use of a voice-changing device for phone calls.

Will dropped into a chair at the dinette table and stared at his laptop screen.

Only one activity could distract him for a few minutes, give him a brief respite from the pressure cooker that had become his life.

Yes, he'd vowed after his previous lapse not to slip again—but he could control his impulses once he was online. Hadn't he done so last time?

He clicked on the bookmarked site, and the familiar page opened.

Give in—or walk away?

But what would he do if he resisted temptation?

Worry? Drink gin? Overdose on sleeping pills?

A wave of depression swept over him, and he moved his finger into position. Suz would be angry if she found out about this, but how would she? And once they reconciled, he'd never touch this site again.

Guaranteed.

As for the bigger dilemma that had dominated his life for months—maybe it wasn't as bad as he thought. After all, glitch or no glitch, his contact wouldn't use the Ivy Hill grounds forever. One of these days, the operation would move somewhere else. Illegal activities always did. Staying in one place too long, no matter how convenient, upped the risk.

If he could wait this out, everything would be fine. Once his contact had no more use for his services, he or she and their organization would disappear—and no one would ever know about the small role a certain security officer had played during their tenure at the school.

At least that's what he hoped would happen before anyone else got hurt.

Except perhaps the unlucky student his contact had asked about.

Cate Sheppard.

10

A S USUAL, ZEKE WAS WAITING FOR HER.
Cate hefted the loaded backpack that seemed to be standard school gear for teens these days into a more comfortable position and entered the library.

Only a few students occupied the tables in the center of the room on this Tuesday afternoon, most wearing earbuds as they worked. None paid any attention to her.

Neither did Zeke. Behind the glass walls of the study cube, he remained focused on the papers in front of him, giving her a few moments to appraise him unobserved.

Eight years ago, he'd been the handsomest man she'd ever met.

That hadn't changed.

If anything, age had enhanced his dark good looks. Even the fading scar on his temple couldn't detract from his magnetism. And other than his slight limp, he appeared to be in excellent physical condition.

From everything she'd observed since their unexpected reunion, his strong work ethic and commitment to justice appeared solid as ever too.

Yet he was also different.

The restlessness that had always been a part of him appeared to have mellowed, and the deep sadness that had some-times added another layer of darkness to his ebony eyes had faded. Nor did he seem as plagued by the personal demons he'd never shared with her but that had always shadowed his smiles.

Were those demons related to the debt he'd referenced during their last meeting?

She expelled an annoyed breath.

It hadn't been fair for him to throw out that tantalizing nugget, then retreat.

Not that she cared about what was going on with his psyche, of course. Those days were past.

Cate tightened her grip on the strap of the backpack as she watched the man who'd blithely tossed aside the love she'd offered him.

Faint furrows creasing his brow, he concentrated on the paper before him and jotted notes with bold, confident strokes.

Bold.

Confident.

Terms that had fit him eight years ago.

Terms that still fit.

A sudden surge of yearning swept over her, so strong she groped for the back of a chair at the nearest table.

No!

She would *not* succumb to his charms again, set herself up for another fall. The old adage about being once burned and twice shy was true.

It was called self-preservation.

Despite Zeke's hint that he'd like to talk to her about more personal matters, she had no intention of—

He looked up, locked gazes with her—and shorted out her respiration.

Oh, for pity's sake.

Letting the man fluster her with mere eye contact was not acceptable.

She tipped up her chin, squeezed the strap on her backpack until her fingernails bit into her palm, and marched toward the study room.

This would be a business session.

Nothing more.

He rose when she entered, as he always did. "Were you waiting long for me to notice you?"

In other words, how long had she been standing there watching him?

"I just got here." Close enough.

She dropped her backpack onto a chair, shrugged out of her parka and gloves, and claimed her usual seat.

"You're dressed for an arctic excursion."

"Or a walk around Ivy Hill in the dead of winter." She fished out her Spanish book and suppressed a shiver. "I hate cold weather."

"I know." Amusement lurking in the depths of his irises, he retook his seat, fiddled with his phone, and set it between them. "Remember the night we had ringside seats at the hockey game and I had to loan you my jacket? You claimed there was a cold breeze whenever a player skated by."

Yeah, she remembered that—and more.

Like how she'd used the chilly temperature as an excuse to cuddle up to her date.

At least he hadn't mentioned that.

But the sudden heat in his eyes suggested that memory had surfaced for him too.

He masked his emotions at once, however, and opened the book. "Anything new with your case?"

Willing her pulse to slow down, she pretended to study the page in front of her and briefed him on her encounter with the security chief and the new foot patrols—though her voice wasn't quite as steady as his. "Does it strike you as a bit strange for him to do that if he believes Stephanie left the premises of her own volition?"

"We do live in a world where violence is prevalent, and this is an isolated location. The administration may have gotten pressure from parents to beef up security. Her disappearance could have rattled them, even if it was innocent."

That was possible.

"Maybe."

"Did you find anything of interest during your walk, or at the barn?"

"A new padlock on the door and newer windows, one of which may have been jimmied—but no evidence Stephanie had been there. I'm going to go back and do a grid search over the next few days. I'm not giving up on the idea she may have dropped something if she ran into trouble. I also saw the camera at the state highway entrance. I assume the DEA has never requested that footage."

"No. If the wrong people found out, it could tip them off we're onto the location. Besides, it's a low-end camera that covers only a small area near the gate, the visits are in the dark, and we've got human eyes with night vision goggles watching the comings and goings—and taking photos."

"That's what I figured. County did request general security footage from the weekend of the disappearance during our initial investigation. According to the report, there's no evidence Stephanie left the dorm, nor was there any activity by the back gate. In light of what I now know about *your* case, it may be worth another review."

"The security cameras are easy to spot—and easy to avoid. She could have left the dorm through a window out of camera range. But if the security tape from the back gate doesn't show any activity, there may not be a link between a cartel delivery or pickup and her disappearance."

"I know—but my instincts tell me there's a connection."

"Instincts don't take the place of hard evidence." One side of his mouth quirked as he parroted her earlier admonition back to her.

"I'll keep that in mind." She tamped the urge to smile at his tease. "What's new on your end?"

"I had lunch with Eduardo."

"I know. I saw you." And it had taken every ounce of her self-control to keep her attention on her turkey club wrap rather than him while she ate. "You still have suspicions?"

"More than ever."

She turned the page in the book as he told her about the man's unexpected visitor and their alarm-triggering conversation.

So *his* instincts had been spot-on.

Maybe hers were too—and a closer review of that security tape could vindicate her hunch.

"Did your people find out anything about this Miguel guy?"

"No. We assume his last name is Hernandez—that's Margarita's maiden name—but he's nowhere to be found in any immigration records. Nor is he on ICE's radar."

She tapped a finger against the page. "No green card or visa information, and the Immigration and Customs Enforcement people haven't tagged him. That would suggest he's here illegally but otherwise clean."

"Or very dirty but managing to stay under the radar. I vote for the latter after the snippet of conversation I heard. That exchange could also suggest Eduardo is involved in criminal activity too."

"Not necessarily. Our research shows he came in legally, has all the proper paperwork, holds a responsible job, and is starting a family. Aiding and abetting anything illicit—let alone a drug ring—doesn't fit."

"Unless he's being coerced."

"How?"

"I don't know—but we're going to put surveillance on his house for a few days. That may turn up helpful information. Anything new with Noah Evans?"

"Not yet, but we're digging deeper on him too. I'm curious about the grounds for his divorce."

"He lived in New York, right?"

Zeke had done his homework on the players—no surprise there. He'd always been a thorough investigator.

"Yes. So the record should be public, unless the court sealed it."

"Unlikely, barring a domestic violence issue."

"I'm not expecting that."

"You going to talk to the ex?"

"Depends on what's in the divorce record." She clicked her pen shut. "Anything else?"

"I think we're up to speed. Same time Thursday?"

"I'll be here." She closed the book, slid it into the backpack, and waved at Kayla on the other side of the glass.

"How goes it with the roommate?"

"I'm making progress. We're studying together today until dinner. But it'll take a while to build a relationship. She hasn't had the best experience with, as she put it, rich white girls." She rose, anger bubbling up inside her again.

"Sad."

"Very. Her former roommates didn't have to treat her like a sister, but would it have killed them to be friendly?"

"I agree." He stood too. "Speaking of sisters—how are Grace and Eve?"

"Fine. Grace is a forensic pathologist in rural Missouri, and Eve has a national radio show. She got engaged over Christmas to—"

Cate stiffened and clamped her lips shut. That was more family history than Zeke deserved to know. More than she should have shared. They had nothing to discuss except their cases.

Thankfully, he didn't press her or ask any other questions.

"I'm glad to hear they're both doing well." He motioned toward Kayla, who was watching their exchange. "I don't want to keep you from your homework."

Without commenting, she stalked out of the fishbowl and joined Kayla, who'd claimed a table against the far wall.

"You didn't have to hurry on my account." The other girl draped her coat over a chair.

"We were done." Cate dumped her backpack on the table and, in true detective fashion, chose a chair against the wall that offered a clear view of the room—though she ignored Zeke.

Kayla, on the other hand, gave the man her full attention. "What were you and Mr. Martinez talking about?"

"Spanish. What else?" Cate sat.

"I don't know." Kayla slid into her chair. "It just seemed kinda like . . . like you were having a fight."

Uh-oh.

If Kayla was picking up less-than-professional vibes between them, others could be too.

Cate forced out a laugh. "Arguing with teachers gets you an F."

"Yeah—but you did look upset."

"He gave me extra homework."

"Oh. That would tick me off too." Kayla opened her trig book. "But it didn't read like that kind of mad, you know?"

Yeah, she did—and she couldn't take the risk anyone else would notice her interactions with Zeke and deem them suspicious.

As long as they were talking cases, that wouldn't be a problem.

So going forward, she'd make it clear to him that all personal subjects and comments were off-limits to protect their investigations and their covers.

Not to mention her heart.

———————

As his burner phone began to vibrate, Wolf muted the TV and picked up the cell from the table beside him. Only two people had this number, and Will Fischer wasn't likely to initiate a call.

He checked the screen.

Yeah. It was Razor.

The man got straight to business. "Sorry to call this late, but you said to let you know once everything was set."

"No worries. I had a busy day and was unwinding with reruns." Wolf smiled as Gilligan and the skipper indulged in slapstick comedy, then picked up the remote and killed the power. "I don't have to know details. All I want is confirmation the job has been arranged."

"I understand, boss. It will be done no later than Friday."

"You have someone trustworthy lined up?"

"Yeah. The guy I mentioned who I've been training to be my second-in-command after you leave for a life of sun and surf. I passed along the photo and the map."

"Is he reliable?"

"He has been so far, but I'm watching him . . . and he knows it. This job will be a test of his skills—and his loyalty."

"It also gives you leverage if he gets out of line."

"That did occur to me."

"I've taught you well."

"Yeah." Razor gave a soft laugh. "You have."

Wolf rose and walked over to the window. Parted the blinds.

All was quiet on this Tuesday night.

Just how he liked it.

"You're certain he understood the instructions?" The less blood on his hands the better, no matter how distant he was from the actual crime.

"Yes. I passed them along."

"Good." Too bad it had come to this—but young women shouldn't be wandering around isolated property alone. In the long run, the incident could save another girl from harm at the hands of someone who had a more personal objective in mind.

A stretch, perhaps, but there was a tiny germ of truth in that justification.

"You want a report afterward?"

"I'll hear about it from other sources." Wolf shut the drapes.

"Got it."

"This new guy you found . . . again, no details necessary . . . share as little as possible until you're certain he's worthy of your trust."

"That's the plan."

"He's not a user, is he?"

"Not anymore. He's gone from customer to colleague."

"Keep an eye on him. No users allowed in management. It's too dangerous."

"I know the rules."

"You haven't told him anything about me, have you?"

"No. All he knows is that I report to the St. Louis boss who has ties to the people in Mexico."

Despite his colleague's reassurance, a niggle of unease tingled through him. While Razor had been a faithful and trustworthy partner for years, doing every job he'd been assigned and handling the dirtier part of the business without a complaint, the fact that someone—anyone—could finger him if they chose was unnerving. Total anonymity would have been far preferable.

But that wasn't how it had worked out, and at this stage fretting about what he couldn't change was useless. All he had to do was hang in another few months and his worries and sleepless nights would be history.

"Keep it that way."

"Naturally. Any firm dates for the next delivery?"

"Not yet. I'll be in touch with details as soon as I have them."

"Okay. Talk to you soon."

The line went dead, and Wolf tapped the end button, set the phone back on the table, and wandered toward the bedroom. Tomorrow would be a busy day, and it was important he remain at the top of his game. No one must ever suspect he was running a side business that was far more profitable than his day job.

At the dresser near his bed, he paused. Surveyed the photos arrayed on top. Homed in on the one from the happiest day of his life.

Bitterness coiled in his gut, and anger coursed through him.

No one on the outside looking in might understand the motivations behind his secret enterprise, but they were real. And legitimate.

Profiting off the backs of users was sweet revenge—and until the day he died, he wouldn't regret hurting any of them.

Only the innocents who'd stood in his way deserved one iota of sympathy.

But he wasn't going to let his conscience put a heavy guilt trip on him or make him rethink his choices.

It was too late for that.

And if more people had to suffer before he reached his goal—so be it.

11

PAY DIRT.

    Pushing aside the dead branches in a pile of brush, Cate bent and retrieved the silver earring.

If the wind hadn't blown aside the fallen leaves for a millisecond . . . if the setting sun hadn't peeked past a pine tree at the ideal moment . . . if she hadn't been situated in the perfect position to catch a glimpse of the shimmer from the shiny surface . . . she'd have missed it.

While the first three quadrants she'd mentally mapped off around the barn had produced zilch, this find more than made up for all the hours spent poking around in finger-and-toe-numbing cold.

Assuming the earring belonged to Stephanie.

A reasonable possibility, given the fleur-de-lis design that was in keeping with the girl's French surname and the excellent condition it was in, which suggested it hadn't been here long.

Her father might recognize it—or perhaps Kayla could confirm it was Stephanie's.

Straightening up, Cate pocketed the piece of jewelry. Not bad for a Thursday afternoon's work.

And with the sun beginning to dip . . . with stray pellets

of ice beginning to prick her cheeks . . . it was time to call it a day.

She adjusted her hood and set off down the trail that led back to the school, a cup of steaming coffee high on her priority list. That would help chase away the chill in her bones.

Five minutes later, as she was planning next steps in her investigation, a twig crunched behind her.

Pulse surging, she swung around and gave the forest a scan.

Inconclusive.

The deciduous oaks and maples had shed their leaves, but the proliferation of cedars and pines restricted her view.

In all probability, a deer was scavenging nearby. There were always a few around during her walks, though in general they kept their distance.

And no one had been skulking about while she was at the barn. Thanks to the high alert she'd maintained there after her close encounter with Fischer, she'd have spotted them.

But dropping her guard during the hike back may not have been wise.

No harm done, however—and a useful reminder to remain vigilant no matter where she was in the woods.

She picked up her pace, gaze sweeping right and left as she hurried through the lengthening shadows. In another fifteen minutes, it would be pitch dark—but her diligence had paid off.

If the earring proved to be Stephanie's—and the girl had been wearing it when last seen—they'd have a solid clue to her whereabouts on the night she'd disappeared.

Rereading the interviews the case detectives had done could be helpful, assuming the last people to see Stephanie had provided a detailed description of her attire. If they hadn't, another chat with them to probe their memories for specific details they may have neglected to mention would—

The tackle came from out of nowhere.

One second she was on her feet, the next she was pitching forward, into a face-plant on the rotting leaves that covered the trail.

Adrenaline surging, she rolled to her side—and gasped as the toe of a hard boot connected with her rib cage.

Despite her down-filled coat, the kick sent pain ricocheting through her.

As she struggled to inflate her lungs, the attacker drew his foot back again.

No!

Her shock morphed into anger.

She was *not* going to be a victim!

As the assailant let loose with another kick, she grabbed his ankle and twisted her body, throwing him off-balance.

He fell with a thud—and a curse.

A Spanish curse.

She jumped to her feet, ignoring the throb in her rib cage.

Fighting with this guy—and based on his strength and build, her attacker was male, even though his black balaclava concealed his features—was a bad idea.

If she wasn't already hurt, she could hold her own in a hand-to-hand altercation—but her ribs had taken a hit.

Besides, without her trusty Sig, if he pulled a knife or gun she was sunk.

Best plan? Disable him enough to get a running start and race toward the school. Once she emerged from the woods, he'd take a huge risk if he followed her.

As he sprang to his feet and lunged at her, she went into attack mode. Pulling out every self-defense move she knew, she aimed for his more vulnerable areas. Heel of hand to his nose, finger poke in the eyes, jab to the throat, and a kick to the groin that doubled him over and broke his hold.

This was her chance.

She took off down the path, running as fast as her aching ribs allowed, hood flopping back.

Seconds later, an object whizzed past her.

What was—

Ow!

She stumbled as something hard collided with the back of her head. Dropped to one knee. Fought a wave of dizziness.

Had she been . . . shot?

No. That didn't make sense. There'd been no sound of gunfire.

She blinked, trying to clear her vision.

A bloody rock on the ground beside her came into focus.

The guy had hit her with a *rock*?

That must mean he didn't have a gun.

But why wait around to find out?

She forced herself back to her feet, took two steps forward— and crumpled as her legs gave out.

Behind her, the crunch of leaves indicated the guy was stirring. Recovering from the blows she'd rained on him. Soon, he'd be back in fighting form and able to do far more than throw a few well-aimed rocks.

Which was more than she could say about herself as the landscape around her tilted.

The blow to the head had done a number on her.

Meaning there was no way she was going to be able to fend him off again—or make it back to safety in one piece.

Cate was late.

Ten minutes late.

Zeke frowned as the digital clock on the far wall in the library flicked to the next number.

This wasn't like her. If she'd been delayed, she would have texted him.

He double-checked his messages.

Nothing.

He tried texting *her*.

Waited sixty eternal seconds.

No reply.

Kayla entered the library, and Zeke rose. Maybe her roommate knew why Cate hadn't shown.

He left the study cube and met up with the girl in the small niche off to the side she seemed to prefer over the long tables where many of the students congregated.

The rich white girls who she'd hinted to Cate had made her feel less than welcome.

"Hi, Mr. Martinez." The girl set her paraphernalia on the table as he drew close.

"Hi. I'm supposed to meet your roommate for a study session, but she hasn't shown. Do you happen to know where she is?"

Twin grooves creased the girl's forehead. "No. She went for a walk about an hour ago. I figured she came straight here afterward."

A sense of foreboding swirled through him. "Do you know where she went?"

It was a logical question, one any teacher would ask, but he already knew the answer.

She'd been to the barn again. Searching for evidence Stephanie had been there.

"She usually takes the trail at the back of school." Kayla played with the drawstring on her hooded sweatshirt, working her lower lip between her teeth. "Do you think there's a problem?"

"I wouldn't worry yet." He tried for a casual tone, but his slight vibrato was telling. To him, anyway. "I'll take a walk around, see if I can find her."

He headed for the library door, quashing his first impulse to barrel outside coatless and race toward the barn.

Not smart if he wanted to protect his cover. As a teacher, of course he'd be concerned about any student who could be in trouble—but he wouldn't go off half-cocked like a man in love would.

Man in love.

Slowly, he exhaled.

Yeah, that was him.

He pushed through the door.

Hard as he'd tried to forget about Cate, hard as he'd tried to convince himself he was in control of his feelings, hard as he'd tried to console himself with the hope that maybe when the time was right he'd meet a woman he could love as much as he'd loved her, it had all been a lie.

He'd never forgotten her.

Never stopped loving her.

And he never would.

Quickening his pace, he detoured toward the teachers' lounge. Snatched up his coat. Sped toward the door at the rear of the school and exited.

Dusk was falling, but there was ample light in the open area around the school.

The woods, however, were a different story.

They were already dark.

And perhaps dangerous.

Drug deliveries and pickups didn't take place at this hour, but that didn't mean there wasn't risk in wandering around the—

Zeke squinted.

There . . . a few yards back in the gloom of the woods. Was that shadowy form weaving about a . . . person?

Moments later, as the figure drew closer to the light, he had his answer—and his pulse rocketed.

It wasn't just a person.

It was Cate.

And she was staggering.

He broke into a sprint.

"Cate!"

As he called her name, she slumped against a tree and peered his direction.

"Stay there! I'm coming."

Accelerating into a full-out run, he reached her in less than half a minute.

Sucked in a breath.

Her pallor and slightly glazed eyes confirmed she'd run into trouble—and twisted his gut into a pretzel.

"What happened?" His question came out in a croak.

She scrunched up her face, as if trying to focus. "There was . . . someone . . . in the woods."

"Are you hurt?"

"I think . . . there was a . . . rock." She lifted her hand toward the back of her head, but the instant she let go of the tree, she swayed.

"Whoa." He steadied her, gently turned her head sideways—and almost lost what little lunch was left in his stomach.

Her hair was dark and matted with blood.

You'd think, after all the gore he'd seen in the field, he could handle a head injury.

But not on Cate.

Legs suddenly shaky, he bent, tucked his arm under her knees, and picked her up.

Her lack of protest was scarier than her appearance.

Unless she was badly hurt, Cate would never have let him touch her, let alone carry her anywhere.

He tightened his protective grip.

She moaned and dropped a cheek to his chest. "Bruised . . . ribs."

Raining silent curses on himself, he loosened his hold. Hurting Cate wasn't acceptable.

Not ever again.

"I'm sorry."

"No . . . worries. I'll . . . live."

Yeah, she would. Cate was a survivor through and through.

He started back toward the school, brain buzzing. They had only a couple of minutes to talk without witnesses, and he needed answers, even if her mind was fuzzy.

"Cate . . . tell me what happened."

"He came . . . from behind." Her voice was muffled against his chest and a bit breathless. As if she was struggling to get a grip on her pain.

He slowed his stride, trying to jostle her as little as possible. "Did you see who it was?"

"No. Face . . . was covered."

"Did he say anything?"

"He cursed—in Spanish."

An excellent clue.

"How do you want to play this?" A few students walking between the main building and the dorms had paused to gawk at them. "We've got an audience."

"I can say . . . I fell."

Not going to work—and if her brainpower hadn't been compromised, she'd realize that.

It was up to him to put together a credible game plan.

"That won't fly. If someone on the inside staged this and you lie about what happened, they'll be suspicious."

"Oh. Yeah."

"Tell the truth—but leave out the part about hearing any Spanish."

Kayla emerged from the main building and watched their approach too.

Kayla.

A plan began to form in his mind.

"I'll offer to drive you to urgent care on my way home. If someone else wants to bring you back, fine. If not, I'll volunteer to wait around. Ask Kayla to come with you. We have to talk—but thanks to the world we live in, a chaperone would be expected. Once we're there, I'll finagle a few minutes alone for us if necessary."

"Okay."

The door from the main building opened again and two figures emerged. "We're about to have company. Tucker and Fischer."

He kept walking as the two men jogged toward them, their complexions almost as pasty as Cate's.

Panting from exertion, Tucker gave her a quick once-over. "What happened?"

"Someone jumped her in the woods."

More color seeped from the man's face. "I'll call the police— and an ambulance."

"No." Cate roused herself. "I'm . . . not hurt that bad."

"An ambulance may be overkill," Zeke interjected. "Why don't I run her to an urgent care on my way home? The police can meet us there."

"Ask . . . ask Kayla to come with me." Cate sent an imploring glance to Tucker. "Please."

She was sticking to the script.

Good girl.

The president hesitated.

"She's back there. In the crowd." Zeke nodded toward the throng that was gathering on the sidewalk. "Having another student go with us would be prudent."

"Yes. I agree." He angled sideways, picked Kayla out of the crowd, and motioned her over.

The girl disengaged from the group and joined them, brow puckered.

"Kayla . . . I have to go to urgent care. Would you come with me? I don't have any other friends here yet." Cate reached out and touched the girl's arm.

Her roommate's features softened. "Sure. What happened?" She directed the question to Tucker.

"She ran into someone up to no good in the woods."

"I told you letting the girls wander around on the property wasn't safe." Will planted his fists on his hips, mouth flat. "Even with the new patrols, we can't be everywhere every minute."

"You're right. Before you leave for the day, let's discuss what kinds of changes we should implement. I can announce any new policies at tomorrow's assembly. Zeke, I'll notify Cate's father about the incident and pick her up at urgent care. If you could stay with her until I get there, I'd appreciate it."

"No problem. Kayla, let's go."

He strode across the frozen lawn, and the girl fell in beside him. The group on the sidewalk parted to let them through, the students' shocked demeanors and quiet murmurs adding to the jittery cadence of this day.

But the worst was over. Barring a severe head injury, which didn't appear likely, Cate would recover.

The real question was why had it happened at all—and why to her? Had she been specifically targeted?

If so, that could mean her cover had been blown.

Yet that didn't add up.

If someone had realized she was here to investigate Stephanie's disappearance, why stop at mere intimidation? Why not take her out? Her attacker had had more than sufficient opportunity to finish the job after she was woozy from the blow to her head.

Cate shifted in his arms, and he dipped his chin to find her watching him, her expression unguarded . . . and filled with longing.

Thanks to her foggy mental state, it took her several seconds to realize what she was conveying and to correct that telling look.

But she couldn't erase the warmth that filled him in its wake.

She still cared for him far more than she was letting on—and it wasn't just hormones.

Her heart was involved too.

That was the best news he'd had in months.

Make that years.

For now, though, he'd tuck away the encouraging evidence she'd given him and put all his energies into getting to the bottom of the illegal activities at Ivy Hill.

Because until both their cases were solved, he couldn't let himself be distracted by the woman in his arms.

Even if that was where she belonged.

12

WHAT A DAY.

Cate grunted as she tried without success to find a more comfortable position on the examining table in the urgent care treatment room.

"Hey. You okay?" Kayla popped up from the chair against the wall and crossed to her.

"I've felt better." She massaged her forehead, where two rock bands were dueling it out. "Sorry I'm such lame company."

Kayla waved her apology aside. "Like you're supposed to be Miss Personality after everything you've been through."

A knock sounded on the door, and the physician's assistant who'd examined her entered.

Zeke left his sentry post in the hall and hovered at the door.

"You can both come in." Cate struggled into a sitting position and swung her legs over the edge of the table.

The woman smiled. "You look like you want to ditch this place."

"Guilty."

"We aren't going to hold you up. I checked the X-rays, and the ribs are bruised, not broken. That's the good news. The bad news is they're going to hurt for three to six weeks. We can prescribe medication to help with the discomfort."

Cate started to refuse.

Rethought that decision.

Pain could be distracting, and it was essential she be fully alert going forward.

"Thanks."

"The staples in your scalp should come out in about seven days. We can do that here, or your own physician can take care of it. We'll give you care instructions before you leave. The cut may throb or feel tender, and you could have a headache. That's normal with staples and/or a mild concussion. We'll also give you a list of more critical symptoms to watch for. You're a boarding student, right?"

"Yes."

"Do you have a legal-age contact in St. Louis who can sign papers for you?"

"I think my dad talked about that with Mr. Tucker, the president of the school."

"He'll be here soon." Zeke stepped forward.

"That'll work." The woman adjusted the stethoscope around her neck. "Why don't you stay in here until he arrives? It's more comfortable than the waiting room. If you need anything before that, let us know."

As she exited, Kayla motioned toward the door. "I'm gonna see if there's a soda machine, okay?"

Perfect. That would give her and Zeke a few minutes alone to chat.

"Yeah. Don't hurry. We could be stuck here for a while. And thanks again for coming. It helped a lot to have a friend with me."

The girl's lips flexed, and she gave a slight shrug. "I think it was kinda cool that you asked me."

She skirted around Zeke and disappeared out the door.

He closed it behind her, leaving a two-inch crack—no doubt to create the illusion of propriety in an era when harassment charges against authority figures were becoming commonplace.

"Let's talk fast. We only have a few minutes." He moved closer but maintained a respectable distance. "What did your handler say?"

"He's sending two of our people here to interview me." Thank goodness she'd had the foresight to text him from the car and alert him to expect a call from Tucker. Forewarned, he could punt until she called him to discuss strategy in more detail.

"I assumed you'd follow standard department protocol for an incident like this to protect your cover."

"Right. They'll be seasoned detectives who've been fully briefed. I'll visit the ladies' room here before I leave to call my handler again and discuss next steps."

"If you were specifically targeted, it's possible your cover's been blown."

"I don't think it was. The people you and I are dealing with play rough, and the guy who attacked me had every opportunity to finish the job. I was down for the count. If he'd come after me, I'd have been toast. Instead, he left."

Her brain was firing on all cylinders again.

"That's the same conclusion I came to."

"I think the attack was either an intimidation tactic to keep people from wandering around in the woods and stumbling onto questionable activities, or I simply ran into someone who—as Tucker put it—was up to no good."

"My money's on the former."

"Mine too—and I happened to be the unfortunate person who was known to take walks in the woods and therefore an easy target."

"The walks in the woods will have to end."

His authoritative tone rankled . . . but she wasn't up to a fight.

Besides, she had what she needed for the moment.

"They might have been over anyway. I found an earring near the barn today that may have belonged to Stephanie." She explained the rationale behind her conclusion.

His eyebrows rose. "How did you manage to find an *earring* in the midst of all the dead leaves and underbrush?"

"I'm thorough."

"And I'm impressed."

She smothered the glow his praise engendered and waved a dismissive hand. "Some of it was luck."

"Whatever the basis for your find, I'm glad you're done with the woodland hikes for now. You should try to lay low for a few days, let your injuries heal."

"Already in the plan, as it happens. Before I started this assignment, I told my boss I wanted the Martin Luther King holiday weekend off. Our story is that my dad planned to come to town to spend it with me and see how I'm doing at school. The hotel room is already reserved. I'm out of here tomorrow after classes."

"That timing worked out nicely. Where are you staying?"

She told him, and his eyebrows rose.

"Nice."

"My dad's rich, remember? He wouldn't stay in a run-of-the-mill place."

"Holing up alone in a hotel room with room service for a long weekend ought to give you a chance to rest and recuperate. Especially there."

"I'm not going to be alone."

The wave of shock that passed across his face was gratifying at a deep, elemental level.

"Oh." He shoved his hands in his pockets. "I, uh, still hope you get some rest."

If she wanted to discourage any intentions he was har-boring about discussing their history down the road—and perhaps rekindling the flame—she ought to keep her mouth shut and let him jump to the wrong conclusion. That would put a stop to any further conversations of a personal nature.

"It's Grace's thirtieth birthday, and I promised her I'd be there. She and Eve and I are having a girls' weekend out."

As the explanation hung in the air between them, she smothered a groan. What on earth was wrong with her? She should have let him stew about her weekend plans.

Yet the relief that chased away his shock and relaxed the taut line of his jaw was gratifying on a different level.

One she refused to acknowledge.

"That should be fun."

"It always is." Through the cracked door, Cate caught sight of her roommate rounding a corner. "Kayla is coming back."

He retreated a few steps, propped one shoulder against the wall, and folded his arms.

The girl knocked. "Can I come back in?"

"Sure."

She entered, two sodas in hand, and held out the Diet Sprite. "I thought you might be thirsty."

"Thank you." Cate rewarded her kindness with a smile as she popped the tab. "This is my favorite."

"I know. You always get it in the cafeteria." She glanced at Zeke. "I would have brought you a drink too, but I didn't know what you liked."

"I'm fine—but I appreciate the thought."

Kayla sipped her Cherry Coke and turned back to her. "I saw two guys in the lobby talking to the receptionist. I think they're here to see you. I heard one of the nurses say they're detectives."

"Detectives?" Cate crinkled the can in her hand, feigning

nervousness. No matter how cool or hip the average teen acted, talking to detectives would be daunting.

"Yeah. I also saw Mr. Tucker pulling up."

"My cue to leave." Zeke pulled out his keys. "Take care of yourself until your father gets here tomorrow, Cate."

"I will. Thanks for helping, Mr. Martinez."

"Glad to be of assistance. Bye, Kayla."

"Bye."

Her roommate watched as he slipped through the door, closing it behind him. "Man, he is *hot*."

"I thought you said he was old."

"Yeah—but when he carried you out from the woods, he looked like one of those heroes on a romance novel cover, you know? The tall, dark, and handsome type."

Cate snorted. "They don't exist in real life."

"They might. Maybe we just haven't met them yet— although Mr. Martinez comes close, don't you think?"

"No."

Kayla dropped back into her chair, eying her. "Your boyfriend treat you bad or something?"

"I don't have a . . . oh." *Rein in the bitterness, Cate. Stay in character.* "You mean the one who moved away?"

"Yeah. Him—or some other guy."

"My ex-boyfriend has nothing to do with how I feel. I just think getting carried away by make-believe and fairy tales and happily-ever-after is dumb."

"There's nothing wrong with dreams."

"Until they turn into nightmares."

Kayla sipped her soda, faint pleats scoring her brow. "Somebody you loved hurt you bad, didn't they?"

Well, shoot.

Either her roommate was way too intuitive or her acting skills were failing her.

In any case, this was *not* a topic she cared to discuss.

Cate swirled her soda. "We all get hurt by people we love, don't we? Are you telling me you've never had a bad experience with a boyfriend?"

A shadow flitted across the girl's features. "Sure. But that doesn't mean all guys are jerks." She sipped her Coke. "Reverend Wilson says love is the most beautiful gift we can give or receive—but not to expect perfection. Because only one man ever loved perfectly . . . and he was the Son of God. The rest of us have to follow his example as best we can. That means forgiving hurts seventy times seven and being compassionate and giving people who are sincerely sorry a second chance."

Words of wisdom—and hope—from a seventeen-year-old who had every excuse to be cynical and disillusioned and hard.

Humbling.

God bless Reverend Wilson for encouraging Kayla in her faith.

"He's a smart man."

"More than smart. He has a heart for God, and he walks the talk. He kind of took me under his wing, says the sort of stuff a dad would. I mean, my dad's fine, and he works hard, but he doesn't talk much, you know? Anyway, I decided if Reverend Wilson could do all the good he's done in spite of all the bad stuff that's happened to him, I should listen to what he had to say."

"What kind of bad stuff?"

"His son was in the Marines, and he got killed in the Middle East. Then his wife was shot in a grocery store by a robber who was high on heroin. Instead of getting bitter, Reverend Wilson kept following his dream to build a rehab center downtown for folks who want to clean up their act but can't afford those fancy, expensive places."

"Wow."

"Yeah." Kayla tipped her chin up and drained the can. "So

see? There *are* good guys out there." She sighed. "Too bad Mr. Martinez isn't younger. I have a feeling he's the hero type too."

Cate gave a dismissive wave. "Only because you saw him carrying me from the woods."

"No. It's more than that. He just comes across as brave and trustworthy and sort of . . . noble. You know?"

Once upon a time, yes.

Now, not so much.

"I think you're getting carried away."

"And I think you have blinders on. Are you still mad at him about that extra homework?"

That was as handy an excuse as any to use, short of telling her roommate the real reason she wasn't enthralled with their Spanish teacher.

"I'm not happy with him about it."

"At least he's trying to help you improve your grades. Not many teachers offer to do one-on-one tutoring."

"I guess. But like you said, he's too old for us anyway."

"Maybe we'll find a younger version of him someday."

"I'm not holding my breath." She rummaged around in her pocket for the perfect excuse to change the subject. "By the way, I found this out in the woods. I remember your old roommate had a French-sounding name. Do you think it could have been hers?" She held out the earring.

Kayla leaned over to examine it. "Yeah. I recognize it. She wore those a lot. I think they were a birthday gift from—"

Another knock, and one of the admin staff members poked her head in. "I have two gentlemen from the police department who would like to talk to Cate."

"That would be me." She tucked her hair behind her ear.

Kayla rose. "I'll wait for you in the lobby—with Mr. Tucker." She slipped out the door, giving the two coat-and-tie-wearing detectives behind the woman a wide berth.

Her colleagues entered, shutting the door behind them.

After a few minutes of chitchat, one claimed the chair, the other leaned against the wall, and both began checking texts and voicemails while they killed twenty minutes to keep up the pretense of their visit.

That left Cate with nothing to do—except nurse her wounds, think over the ramifications of Kayla's confirmation about the earring's owner, and consider her roommate's take on Zeke.

It mirrored her own eight years ago . . . until he claimed her heart, then trampled on it.

As for how her roommate's philosophy about love and forgiveness and second chances applied to her own life—she'd borrow a rule from Scarlett O'Hara's playbook and think about that tomorrow.

"Miguel!" Margarita grasped the edge of the counter and put a protective hand over her stomach, shock flattening her features. "What happened to you?"

As his wife asked the question, Eduardo swung toward the hall doorway—and almost lost his grip on the dinner plates he'd retrieved from the cabinet.

Despite the baseball cap pulled low on his forehead, his brother-in-law couldn't hide the evidence of a recent violent encounter.

One black-and-blue eye was swollen shut. His nose was puffy, as if it had sustained a punch. There were also two long parallel scratches on his cheek—the kind fingernails could leave.

First drugs, now violence.

The situation got worse with every day that passed.

Miguel lowered himself gingerly into his place at the table, as if every motion hurt—but remained silent.

Eduardo set the plates on the counter and moved to the

table. He didn't have much leverage at this stage, but putting his wife and unborn child in physical danger was unacceptable.

"Margarita asked you a question." He wrapped his fingers around the top of the chair. "We're waiting for an answer."

"I don't want to talk about it." Miguel picked up his glass of water and took a small sip, grimacing as he swallowed. As if his throat hurt.

"Too bad." Eduardo glared at him. "I won't have violence in my home."

"The violence didn't happen in your home." Miguel gave a dismissive wave.

"Not this time—but it could follow you here. I won't put my family at risk."

The twist of Miguel's lips didn't qualify as a smile. "What are you going to do about it?"

They were back to that.

"Don't push me, Miguel."

"I've already pushed you, dear brother-in-law. You're in a corner and there's no way out. Not if you want to protect the life you've built in this adopted country of yours." He put his napkin on his lap. "Thank you for the photo you provided, by the way. It will be helpful."

Eduardo squeezed the back of the chair and fought off a wave of desolation and panic.

He should have resisted Miguel's demand that he snap a photo of the new Spanish teacher after his brother-in-law had shown up at Ivy Hill—but what could he do? Margarita's brother was running the show . . . as that visit had proven. It had done exactly what the man intended—attracted the attention of school security, put him in an uncomfortable position, and demonstrated who was in control.

Except Miguel wasn't in total control, as his condition tonight indicated. It also proved that people were getting hurt in whatever he was involved in. How Zeke Martinez fit into the picture was a mystery—but if Miguel wanted his photo, the man could be in danger.

The whole mess kept getting worse and worse.

Margarita came up beside him and slipped her arm in his. "I am so sorry, mi amor. This is all my fault." Her voice was thick with tears.

He patted her cold hand. "No, it's not. Your brother bears full responsibility for all the trouble he's caused. Never be sorry for being kindhearted."

"What a sweet picture of domesticity and love." Miguel sneered as he made the saccharine comment. Then his tone changed to a low, menacing growl. "And if you want to keep your happy home, you'll both continue to be hospitable hosts. Let's eat dinner."

Margarita glanced at him, and after a moment Eduardo nodded.

They'd play by Miguel's rules for tonight.

But now that violence had entered their home, the rules were going to have to change. He would not put Margarita and his child at physical risk.

Miguel had crossed a line.

How, exactly, he would solve this problem wasn't yet clear to him. He and Margarita would have to discuss it behind their closed door, examine the options, and weigh the consequences of any actions they were considering.

In the end, though, they'd defeat Miguel.

They had to.

If they didn't, their lives would be ruined.

Yet as Margarita dished up their enchiladas, the savory, spicy aroma that usually made his taste buds tingle turned his stomach instead.

For defeating Miguel was a daunting task—and even if they succeeded, their lives could still end up in ruins.

13

"CATE! WAIT UP!"

As Noah hailed her from down the hall, Cate carefully lowered her backpack to the floor. Carting around the half-empty satchel eighteen hours after the injury to her ribs was uncomfortable, but it was better than the fully loaded version. That would have been torture.

Truth be told, she'd much rather curl up in her bed than attend classes and sit through an assembly.

But her reprieve with Grace and Eve was only six hours away. She could hang in that long.

Besides, with the attack fresh on everyone's mind, it was possible she'd pick up a bit of helpful scuttlebutt if she kept her ear to the ground at school today.

Noah joined her, concern etching his features. "I was hoping to run into you. I heard about what happened yesterday. I'm so sorry."

"Thanks. Me too."

"How are you doing?"

"Hanging in—but I'm pretty sore."

"I'll bet. Did they give you any pain medication?"

She made a face. "Yeah, but it makes me feel sick. I'd rather put up with the aches." Kayla appeared down the hall, moving her direction, and Cate waved at her.

Noah looked over his shoulder and lowered his voice. "Why don't you stop by my office sometime today? It often helps to talk about traumatic experiences. They can leave a lasting mark if they're not worked through."

Cate hesitated. Chatting with the guidance counselor wasn't high on her agenda today—but he *was* on her suspect list. She ought to take advantage of every opportunity to interact with the man.

"I have to go over my notes before trig class, but I can stop in for a few minutes after the assembly."

"That works. I'll see you later this afternoon." He touched her arm and continued down the hall.

Kayla joined her, frowning at Noah's back. "What did he want?"

"He asked how I was doing and offered to talk with me later."

"You going?"

"For a few minutes."

"Be careful."

"You keep saying that, but I don't get why."

Kayla chewed on her lower lip, then picked up the slimmed-down backpack and motioned toward an empty classroom. "Let's go in there for a minute."

"I can take that." Cate reached for her bag.

Kayla swung it away. "I've got it. I saw your ribs last night while you were putting on your sleep shirt, and that bruise is nasty."

Yeah, it was. Even breathing hurt.

Cate gave up the fight. "Thanks."

She followed the girl into the classroom, and Kayla closed the door, leaving it open a crack. "Look—I don't want to get into trouble, okay? This has to stay between you and me."

Not a promise she could make.

But protecting the identity of sources was important, and she *could* do that by sharing information only with trusted colleagues.

"I don't snitch on my friends. Did you break a rule?"

"No. But my last roommate did, with Mr. Evans's assistance."

"Why didn't you tell someone?"

Kayla barked out a humorless laugh. "Get real. In a my-word-against-his battle, who do you think would've won?"

Sad to say, she had a valid point.

A surge of adrenaline quickened her pulse—as it always did whenever she sensed a breakthrough was near—but Cate maintained a relaxed stance. "What did he do?"

Kayla peeked through the crack in the door, closed it another inch, and lowered her voice. "He gave her weed."

Cate stared at her.

The guidance counselor was a drug dealer?

This was surreal.

If it was true, though—did that mean Evans was the Ivy Hill connection to the Mexican drug cartel pipeline?

Had he been involved in Stephanie's disappearance?

Could he be linked to both?

Impossible to know without more concrete evidence.

Cate leaned a shoulder against the wall. "Are you sure she got it from Mr. Evans? Did she tell you that?"

"Not directly—but she visited him every week. He always talks to the new girls, and he takes a special interest in the ones who are having problems. Stephanie was mad at her parents for sending her here, and she hated everything about the place—the location in the sticks, the teachers, rooming with me. He was the only adult she spent any time with. She said he helped her relax. After their meetings, she'd go out to the woods—and she always reeked of weed when she came back. I did the math."

"You think she was paying for it?"

"I don't know."

"Could he have been hitting on her—and the weed was her reward for cooperating?"

Twin crevices appeared on the girl's brow. "I doubt it. She was tight with her boyfriend. As far as I know, all she and Mr. Evans did was talk. It was more like—" She cocked her ear. "Someone's coming. Listen—if you go see him, don't let him talk you into doing anything you don't want to do. And stay away from drugs. They're a dead-end street. I'll see you later."

After one more survey of the hall, she slipped through the door.

Cate gave her a thirty-second lead, then picked up her backpack. It appeared Zeke's suggestion to ask Kayla to accompany them last night had opened the door to friendship—and was already paying dividends.

And if her roommate's suspicions were correct, one of Ivy Hill's guidance counselors was providing the wrong kind of advice.

Her to-do list was growing by leaps and bounds. Chat with Evans to see if she could lead their discussion in a revealing direction. Block out a few hours during the birthday festivities this weekend to dig deeper into his background. Scrutinize the security footage from the surveillance camera by the entrance to the property near the barn from the night Stephanie went missing.

It was possible none of those would produce a solid lead. But a breakthrough was imminent. She could feel it in her bones.

Someone at Ivy Hill was neck-deep in either Stephanie's disappearance or a Mexican drug cartel pipeline.

Perhaps both.

The question was who?

Maybe he ought to talk to Reverend Wilson.

As Will watched the students spill out of the auditorium after the assembly and the interdenominational service the minister had conducted, he homed in on Cate Sheppard.

Her movements were stiff, as if she was hurting, and it was impossible to miss the dressing on the back of her head.

His stomach knotted.

He had to escape from the corner he'd painted himself into before anyone else got hurt.

But how? The guy who was calling the shots had all the power.

Maybe there was a strategy he hadn't thought of, though. Another brain working his predicament could be helpful. And men of the cloth had the equivalent of attorney/client privilege. Reverend Wilson wouldn't call the cops on him.

Nevertheless . . . telling someone the whole story, admitting his faults and weaknesses and just how deep he was involved in an illicit activity, required courage. More than he'd been able to muster during his futile attempt to solicit a loan from a few friends without revealing the source of his money crisis.

He was still wrestling with his dilemma as he trudged to his car an hour later, at the end of the workday.

Carrying this burden alone was hard, and finding a way out elusive. Suz had always been his sounding board for any dilemmas he faced, but talking to her about this was out of the question. If she learned of the mess he'd gotten himself into, the six-month separation would become permanent and he'd be—

"Will! Hold on. I'll walk out with you."

As Reverend Wilson hailed him, Will paused in his trek toward the parking lot and turned back toward the main building.

The minister waved, offered his usual sunny smile, and picked up his pace until he drew close. "I stopped by the front desk to say hello when I arrived, but you weren't there."

"We've added foot patrols, day and night. I was tramping through the property."

The minister's demeanor grew more serious as he fell in beside him. "Yes, Richard told me about that and filled me in on yesterday's attack. Increased security measures are wise in this crazy world we live in, but it's a sad state of affairs." He shook his head. "Even Ivy Hill isn't immune from violence, despite its bucolic setting."

"Nowhere is safe anymore."

"Isn't that the truth?" The minister laid a hand on his shoulder. "How goes it with your wife?"

The separation was the one personal piece of information he'd shared with the man, although he'd offered no details about what had prompted it to him or anyone else on campus.

"The six months we agreed to are almost up."

"Do you think she'll come back?"

Yeah. Their finances were in order now. The debts were paid off, and once she let him come home he'd stick to his promise and *keep* them out of debt—even if he'd taken a few detours to the dark side recently.

But she wouldn't stay long if she got wind of his latest quandary.

"I hope so."

"Hope is a wonderful thing. Remember the story in Job, about the tree that's cut down, how its stump dies in the dust. Yet at the first whiff of water, it sprouts and puts out branches like a young plant. There's always hope, my friend—even when all appears to be lost."

Lost was the perfect description for his current mental state. Once again, uncertainty assailed him.

Should he talk to the minister? Seek his counsel? With all the work the man had done at his church in the city and the rehab center he'd founded, he'd no doubt brushed up against his share of criminal activity. Perhaps offered advice to offenders. It was possible he could share an insight or two that would provide direction.

Yet short of a suggestion to refuse any future demands from his so-called savior and take the consequences, what could the cleric offer other than an empathetic ear?

"You seem worried, Will." Reverend Wilson stopped beside his older-model car and pulled out his keys, eyes caring and filled with empathy.

Talk to him, Will. Just tell him.

For a moment he wrestled with that temptation—but in the end, he shoved his hands in his pockets and stifled the urge to spill his guts. "The security around here is on my mind. I don't like people being hurt on my watch."

"Well, you've taken positive steps to safeguard the girls going forward. What happened yesterday wasn't your fault."

Except it was.

He balled his hands. "Yeah."

"If you want to talk anytime, don't hesitate to get in touch. You have my cell number—and my ear's always available."

"Thanks. Have a good evening."

"You too."

Not likely.

Heart heavy, he continued toward his own car as the minister slid into his. Compassionate as Reverend Wilson was, sympathetic as the man might be to the plight of a lost sheep, he couldn't fix the problem.

Will sighed.

He was in this alone.

And the violence was escalating.

First Stephanie and her boyfriend, now Cate Sheppard.

Who would be next?

Waiting his contact out, hoping those involved grew tired of using this location, no longer seemed like a viable plan. Not if he wanted to be able to live with himself.

Yet if he wanted to live, period, reneging on the arrangement or alerting law enforcement to the next delivery and pickup dates wasn't viable, either.

These people played rough.

At the crunch of tires on the pavement behind him, he moved aside.

Reverend Wilson rolled by, waving as he headed for the exit.

Will lifted a hand in response and watched the car gain speed.

If only he could drive away from all his difficulties as easily as he drove away from Ivy Hill at the end of his shift.

But that was wishful thinking.

As for the hope Reverend Wilson had referenced?

His was fading fast.

———

"Cate." Noah glanced up as she hovered in his office doorway. "Come in. Have a seat."

"I can't stay long. My dad's picking me up soon."

"That's fine." He rose and circled around the desk, closed the door as she sat, and took the chair beside her. The desk put too much distance between them and created both a physical and psychological barrier. Not conducive to encouraging a girl to open up.

And getting girls to confide in him was essential.

"I was surprised to see you in the hall today. I thought you'd be recuperating in your room."

"I didn't want to be alone . . . you know?" She fidgeted in her seat.

"That's understandable."

She began to jiggle her foot. "I've been pretty wired all day."

"Also understandable. A trauma like that takes a toll."

"Yeah." She toed aside the backpack she'd set on the floor . . . and a pack of cigarettes slipped out of one of the pockets. After shooting him a guilty look, she snatched it up. Shoved it back inside. "I know smoking's not allowed, but it helps calm me down. And I really need that right now. You won't tell anyone, will you?"

"No." The poor girl was almost trembling with anxiety. A lot like Stephanie had been when she'd arrived—except her agitation had been caused by anger rather than nerves. Neither emotion, however, was healthy. "After all you've been through, I can see why you're seeking relief."

"I wish I had something stronger that would help more, though."

"You mean like alcohol?"

"I don't know." She shrugged. "Whatever works. All day I've felt like I'm going to jump out of my skin, you know?"

"Yes, I do." Some of the girls who came to Ivy Hill required counseling in the beginning. Boarding school was a huge adjustment for a fair number. But an empathetic ear wasn't always enough. A few required a bit more help to chill out. To feel happy and content.

The kind he could provide once he got to know them—if they could be trusted to keep the secret.

It was too soon to know yet if Cate was a candidate for that sort of help.

"So you're a counselor. What do you recommend?" Her eyes were wide. Beseeching.

She wanted him to help her. Believed he had the power to make her life better.

And he could.

In time.

But not yet.

"Let's start by talking about what you're feeling. Putting it into words often helps relieve anxiety."

They chatted for a few minutes, and he followed the textbook script for such sessions. He listened, offered nods of encouragement, made a few suggestions.

As their conversation waned, she twisted her wrist and scanned her watch. "I have to go or I won't be ready when my dad comes."

"We can pick this up after the holiday weekend." He stood as she reached for her backpack. "Let me get that for you. You have to be hurting."

He lifted it and helped her settle the weight on her shoulder, offering a pat of encouragement. "Hang in. We'll sort this out. Come and see me next week."

"Okay. Thanks."

He waited at the door as she traipsed down the hall, then returned to his chair and picked up a pencil, turning it end to end on the desk.

Cate was a nice kid. Troubled, but she had potential—if she could get past this rough patch in her life.

He couldn't help her much while he was in transition mode, but if she continued to see him—and if he was confident she was trustworthy—she could end up being one of the lucky ones who benefited from his largesse after the next shipment arrived.

Rocking back in his chair, he pressed his fingertips together, lips curving up. It was energizing to finally feel back in control after the messy, ego-shattering divorce.

In hindsight, however, parting from his wife had been for the best. She'd never been that supportive of his endeavors. He was well rid of her.

In fact, living in St. Louis and working at Ivy Hill was far preferable to the life he'd had with her.

With a cadre of girls who flocked to his door and gave him the respect and gratitude he deserved—and an extracurricular activity that paid huge personal dividends—what more could a man want?

14

AT THE KNOCK on her hotel room door, Cate braced. Didn't matter which sister had arrived first—Eve and Grace would both be all over her once they realized she was hurt.

And there was no hiding that fact.

Even if she'd been a whiz at hairstyling, it would have been impossible to conceal the staples completely—and their usual hugs were out of the question.

She rose from the couch, pressing her fingertips to the upholstered back to steady herself as pain shot through her ribs.

Maybe, now that she was among friends, she'd cave and take the pain meds from the urgent care center. It wasn't fair to throw a damper on Grace's big birthday just because she was hurting.

Moving carefully, she crossed to the door and peeked through the peephole.

Her two sisters stood on the other side of the fish-eye lens, making goofy faces.

Lips twitching, Cate flipped the lock. Injured or not, she was going to enjoy this weekend—even if part of it had to be devoted to work.

She opened the door and stepped back, letting her sisters hurry through.

After securing the lock behind them, she turned to find them both staring at her.

"What happened to your head?" Grace dropped her overnight bag to the floor with a thump—suggesting she didn't intend to move until she had answers.

So much for her camouflage efforts.

"I ran into a bit of trouble yesterday. After you both get settled we can—"

"Forget it. I'm not budging until you tell us what happened." Grace circled around behind her to examine the gash. "That is one nasty cut. Do you have a concussion?"

"Mild. I'll be fine. Why don't we sit?" She motioned toward the living room in the two-bedroom suite the department had booked under her "father's" name.

"Wow." Eve gave the spacious accommodations an appreciative perusal, juggling her bag in one hand and a small cake box in the other. "Some big bucks are being spent on this case."

"I told you my assignment was cushy."

"You didn't mention the dangerous part." Grace folded her arms. "Where else are you hurt?"

Leave it to a forensic pathologist to wonder about hidden damage.

"I have bruised ribs. So expect a very gentle birthday hug."

"I can do gentle. Tell us what—"

"Grace." Eve nudged their sister. "We'll get to that. Cate probably would be more comfortable sitting—and I have to put this hazelnut white chocolate cheesecake in the fridge." She lifted the box.

Grace swung toward her, face lighting up. "Is that from Hank's?"

"Where else?"

Her sister gave a little squeal and clapped her hands. "Thank you for splurging."

"Hey, thirtieth birthdays only come around once. And since Cate said our meals would be covered by room service, we won't have to shell out big bucks to take you to dinner. This is the least I could do."

"Maybe I'll order caviar." Grace grinned.

"Let's not get carried away." Cate motioned toward the bar area. "The cheesecake can go in there. The bedroom on the right has a king bed. I hope you two won't mind sharing. I claimed the queen in the other room. In light of my sore ribs, I figured that would be safer, knowing how a certain birthday girl sometimes thrashes around in her sleep."

"Do not."

"You did last time we shared a bed."

Grace sniffed. "That was years ago, when I was going through a growth spurt. At least I don't snore."

"I don't either."

"Yeah? You sure about that?" Grace's hazel irises twinkled with mischief. "You have any witnesses to prove you're a silent sleeper as an adult?"

Cate managed to hang on to her smile. "Do you think I'd tell you if I did?"

"I'll take that as a no, given the strict moral code Mom and Dad drummed into us." Grace picked up her bag and headed toward the bedroom. "You have a five-minute reprieve. Then I want the whole story about what happened to you." She disappeared through the door.

Eve left her bag in the living room and toted the cheesecake to the refrigerator. "Bossy little thing, isn't she?"

"I suppose we should cut her some slack." Cate followed her middle sister. "She can say whatever she wants to her clients and none of them ever talk back or take offense."

"Yeah—but dealing with dead bodies all day would give

me the creeps." Eve slid the confection into the fridge, shut the door, and retraced her steps to the living room. "But I'm in her camp on this one. Be prepared to brief us ASAP."

Bag in hand, she followed Grace into the bedroom.

Now that they were out of sight, Cate let her shoulders slump and plodded toward her own room.

Time for that painkiller.

Past time.

Too bad there wasn't a pill that could also assuage the regrets Grace's snoring-related comment had stirred up.

When she returned, both of her sisters had helped themselves to drinks and dived into the bowl of snacks the hotel provided for suites.

"This is the life." Eve leaned back on the couch, propped her feet on an ottoman, and opened a bag of chips.

"But it's not worth the price Cate's already paid." Grace selected a bag of Fritos and waved it at them. "These are my downfall, you know."

"It's also your birthday weekend. Forget about calories—as if you have to worry anyway." Cate sipped her can of Diet Sprite and sat gingerly in the chair across from her sisters.

"I brought a bunch of chick flicks for us to watch—and a deck of cards, if we want to have a Kings Corners tournament." Eve munched on her chips, scrutinizing her. "The red streak in your hair is . . . interesting. What are you supposed to be, a punk-rock groupie?"

"Nope—and don't bother trying to guess. Even I didn't believe the part they wanted me to play at first." Cate considered the bag of M&M's in the bowl. Resisted the temptation. It would hurt too much to lean forward and retrieve them.

A fact she didn't intend to share with her sisters.

"It doesn't have anything to do with that human trafficking investigation you were involved in, does it?" Grace pinned her with a worried look. "That had to be super dangerous."

"But she didn't get hurt on that one—or not that we know of." Eve arched an eyebrow at her.

"No, I didn't get hurt during that job, and no, my current assignment has nothing to do with the previous investigation." Since the two of them didn't seem inclined to end their cross-examination, she'd have to toss them a bone. "I can't discuss an in-progress case, as you both know. All I can tell you is I got jumped and no one was around to help." Until she stumbled out of the woods and Zeke had been there to catch her.

"You weren't carrying?" Grace stopped eating the Fritos.

"Not on this assignment."

Her two sisters exchanged a look.

They didn't have to say what was on their minds, because it was on hers too.

However—since she had no plans to go into the woods alone anymore, there should be less risk going forward.

She hoped.

"How close are you to wrapping up?" Eve asked.

Not close enough.

"Getting there. I have several solid leads I'm investigating. In fact, I have to work tomorrow for a couple of hours, so I booked a spa appointment for both of you. Facials and a manicure or pedicure. Happy birthday, Grace."

"It's not *my* birthday." Eve chomped on another chip.

"You're there to keep Grace company. It's no fun doing a spa alone."

"Can't you come too?" Grace popped a Frito into her mouth.

"Nope. I have to stay sequestered here. I can't risk running into the wrong person and blowing my cover. Not that there would be much likelihood of that, but you never know."

Grace shivered. "I don't know how you can live like this. Sneaking up here in the freight elevator while a detective kept watch to ensure we weren't being followed gave me the shakes. I'm definitely not cut out for skullduggery."

"Neither am I—and after this, I'll be back to regular detective work." Cate sipped her Sprite.

"Like that's so much safer." Grace rolled her eyes.

"Do you really think you're making progress on the case, Cate?" Eve swiped at the condensation on her can, watching her as if trying to discern whether she was being truthful. "You're not just saying that to reassure us?"

"No. I'm finding out more every day. Trust me, I want this to end as much as you both do. Any more questions before we move on to pleasanter topics?"

"Yeah. A bunch. But you won't answer them anyway." Grace gave her a disgruntled look.

"True. So what do you say we get this party rolling?"

"I vote for that." Eve rose and picked up the room service menu. "Let's start by deciding on dinner, then we can pick out a movie."

As her two sisters bent their heads over the offerings, Cate continued to sip her soda. Now that they were past the Q&A, she could relax and enjoy the rest of the weekend. No watching over her shoulder. No playacting. No constant red alert.

For the next forty-eight hours, she would be totally safe.

———

Cate wasn't going to be happy about him crashing her sisters' birthday weekend—but after the latest development, he wasn't inclined to wait three days until their usual Tuesday meeting in the library to compare notes.

Unless she refused to see him.

Zeke pulled out his cell, called the hotel's main number, and asked the operator to put him through to her room.

She answered on the second ring.

"Cate, it's Zeke. Sorry to interrupt your weekend, but if you can spare half an hour, I'd like to drop by. I have news."

Positioning it as a purely professional call should make it harder for her to refuse.

Several beats of silence ticked by.

"Can we do this by phone?"

"I'd rather talk in person. That would be more secure." True—but as far as he knew, no one was hovering nearby listening to this call. Nor was it likely anyone had tapped into his burner phone.

Cate didn't need to know that, however.

"Isn't it just as risky for you to come here?"

"I dressed for the visit, walked from my rental unit to a different location, and took a cab from there." Slipping out the back door of the building that was his temporary home and hoofing it to a nearby Starbucks may have been overkill—but it never hurt to take extra precautions.

"Where are you?"

"In the lobby. I have information to share."

A beat of silence passed.

"It must be important if you went to so much effort to talk to me."

"It is."

"As it happens, I have info to share too. My sisters are at the spa, so you lucked out with your timing. I can give you half an hour." She relayed her room number.

Finding Cate alone was a stroke of luck. If necessary, he'd have bought them a few minutes of private time by claiming they had confidential case matters to discuss, but this was simpler.

"I'll be up in three minutes."

He ended the call, pocketed the phone, and caught the next elevator.

Stopping two floors short of her room, he exited and took the stairs the rest of the way up.

Before he could even knock on her door, it opened.

He slipped inside, and she closed it behind him, eyeing the knit cap pulled low over his forehead, the worn jeans, and the fake glasses he'd donned.

"Not a bad disguise." She turned to lock the door.

He pulled off his cap and glasses, running his fingers through his hair as he gave *her* a quick scan.

She was still too pale—and while she'd tried to disguise the staples, the angry welt in her scalp was hard to miss. The bruised ribs, however, were no doubt hurting more.

"How are you feeling?"

"I'll be fine. We can sit over there." She motioned toward the dining table in the suite, where a laptop had been set up with papers spread out around it, and walked across the room.

If her stiff gait was any indication, she was nowhere near fine.

He followed her, dropping his leather biker jacket on the couch as he passed.

She eased into a chair, and he took the one beside her. "You want a soda? We have a stocked refrigerator." She indicated the small kitchenette.

"No thanks."

"So what do you have?" She straightened up the papers on the table, avoiding eye contact.

Being alone with him in a hotel room made her nervous.

Because she didn't trust him?

Or did she not trust *herself*, thanks to the electricity sparking between them?

Difficult to gauge . . . but she had no worries from his side. He didn't intend to do anything to jeopardize the opportunity fate . . . or luck . . . or God . . . had laid at his feet with their unexpected reunion.

"I told you we were going to put surveillance on Eduardo. A man matching the description of his brother-in-law was spotted leaving Eduardo's house about ten. It appears he lives there. My contact texted a photo, and I made a positive ID. Hernandez had a black eye and a puffy nose."

Her attention snapped to him. "You think he's the one who attacked me?"

"I think it's a reasonable possibility."

Her forehead bunched. "The pieces aren't fitting. Eduardo's worked hard to establish a life here legally. Why would he harbor a criminal? Maybe even become involved in criminal activity?"

"Blackmail? Extortion? Threats? Family loyalty? There could be a host of motives."

"I assume you'll continue to watch him."

"Both of them. Closely. Be careful around Eduardo until we learn more." He waved a hand over the material spread out on the table. "What do you have?"

She stared at him. "That's it? You went to all that effort"— she indicated his disguise—"to pass on one piece of information? You could have told me this by phone."

Yeah, he could.

But a phone call wouldn't have let him appraise her physical condition—and after cleaning her blood off the lapel of his dress coat last night while his stomach churned, that had been a high priority.

Plus, he had another topic to discuss that required an in-person conversation.

He said none of that, however.

"Warnings are better passed on in person." Again, he motioned to the material on the table. "So what do you have?"

After assessing him for another moment, she leaned back in her chair. "I've been digging deeper on Noah Evans in light of new information that surfaced yesterday."

He listened as she filled him in on Kayla's revelation.

"A guidance counselor providing marijuana to students and

somehow managing to stay under the radar?" He mulled that over. Shook his head. "Seems like a stretch."

"I agree. I stopped by after school and pulled out every acting trick I know to create the perfect opportunity for him to offer me some, but no go. He followed the counselor's handbook to the letter."

"You've only been on campus two weeks. He may not know you well enough yet to be willing to take a risk."

"I came to the same conclusion. But I've been digging into his background. The divorce appears to have been acrimonious. Evans contested it, so they negotiated a six-month separation agreement. He may have hoped they could patch up their marriage. Didn't happen. After the agreement expired, the divorce was granted on the grounds of an irretrievable breakdown in the relationship. His wife stayed in Syracuse, and he took the job here."

"No trouble at his previous job?"

"None that I can find—but I thought the drug connection would interest you."

Zeke leaned back. "He's too new in St. Louis to be the lead man in this operation, and Syracuse isn't a hotbed of cartel activity. There *is* a gang issue and drug trafficking there— primarily cocaine and heroin. A twelve-month investigation nailed more than fifty of the players two or three years ago. Marijuana dealing is much lower level, though."

"He could be into more than that. The Stephanie connection may be just the tip of the iceberg."

"Too bad he didn't offer you weed. That would give us the grounds for a warrant to dig deeper into his personal data— and his computer."

"I plan to try again on Tuesday."

"You think Kayla could be wrong?"

"No. She's smart and observant. I trust her judgment."

"In that case, it's worth another attempt. If you can fake

a meltdown, he may take pity on you and waive any self-imposed timeline he has for offering new students drugs."

"That's my plan. I'm also going to touch base with the Syracuse PD, see if one of the detectives will have a chat with the ex-wife. She may know about any previous drug dealings. In view of their less-than-amicable parting, I'm not too worried she'll tip him off to that conversation."

"Are you thinking he may have been responsible for Stephanie's disappearance?"

"It's possible, if she threatened to expose him—but I think the odds of that are low. All he would have had to do is deny her charge. Unless she could produce proof of her claim, she wouldn't get very far—and I doubt he'd hand over joints in front of witnesses. He's too smart to be that sloppy."

"Agreed. Besides, a mere threat that would likely lead nowhere doesn't seem like grounds for murder. If he's involved with the cartel, though, and Stephanie and her boyfriend stumbled into one of the deliveries or retrievals—that's a different scenario."

"Very. And since Kayla verified the earring I found belonged to Stephanie, that seems more and more plausible."

"A providential find—at a high cost to you."

"I'll heal." She angled her computer toward him. "Evans isn't the only one with a shadow hanging over his head." She tapped a few keys, and a nighttime video appeared on the screen.

He leaned closer. "That's from the surveillance camera at the back road into Ivy Hill, near the barn."

"Yes. Notice the date."

He squinted at the small date/time stamp in the bottom right corner. "This is from the night Stephanie disappeared."

"Correct. Look at this." She rewound the video for a few seconds and hit play.

He concentrated on the screen as a silent minute ticked by. Two. Three.

There was no activity.

"How long am I supposed to watch this? Nothing's happening."

She stopped the video. Rewound it again. "Watch it again—but focus on the date/time stamp." She started it over.

After a minute and a half, the time changed from twelve-thirty to one-thirty.

A full hour of the tape had been deleted.

Zeke shifted his attention to her. "Your people missed this?"

Her shoulders stiffened. "So did you, on your first viewing. How often do you pay close attention to the date/time stamp while you're watching surveillance video, unless there's activity you have to document?"

She had a point. Rarely did detectives or agents watch hours of video at normal speed. The usual method was to fast-forward through until something caught your attention.

And there'd been no activity on this video.

"You're right. How did *you* find it?"

"I fast-forwarded too—but I checked the date/time stamp every ten minutes, beginning at ten-thirty."

"So someone doctored this video. Will Fischer—or one of the other security people—are the obvious suspects. They'd have easy access to this."

"And motive, if they're tied up with your drug pipeline."

"All of them came back clean in our background check, though."

"Ours too. But I think we should dig deeper."

"I agree. You want to handle this, or should we?"

"We'll tackle this one." She shifted her weight, as if seeking a comfortable position.

Her slight grimace suggested the attempt hadn't succeeded.

"Why don't we finish this discussion over there?" He nodded toward the cluster of upholstered furniture. "That would be more comfortable."

"I think we're finished—unless you have other information to share."

"I do."

She narrowed her eyes, studying him. "Case related?"

He hesitated.

If he told her the truth—that he wanted to venture into personal territory—she could shut down. Throw him out.

But until their cases were over, it was doubtful they'd have another opportunity for a private conversation—and he wanted to give her food for thought so when their investigations *did* end, the hardest confessions would be behind him and they could move forward.

Or not.

He'd prefer to ignore that disheartening possibility, but the truth was Cate held all the cards in this relationship. He'd hurt her, and unless he made a compelling case for the rationale behind his choices eight years ago—and she could find it in her heart to forgive him—they were doomed.

First, however, she had to hear him out.

"No." He fought the temptation to take her hand, linking his fingers on the table instead. "This is personal history I've never told anyone—but I'd like to share it with you. Whether or not it changes anything between us, you deserve to know. I should have told you the day we broke up. I'm asking you to let me explain now. To listen to what I have to say. Please."

Her gaze dropped to his hands.

His did too.

Every knuckle was white.

He didn't bother to loosen his grip. It accurately portrayed the state of his emotions.

Her cell began to vibrate on the table, and she jumped to her feet. Winced. "I'll take this in the bedroom. Excuse me for a minute."

Without waiting for a reply, she snatched up the phone, escaped to the adjacent room, and closed the door.

Letting out a slow breath, Zeke stood too and wandered over to the picture window that offered a panoramic view of the blue sky. A welcome change from gray.

But whether the sky in his personal world was destined to morph from gray to blue remained to be seen. At this point, it was in God's hands.

A prayer couldn't hurt, though.

He watched a puffy cloud scuttle along in the vast blue expanse of the heavens.

Solid as his core faith was, prayer hadn't been a big part of his world for years. Not after all the horrendous violence he'd witnessed.

Yet at this pivotal moment that would determine the direction of his life, he reached deep into his soul and sent a plea to the Almighty for courage to open his heart to the woman who'd claimed it long ago—and for a positive reception to the leap of faith he was about to take.

15

A S CATE ENDED THE CHECK-IN CALL from her handler, she sank onto the edge of the bed. Examined her trembling fingers. Blew out a wobbly breath.

Evidence didn't lie.

She had a bad case of the shakes—and her phone call hadn't prompted them.

The man on the other side of the wall, waiting to shift the conversation from professional to personal, took the credit for her jitters.

She was so not ready to talk about their past.

Yet from the moment he'd made eye contact with her for that fleeting instant the first day in his Spanish class, she'd known this was coming.

And based on the hints he'd dropped in their subsequent meetings, it was clear he wanted, at minimum, to resolve the issues around their parting and mitigate the animosity she still harbored.

At best, he wanted to explore the possibility of picking up where they'd left off.

He may not have verbalized any of that, but close as they'd once been, she knew how to read his nuances—and see into his heart.

She pushed herself to her feet and began to pace.

The temptation to take another chance on Zeke was powerful. There was no denying that. But the risk of making that leap rattled her to the core.

Meaning a personal conversation was a bad idea.

Still . . . his reference a week ago to paying back a debt was intriguing.

Could he, by some remote stretch of the imagination, have had a valid excuse to walk out on her?

Was it possible their breakup had been prompted by more than the offer of an enticing job and career ambition?

Did he harbor as many regrets as she did about the loss of the dream she thought they'd shared?

She paused at the window and scanned the cloudless blue sky.

No answers appeared in the heavens—but perhaps if she agreed to listen to him today, he'd provide some. It wasn't as if she had to respond to anything he said. He'd asked nothing from her except to hear him out.

But if you listen . . . if he infiltrates your defenses . . . will you cave? Set yourself up for heartbreak all over again? End up with even more regrets?

Maybe.

Yet after that beseeching *please* from a man who was used to being in command and control, who showed his softer and more vulnerable side to only a select few—how could she say no?

As long as she fortified herself against his dark, compelling eyes and kept her emotions in check, she'd be fine.

Wouldn't she?

Cate began pacing again.

If she could manage to pull off undercover work, play roles that required her to insulate her real persona from the activities around her, she ought to be able to passively listen to Zeke and keep her distance.

And if he had an explanation that could soothe the hurt his reappearance had resurrected, why not give him the opportunity to offer it?

She stopped. Squared her shoulders.

Yes.

She could do this.

Altering her course, she detoured to the bathroom, picked up a brush—and glared at her image in the vanity mirror.

Primping for Zeke?

Oh, for pity's sake.

She slammed the brush onto the marble top and marched toward the door. If he didn't like how she looked, tough.

As she reentered the living room, he rose from the couch.

"You have fifteen minutes." After delivering that brusque ultimatum, she chose an upholstered chair at a right angle to the couch and sat.

In truth, he had more than that. Grace and Eve wouldn't be back for another hour—but why test the limits of her emotional fortitude?

"In that case, I'll give you the condensed version of my story." He retook his seat. After lacing his fingers, he leaned forward and rested his forearms on his thighs. "I'll begin by repeating the apology I gave you eight years ago. I never meant to hurt you, Cate. And I'm as sorry now as I was then. Not a day has passed that I haven't regretted the pain I caused you."

A pretty apology—but it didn't make up for years of feeling betrayed.

Her spine stiffened, but she kept her expression neutral and remained silent.

"I know you assumed my ambitions caused our breakup, that I chose career over you—and I let you. But that wasn't true. I took the DEA job because it was an opportunity to redress a wrong. Repay a debt."

There was that word again.

"What kind of debt?" The question spilled out before she could stop it.

So much for just listening.

Zeke's Adam's apple bobbed. "To answer that question, I have to go back into my earlier history. To a place I never told you—or anyone—about. A place that, to this day, makes me sick to my stomach to think about, let alone share. It wasn't my finest hour." He wiped a hand down his face and fell silent.

Five seconds passed.

Ten.

He continued to stare at his hands.

Had he changed his mind about sharing his story?

She gritted her teeth.

That wasn't fair.

After all the grieving she'd done in the wake of their breakup, she deserved to hear a less emotionally devastating explanation for his desertion than he'd offered her back then—assuming there was one.

When the silence dragged on, she finally spoke. "You asked me to listen. I'm listening. But the clock is ticking."

He looked over at her, and the indecision in his eyes, their haunted air, jolted her. Never had she seen confidence desert this usually decisive man.

Her stomach twisted.

Whatever had happened in his past must have been very, very disturbing. Perhaps life-changing, if its repercussions could echo all these years later.

Not that any past trauma would excuse what he'd done to her. Forgiveness wasn't on her agenda this January Saturday, even if that virtue was a basic tenet of her faith.

Heck, she hadn't yet forgiven *herself* for the biggest mistake she'd made in their relationship—next to trusting Zeke, of course.

He concentrated on his linked fingers again, and when he

resumed speaking, his cadence was choppy, like a sea rocked by turbulence. "You know I came from a single-parent household. That we didn't live in the best part of town. Putting food on the table was a struggle after my dad walked out on us when I was thirteen and . . . and Michael was eleven."

The brother who'd died young, in an accident. The one he never talked about.

"Yes. You told me all that."

Zeke focused on his hands again. "What I didn't tell you was that Michael took Dad's abandonment hard. We both did. Mom worked two jobs to feed us and keep a roof over our heads, leaving us on our own alone for long periods. Not the best situation for hurting kids. I started to hang with a rough crowd, and Michael wanted to tag along. For whatever reason, he viewed me through a lens of hero-worship. That fed my ego, so I let him join my group. By the time I was fifteen, I was out of control—and Michael had followed in my footsteps. We were smoking, drinking—and beginning to dabble in marijuana."

The coil of tension in Cate's stomach tightened.

Who could have guessed the honorable, stalwart, straight-arrow County detective she'd fallen in love with had spent his youth on the wild side?

And it didn't take a genius to figure out where this story was heading—or why Zeke had never wanted to talk about his brother.

"One day, after I'd skipped out on school again and was close to being expelled, my mom dragged me to her church and turned me over to the youth minister. I had no intention of listening to whatever he had to say. But instead of lecturing me or quoting Scripture or trying to scare me into cleaning up my act, he talked about sports. He zeroed in on my interest in basketball and invited me to play a round in the gym. After forty-five minutes of heavy-duty exercise, he offered me a soda and chips, then got me to agree to come back the next night."

"Smart man."

"Very. The basketball games kept me off the street and became a pattern. I ended up liking the guy, which meant I became more and more receptive to his message—and more and more aware I was headed down the wrong path."

Cate stroked a finger along the nubby upholstery that appeared rough but was soft to the touch. "So shooting hoops helped you turn your life around. Amazing how God often works through ordinary activities to bring about extraordinary results."

"In light of where I was in my life, it was nothing short of a miracle."

"What happened with Michael, Zeke?"

A muscle ticced in his jaw. "I tried to get him to come with me to the basketball sessions. He had no interest—and I didn't have the smarts back then to realize the brilliance of the youth minister's subtle approach. I was too heavy-handed with him—and it didn't work."

"He got more involved in the drug scene."

"Yeah. He graduated from marijuana to meth and heroin and cocaine—whatever was available. He came home stoned more often than not, and began to steal to feed his habit. My mom was sick with worry over his situation—literally. She ended up calling the juvenile authorities for help, but he eluded them and ran away. I combed the streets for him, but he knew how to hide."

"How old was he then?"

"Sixteen."

The ache in Cate's heart for both Zeke and his brother swelled. During her tenure with County, she'd seen this story played out over and over again . . . usually with tragic results.

"At that point I'd straightened out and earned a scholarship to college. I tried once more to find him before I left, but he'd disappeared. Two years later, the police—" His voice rasped, and he swallowed. "They found him in an alley behind an abandoned warehouse downtown. Dead from a drug overdose. Three years after that, my mom died at fifty-one of a heart attack."

In the silence that followed his devastating tale, Cate closed her eyes. Fought for control as pressure built in her throat.

When she opened them, Zeke was watching her, the desolation in his dark irises so acute it took her breath away.

"I never got over those losses. How could I? They were my fault. I pulled my brother into a life of drugs, and his death killed my mom. That's why I went into law enforcement. I wanted to do everything I could to atone for my mistakes. To keep young people from throwing away their lives. To save other families from similar trauma and tragedy."

Cate willed away the tears clouding her vision. Tried to think of a response.

But how did you comfort someone in the face of so much wasted potential? So much heartbreak? So much guilt?

"I'm sorry, Zeke. I don't—"

"No. Wait. There's more." He held up a hand, his expression grim. "Let me finish. While I worked for County, I always asked to be assigned to drug cases. I thought cleaning up the drug problems in the city would help me make amends for failing my brother. But you know how frustrating that work can be. There are days it's hard to feel as if you're having any impact."

Yeah, she knew. No matter how many criminals were arrested, there were always more waiting in the wings to take their place—one of the many contributing factors to the elevated burnout rates among law enforcement personnel.

The only consolation was that every criminal they took off the streets was one less lawbreaker to disrupt society . . . or point a lethal weapon at an innocent person . . . or sell drugs to underage kids.

But that didn't explain why Zeke had moved from police detective to undercover DEA agent—an even higher-stress job.

"If you were burned out, why did you take the DEA job?"

"To fight the war at the source. Work to disrupt the cartel pipeline and keep the drugs from ever getting to our cities." He raked his fingers through his hair. "You remember how I got assigned to the DEA task force while we were dating?"

"Yes." An appointment she'd considered an honor for him at the time but lived to regret after the agency took him away from her.

"I was shocked by their offer of an undercover job. I would never have sought out that type of work. But they made a compelling case for why I could be effective, how my coloring and language skills would give me a leg up on infiltrating the Mexican cartels. I began to wonder if God was nudging me to fight drugs on the front lines. To give that my top priority. I prayed about that job harder than I'd ever prayed about anything in my life, other than my brother."

"Why didn't you tell me what you were going through?"

His eyes grew bleak. "I was ashamed to admit why I was interested in the job. I didn't want you to know I'd failed my family. If I hadn't led my brother into the drug scene, he'd be alive today. So would my mom."

"You don't know that. You said yourself you lived in a tough environment. He could have gone down that path anyway and—" Cate frowned.

Why on earth was she defending the man who'd left her in the lurch after taking everything she had to give?

"No." Zeke shook his head, and his broad shoulders sagged. "I know in my gut that if I'd been a better mentor—and brother—he would have made it through the fire, like I did." He released a ragged sigh. "I wanted there to be an *us* more than I'd ever wanted anything in my life, but deep inside I never believed I deserved you . . . or any chance at happiness after how I corrupted my brother."

"Then why did you date me? Let me think you had serious intentions? I would never have—" Her voice choked, and she mashed her lips together. Fought for control.

Hold it together, Cate. Don't let him see how much you still—

"Cate." He took her hand, and her lungs deflated.

She tried to pull away, but he held tight until she looked at him.

"I know what we did that night went against everything you believed. I knew you were giving me a precious gift, that you would never have succumbed to temptation unless you were absolutely certain we were destined for the altar. That's where I thought we were headed too."

The warmth of his familiar touch seeped into her cold fingers, bringing with it a cavalcade of sweet, long-buried memories from the golden months this man had been the center of her world.

"Yet you walked away."

Brackets of tension formed around his mouth. "I didn't want to. I didn't plan to. I was working hard to tame the guilt demons that had plagued me since my brother's spiral into drugs. By the time we spent that night together, I was certain I'd succeeded. In fact, I was planning to propose the next weekend."

Cate stared at him.

Zeke had come that close to committing to her?

"Yeah. I was ready to pop the question." He spoke as if he'd read her mind. "But three days later, the DEA offer came along and made me second-guess everything. It reminded me my debt was far from paid—and that giving up a personal life, living in the midst of hell, facing death every day, was what I deserved. If I'd deprived my mom and my brother of a happy ending, I shouldn't have one either."

"What about *my* happy ending?"

Pain ricocheted through his eyes. "I wanted to be your happy ending, Cate. With every fiber of my being. But I felt compelled . . . driven . . . to accept that job. And I couldn't take you with me. Not to the places I was going." He shook his head, and the shiny white scar at his temple caught the light. "I assumed you'd eventually move on, meet someone new, get married. With all you have to offer, I still can't believe men weren't lining up to date you after I left. That you stayed single."

How to respond?

Should she be honest . . . or blow off his comment? Close in on herself, take the safe route?

But that's what Zeke had done eight years ago—and look where that had led.

Perhaps there'd been enough concealment in this relationship. Whatever the future held, why not put as much as possible on the table—especially in light of all Zeke had shared with her?

She took a steadying breath. "After you left, I lost interest in romance—and I didn't trust my judgment with men anymore."

His features flexed, as if he was in physical pain. "I'm sorry for that too. And for the guilt I know you've carried about that night—just as I have. I should have backed off before it went too far and—"

"Stop." She gave him her fiercest scowl and pulled her hand free. Carried away as she'd gotten that night with the man, the mood, and the moonlight, her mental faculties had been in full working order. She'd known the exact instant her control had begun slipping. And she'd let it. End of story. "I'm a big girl, and I make my own decisions. I could have put the brakes on too—but I chose not to. That's my guilt to bear, not yours."

He studied her, then gave a curt nod. "Message received."

Then he leaned forward again and switched gears. "I know my time is running out, so let me cut to the chase. I never forgot you, Cate. Never stopped thinking about you. Never stopped missing you—and wishing we could have had our happy ending. But I assumed that was an impossible dream . . . until we met again at Ivy Hill."

She snatched up a throw pillow and hugged it against her chest, easing it back a hair after her ribs protested. Zeke would no doubt pick up on her I'm-going-into-protective-mode body language—and that was fine. She wasn't taking any more frivolous chances with her heart.

"The intersection of our cases was pure coincidence." Her assertion came across far more confident than she felt.

"Was it?"

"What do *you* think it was?"

"A second chance?"

She squeezed the pillow. "I'm done taking chances."

"The odds are in our favor this time."

Maybe.

He did seem to have subdued his demons. Appeared comfortable he'd paid off most of the debt that had burdened him for almost two decades.

And it wasn't as if their unexpected reunion had been the catalyst for his career-related soul searching. At their first meeting in the library, he'd told her he was already thinking about returning to regular agent duty back in the States.

Could they make a new start?

"I'm not asking for an answer today, Cate. I'm just asking you to think about the possibilities."

She played with the cording on the edge of the pillow. Now that she knew the real basis for his decision to leave her for the DEA, it was harder to hold on to the animosity she'd nurtured for eight years—especially since it was obvious the situation had been as traumatic for him as it had been for her.

But she wasn't ready to offer any assurances.

"I have to think about it, Zeke."

"Of course. But I'd like you to think about this too." Once more he clasped her hand.

A swarm of butterflies took flight in her stomach, and her lungs balked.

She waited for his request—but he didn't speak.

At last she moistened her lips. "Th-think about what?"

Drat that catch in her voice.

"This." He lifted their joined hands. "The electricity in this simple connection. And don't deny it. Your pulse is pounding. I can see it here." He touched the hollow of her throat.

Which only jacked up her heart rate more.

Denying the attraction would be stupid—but she didn't have to admit *all* of the reasons for it. Like the fact that her attitude toward him was beginning to soften.

"Hormones aren't enough."

"We had more than that eight years ago. We could have it again."

"Why are you so certain?"

"Because I know how I feel—and I can guess how you feel. It's in your eyes. In your body language. In your actions." He stroked his thumb over the back of her hand, upping the voltage between them with the sweet friction. "You went undercover to try and understand why I left you for that type of work, didn't you? And you'd only do that if you still cared. All of that is compelling evidence."

Instead of waiting for her to respond, he stood and gently tugged on her hand. "Walk me to the door?"

He was leaving?

Now?

She struggled to her feet, mind whirling, emotions in chaos. Not good.

She had to keep her wits about her. Regroup. Settle down. Splash cold water on her cheeks. Be logical.

As he released her hand to retrieve his jacket and slip his arms into the sleeves, she kick-started the left side of her brain.

Zeke's decision to leave the hotel suite was sensible. Prolonging this exchange in her present state would *not* be prudent. She should be glad he was being rational.

And she was working on that.

Hard.

He claimed her hand again and walked toward the door.

Halfway there, he stopped. Pivoted toward her.

Oh man.

His broad chest, where she'd often rested her head, was inches from her face—and a hint of five o'clock shadow was beginning to darken his jaw, the memory of that stubble against her fingertips as distinct as the familiar aftershave tickling her nostrils.

She raised her gaze a tad higher, to the firm, strong lips that could demand, cajole, caress in equal measure until the world melted away.

Higher still, his dark eyes sizzled, the heat simmering in their depths more than sufficient to chase off the coldest chill of a St. Louis January.

And then the distance between them began to shrink as he slowly lowered his mouth toward hers.

Run, Cate! Fast! Stop this craziness!

It was the same warning that had strobed across her mind on the fateful night she'd chosen to let love override the moral values that had always been the bedrock of her life.

She'd ignored it then.

She ignored it now.

This was a kiss, nothing more. It would go no further.

His mouth hovered above hers, a whisper away, as if waiting for a green light to complete its journey and claim hers.

Inching closer, she slid her arms around his neck and rose on tiptoe until their lips touched . . . and the world disappeared.

"Whoops!"

Somewhere in the distant depths of her consciousness, the startled exclamation registered.

But the full realization that they were no longer alone took a few seconds to fight its way to the surface.

Once it did, she gasped, broke the lip-lock with Zeke, and peeked around him to find Grace and Eve gawking at them as if they were watching a sideshow in a circus.

A word she never, ever said flashed through her mind.

It took Zeke longer to emerge from the kiss, but as he angled toward her sisters he managed to find his voice faster—and it was remarkably calm, given the passion that had been seething between them moments ago.

"Grace. Eve. Long time no see."

Eve managed to snap her jaw shut first. "Uh, Zeke?"

"Guilty."

"Hi."

"Hi back."

No response.

For once her smooth-talking radio-show-host sister was at a loss for words.

Cate could relate.

"Um . . . we can, uh, come back later." Grace fumbled for the doorknob behind her.

"Don't leave on my account. Cate and I were just saying goodbye." Zeke turned to her. "See you next week. Enjoy the rest of your get-together." He crossed to the door, and her sisters parted like the Red Sea to let him pass. "Happy birthday, Grace."

"Um . . . thanks."

He slipped into the hall and shut the door behind him.

Her sisters swung toward her in unison—and moved in for the kill.

The flush on her cheeks grew hotter as they swooped in on her.

Best plan? Go on the offensive.

"What are you guys doing back so soon?" She twisted her wrist and tapped her watch. "You should be in the spa, indulging in a glass of lemon-infused water between your facials and pedicures."

Eve elbowed Grace. "Deflection."

Grace cocked her head. "I noticed."

"I also smell an ulterior motive for me being included in your birthday treat." Eve grinned. "Cate wanted the suite all to herself for a couple of hours."

Cate propped her hands on her hips. "For the record, I had no idea Zeke was going to stop by until forty-five minutes ago."

"Whatever." Grace waved off the explanation with a flip of her hand. "What I want to know is when you and your old flame got back together."

"We haven't."

"Yeah?" Her youngest sibling didn't attempt to hide her skepticism. "That kiss seemed pretty together to me."

"I'll say." Eve smirked at her. "It looked like you two were trying to make up for lost time."

"Appearances can be deceiving. We ran into each other a couple of weeks ago in the course of our jobs. Pure coincidence. Turns out he's interested in rekindling the romance."

"That kiss would suggest the interest goes both ways." Grace waggled her eyebrows.

"Don't jump to conclusions too fast."

"Is he still with the DEA?"

"Yes."

"Why did you two break up, anyway?" Eve scrutinized her. "You were always closed-mouth about the whole affair."

Cate tried not to cringe at her sister's innocent use of that term. "Long story."

"That's what you said then."

"Still true—and not one I care to discuss."

"Hmph." Grace expelled a breath. "All I can say is, you got the best birthday present of the day and it's not even your birthday. If you see any other hot guys hanging around, send them my way."

Eve grinned. "Be careful. You're beginning to sound desperate."

"I *am* desperate. Do you know how long it's been since I had a date with a swoon-worthy guy?"

"Your social life is lacking because all the guys you hang out with are stiffs. I warned you there'd be consequences for spending your life in a morgue."

"To each his own. At least I don't have fanatics plotting to kill me."

"That chapter of my life is over—and if it hadn't happened, I wouldn't be an engaged woman." Eve wiggled her ring finger. "All's well that ends well."

"Now that we've dissected each other's love lives, I'm going to take a nap while you two ladies finish your spa treatments." Cate faked a yawn. "You never did tell me why you came back early."

"We had a few minutes before our pedicures and thought you might be lonely." Eve hooted. "Boy, were we wrong."

Cate walked to the door, peeked outside to verify the hall was empty, and pulled it open. "Knock when you get back. I'm going to bolt it for extra security."

"I think we're being dismissed." Eve ambled toward her.

"You know . . . I bet Zeke would have hung around and played bodyguard if you'd asked." Grace joined their sister.

"At the very least." Eve linked arms with Grace and they sashayed into the hall.

"Don't hurry back." Cate closed and bolted the door behind them, but their laughter seeped through the cracks.

She let out the groan she'd been holding back.

Of all possible moments for her sisters to return.

The scorching kiss they'd witnessed was going to be a hot topic until she offered them more details—and an indication of where her relationship with Zeke was going.

Trouble was, she had no idea.

He'd given her a lot to ponder—and process. After all these years apart, a reconciliation wasn't going to happen overnight . . . assuming one was even in the cards.

But as she wandered toward the bedroom to rest her aching body, Eve's all's-well-that-ends-well comment replayed in her mind.

Could that be true for Zeke and her?

Now that she'd heard his full story, could she replace the enmity in her heart with empathy? Have compassion for all he'd gone through in his life, and the guilt that had driven him to sacrifice what he claimed he'd most wanted in reparation for perceived sins?

It was too soon to know for certain, given her tumultuous emotions. And that kiss, which told her more eloquently than words the depth of his feelings, only muddled them further.

She sank onto the side of the bed.

At least they had time on their side. There was no reason to rush a decision. If he stuck around, proved he could be trusted to stay the course, maybe she'd think about giving this another go.

If he didn't . . . she'd go back to the solitary life she'd created for herself.

Even if today's brief taste of romance had whetted her appetite for much, much more.

She stretched out on the bed, every nerve in her body pinging.

Funny the twists life could take.

Last night she'd been certain that for the next forty-eight hours she'd be safe.

But who could have predicted Zeke would show up at her door, bringing with him a danger even her trusty Sig couldn't protect her from?

16

AS THE BURNER PHONE buried deep in his pocket began to vibrate, Wolf's pulse stuttered.

If Razor was calling, there was trouble.

His chief lieutenant had been instructed to contact him only during certain hours unless there was an emergency, and the man had always abided by that rule.

Angling toward the wall, Wolf pulled out the cell and pressed it to his ear. "Give me a minute." He palmed the phone, strode a few yards down, and slipped into the men's room. Checked the stalls.

Empty.

He put the phone back to his ear. "What's up?"

"We've got a federal agent on our tail. Currently goes by the name of Zeke Martinez."

Wolf hissed a breath through his teeth.

This wasn't the sort of news he wanted on a Sunday morning—or anytime.

"Tell me what you know."

"The guy I'm grooming to be my second saw him at the school. He thought he recognized him from a confrontation in Mexico a year ago, so he managed to get a photo of him and send it to his contacts in Mexico. They confirmed his ID."

Razor's news raised several questions.

Wolf focused on the most important one first.

"How do you know Martinez is a federal agent?"

"He managed to infiltrate the top levels of our supplier's organization and was brokering a major deal when the Mexican Feds showed up and blew his cover. A bunch of people were shot—including Martinez. After that he disappeared."

A gunshot wound would explain Martinez's slight limp.

The man must be an undercover agent. Likely DEA.

"Why would your guy tell you about this, unless he knows we have a connection to the school?"

"He doesn't know anything. I think he was trying to prove he keeps his eyes open, has contacts in Mexico, and would be an asset to our organization."

Possible.

"Why was he at the school?"

"Family business. He was paying his brother-in-law a visit. Dude by the name of Eduardo Garcia. You know him?"

"I know who he is." Wolf inspected a cracked tile above the sink. "Why am I just now learning about your man's connection to the school?"

"I didn't know about it either until this morning. His link to the school was a lucky break for us."

Wolf frowned.

If that was true, why was his anxiety meter rising?

"How did your guy get Martinez's photo?"

"He didn't. He asked his brother-in-law to take it."

That didn't fit with his impression of Garcia. Near as he could tell, the man was a straight arrow.

"Why would he do that?"

"I don't know. Family loyalty, maybe. My guy lives with his sister and her husband."

"What explanation did he give Garcia for wanting the photo?"

"I didn't ask, he didn't say. I got the feeling he and his sister's husband don't always see eye to eye and have limited contact."

Making Garcia's cooperation even more suspect.

The band of tension around his midsection tightened.

"Don't let anything slip about our association with the school."

"Goes without saying. What are we going to do about Martinez?"

"Nothing yet."

"But if he knows we have a connection to the school, he may also know who we are."

"No." Wolf's brain shifted into analytical mode. "If he did, his agency would have shut us down and we'd be under arrest. They're waiting to see if they can identify the major players."

"So what do we do? We have a shipment coming soon—and no other location set up to receive it."

Wolf cracked the door to the hall.

Still clear.

"Let me think about this and call you back."

"Should we get rid of Martinez?"

"To what end? That would tip them off we're onto their investigation. We're one step ahead of them at this point. Let's keep it that way." He peered through the crack in the door again. Traffic in the hall had picked up. "I have to go. I'll be in touch soon."

He repocketed the phone. Filled his lungs.

For years he'd been able to stay under the radar with careful planning and a well-orchestrated cover. It had been an incredible run of good luck.

But fortune was fickle—and luck always ran out. That's

why you had to stay alert. Tune in to signs fate was beginning to turn against you.

Like two teenage lovers who stumbled into the wrong place at the wrong time . . . an innocent schoolgirl who happened to enjoy taking walks in risky locations . . . an undercover agent in their midst.

Wolf straightened his shoulders and grasped the door handle. He had commitments to keep, people to see.

But later this afternoon, alone in his living room, he'd spend a quiet hour rethinking his strategy—which might have to include handing over the reins of his organization and disappearing before he'd quite reached his monetary goal.

He was close, though.

And cutting back a tad on the lifestyle he'd planned was a small price to pay if it saved him from a far more austere existence.

Like the kind he'd have in prison.

———————

"Mr. Evans—do you have a minute?" Cate paused on the threshold of the guidance counselor's office on Tuesday morning, tone tremulous, story ready.

If he was giving students marijuana, she was going to get herself on his list. Today.

And if he'd had anything to do with Stephanie's disappearance, she would ferret that out too.

"Sure. Come on in." He motioned to the chair across his desk.

She blinked to call attention to her teary eyes—courtesy of the drops she'd put in moments ago—pulled out a tissue, and swiped at her lashes as she sat. "Sorry. I didn't have a great weekend."

"You and your father clashed?" He circled the desk and dropped into the chair beside her, radiating empathy.

"Yeah. So what else is new? He is, like, totally out of touch with my life. I mean, he yelled at me for taking a walk in the woods, when he's the one who said I should get more exercise. Like this is my fault?" She waved a hand over the staples in her head.

"Is it possible he was just upset about what happened? Sometimes people overreact if they're stressed."

Cate put on her best pout face. "I should have figured you'd side with him. All adults stick together." She reached for her backpack. Playing the walk-out card was a risk—but she had to accelerate whatever timetable he was on.

Thank heaven he put out a hand to stop her.

"Wait. I'm on your side. Believe me. As a counselor, my primary concern is the students. Why don't you tell me more about what happened this weekend?"

She hesitated, as if debating whether to continue, then released the strap of the backpack. "It wasn't fun. And I was hurting. I finally took the pain pills, but they made me sick. I couldn't even eat the room service food Dad ordered. And I had nightmares both nights."

"About the attack?"

"Yeah—and other scary stuff. I don't think I got more than four hours' sleep the whole weekend." She jiggled her foot rapid-fire. "I'm totally creeped out by what happened, you know? I need to chill, though, or I'll be too tired to study— and if I get bad grades, Dad will have a hissy. But how can I study with these jitters?" She sniffed and pulled out her tissue again. "Sorry."

"Don't apologize." He watched her for a few moments. "Were you able to sneak in any smokes during the weekend?"

"No. Dad can smell tobacco a mile away—and he only left our suite to go to the Starbucks in the lobby. Besides, a cigarette wouldn't have helped enough."

Evans rose, circled back around his desk, sat—and asked the question she'd been waiting for.

"Have you ever tried anything stronger than tobacco to help get you through the rough patches?"

She feigned innocence. "Like booze?"

"Anything."

"Is this just between you and me?"

"Yes. What's discussed in this office stays in this office—and that works both ways. Everything we share here is confidential. Agreed?"

"Sure. I mean, it's not like I tell my dad *anything*, and I don't have any friends here yet."

"You will—but that doesn't mean you have to share everything with them. Two friends can keep secrets from their other friends. Trust is an important part of any relationship. Do you agree?"

"Yeah. Of course."

"I'd like you to consider me a friend."

"I do. You're different than all the other adults here. I mean, I can talk to you, you know? You're the only one who understands what I'm going through. I wouldn't do anything to hurt our friendship." She put as much passion as she could muster into her declaration.

He leaned back in his chair, rested his elbows on the arms, and steepled his fingers. "I can imagine how you feel. Your father uproots you, takes you away from all your friends. He leaves you here, among strangers, and goes back to the East Coast. Everything is new and different. Cliques are already formed at Ivy Hill, and it's hard to break in. The classes are demanding, and it's difficult to get up to speed midyear. Then someone jumps you in the woods. That's a boatload of stress within a very short period."

"Exactly. See what I mean? You get it." She exhaled and slumped back in her chair. "But how do I fix it?"

Come on, Evans, take the bait. Give me what I need.

"Let me go back to the question I asked a minute ago. Have you ever tried anything stronger than tobacco?"

"Yeah. I gave booze a shot once. Not here, but at a party back home. Two of the guys sneaked in scotch and gin and other stuff. It was fine while I was drinking it, but I didn't like being out of control—and I was sick as a dog the next day." She grimaced. "Booze didn't work for me."

"Have you ever smoked anything other than tobacco?"

Yes!

"Like . . . marijuana?"

"Mmmhmm."

"No. I mean, it seems lit and all, but I was always afraid I'd get caught—and I didn't want anything to do with the drug scene, you know? There was a guy in my class back home who got hooked on coke, and he ended up stealing to buy drugs. Last I heard, he was locked up in a detention facility." She gave a tiny shudder. "I don't want any part of that."

"Hard drugs like coke and meth and heroin are bad news—but marijuana is different. It has a very low addiction rate and is legal in a number of states. Unlike alcohol, it doesn't erode your self-control—and it has a lot of beneficial effects. Relaxation, mild euphoria, heightened awareness."

"Yeah? How do you know all that?"

"I discovered marijuana back in college. Used in moderation, it's a relatively safe recreational drug—and much more enjoyable than a plain cigarette. One of these days, I expect it will be legal everywhere."

"Is it legal here?"

"Not yet."

She gave an exaggerated sigh and dabbed at her lashes again. "That sucks. I bet it would help me."

Evans picked up a pen. Rolled it between his fingers. "I

don't like to see any of my girls hurting. Especially ones I've gotten to know well."

My girls.

An odd phrase for a guidance counselor to use.

Was he suggesting the two of them could have a relationship that went beyond the normal scope of a counselor's job? One that was more . . . personal? Where favors were exchanged, perhaps?

Cate went into full alert mode.

"You seem like a nice guy. I like coming here, talking to you. You make me feel sort of—special."

"You *are* special."

"I don't *feel* very special anymore." She let her shoulders sag. "And these stupid staples in my head aren't helping. Everybody stares at them."

He stood again and retook the chair beside her. "The staples will be gone soon, and after that no one will pay attention to your head—other than this." He fingered the ends of her red swath of hair.

Inappropriate.

But an instant later he let the strands drop.

"My dad hates my hair."

"Parents should learn to pick their battles."

"Isn't that the truth."

"Let me think about how I may be able to help you chill out and reduce your stress. Give me a day or two. Can you hang in that long?"

"What choice do I have—except run away, like that other girl did. Stephanie whatever."

"That was a bad decision. For all we know, she ended up in trouble."

"Hasn't anyone ever heard from her?"

"Not that I'm aware of."

Cate shrugged. "Maybe she and her boyfriend are living on a beach somewhere."

"With limited education and finite money, life isn't going to be a beach for them long-term."

"I guess not—but after everything that's happened to me here, anywhere else would be an improvement."

"I'll tell you what." He touched her arm. "Promise me you'll hang in for a couple of days and I'll see if I can improve your situation. Deal?"

"You have a magic wand or something?"

"Something."

"Fine. I'll stick it out for a while. I don't want to do anything stupid."

"Good girl. I knew you were smart—and mature for your age." He squeezed her arm and lifted her backpack for her. "Get some rest."

"Thanks. I'll try."

But as she exited his office and hurried toward her next class, rest wasn't on her to-do list.

If Evans offered her weed, as she expected him to, they'd have grounds for a warrant to search his house and computer.

She swallowed past her disgust.

However . . . repugnant as providing drugs to students was, it didn't necessarily implicate him in either Stephanie's disappearance or Zeke's drug cartel pipeline—their primary purposes for being at Ivy Hill.

And if he wasn't involved in those situations, exposing him too soon could generate shock waves throughout the school—and perhaps jinx their investigations. Push the real culprits into lay-low mode.

Tucking her hair behind her ear, she eased the backpack into a more comfortable position.

She and Zeke had much to talk about this afternoon in the library.

But before that, she had two tasks to do.

First, touch base with her handler to see if their counterparts in Syracuse had followed through for them and contacted Evans's ex-wife.

And second, come up with a strategy for dealing with Zeke after the toe-curling kiss that was far more responsible for her lack of shut-eye the past three nights than the ache in her ribs or the throb in her head.

For once, Cate had beat him to the study room in the library.

Zeke stopped on the threshold as she glanced his direction. Cell to her ear, she waved him into the fishbowl they shared twice a week.

He opened the door as she continued her conversation. "Hold a minute, Dad."

Her handler was on the line.

"Could you activate the white noise?" She motioned toward his pocket as he shut the door, keeping her voice low.

He extracted his phone, took his seat, and set the app. Though he pretended to work in case they had an audience, he kept his ear tuned to her end of the conversation.

"Sorry about the interruption. Did she talk to them? . . . How so? . . . Did she think he was involved with any of them romantically? . . . What about the drug issue? . . . Yeah, that fits . . . Not that I've established. We may want to hold off on warrants . . . Right. That's my concern too. Thanks for the update." She pressed the end button, flipped open the Spanish text in front of her—and avoided eye contact.

Understandable, after their hot kiss on Saturday. It wasn't wise to mix business and pleasure—and he should have thought about that before he initiated the fireworks.

At least it had given her a compelling incentive to think

about the possibilities for the two of them after this job ended if she was willing to give their relationship another try.

They didn't have to discuss that yet, though. Their cases deserved their full focus for the duration.

"Was that call about Evans?" He kept his attention on the textbook in front of her and pointed to a random word.

"Yes. I have news on that front, beginning with an encounter I had with him this morning."

He listened as she relayed the conversation that had taken place in the man's office.

"It's surreal, isn't it?" She finally looked over at him. "A high school counselor supplying girls with joints in the interest of helping them cope with stress."

"I've heard of and seen stranger things. What's the story on his wife?"

"A detective from Syracuse visited her. She said he loved his job—and the girls at his school—more than he loved her. Spent far more hours there than the position warranted. She suspected he'd had a romantic relationship with a few of them, which he always denied—and his alibis were solid. But she says he talked about the girls so much it was weird."

"He sounds like a piece of work." Zeke leaned over to turn the page in the textbook—an excuse to inhale Cate's fresh scent as much as to preserve their cover. "She know anything about a drug connection?"

"She was, uh, less forthcoming on that subject." Cate cleared her throat—as if their proximity was having a pulse-pounding effect on her too. "Could be she uses too and doesn't want any hassles with law enforcement. When pressed, she did admit Evans had smoked weed on occasion."

"I'd say County will have grounds for a warrant soon."

"Yes—but I don't want to derail the other investigations. If Evans doesn't have any role in either of them, and cops start

swarming the school, the people we're after could get spooked
. . . and disappear."

"Agreed. Until we have a handle on how all the players fit
together . . . and who may lead me to the key people I want
to nail . . . it may be best to defer any action with Evans."

"Any news on your end?"

"You mean other than the new ground we broke Saturday?"
Why dance around the elephant in the room?

Soft color rose on her cheeks as she gripped the textbook
in front of her. "I was talking about case news."

"So was I." Sort of . . . but the skeptical peek she slanted
at him suggested she wasn't buying his response. "We're continuing to keep Eduardo and his brother-in-law under surveillance, but neither has done anything suspicious. My gut tells
me Hernandez could lead us to key people, now that we have
him in our sights . . . thanks to your unfortunate experience
in the woods. How are the ribs?"

No reason to ask about the gash in her scalp, visible for all
the world to see. It was nasty—but appeared to be healing
without complications.

"I'm coping."

In other words, both injuries hurt like blazes.

Cate had always been a master at understatement if any
question arose about her physical or emotional condition.

Much as he'd like to wrap up this investigation ASAP, he
could tolerate a few quiet days on the case if that helped her
heal.

"Try to take it easy."

"Yeah. You have anything else?"

"No." Not case related.

"Short meeting." She twisted her wrist. "I can't leave yet.
That would be too fast for a tutoring session." She pulled out
a notebook. "Guess I'll have to tackle my Spanish homework.
You can pretend you're coaching me."

With that, she dived into the assignment he'd given in class today.

For the next twenty minutes, she played her role to perfection. Not until the clock on the library wall flipped to the half hour did she close her book.

"I'll let you know what happens with Evans." She tucked the weighty tome into the backpack on the table, secured the latch, and stood. "Watch your texts. If I think we should talk sooner than Thursday, I'll use the code word somewhere in my message."

"Got it."

She slid the backpack onto her shoulder, and though she didn't wince, the sudden tautness in her body spelled pain in capital letters.

Given the extent of her injuries, she should be on medical leave.

But that wasn't Cate. Never had been. Not if she was in the middle of a case.

And suggesting she stick close to her room for a few days wouldn't endear him to her. She'd always thought he was too protective.

"See you around." She walked toward the door, posture stiff. As if moving hurt.

No doubt it did.

"Count on it." He let his voice go husky.

Her step faltered, and she gave him her full attention. "Don't push me, Zeke."

"I'm not. I'm just letting you know where I stand."

"You already did that—on Saturday."

"So did you. We were both all in."

Faint color stole over her cheeks. "That was hormones."

"Believe that if you want to. For now."

She opened her mouth. Closed it. Turned on her heel and escaped through the door.

Zeke didn't hurry as he gathered up his papers and followed. Cate would be long gone already.

But she couldn't hide from him . . . or the magnetism between them . . . forever.

He'd made his position clear. She knew what he wanted as soon as their cases wrapped.

All he could do was hope that in the days to come, she'd think about that kiss . . . remember what they'd once had . . . dig deep for forgiveness . . . and let him prove to her that this time around, he was here to stay.

17

YES!

It had taken him two days, but Evans had followed through on his promise.

Cate reread the typed note the man had slipped her without comment as he'd passed the table she'd claimed in the cafeteria for a solitary late-afternoon snack.

Relaxation is healthy for mind and body. It can be found at the bench in the gazebo behind the school. Best done alone. Enjoy.

This was what she'd been waiting for.

He'd been more subtle than she'd expected, more careful, but that was understandable. Giving drugs to minors wasn't only unethical, it was illegal.

At least he hadn't compounded the crime by attaching any personal strings to his gift.

Yet.

She shoved her arms into the sleeves of her coat, hefted her backpack, and made a beeline for the exit.

Halfway down the hall, though, she slowed her pace.

Whatever he'd left for her wasn't going anywhere, and wandering around the grounds in this weather, toting a backpack, could raise a few eyebrows.

It would be smarter to drop her books in her room before moseying out to the gazebo.

Fifteen minutes later, she braved the cold again after donning latex gloves under her Sealskinz version and retrieving a small ziplock bag during her detour to the dorm.

Dusk was descending, that nebulous interval between day and dark that camouflaged movement. Perfect cover for her to poke around the shrub-rimmed gazebo on the expansive back lawn, in the center of gardens barren save for a few desiccated plants.

It took less than five minutes to find the small, lightweight, cylindrical packet wrapped in brown paper that was taped under one of the benches inside the structure.

No question about the contents.

And despite Evans's instruction, no one was going to be enjoying this baby except the people in the police lab.

Cate slipped the package inside the plastic bag, tucked it in her coat, put her gloves back on, and checked her watch.

Drat.

Zeke would be gone by now, since she'd texted him after Spanish class that she had to cancel their tutoring session to prepare for a trig exam tomorrow.

Yeah, yeah, she'd chickened out.

Not her usual style—but all the rules were different with Zeke.

Because if Evans hadn't come through, today's tutoring session would have been a repeat of Tuesday's. Unless he'd had news to share, they'd have finished their business in less than five minutes and she would have had to sit beside him for almost half an hour pretending to study.

Pretend being the operative word.

It was impossible to get any actual work done with Zeke mere inches away, the air crackling between them, the scent of his subtle yet potent aftershave invading her space.

Skipping out had been the safest course.

She slipped through the door to the dorm and paused to let the warm air chase the chill from her cheeks—and to plan her strategy.

A call to her handler was top priority. It was critical to get the evidence in her pocket to the lab ASAP. If that required another weekend visit from her concerned father—and two more days away from school—that was fine by her. Much as she wanted to solve her case, another forty-eight hours to recuperate would be bliss—not that she'd admit that to anyone. But if the opportunity arose, why fight it? Every breath still hurt.

She pulled out her phone. Hesitated.

Should she text Zeke first? She *had* said she'd let him know if Evans followed up on his promise.

Yeah, that would be the professional approach.

Thumbs flying over the screen, she typed in a brief message.

> —Making progress, but need help with homework. Reschedule study session 2 2morrow?

That would tell him there was news.

And while she was waiting to pass it on, she'd arrange the handoff of her very important package.

Zeke ignored the vibration from his phone as he swung into the parking garage at his condo, steadying the cardboard tray on the seat beside him that held his takeout dinner and beverage.

Whoever was texting him could wait five minutes until he carried his food into his kitchen and ditched his coat.

It sure wasn't Cate—the only person he was interested in talking to at the moment. Not after she'd bailed on their study session.

The urge to try and persuade her to keep their date had been strong—but she was running scared . . . and pushing could do more harm than good.

He pulled into his assigned spot, set the parking brake, picked up his food, and slid out from behind the wheel.

On the plus side, if she was scared, that must mean she was fighting the temptation to consider his proposition, that her feelings ran as deep and strong as his did—and she wasn't clear how she felt about that yet.

He walked toward the door, fishing for his security card.

As long as the verdict was positive in the end, he could wait for her to—

All at once, the hairs on the back of his neck rose—and a red alert began to strobe through his mind.

An attack was imminent.

He could feel it in his gut.

Dropping his dinner, he dived for cover—and felt the vapor bulge of a bullet that had come much too close for comfort before it ricocheted off the concrete wall behind him, sending chips flying.

He rolled behind the nearest car as another shot ripped through the air, the silencer not all that silent in the echo chamber of the garage.

It took him too long to yank the compact Glock from his concealed carry holster, but by then he'd spotted the shadowy figure fifty feet away who was using cars for cover as he worked himself closer for the kill.

Not happening.

Zeke kept his Glock trained on the amorphous outline of his attacker.

When the guy attempted to gain another few feet, Zeke fired.

The shadow scuttled back into the darkness as the pop reverberated in the cavernous space.

Zeke repositioned himself into a crouch, ignoring the protests from his leg.

His turn to be the aggressor—after he called in backup.

Keeping his focus on the car where the guy had taken cover, he pulled out his cell and punched in 911 to report an active shooter.

Although the operator advised him to stay on the line, he ended the call.

And when the guy darted away, keeping low to the ground, he followed.

No way was he letting the man get—

The door from the building to the garage opened, and a woman with two small children in tow exited ten feet in front of him.

Between him and his attacker.

Zeke muttered a word he rarely used.

The man fired again and bolted, weaving in and out of the cars.

The woman screamed.

The kids started crying.

"Get back inside!" Zeke dashed forward and put himself between the woman and the fleeing man. Grabbing her arm, he propelled her toward the door. Pushed her and the kids through. "Go back to your condo. Help is coming."

Once she was secure, he sprinted in the direction the guy had run.

But the man had vanished.

In the distance, sirens pierced the night air.

Too late.

Zeke exhaled, his breath a frosty puff in the cold air, every taut nerve in his body vibrating as he powered down self-defense autopilot, kicked his brain into gear, and pulled out his cell to call his handler.

For the sake of the DEA investigation, this would have to

be positioned as an attempted robbery. The brass could make that happen.

But the truth was, he'd been targeted.

And that could mean only one thing.

His cover was blown.

Someone knew his real identity.

The question was whether that someone was an old enemy who'd happened to recognize him—and he had an abundance of those from both his DEA and St. Louis PD days—or an operative in the local cartel pipeline distribution organization.

Yet how was the latter possible? No one on campus other than Cate was aware of his position with the DEA.

It didn't make sense.

All he knew was that depending on how his people wanted to play this, his undercover gig at Ivy Hill Academy could be over.

"He's back, Eduardo."

From his seat at the kitchen table where he was paying bills, Eduardo looked over at Margarita, who stood beside the back window, watching the alley through a slit in the blinds.

His stomach clenched.

Miguel was a blight on their days, and every moment he spent under their roof inched them closer to a dangerous precipice.

"He's not coming in." Margarita remained at her post.

"What's he doing?" Eduardo gathered up the bills and pocketed the checkbook he'd begun keeping on his person. He wouldn't put it past his brother-in-law to forge his name and empty out their meager savings.

"Sitting behind the wheel."

Odd.

No matter how high you cranked the heater, cars weren't

the warmest place—and most people didn't linger in them if the temperature was in the teens.

"I think he's been up to no good." Margarita sent a worried look toward the table.

So what else was new?

But an odd nuance in her tone put him on alert. As if there was a basis for her heightened concern.

"Why?" Eduardo crossed to her.

"He was wearing strange clothes when he left earlier."

"Strange how?"

"All black."

"I've seen him wear black before."

"But he was also carrying a black knit cap. The kind that covers the whole face. Like people use for skiing."

Or to hide their identity, if they had an illegal activity in mind—as Margarita must suspect.

His anxiety rose a few more notches.

"Did he say where he was going?"

"No."

Of course not.

He squinted through the slit. As he watched, Miguel got out of the car. Walked down the alley. Stopped.

"He's waiting for someone." Eduardo strode across the kitchen and snatched his coat and hat off the hook by the back door.

"What are you doing?" Fear raised the pitch of her voice.

"I'm going to see if I can listen in on the conversation. We have to find out what he's up to."

She latched on to his arm as he headed toward the front door. "No, Eduardo! It could be dangerous."

"It's more dangerous waiting around for Miguel to pull his next trick—and I'm tired of being a puppet. Maybe I'll hear something that will help me figure out how to get us out of this mess."

"But . . . but what if they see you?"

"They won't." He started forward again. "I'll be back in a few minutes."

He let himself out the front door, crept along the face of the unit, and hugged the wall as he rounded the corner. Thankfully there were large cedar trees along the side of the property, which gave him cover.

As he approached Miguel, a car without headlights swung into the alley and stopped a few feet from his brother-in-law.

The man in the bulky coat who'd become a frequent visitor got out, a hat pulled low on his forehead. As usual.

"Sorry to keep you waiting. I got stuck in traffic." The guy joined Miguel and handed over a packet. As usual.

"No problem. I only got home a few minutes ago myself." Miguel stuffed the parcel in his jacket. As usual.

"Out having fun?"

"I wish. I had a job to do—but unfortunately it didn't go like I planned."

"What kind of job? I thought you were working for us."

"I am. This was a personal job. You remember the man I told you about, who was trying to set up my friends in Mexico and was shot in the raid? The one they identified after I sent them his photo?"

"Yeah. Martinez."

Eduardo's heart missed a beat.

Dear Father in heaven!

Did he mean Zeke Martinez? The Spanish teacher from Ivy Hill?

Now the reason for the photo Miguel had demanded became clear.

Except . . . if Martinez had been in Mexico trying to shut down a drug ring, he wasn't a teacher at all. He was a law enforcement officer, working at Ivy Hill undercover.

Why?

"I decided to take him out. Payback for my friends. But he had a gun—and he used it. Once a Fed, always a Fed, I guess."

His brother-in-law had tried to *kill* Zeke Martinez?

The other dude uttered a string of obscenities that scorched Eduardo's ears.

"Hey, man—it's no big deal, okay?" Miguel sounded conciliatory—and puzzled. "I'll get him next time. No harm done."

"Plenty of harm was done, you idiot!" More curses followed, and the other guy stalked away.

"Hey!" Miguel lunged after him. Seized his arm. "What's your problem, man? Why do you care if I waste a cop? It's not like those guys are friends of yours, either."

"No, they're not—but this will cause major trouble for our operation. And my boss is going to be very unhappy. You may just have cost yourself the second-in-command position I was grooming you for after he retires."

"How? Why?" A thread of panic wove through Miguel's voice.

Eduardo didn't wait to hear any more. He'd learned enough to know what he had to do.

Ducking low and using shrubs for cover, he worked his way behind the visitor's car. Peered at the license plate. Memorized the numbers and letters.

Then he hightailed it back toward the house, staying in the shadows as his mind processed the conversation he'd heard.

Several facts were clear.

Martinez was a federal agent, stationed at Ivy Hill as part of a drug-related investigation.

His brother-in-law had tried to kill a law enforcement officer and was involved with a local drug ring that appeared to have ties to Mexico.

And he and Margarita could no longer sit on the sidelines while this drama unfolded around them. Not if attempts were being made on people's lives.

He'd discuss it with her tonight, but as he hurried across the frozen ground, the frigid wind whistling past his ears, his course was clear.

Even if following it could destroy the life he'd worked so hard to create in his adopted land.

18

ODD.

As Cate scanned the number of the incoming call on her cell, she frowned.

She'd talked to her handler less than an hour ago about another paternal visit. Why would he contact her again?

Brow still furrowed, she maneuvered herself into a sitting position on the dorm bed.

"Is that Mr. Martinez?"

At the out-of-the-blue question from Kayla, she looked up. "Why on earth would you think that?"

"That's the expression you always get when his name comes up. Like you can't quite decide how you feel about him."

"I *know* how I feel about him."

"Yeah?" Kayla angled sideways on her desk chair and grinned. "I think that tall, dark, and handsome thing he has going is getting to you."

She held up the phone. "It's my dad."

"Oh." Kayla shrugged. "Well, you're not sure how you feel about him either."

"Yes, I am. I'm mad at him for sticking me in the boonies and ruining my life."

"Uh-huh. You should get that." She waved toward the phone and went back to studying.

Cate pressed the talk button and struggled to her feet.

A whole weekend of rest would do wonders for her aching ribs, if she could hang in twenty-four more hours.

"Hi, Dad."

"People around?"

"Yeah." She walked toward the door. "What's up? I'm on my way to the bathroom." She exited into the hall.

"Let me know once you're in a place to talk."

"You got it."

She walked down the corridor toward the communal bathroom, but halfway there detoured to the stairwell. After slipping through the door, she listened for footsteps.

Silence.

"All clear."

"I have news."

As the man briefed her on the incident with Zeke, her lungs stalled.

"Is he hurt?"

"No."

But he could have died.

A wave of nausea swept over her, and she groped for the stair rail to steady herself.

"You there?"

"Yes." She forced herself to take a deep breath. To compose the next logical question. The one a person without the history she and Zeke shared would ask. "What's the plan?"

"The incident will be classified as an attempted robbery to the press."

"But it wasn't." She knew that as surely as she knew it was a miracle Zeke had survived the ambush.

"We agree—and so does the DEA. But we're both going to pretend we think it *could* have been. Because the pieces don't quite fit."

Cate forced herself to think through that comment—and came to the same conclusion.

If the local distribution organization knew who Zeke was, the smart response would have been to find a new location for deliveries. Killing him served no purpose—and could put the ring under more intense scrutiny.

"You're thinking someone knows his real identity, but this hit may not have been ordered by the organization under investigation."

"It's possible."

"Who else would want him dead?"

"Lots of people, according to Sloan. They're working hard to get an ID on the subject—starting with the security footage at the garage."

"Even if the organization under investigation wasn't involved, they'll hear about this. It could spook them."

"Also possible. For the immediate future, though, he'll continue to play his role while they assess strategy. Try to keep the other side off-balance, wondering how much we know. But he wanted you in the loop sooner rather than later."

"I appreciate that. Are we still on for the weekend?"

"Yes. See you tomorrow night."

They said their goodbyes, and Cate exhaled. Tried to stop shaking.

This game was becoming deadlier by the day.

First an attack on her, now an attempt on Zeke's life.

Were the two connected?

And if they were, did that mean her cover had also been blown?

Her head began to pound as she reentered the hall.

Man, she could use a long vacation to recuperate and get back in fighting form.

But she'd have to make do with the weekend break.

One thing for certain—they had to get their arms around all the moving parts in the two cases ASAP.

Because if the investigations dragged on much longer, someone could die.

Either Razor or Fischer was calling.

His money was on his number two man. Fischer never initiated conversations.

Wolf skimmed the screen, verified his assumption, and put the phone to his ear.

"We've got more trouble."

At Razor's greeting, he squeezed the phone. "These kinds of conversations are getting old."

"I hear you. I'm not happy about this either."

Silence.

Wolf's stomach began to churn. If Razor was hesitant to spill the news, it must be bad.

Worse than discovering they had a Fed on their tail.

"Just spit it out. Badness only festers unless it's dealt with."

"You're not going to like it."

"I already figured that out." He braced. "Tell me."

Razor complied, in a few brief but world-rocking sentences.

"I told him he could be hosed," Razor concluded. "But in his defense, he had no idea his action would have any impact on us. I think he hoped it would demonstrate his willingness to take on dirty jobs and go to any length in service of friends."

Wolf groped for the arm of the easy chair in his living room and sank onto the cushioned seat. "Doesn't matter. Martinez will assume it was us."

"That's not the official verdict. I checked with my PD contact. It's being classified as an attempted robbery."

"He knows better."

"Maybe not. He has to be thinking like us. That doing anything at this point to alert him we know who he is would be stupid. It would give him the upper hand, instead of us. And if we took him out, the investigation would continue—at a more intense pace than ever. They may really think it was a robbery attempt—or one of his other enemies trying to settle a score. A man with his background would have a lot of enemies."

Wolf let his head drop back against the plush fabric and stared at the dark ceiling.

He'd like to believe the argument Razor had offered—and it did have merit.

But he'd have to do some heavy thinking before the next delivery. If they guessed wrong, they'd all be brought down.

And he was too close to his goal to let that happen.

Just one more delivery, that's all it would take.

He wouldn't end up quite at the target goal he'd set years ago, but greed had never been part of the equation. All he wanted was enough money to live comfortably the rest of his life.

He deserved that much at least.

"So what should we do, boss?" Razor sounded rattled.

Bad sign. The man was always cool under pressure.

Wolf rubbed his forehead. "I don't know yet. I have to mull this over and—"

His other burner began to vibrate, and he stiffened. Sprang to his feet.

Of all times for his Mexican contact to call.

But this could be information about the next delivery—and it would help to know how many days he had to work through the issues and plan his strategy.

"I have to go. A call is coming in from our friends down south. I'll get back to you." He ended the conversation with Razor and pulled out the other burner phone. "Buenas tardes."

The man returned the greeting, then switched to English. "I have a delivery date. January 29."

Wolf stifled a curse.

That was much too soon. He'd expected to have at least a week more than that.

"That's in five days."

"Yes. Is there a problem?"

He couldn't admit that.

All it would take for his suppliers to divert the shipment elsewhere was one whiff of danger—and local customers wouldn't be happy if a delivery didn't arrive within the expected window.

Not a position he wanted to be in.

Unhappy customers in this business tended to express their displeasure in unpleasant ways.

"No. The timing is a bit short, though."

"We were alerted to a possible raid on our end and had to move the merchandise quickly. You understand."

Only too well.

"We'll be ready."

"Same arrangements as on the previous trip?"

"Yes."

"A pleasure doing business, as always."

The line went dead.

Wolf slowly lowered the phone. Pressed the end button. Eased back into the chair. Tried to apply logic to the situation.

Zeke Martinez was a federal agent. That much was clear. And if he'd been sent to Ivy Hill undercover, the Feds were aware of the school's connection to the cartel pipeline. Perhaps had even observed deliveries and pickups.

Yet they hadn't moved in—because they wanted to identify the leadership first.

A goal not yet attained.

So far, so good.

The man Razor had tapped to mentor, however, was proving to be a loose cannon—and Martinez's agency was going to dig deep to try and identify him . . . along with his connections. If they linked him to Razor, they'd have one of the two key people in the St. Louis distribution organization.

And while Razor had vowed never to betray him, Wolf knew history—and human nature.

Even the most loyal of friends could turn their back on you if they felt threatened.

But what could he do? The delivery was scheduled, and he couldn't cancel it.

In fact, he ought to alert his Ivy Hill contact of the timetable ASAP. The preparation window was short.

That didn't mean he was without options on a personal front, however.

He rose and hurried toward the bedroom, where he kept his most important documents in an envelope taped behind the dresser.

It was best to be prepared to move fast.

Just in case.

Not again.

Will groaned as his so-called savior passed on the next delivery and pickup dates.

A mere five days away.

"That's short notice."

"On our end too. You'll want to assign yourself to night duty on those days so you can handle the evening patrol and take care of other details."

"The schedule's already done for next week."

"You're the boss. You can change it."

"Not without raising questions."

"Find an excuse. And here's an incentive to guarantee there are no glitches—after next week, we won't require your assistance again."

Will's pulse stuttered. Was the nightmare really coming to an end?

"Are you serious?"

"Yes. Do what has to be done once more, and you'll be a free man—as long as you keep our arrangement to yourself."

"Of course." Who could he tell, without implicating himself?

"And try not to let vice rule your life in the future."

Will glanced at the screen of his open laptop on the kitchen table, a wave of guilt crashing over him.

That wasn't a site he should be visiting.

Nor would he again—not ever.

Suz was coming back soon, he was debt-free—and the stressful situation that had driven him to once again dabble in an activity best avoided was about to become history.

"That won't happen."

"Glad to hear it. Next time, there may not be anyone to bail you out. So long, Will."

The faceless person on the other end of the line disconnected the call, and Will drew a long, slow breath.

In less than a week, the yoke that had been around his shoulders for months would be lifted.

If he were a praying man, he'd drop to his knees and thank God for deliverance.

As it was, he simply thanked his lucky stars.

Spirits soaring, he crossed to the table, closed the tempting site, and continued to the fridge for a celebratory beer.

The nightmare was winding down.

All he had to do was come up with a valid excuse to change the work schedule for next week—back-to-back medical tests, or unexpected personal business that had to be handled during normal business hours—do a patrol in the vicinity of the barn each night, and doctor two tapes to erase the hour in question.

Piece of cake.

As he wandered back to the table, he popped the tab on the beer. The gas hissed out, releasing the pressure inside.

He could relate.

After months of mounting stress that had knotted his stomach and kept sleep at bay, the end was in sight. In a handful of days, all his tension would dissipate, as the carbonation in the can had.

A few more simple tasks to complete, and he'd be home free.

19

I THOUGHT YOU'D GET BACK TO ME last night." Zeke pulled into a parking space at Ivy Hill and set the brake as he took the call from his handler. "What do you have?"

"The security cameras at the parking garage didn't yield anything usable. But Hernandez left his brother-in-law's house yesterday about three. Drove to a mall. Our people followed him inside, but it was a mob scene, thanks to a special event. The guy's slippery. He melted into the throng."

Zeke shut off the engine.

Cold instantly seeped into the car.

"I'm guessing Hernandez's whereabouts are relevant to last night's incident."

"The mall is less than ten minutes from your condo."

Too close to be coincidental—especially since circumstantial evidence already linked the man to the attack on Cate.

"So our people lost him in the mall." He tried to curb his irritation. "I assume they watched his car?"

"Yes. He came out about an hour later and drove home. Minutes after that, he had a visitor."

"Who?"

"Unknown. The agent assigned to him was at the wrong end of the alley. He alerted the agent watching Garcia, who was in front of the building, but by the time he got to the other side of the alley, the person had driven away."

Zeke gritted his teeth. "We need more eyes on this."

"We don't have unlimited resources, you know." The man seemed a bit annoyed. "We've already got two surveillance units assigned to that house to cover both men—on top of the unit watching the back road to the school at night. The special event in the mall was just bad luck."

Or crafty planning by Hernandez.

But if the man was part of the St. Louis distribution organization . . . and the leaders were as smart as they seemed to be . . . why would they have sicced him on a federal agent? They had to know that launching an attack on an undercover operative would increase law enforcement scrutiny.

While the evidence suggested Hernandez was behind the attacks on both him and Cate, the rationale didn't fit.

They were all missing a vitally important piece.

"Anything else?" Tamping down his frustration, Zeke picked up the briefcase from the seat beside him.

"No."

"Let me know if there are any new developments."

"You'll be my first call. Watch your back."

"Goes without saying."

Zeke pressed the end button, locked his car, and walked toward the entrance to the school. Or rather, limped.

Yesterday's dive and roll had taken a toll on his leg.

On a brighter note, he had an afternoon study session with Cate to look forward to—and today they'd have far more to discuss than during their previous meeting.

He checked his watch and headed for his office. With forty-five minutes to kill before his first class, a large coffee was his top priority. Thank goodness his predecessor had stocked her digs with a personal coffeemaker and—

"Zeke!" Richard Tucker waved from down the hall and hastened toward him. Based on the man's harried demeanor, he was still reeling from the news about the "mugging" Zeke had shared with him in a phone call last night.

"Morning, Richard."

"Why are you here? You should have taken the day off."

"No reason to. As I told you last night, I'm fine."

"But shots were fired!"

"Fortunately for me, the guy's aim was bad."

Richard pulled out a handkerchief and mopped his brow. "I don't know what to think. A student runs away and disappears . . . another student is attacked in the woods . . . one of our teachers is almost robbed at gunpoint . . . this is all very, very distressing."

From both a personal and professional standpoint, no doubt.

No matter how concerned Richard was about the victims, he had to be viewing the incidents from a recruitment perspective too. Repeated mayhem at the school wouldn't help enrollment—and a large student body paid for all those high-end furnishings in the office area and the top-tier salaries of the staff.

"A run of bad luck. Nothing that reflects badly on Ivy Hill." Other than Noah Evans's indiscreet activities, if Cate's text about getting together today meant the man had actually offered her marijuana.

"Worrisome, nonetheless. If you want to go home early, let me know. That won't be a problem."

"Thanks. But what I could use most at the moment is a hefty dose of caffeine." He motioned toward his office.

"I won't hold you up. I'm glad you weren't hurt—and take it easy today."

"Thanks. I will."

As the president pivoted and hurried back toward the administrative suite, Zeke entered his office, dropped his briefcase on the desk, and set about brewing his coffee.

"Excuse me . . . Mr. Martinez?"

Zeke swung around.

Eduardo Garcia stood on the threshold of his office.

His pulse picked up. "Good morning, Eduardo." After the man's perceptive comment about his Spanish inflection, he stuck with English.

"I don't mean to intrude . . . but I wondered if I could talk with you for a few minutes." Sweat beaded on the man's forehead.

Zeke went from yellow to red alert—though he maintained a casual air. "Sure. I have forty minutes until my first class. Come on in."

The man complied—and closed the door behind him.

Another indication this wasn't a casual visit.

Zeke pushed the button on the coffeemaker. "Would you like coffee? It will be ready in a few minutes."

"No, thank you."

He took one of the two chairs in front of his desk and motioned to the other one. "Please—make yourself comfortable."

After a brief hesitation, the man sighed—and sat. "I have not been comfortable for many months."

"Why is that?"

Eduardo linked his fingers and stared at his hands. "I know you are a federal agent."

Crossing an ankle over his knee, Zeke kept his tone conversational. "Why do you think that?"

"Last night, I heard my brother-in-law speak with a man behind our house. He said he tried to . . . that he tried to kill a Fed. A man named Martinez." Eduardo looked at him, his eyes leeching anguish—and fear. "That is when I knew I could no longer remain silent."

Eduardo's story fit with what the agents covering Miguel had observed.

Could this be their long-awaited break?

"Why are you coming to me now?"

"Because even though I am afraid, I cannot be a part of anything that hurts people."

"Why are you afraid?"

"Miguel . . . he said he has hidden drugs in our house. That if I go to the police he will tell them I am a drug dealer." He swallowed and wiped a hand down his face. "I have worked hard to be an American, and I was afraid I would lose everything. I don't care as much for myself, but I want my wife and unborn child to have a future here. And I had nothing to offer but suspicion. So I stayed silent. But now I have heard my brother-in-law speak of murder . . . and I have this." He pulled a scrap of paper from his pocket and held it out.

Zeke took it. Scanned the notation. "A license plate number?"

"Yes. From the car that belongs to the other man. I snuck outside and listened to their conversation—and wrote this down."

Eduardo had accomplished what their own people couldn't.

Since the man had overheard last night's conversation, there was no point in keeping up the pretense of his role play.

"I appreciate this." Zeke lifted the paper. "We'll run the plates immediately."

"So what I heard . . . it is true?"

"Yes. I'm an undercover DEA agent—but please keep that information to yourself."

"Of course. And I have more. Do you remember the day my brother-in-law came here?"

"Yes."

"Afterward, he asked me to take a photo of you. He thought he recognized you from Mexico, but he wanted to see if his contacts there agreed."

So that was how his cover had been blown.

"That fits. I've done work in Mexico."

"But why are you here?" Eduardo swept a hand around the office.

"As part of an investigation." No need to share details. "Has your brother-in-law ever mentioned the school?"

"No. He came here the day you met him to cause me discomfort. To let me know he had power over me. But he has never talked of the school. Do you think he is involved in whatever you are investigating?"

"Perhaps on the fringes. How long has he been mixed up with the person who owns this car?" Zeke lifted the slip of paper again.

"I first noticed the man coming around about six months ago. They always meet in the alley behind our house, and the man gives Miguel a small package. I believe it is drugs."

That would be a safe bet.

"Do you know anything about this man?"

"No—but I think he is important. He said he was training Miguel to be second-in-command, after his boss retires."

Zeke's pulse skyrocketed.

They had the license plate for the number two man in the ring—who had to know the identity of the leader.

Finally they were getting a real break.

"Could you identify this man if you saw him again?"

"No. It was dark, and he wore a hat down over his face."

But they had his license plate.

That was huge.

"Thank you for coming forward, Eduardo."

He nodded—and twisted his hands together. "What will happen to me and my family?"

"I'll discuss it with my boss—but I doubt anything will happen. You've brought valuable information to us without prompting, despite what you perceived to be significant risk. I'd ask you to continue on as you've been doing. Don't mention this meeting to anyone."

His face went blank. "You mean—I don't have to worry about being deported?"

"I think we can safely assume that isn't a concern. We dug into your background as part of our investigation, and from

226

what we've seen, you've followed all the rules since you came to the United States."

His irises began to shimmer, and he swiped the back of his hand across his eyes as he rose. "Thank you."

"Thank *you*." Zeke held out his hand, and the man returned his firm grip. "Do you think you'll have any difficulty keeping up the business-as-usual pretense with your brother-in-law?"

"No. I have learned over many months to live with his threats and deceptions. I can continue to play my part, as you are playing a part here."

"Good. I'll let you know if we require any additional help from you." Zeke opened the door, and Eduardo slipped into the hall.

As the man disappeared from view, Zeke pulled out his cell and punched in his handler's number, inhaling the aroma drifting across the room from the brewing coffee.

But he didn't need the caffeine anymore.

He was already wired.

Zeke's limp was more pronounced.

But he was alive.

As he crossed the library toward the study cube, Cate let out a slow breath. Seeing him in person chased away the last of her fears that he'd fared worse in the violent encounter than he'd let on. Other than the more noticeable limp, he appeared to be fine.

He entered the booth, shut the door behind him, and held up his index finger as he pulled out his phone.

After activating the white noise app, he set the cell between them and took the seat next to her.

"You had some excitement." An understatement if ever there was one.

He shrugged. "All in the line of duty. I'm fine."

"Your leg took a hit."

One side of his mouth rose. "You've been looking at my legs?"

She rolled her eyes and opened her Spanish book. Enough personal talk. "I'm leaving for the weekend in less than an hour. A visit from Dad was the best excuse we could come up with to pass on the gift I received."

"Reading between the lines of your text, I assumed your subject had come through. Any hints he has a connection to Stephanie's disappearance?"

"No—but the whole setup is still troubling."

"At the very least."

"I also have other news. Like I promised last weekend, after the missing hour on the tape gave us grounds to dig deeper into the security personnel, our people have been taking a closer look at their backgrounds. All of them are squeaky clean—except Will Fischer. Turns out he's been dealing with financial issues over the past eighteen months."

"What sort of issues?"

"He took out a second mortgage on his house, racked up significant credit card debt, refinanced his car, and applied without success for a few personal bank loans."

"His wife left him too. Not a stellar year."

"No. The financial dilemma could have been a contributing factor in their separation. But here's where it gets interesting. Four months ago, he paid off all his debts."

Zeke's eyebrows shot up. "Any indication how he came into the money?"

"No—but I can offer an educated guess. In return for a bailout, he's doing someone a few favors. Like facilitating the use of Ivy Hill property and editing security tapes."

"We're tracking the same direction—but if it's a blackmail situation, I doubt he knows the identity of the main man. However . . . I have a new lead that may give us that answer."

She listened while he briefed her on Eduardo's visit to his office this morning.

"Who's the car registered to?"

"A Jackson Jones, age thirty-five. Ex-military, six-year tenure with a container manufacturer downtown, solid credit rating."

"He sounds legit."

"Aside from his drug-related run-ins with the law post military and pre current job."

"Selling or using?"

"Using." Zeke turned a page in her textbook. "But he's cleaned up his act since—on the surface, anyway."

"Nevertheless, he has contacts in the drug scene and a solid cover with his day job."

"Bingo."

"I take it your people are watching him."

"Yes. We moved the team that was on Eduardo to him today. If he's the number two guy, as we suspect, he could lead us to the top gun."

"What if he doesn't?"

"Best case, we wait until we catch him in an illegal act—like handing over drugs to a dealer—and pull him in. See how loyal he is if his neck is on the line. The threat of prison can be a powerful bargaining chip." He flipped another page, keeping up the pretense of tutoring. "Are your sisters spending the weekend with you again?"

"No. This was too unexpected to coordinate a get-together. Eve and Brent are starting a DIY project at her house, and Grace is backlogged. She claims she's going to work straight through. Personally, I think she's keeping her distance so Eve doesn't rope her into helping paint or strip wallpaper or whatever's on the rehab list. She hates that kind of stuff."

"So you'll be alone all weekend."

"Yes. The only item on my schedule is getting my staples out."

"Same cushy digs as last time?"

"Yes. Even the same room."

He waited, but she clamped her lips together. If he was hoping for an invitation to stop by, he was out of luck. She couldn't take the risk. Not after that kiss on his last visit had turned her brain to mush and sent a tingle clear down to her toes.

Until she got a handle on how—or if—she wanted to give him a second chance, arranging a rendezvous in a hotel room would be downright foolish.

"Well . . ." He began to collect his papers. "Enjoy your break—and try to rest."

"That's the plan."

He turned off the white noise app and stood. "You know how to reach me if anything comes up we should discuss."

"Yes. Likewise."

Without lingering, he left the study cube, limped to the library door, and disappeared.

Huh.

He hadn't pushed for an invitation.

A surge of disappointment swept over her—even as hope bubbled up that he'd appear at her door anyway.

Huffing out a breath, Cate shoved the Spanish text into her backpack.

How ridiculous was that?

A weekend alone was exactly what she needed to rest, relax, heal—and think.

About her case . . . and about how to deal with a man from her past who wanted to be part of her future.

20

THE PHONE DEEP IN HIS POCKET began to vibrate, and Wolf tensed.

It had to be Razor again. Calling two Sundays in a row—at the worst possible time.

He held on to his smile and ignored the summons as he continued to circulate and chat.

Putting an end to his increasingly complicated double life couldn't happen fast enough.

But in the meantime, he had to return this call and deal with whatever new crisis had arisen.

After edging toward the door, he finally managed to slip into the hall.

The outside exit was a few yards away—but it was cold today. Too cold to linger without his overcoat.

So he'd tell Razor to be quick with the facts and promise to call him back after he'd formulated a damage control plan.

The wind nipped at his cheeks as he left the warmth of the building behind, and he tucked himself into a small alcove, keeping his back to the arctic gusts.

Ten seconds later, Razor answered his call.

"I wasn't in a position to talk. I'm outside now, but it's cold. Make this fast."

"I think I'm being watched."

A cold chill that had nothing to do with the frigid wind snaked through him.

That was very bad news.

All these years, they'd managed to stay under the radar. Their operation had been smooth. Seamless. Anonymous. No one but Razor knew who he was—and only a few people were aware of Razor's real identity, all of them long, trusted, proven lieutenants.

Except for the newest member Razor had recruited to his inner circle.

Wolf's eye twitched. "This is your man's fault. He's made mistakes."

"They were innocent mistakes."

"It doesn't matter." He spat out the reply . . . but getting angry wasn't going to fix the problem. Reining in his temper, he moderated his tone. "A mistake is a mistake. If the Feds identify him, he could lead them to you."

"He said he wore a ski mask in the garage and there were no witnesses. If they knew who he was, they'd have grabbed him already."

That was true.

"Okay. Let's back up a minute. Maybe we're overreacting. Why do you think you're being watched?"

"I noticed a car with dark windows parked at the end of the block yesterday. I saw it again while I was out running a few errands."

"You're certain it was the same car?"

"Not 100 percent—but I got a bad feeling about it. And I don't ignore my instincts."

"I'm with you on that." His own instincts had saved him on more than one occasion. "This isn't great timing for a tail—not with a pickup planned for Wednesday."

"Tell me about it. You want me to hand off the job?"

That was one solution.

But not the best one.

Considering Razor's bad judgment with Miguel, who knew if the other members of his inner circle were also walking time bombs?

"I'd rather not do that. You know the layout at the school best—and I trust you to get the job done and deal with any complications . . . or unexpected visitors."

"Like that girl and her boyfriend?"

"Her name was Stephanie."

"Whatever. But we shouldn't have to worry about that happening again, right?"

"Right. My inside guy will keep the area clear. As for the tail—to be safe, we'll assume you have one. You'll have to figure out how to lose it. Use a roundabout route to get to the van, and—"

Was that a squeak?

He swung around.

The area was empty.

Must have been the wind rattling a shutter.

"You there?" Razor's curt question pulled him back to the conversation.

The man was definitely stressed.

That made two of them.

"Yes. Sorry. I heard a noise, but there's no one here." If this kept up, they'd both be paranoid and jumping at shadows.

Nevertheless, it paid to be cautious.

"I can lose a tail, now that I'm onto them. But what if the Feds are watching the access road to the barn? What if they move in during the pickup?"

"I think we can assume they've watched deliveries and pickups before, since they sent an undercover agent in. But until they identify us—and can link us to the operation—they aren't going to disrupt a pickup. That's why it's imperative you lose the tail before you get the truck. As long as you're certain you can do that, let's proceed as planned. We'll shift locations for the next delivery."

"What if they do make a move? If I *am* on their radar . . . and if they pick me up . . . our operation will be history."

"The odds are in our favor—as long as you lose the tail and they don't know it's you making the run. They aren't going to pick up a mere delivery guy. One piece of advice going forward. Find someone new to train as your second. The man you had in mind may be fine as a street dealer, but trying to take out a federal agent doesn't give me any confidence in his judgment."

"Already done."

Sleet began bouncing off the flagstones, and Wolf started back toward the door. "I have to get inside or I'll freeze. I'll confirm the delivery on Tuesday night and touch base with you Wednesday morning."

"That works. And I'll come up with a plan to lose my tail. Trust me—I'll handle it."

"I've always trusted you."

More or less.

But no one was completely trustworthy. Everyone had their breaking point. Everyone was capable of betrayal.

Yet Razor had always been loyal, and worrying about the man's allegiance at this late stage was fruitless.

Wolf secured the cell deep in his pocket, rubbed his icy hands together, and strode back to the door. It would take him an hour to warm up.

Lord, he hated winter.

But very soon, he could kiss this icebox goodbye forever.

Assuming everything went according to plan.

And there was no reason it shouldn't. Razor was smart. He would come up with a plan to lose his tail on Wednesday night—assuming he had one. Their customers were waiting, cash at the ready. Money would soon begin flowing into his account. And once this shipment was taken care of, they could regroup. He'd help Razor find a new delivery location. Vet someone in the organization who had potential, and put him in charge of the next pickup so Razor could lay low in case he *was* being watched.

Then he was wheels-up to a tropical climate.

And he was never coming back.

Wolf put his game face back on and reentered the room, his hands warming.

Yet he couldn't shake the coldness that had seeped into his core.

Or the nagging fear that despite all the care being taken to elude law enforcement, his house of cards was about to collapse.

———

She hadn't invited him to the hotel—and there was a strong possibility she'd shut the door in his face—but passing up an opportunity to see Cate alone, away from their role plays, had been impossible to resist.

Zeke took a deep breath and knocked on the door to her room.

Twenty eternal seconds ticked by.

Was she ignoring him . . . taking a Sunday afternoon nap . . . in the shower?

A delicious image of her wrapped in a towel flitted across his mind.

He erased it at once.

Inappropriate.

He was here to discuss business . . . or that would be his excuse if she ever opened the door.

And he did have an update to pass on. One that could have been handled by phone, true—but what fun was that?

He lifted his hand to knock again as a bolt turned on the other side and the door swung open.

Cate wasn't wrapped in a towel—but her hair was.

The shower image resurfaced.

"Sorry." He lowered his hand and redirected his thoughts. Again. "Looks like my timing wasn't the best."

"Why are you here?"

Not the most encouraging greeting.

"Case update."

"You could have called."

Impossible to deny.

"I was in the neighborhood."

She lifted an eyebrow.

"I was." To see her. But why admit that? "May I come in?"

After a tiny hesitation, she backed up and pulled the door wide.

He entered and gave the suite a sweep. With only one occupant versus three, fewer personal items were strewn about this week. Cate's laptop was up and running on the table, suggesting it had been a working weekend rather than one devoted to rest and recuperation.

"So what do you have?" Cate positioned herself behind an upholstered chair and rested her hands on the back.

He didn't miss the significance of the physical shield.

"Do you want to sit?" He motioned toward the couch.

"No."

He called up a grin. "If you stand, I'll have to do the same—and to be honest, I'd like to take the weight off my leg."

Shooting him a narrow-eyed look, she circled the chair and sat. "I'd offer you a soda, but I doubt you'll be here long enough to drink it."

No subtleties about this woman.

She wanted him gone.

Because she'd decided she wasn't willing to give him another chance—or because she didn't want to risk another toe-curling kiss that could convince her otherwise?

His money was on the latter.

And since it was doubtful they'd have another excuse to be alone together in private until their cases wrapped, he had to maximize this opportunity. If a kiss was in the cards, great. If all they did was talk, he could live with that.

But he wasn't leaving here without a few minutes of personal interaction. He had career decisions to make, and while he'd ruled out any more undercover fieldwork, he did have to decide where to establish a home base.

And that decision depended on Cate.

After all the years he'd been away from St. Louis, she was his sole tie to the city. If she intended to cut him out of her life once their cases were over, working out of this office could be awkward down the road if an assignment brought them together again.

He took a seat on the couch.

Business first.

"We got a tip that there's a sizeable drug shipment coming our direction from Mexico, heading for Chicago. We think they could detour to Ivy Hill en route, sometime this week."

"What's your plan?"

"Observe, as we've been doing—and hope they use the school as a drop spot. Now that my cover's blown, they have to know we're watching the place. They may change locations—unless it was too late to make other arrangements."

"What if they do switch drop sites?"

"Our ace in the hole is Jackson Jones. We can also pull Fischer in for questioning. I doubt he'll be of much help bringing the ring down, but if he realizes he's going to be charged as an accessory, I expect he'll tell us what he knows. He may offer a useful nugget."

"Speaking of Fischer"—she took the towel off and finger-combed her hair—"we did more digging into his credit card charges . . . and we've uncovered the source of his financial issues. Online gambling.”

“Ouch.” He winced. “That can rack up debt fast—which could have set him up for extortion.” He leaned back and tapped a finger on the cushioned arm of the couch. “It may be time to reel him in. If he's the Ivy Hill inside connection, he'll know when the delivery is going to happen. That would be helpful information to have.”

“As long as you aren't concerned he'll alert his contacts.”

“Once he knows he's on our radar, he'd have too much to lose by doing that. Keeping his mouth shut will be safer for him all around.”

“It's worth a try.” She gingerly crossed her legs. “I also have an update on Evans. The lab confirmed that the package did contain a joint. We'll be launching a separate investigation into his drug dealings—but we're holding off taking any action until you're finished at Ivy Hill.”

“Are you still thinking he may have been involved in Stephanie's disappearance?”

“Less and less. He'll remain on the suspect list, but after interacting with him, I don't think he's a kidnapper or a killer. As his wife said, he loves his girls too much. And during our last conversation, he seemed concerned about what may have happened to her. Unless he's a stellar actor, he's not our man.”

“Then who is?”

“I'm no closer to that answer than I was the day I stepped onto campus. However . . . I'm convinced my attack and the attempt on your life are connected to each other—and to the ring you're investigating. Since the barn is a drop spot, and we know from the earring I found that Stephanie was there, I suspect our investigations are also connected. I think answers on one front will lead to answers on the other.”

“I agree. Let's stay in touch until our study session Tuesday.”

"Tuesday's not happening. There's an assembly in the afternoon that overlaps our tutoring gig."

"Then I'm doubly glad I stopped by today."

She began toweling her hair dry. "Anything else?"

"Case related?"

Her hands stilled as she watched him. "Yes."

"No."

"Fine. I'll walk you out." She rose and dropped the towel on the chair.

"Not yet." He stood more slowly.

She angled toward him, keeping her distance. "I'm not kissing you again, Zeke."

"I didn't ask you to."

"No—but it's on your mind."

"I'll take the Fifth—but our last kiss *was* pretty spectacular."

"Also confusing."

"Confusing—or illuminating?"

"I'll stick with confusing."

"Why did it confuse you?" He stayed where he was. One step toward her, this conversation would be over.

She played with the damp ends of her hair—but she didn't shy away from his gaze. "It makes me want what may not be in my best interest."

That was honest.

"Meaning me."

"Yes." She shoved her fingers in the pockets of her jeans, never breaking eye contact. "You seem determined to have this conversation, so let's have it. I cared for you once. More than I've ever cared for any man. I gave you my heart . . . among other things. I believed you loved me. And you walked away."

"I didn't want to. Leaving you was the hardest thing I've ever done. I hoped when I told you the background you might be able to understand why I took the job."

"I do—and I'm sorrier than I can say for all the trauma you've had to deal with in your life. But love—real love—should triumph over that. You made a commitment to me, Zeke. Maybe not in words, but in every other way. Yet your feelings weren't strong enough to chase away your demons or override what you thought was a God-sent opportunity to right a wrong. You've reassured me that won't happen again, but how can I be certain of that?"

It was a fair question. In her place, he'd have similar fears.

And based on her comments, winning her back—if that was even possible—would be a very long process.

That was fine—as long as there was hope.

"I could promise you again it won't—but I understand your concerns in light of our history." Zeke fought another urge to close the distance between them. "I'm not asking you to marry me today, Cate. I realize that possibility is a distant speck on the horizon—but I *have* decided to ask for a job in a domestic field office. The question is where. There are two openings in St. Louis, and given my tenure with the agency, I believe one of them could be mine if I put in for it. But you're the only reason I'd stay here."

She folded her arms across her chest. "No pressure there."

"I'm not asking for a lifetime commitment. Just a chance to prove I have staying power this time around."

"What if it doesn't work out?"

"I'll move to another location. You won't ever have to worry about running into me again."

He'd keep that promise too—even if it killed him to walk away.

She bit her lower lip. "I don't know, Zeke . . ."

"You can set the pace—and the rules. I'll see you when and where you say. On the schedule you set. No kissing until you initiate it. We'll do this your way for as long as it takes you to be certain about your decision."

She swallowed. "You haven't left anything on the table to negotiate. Everything in your proposition is in my favor."

"I know." A purposeful decision.

"You make it hard to say no."

Exactly.

"Is that a yes?"

In the silence that followed his question, he held his breath. This was the moment of truth. The point where the road diverged, and she could go either direction.

Lord, let her go my way. Please.

When she spoke, her voice was so soft he had to lean close to hear her. "If I let you back into my life, it won't take much effort to rekindle the romance. And if you walk out again, I don't know what I'd do. After you left eight years ago, it was as bad as . . . as after Mom died." Her breath hitched.

Zeke's stomach knotted, and a fresh wave of remorse twisted his gut. "I won't walk out again."

"You're that certain?"

"Yes."

After scrutinizing him, she pivoted away and unlatched the door. "I have to think—and pray—about this. I'll have an answer for you by Wednesday."

Not what he'd hoped to hear, but at least she hadn't said no outright.

"I can live with that."

He crossed to the door as she pulled it open. Stepped into the hall. Turned back to say—

Whoa.

A shot of testosterone zipped through him, and it took every ounce of his willpower not to pull her into his arms and claim another kiss.

Because if she was facing a mirror and could see the love and longing in her eyes, she'd know that's where she belonged. She'd know what her answer should be.

But he could wait until she came to that conclusion on her own, now that he'd had a clear indication of her feelings.

Unless fear kept her from saying yes.

He cleared his throat. "I may approach Fischer tomorrow. If we need to talk afterward, I'll text you."

She blinked, clearly thrown by the abrupt change of subject. "Uh . . . okay. Fine. That w-works."

"See you at school." He lifted his hand in farewell and walked down the hall.

After pressing the call button for the elevator, he glanced over his shoulder.

She was watching him.

But she ducked back into the room and shut the door at once.

The elevator arrived, and Zeke entered. Pressed the button for the lobby.

Yet as he descended back to earth, his spirits soared.

Cate wanted to say yes. Wanted to trust him. Wanted to give their relationship another go.

And if she listened to her heart, she would.

He'd done everything he could to convince her he was in for the long haul.

Now all he could do was wait—and pray.

"This history assignment sucks." Kayla shoved the book on her desk aside, stood, and stomped over to her bed.

Geez, her roommate was in a funk tonight.

And after her emotional encounter with Zeke this afternoon, Cate wasn't in the mood for moodiness.

She lowered her trig book and adjusted the pillow behind her head. "What's with you, anyway? You have a bad weekend?"

"I didn't get to spend it in a cushy hotel room, that's for

sure." She sat cross-legged on the mattress, snatched up the tattered teddy bear that was always propped against the bolster, and hugged it against her chest.

"You also didn't have to spend it putting up with a father who is totally out of touch."

"You know what?" Kayla glared at her. "You ought to be glad you have a father who cares enough to fly halfway across the country to see how you're doing. Get some perspective, girl."

O-kay.

This conversation wasn't about her weekend hotel junket or her complaints about her father.

Something had seriously upset Kayla.

Cate put her book down. "Hey. I'm your friend . . . remember?"

"I don't know who my friends are anymore."

"What does that mean?"

No answer.

Cate inspected her. "Did you go home yesterday, like you planned?"

"Yeah."

"You have an argument with someone?"

"No."

"Was somebody mean to you?"

Kayla barked out a laugh. "Girl, mean is the name of my neighborhood."

As a suspicion began to niggle at her, Cate sat up. Gentled her voice. "Did someone hurt you, Kayla?"

"Do I look hurt?"

"Not all hurts show on the outside. And you act like you're hurting."

"I'll get over it."

"You want to talk about whatever happened?"

"No. I wanna think about it."

She lay back on the bed and curled up facing the wall, the bear pressed against her chest.

Cate stared at her.

This was *not* Kayla. The girl was mature and controlled beyond her years.

What could have happened to knock her so far off-balance?

Judging by Kayla's back-off body language, that wasn't a question destined to be answered today.

Frowning, Cate sank back on her own pillow.

Solving Stephanie's disappearance had to be her first priority, but Kayla needed a friend to help her deal with whatever had happened.

So while she'd continue to work the case hard, she'd also do her best to find out what was troubling her roommate . . . and to fix whatever problem was causing her such distress.

21

ZEKE CHECKED HIS WATCH, picked up his coffee from the desk in his Ivy Hill office, and stood.

It was time to have a chat with Will Fischer.

Everyone in his chain of command had agreed there was little downside to that strategy at this stage—but significant upside potential.

And if the man had to be coaxed to cooperate, they had bargaining power on their side, thanks to all they'd uncovered about him.

Maybe they couldn't prove he was the one helping the St. Louis distribution ring, but they could make it clear they'd be watching him going forward—so future assistance would be quickly detected. As a result, it would be smarter to switch allegiance, tell them what he knew, and negotiate a deal.

That was the argument Zeke intended to offer on this Monday morning.

He took a swig of his java and headed down the hall toward the security desk near the entrance.

Perfect timing. Fischer was handing over the reins to his counterpart for the day shift.

The man looked up as Zeke paused at the desk. "Can I help you?"

"Yes—but I'll wait until you're done there. No rush." He sipped his coffee, as if the matter was of no great consequence.

Fischer finished briefing his replacement, then came out from behind the desk that displayed feeds from the five surveillance cameras on the premises. "What can I do for you?"

"I hoped you could give me a few minutes to discuss a security issue."

"Of course. After what happened to you Thursday, I imagine safety is top of mind."

"Yes, it is. Since this is a private matter, would you mind if we talked in my office?"

"Not at all."

Fischer followed him back, and once inside, Zeke closed the door and took the chair behind his desk. "Please . . . have a seat." He motioned across the expanse of polished mahogany. "I'm going to share some information that I trust you'll keep confidential."

"I deal with confidential matters every day. Believe me, after all my years in this business, I know how to be discreet." He settled into one of the chairs.

"I have no doubt of that." Zeke pulled out his credentials, flipped open the case to display his badge and ID card, and set it on the desk between them. "My real name is Zeke Sloan."

The man stared at the official ID. Lost several shades of color. Lifted his gaze. But he managed to hold on to his composure. "You're a DEA agent. Undercover."

"Yes."

"Why are you here?"

"I think you know."

"I have no idea what you're—"

"Will—let's not play games. We know the barn here is being used as a transit stop for drugs from Mexico."

"What are you talking—"

Zeke held up his hand. "We know about your gambling debts. We know you came into a chunk of money a few months ago that allowed you to repay those debts. We know you instituted night patrols here, and that you have a special interest in the barn area. We know the security tapes for the camera on the road that leads to the barn have been altered on delivery and pickup nights. You have no police record, so we assume you're being blackmailed to cooperate by whoever gave you the money to pay off your debts."

The man laced his fingers together in his lap. "I think I should get a lawyer."

"That's your choice—but we're on a tight timeline and we're willing to offer you significant consideration for your cooperation. If you tell us what you know about the activities taking place here—and the people involved—that will factor in to how your case is handled."

"I don't know anything."

"You don't know anything—or you're not willing to share what you know?"

"I don't know anything."

Not what he wanted to hear.

"Why don't you tell me what you do know—and how you got involved?"

Will massaged the bridge of his nose.

Ten seconds ticked by.

Twenty.

Zeke waited him out, willing him to cave. A lawyer would muddle up the situation and slow everything down.

"It started with a phone call."

Thank you, Lord.

"From who?" He pulled out a lined notepad and a pen.

"I don't know. I don't even know if it was a man or woman. They were using voice-changing software."

"What did they say?"

"That they knew about my financial issues and were willing to bail me out in exchange for a favor."

"Facilitating their use of Ivy Hill property."

"Yes."

"How did they know about your money problems?"

"They didn't say—but I'd applied for loans at several banks, and asked a few friends for help. It wasn't a closely guarded secret."

"Did you suggest the barn?"

"No. They already knew about it—which was strange. It's not on any of our brochures."

Interesting—and worth further deliberation.

"What did they ask you to do?" Zeke jotted more notes.

"They wanted me to leave a key under a rock for the lock on the access road gate and to delete the security footage for certain hours."

"And you agreed."

"Yes." He lifted a hand to massage his temple. "My wife and I had separated not long before. She gave me six months to stop gambling and get out of debt. The call seemed like a gift from heaven."

"Only it wasn't."

"No." The man's features contorted. "It was a nightmare that led straight to hell. Once I helped them, they had blackmail material. I was at their mercy."

"How many times did you assist this person?"

"Three so far. But there's another delivery and pickup scheduled for this week."

"We know—but not the exact dates."

"Delivery tomorrow between eleven and midnight, pickup the next night during the same hour."

He wrote down the information. "Why did you begin doing night patrols?"

"They told me to, after . . . after Stephanie Laurent and her boyfriend disappeared."

Zeke stopped writing. "What do you know about that?"

"Nothing." Panic flared in the man's eyes. "I don't know anything. Except . . . except they disappeared the same night as one of the pickups."

So the DEA case and Cate's were, indeed, linked—as they'd suspected.

"What do you think happened to them?"

The man swallowed. "I don't know. I asked once but didn't get an answer. I have to think . . . to think there was a connection."

"What about the attack on Cate Sheppard?"

The rest of the color drained from his complexion. "I think I should . . . I should wait until I have a lawyer to answer that."

Translation? He had more to do with the attack on Cate than with the one on Stephanie.

Zeke tamped down the spurt of anger that jacked up his pulse.

"You can do that . . . but we'll be asking the same questions. And whether you choose to cooperate or not, we'll find the answers in the end. It would behoove you to work with us."

Sweat beaded on the man's brow. "The Cate Sheppard incident . . . that was my fault. Indirectly."

"Explain."

"I mentioned to my contact that I'd seen a student wandering around near the barn. That she walked every day. They asked for her photo. Said they'd give me an excuse to restrict access to the woods."

Zeke clenched his teeth. "You had to know what they were going to do."

"No. Not exactly. But I . . . I was worried sick."

"Yet you provided the photo."

"Yes."

"And Cate Sheppard was attacked."

"Yes. I'm sorry. So sorry for everything." The man's voice broke. "I just wanted Suz to come back. I never meant to get involved in anything like this."

"How did you get Cate's photo to these people?"

"I texted it."

"You have a phone number?"

"Yes. I can give it to you." He pulled a slip of paper out of his pocket and recited it.

Zeke jotted down the digits.

They'd check it out, but the number likely wouldn't lead anywhere. Most people involved in the drug trade relied on untraceable burner phones.

"Do you have names for any of the people involved in what's going on here?"

"No—but my contact did tell me during our last conversation that they wouldn't be calling me again."

In other words, they were changing the delivery/pickup location after this because they knew the Feds were on their tail.

Meaning the DEA had to move this week, round up the players they had.

Jones in particular.

But the ideal scenario would be to catch the man in an illegal act, hold the threat of prison over his head while they questioned him. That was far more effective in getting criminals to rat on their friends.

They'd have to go with what they had, though.

"Okay." Zeke wrote his cell number on a slip of paper and held it out. "If you think of any more details, let me know."

The man took the paper. "So . . . what happens next?"

"Continue business as usual until the delivery and pickup are finished. Follow the instructions you were given. We'll talk later in the week. And do yourself a favor—keep this conversation confidential. If there are any leaks . . . or any changes in plans . . . we'll know who to blame."

"I won't say anything." Will rose, his face a study in misery. "For the record, if I had it all to do again, I'd find another way to deal with my debts."

If the guy was hoping for sympathy, he'd come to the wrong place.

"That doesn't bring Stephanie or her boyfriend back. Or heal Cate Sheppard."

"I know—but I never . . . when I got involved in this, I thought it would be a one-time deal. And I never expected anyone to get hurt."

"I don't think hurt comes close to describing what happened to Stephanie and her boyfriend, do you?"

"No." His response came out in a choked whisper.

"I'll let you get home." Zeke rose.

"It's not much of a home these days."

"It's better than the one Stephanie and her boyfriend have."

The man winced, as if he was in physical pain.

Tough.

People who covered their butts at the expense of others didn't deserve to be cut any slack.

Fischer left the office, head bowed.

Zeke closed the door behind him, circled back around his desk, and pulled out his cell. Hesitated. He had to let Cate know about the confirmed link between their cases—but that was best done in person.

A brief student-teacher conference after Spanish class this afternoon would give him an opportunity to pass on the news.

In the meantime, a call to his handler was top priority. Now that he had pickup dates, they needed all hands on deck for the takedown. Every dealer they'd identified, the people who showed up here on Wednesday night, and Jackson Jones had to be rounded up simultaneously.

And once Jones was in custody, they'd use every available legal means to convince him to share the name of the man who called the shots for one of the largest drug rings in the St. Louis area.

"Hey . . . are you ever going to tell me what's going on?" Cate stopped beside Kayla's desk as the other girl stowed her book after Spanish class. "You hardly talked this morning while we were getting dressed, and you wouldn't eat breakfast with me."

"I wasn't hungry."

"Are you sick?"

"No. Upset. Trying to figure out what to do." She looped the strap of her backpack over her shoulder. "I'm sorry. I didn't mean to be rude."

"Forget it—but I wish you'd let me help. Maybe between the two of us, we could come up with a plan of attack for whatever the issue is."

"No. It might be nothing more than a misunderstanding, and I don't want to ruin a relationship over a wrong interpretation. I don't have all that many friends as it is. I want to think it through a little more."

"If it could be a simple misunderstanding, why don't you talk to this person? Clear the air? Open communication can solve a host of problems."

As the advice left her mouth, Cate curbed an eye roll.

Like she was such an expert on opening up.

Since being burned by Zeke, she hadn't communicated with anyone other than her sisters about personal subjects—and even they weren't privy to all her secrets.

"I don't know." Twin grooves dented Kayla's brow. "I don't want to—"

"Ms. Sheppard? Sorry to interrupt, but if you have a few minutes, I'd like to discuss the last assignment you turned in."

"You go ahead. We can talk later." Kayla edged past her and hurried toward the classroom door.

Zeke followed the girl, closed the door halfway, and motioned toward the far side of the room. "Let's claim a couple of desks and discuss your homework." Without waiting for a response, he crossed the room.

Cate glanced out the door as Kayla disappeared around a corner in the hall. Sighed.

So much for that conversation.

She joined Zeke and sat at the desk beside him. "Your timing stinks."

"Sorry. What's up with Kayla? She seemed zoned out during class."

"She's been on edge since I got back yesterday—and I have no idea why. She went home Saturday for her mother's birthday, and I think she had a run-in with someone she cares about that's eating at her. I was trying again to get her to open up about it when you interrupted us."

"I'd repeat my apology, but I think you'll agree my intrusion was justified after you hear my news." He set a homework paper in front of her. "I met with Fischer this morning."

"Did he know anything?"

"He had delivery and pickup dates. He also confirmed that Stephanie and her boyfriend disappeared on a pickup night."

Cate closed her eyes. It was what they'd feared all along, but hearing their suspicions validated made her sick to her stomach.

"Does he know what happened to them, or who was involved?"

"No—but I think we can safely conclude it wasn't a runaway situation."

"Her father will be devastated."

"It's always hard to pass bad news along—but he has to suspect, after all these months, that foul play was involved."

"That doesn't make it any easier to accept—nor is my job over until I find the perpetrator. But from all we've learned, I don't think the clues to that person's identity are at Ivy Hill."

"I agree."

"I'll touch base with my handler, see how our people want to deal with this."

"One favor. Until the pickup on Wednesday, I'd prefer to maintain the status quo. Any abrupt changes here this close to a delivery could have negative repercussions."

"I don't see why there'd be any objection to me continuing my role play until Thursday."

"I also got confirmation that your attack was part of the plan to discourage people from wandering in the woods—in order to prevent another Stephanie situation." He filled her in on Fischer's role.

Cate scowled. "What a prince."

"Quite a contrast to Eduardo, who followed the honorable course and came forward at what he thought was immense personal risk."

"And then we have Noah Evans."

"Who apparently had no role in the larger intrigue—other than supplying your victim with joints."

"We'll see. There's a search warrant in the works for his office, his apartment, and his computers that will be implemented bright and early Thursday morning, now that you have a pickup date." She twisted her wrist to display the face of her watch. "I have to bring my handler up to speed and get to my next class. Do you think Fischer will stay mum about your identity?"

"I laid out what would happen if he didn't. I think we're safe."

"Let's hope you're right." She stood. "Are your people going to do anything with the crew from Mexico that delivers to-morrow?"

"Follow them. Once we get the people we're after in St. Louis, we'll grab them and the truck. But they're delivery guys, not key players. The cartel won't be happy about the loss of merchandise, but it won't bankrupt them, sad to say. Or affect their leadership."

"Good luck."

"Thanks. Be careful until this wraps."

"My work here is done—but I'm hoping one of the people you pull in during your sweep will either know what happened to Stephanie and her boyfriend or end up being the perpetrator."

"If that happens, both of our cases will conclude at the same time. Wednesday could be a big day on the personal *and* professional front."

He didn't have to spell out what he meant.

She'd told him she'd give him an answer by Wednesday about whether or not he should seek a job in St. Louis.

But Wednesday was approaching much too fast.

"Given how hectic life will be for the duration, it may be wise to move the personal deadline to Thursday."

"Stalling?"

"Being practical. We won't have an opportunity to talk on Wednesday."

"I'll extend the deadline if you agree to have dinner with me Thursday night to give me your answer."

"What if my answer is no?"

"Then I doubt I'll be in the mood to eat much. But I hope it won't be. Because I can promise you this—if anyone walks away this go-round, it will be you."

It was hard to doubt his sincerity.

But were her emotions clouding her judgment?

Hard to say.

She backed toward the door. Fumbled for the knob. "I'll pencil you in for Thursday." She turned and fled.

Her dilemma, however, followed her down the hall.

Zeke wasn't asking for a commitment—just a chance to prove he had staying power.

The request was reasonable.

Yet there was real danger.

For as Cate searched for an empty classroom to call her handler, she admitted the truth.

Despite her best efforts to shore up her defenses, she was already half in love with Zeke again. If she agreed to his proposal, if she let him woo her, she'd be head over heels faster than the weather could change from cloudy to sunny on a Missouri autumn day.

But what if history repeated itself?

As she'd told Zeke at the hotel yesterday, she'd survived losing him once—but the very thought of facing that trauma again sent a cold chill snaking through her.

So before their tenure at Ivy Hill wrapped up on Thursday, she had to decide how much she was willing to risk in the pursuit of a possible happily-ever-after.

22

OF COURSE, MS. BROWN. I'll be happy to meet with you on Thursday to discuss the arrangements for the service." In his peripheral vision, Reverend Wilson caught a movement. He angled toward the door of the Ivy Hill chaplain's office, cell pressed to his ear.

Kayla Harris hovered on the threshold.

He waved her in as he resumed his conversation. "One o'clock will be fine. Please accept my deepest sympathy on your loss, but take hope in the knowledge that your dear sister is with the Lord."

As he ended the call, he turned to the girl and offered her a smile. It was heartening to see how she'd blossomed in Ivy Hill's academically challenging environment.

"Come in, my dear. How are you?" He met her halfway and cocooned her hands between his.

"I-I don't know."

At her shaky answer, he studied her more closely. Her shoulders were stiff, her features taut, and her fingers were trembling.

The poor girl appeared to be in acute distress.

"Please, sit down." He led her to one of the comfortable

chairs in the corner of the office. Took the seat across from her. "You seem very worried. Tell me how I can help you."

She twisted her hands in her lap. "I-I don't know where to begin."

"Begin wherever you're comfortable. Has someone upset you?"

"Yes. Someone I . . . I care about."

"What happened?"

Tears spiked her lower lashes. "This is hard."

"It doesn't have to be. You know you can talk to me about anything. Haven't I always told you that?"

"Yes, but I . . . I don't want to offend you."

"My dear, I've been in ministry for many years. I've heard more shocking stories than I can count. You can share anything with me. How long have we been friends?"

"Six years. Since we started going to your church and you invited me to come to the after-school program. You took me under your wing from the beginning. That's why this . . . why it's so upsetting."

"It doesn't have to be. Why don't you tell me what's wrong? Talking through an issue can often bring clarity."

"That's what my roommate said this morning too. That if I was confused about what I'd heard, I should discuss it with the person involved. I know there must be a simple explanation."

The girl was talking in riddles. "An explanation for what?"

"For your phone conversation on the terrace Sunday—after the worship service."

Somehow he managed to hold on to his expression of calm, sympathetic concern.

But inside, an alarm siren began blaring.

The squeak he'd heard while talking to Razor hadn't been a shutter being pummeled by the wind.

Kayla had been out there.

His heart missed a beat, and his lungs locked.

This was a disaster.

Or . . . was it?

He studied her earnest, hopeful face. Kayla trusted him. It was clear she didn't *want* to believe that what she'd heard meant what she was afraid it did. She was open to persuasion.

And he was excellent at pleading his case—a skill he'd polished through the years. One that had allowed him to wheedle generous contributions from heavy hitters for the drug treatment center downtown.

But he'd never needed it as desperately as he did now.

He smoothed a hand down the front of his jacket.

Play this cool, Tyrone. If the conversation on Sunday was of no consequence, you'd barely remember it. You'd be confused by Kayla's comment. Keep up that pretense—and buy yourself a few minutes to think through the best way to handle this.

Summoning up every ounce of his acting skills, he put on a puzzled frown. "This is about a phone conversation I had?"

"Yes." She twisted her hands together in her lap, anguish darkening her eyes. "I was coming out of the bathroom, and I saw you go out onto the terrace without your coat, holding your phone. I thought it was an emergency call you had to take, and I knew you'd get cold. I followed you to ask if you wanted me to get your coat. But after I heard part of the conversation, I . . . I didn't know what to think—and I got scared."

"I'm trying to recall the exchange, Kayla—but I get dozens of calls every day. Tell me what you heard, and I'll be happy to clear up any misunderstanding."

She swallowed. "You were angry—and you mentioned the Feds. It sounded like the person you were talking to was being watched. You said there was a pickup Wednesday, and that wasn't the best time for a tail. Ivy Hill was involved somehow—along with someone here. An inside person, I think you said. You also talked about Stephanie. I got the feeling she'd walked into a bad situation—and you knew about it." She picked at her cuticle. "It was all very confusing—and upsetting."

As she finished, he maintained the concerned demeanor that had been his stock in trade for decades in his day job.

But this was worse than a disaster.

Kayla remembered his end of the conversation with Razor almost word for word.

And how much had she shared about what she'd heard—and her suspicions—with the roommate who'd advised her to speak with him?

She peeked up at him, waiting for him to respond. It was clear from her expectant look that she was eager to have him explain away what she yearned to believe was an innocent exchange.

He wanted to accommodate her. Wanted to call up the smooth eloquence that usually came to him with no effort.

But fear was muddling his mind.

Get your brain in gear, Tyrone. Whatever you say next is critical.

Despite the panic simmering below his placid façade, he coerced the left side of his brain to engage.

"Now that you've refreshed my memory, I do recall that conversation, Kayla. Mostly because it was freezing out there." He forced up the corners of his lips to lighten the atmosphere, then adopted a more sober demeanor as he began to spin his yarn. "I was talking with one of the clients from my drug rehab center. The man has potential, but he's in trouble with the law, which upset me. I'd managed to get him a delivery job—in fact, he has a pickup here this week—so having issues with law enforcement isn't ideal."

Kayla was watching him. Searching his face. From all indications, she bought the story he was fabricating.

"What about Stephanie?"

The gears in his brain revved into warp speed.

"I'd mentioned to him once that a girl here had gone missing—and speculated she may have put herself in a bad situation. I reminded him of that to encourage him not to be foolish. To keep his nose clean."

"And the inside guy?"

"I was reassuring him I'd keep my promise to talk to the security people here. He was concerned he'd be hassled by law enforcement during his delivery, and I wanted him to know that once he was on school grounds, he wouldn't have to worry about that."

Not a bad off-the-cuff explanation—but there were definite holes if Kayla thought through his story.

She fiddled with the edge of her sweater. "I guess that explains it."

But she didn't seem entirely convinced.

And she wasn't making eye contact.

Already she must be identifying the flaws in his account.

The dress shirt under his suit jacket began to stick to his back, and he flexed his shoulders to loosen the damp fabric.

He could plug the gaps if he had a minute to think. Kayla would be receptive to any further clarifications he offered.

But what if she wasn't the only one wondering about his conversation on the terrace?

How much had she shared with Cate Sheppard?

Better try to find out.

"I can see how worried you've been about this, Kayla." He leaned forward and clasped his hands together, giving her his full attention. "I'm sorry you were upset. Your roommate gave you excellent advice. Talking concerns through is always the best approach. What did she think about the conversation you overheard?"

"I didn't tell her any details. It wouldn't have been fair to you. Casting doubts about good people is wrong."

The coil of tension in his gut loosened a hair.

"You've been listening to my sermons." He called up a smile—and hoped it didn't appear as stiff as it felt.

"They're easy to listen to."

"Thank you." He ignored his clammy shirt and leaned back. It appeared he was in the clear with the roommate, but it couldn't hurt to reiterate the importance of discretion. "I appreciate your consideration. Lives can be ruined by sharing groundless fears. They can plant seeds of doubt in people's minds—even if the other person is later proven innocent."

"I know—but Cate wouldn't judge someone based on stories about them. She'd decide for herself."

"She's a smart girl."

"Yeah—except in Spanish." Her lips bowed. "That's not her subject. She's lucky Mr. Martinez is tutoring her—even if she complains about the extra sessions."

His pulse stuttered.

Kayla's roommate had study sessions with the federal agent who was posing as a Spanish teacher?

What if Kayla ended up telling her about their conversation in a moment of shared confidences, and she, in turn, mentioned it to Martinez?

Kayla might buy his explanation for the phone call on the terrace, but if a federal agent got wind of the exchange, all kinds of red flags would go up.

It was more important than ever that Kayla keep what she'd heard to herself.

"I get the impression you two have become close."

"Yeah. It's nice to have someone to share stuff with. Stephanie never talked to me, but Cate's different. She's a new friend, but a good one."

"Good friends are a treasure. More precious than gold. But friends don't have to share everything. It's fine to keep parts of our life private. Like our chat today. She doesn't know me like you do, and the gossip mill around here is already too active."

"Cate doesn't gossip."

"I'm glad to hear that. Still, let's keep this between you and me, okay?"

"Sure. I wasn't going to tell her about it, anyway. We don't share *everything*."

"Perfect. But I'm glad you found someone here you feel comfortable talking with. Friends are important." He checked his watch. "I have to run, but why don't you think about our chat, and I'll call you later tonight to see if you have any more questions? I don't want you to worry, and I surely don't want anything to hurt our friendship."

Her irises began to shimmer. "Me neither. I owe you so much. I would never have gotten a scholarship here if you hadn't gone to bat for me."

"I've always believed in helping those who are willing to work hard and who stay away from the vices that are rampant in our society today."

That much was true, at least. It was how he'd lived his life.

"I know. *Everyone* knows that." She stood. "Thank you for not being angry."

"Anger is a wasted emotion." He stood too. "May I call you about nine? To clear up any other questions that come to mind?"

"What if I don't have any?"

He winked. "Then I expect it will be a short conversation."

The corners of her mouth tipped up. "Okay. I'll talk to you later."

He crossed to the door and pulled it open. "Take care—and God go with you."

The standard send-off he gave those who came to him in search of guidance tripped off his tongue. Most people found comfort in it.

Truth be told, he could use comforting himself on this Tuesday afternoon.

For as he watched Kayla walk away, unease slithered through him.

Yes, she'd seemed to accept his explanation.

Yes, she'd assured him she hadn't told anyone about her concerns.

Yes, she'd agreed they were friends.

Plus, he was poised to do more damage control later to chase away any lingering doubts.

The situation appeared to be under control.

But what if she decided to share her experience with someone else she trusted, despite his request to keep their exchange confidential?

Someone like her roommate.

A girl who didn't know him and who could be more prone to suspicion.

A girl who could mention it to Martinez.

That would create a very, very dangerous situation.

Tyrone drew in a long, slow breath and circled around his desk.

There had been too many glitches in the past few weeks. Too many complications. Too many developments that could jinx their operation.

Much as he wanted the income from tomorrow's shipment, waiting around until the money came in suddenly felt far too risky.

Maybe he should get out even sooner than the accelerated departure he'd already been contemplating.

Much sooner.

Exactly when depended on the vibes he got from his conversation with Kayla tonight.

He slid his papers into his briefcase. Put on his coat. Flipped off the light in his office.

His first order of business as soon as he got home?

Prepare his contingency exit plan for immediate execution in case Kayla didn't keep her end of their agreement and spilled what she knew to her roommate.

And if she did, he'd also have to figure out how to silence her—and Cate Sheppard—so he could escape.

———————

"That was a fast call." Cate yawned and shifted around on her desk chair as Kayla reentered their room. Studying every night was getting old—but with the end in sight, she could keep up the pretense for another thirty-six hours.

Brow puckered, Kayla set her cell on her desk and dropped onto her bed. "Yeah."

"You still upset about whatever happened over the weekend?"

"Not as much—but some."

More than some. The girl who spent every minute outside of class cramming and doing projects for extra credit had hardly opened a book the past two nights. "You want to talk about it yet?"

"I don't think I should."

"Why not?"

"It feels sort of . . . disloyal."

"I know how to keep secrets."

Kayla picked up her teddy bear. Played with a loose thread on one of the seams. "I followed your advice. About talking to the person I had an issue with."

"Did it help?"

"At first. But the more I think about the explanation he offered, the more I feel like he could be . . . that he's not telling me the whole truth."

The knot of tension in Cate's stomach loosened.

If this was a guy problem, it may not be as bad as she'd thought. Teens tended to overreact to romantic tribulations.

Except . . . Kayla had been clear in their chats that she wasn't dating anyone special.

"I didn't think you had a boyfriend. Did you meet someone at home?"

"It's not that kind of guy problem."

"Then what kind of guy problem is it?"

"An adult guy problem."

Cate froze. "Has someone been hitting on you?"

"No." She waved off the question. "I could handle that. This is . . . it's more like being let down. And I don't have any idea what to do with what I know. Or if it means anything. I'd hate to cause an innocent person hassles—but what if they're not innocent?" She wrapped her arms around the teddy bear. "It totally sucks to start doubting someone you care about."

She could relate.

But this wasn't about her and Zeke. It was about Kayla.

"Someone from home?"

"Yes . . . at least that's where we met. What really freaked me out was when he mentioned Stephanie."

The nerves in Cate's fingers began to tingle—like they often did as she was closing in on the solution to a case.

Was it possible Kayla had come across information that was relevant to their investigations?

If so, could she be persuaded to share it? To trust a room-mate she'd known less than a month?

How could she make that happen?

Demonstrate your trust in her, Cate—by confiding in her. Actions do speak louder than words.

Yes.

That could work.

It involved a bit of risk, but if her instincts were correct, it could be worth a slight gamble to find out what Kayla knew.

Decision made, Cate crossed to the girl and sat beside her. "Can you keep a secret?"

Kayla gave her a wary glance. "Yes."

"Speaking of adult guy problems—remember how you told me Mr. Evans gave some of the girls joints?"

"Yeah."

"He offered me one."

"For real?"

"Yes."

"You didn't take it, did you?"

"Yeah. I did."

Alarm flared in her irises. "Why? You could get expelled!"

"I did it because what he's doing is wrong—and illegal."

"I know! That's why you should have said no and run the other direction!"

"I ran to the police instead."

The girl gaped at her. "Seriously?"

"Yes. I reported him."

"But . . . he's still here. I saw him today."

"He won't be by the end of the week. The police are getting search warrants for his house and office and computers."

"Wow."

"Here's the thing—I have a feeling the person you're worried about may be breaking the law too. If he is, you should do what I did. Report him."

The twin creases on her roommate's forehead deepened. "But Evans is different. I mean, the guy's a jerk—and he didn't mean anything to you. You also had absolute proof he's guilty. It's not as easy to know what to do if you're not positive. I don't want to sic the police on someone who may be innocent. That could ruin his reputation forever."

"Kayla." She touched the girl's arm. "You're smart and you have your head on straight. If this guy's story seems sketchy to you, it probably is."

She dropped her chin to the top of the teddy bear's head.

"I just can't believe what I'm thinking is true. It doesn't fit with everything I've seen."

"Some bad people are good actors. They know how to play a part. Make you believe what they want you to believe."

"No." She shook her head. "He's not like that."

"Or he is, and you're too close to him to be impartial. If he has information about Stephanie, don't you think it's important to let someone know? What if she didn't run away? What if she got snatched? What if she got hurt? Shouldn't someone investigate that?"

"I don't know." She blew out a breath. "I'll sleep on it, okay?"

No. It wasn't.

But if she pushed any harder, Kayla could shut her off.

"Whatever." Cate stood.

"Besides, he's going to pick me up after school tomorrow. We're going to have coffee and talk again. That might clear up my doubts."

A coffee date.

Cate jotted that on her mental calendar. If Kayla wouldn't share the man's name, surveillance of the pickup could be in order. Best case, she'd get a glimpse of the guy and his license plate—but a license plate alone would do the trick. The mini binoculars she'd brought along on this gig were going to come in handy.

"Where are you going?"

"Starbucks."

"Well, I hope that puts your mind at ease. I hate to see you so stressed. And I'll be here if you decide you want to talk."

"Thanks."

Cate returned to her desk but kept tabs on Kayla in her peripheral vision.

For the remainder of the evening, her roommate didn't crack a book—despite their history exam tomorrow. Nor did she work on her extra-credit paper for English lit.

All she did was hold her bear and stare at the wall.

An hour later, when Kayla turned in for the night, Cate doused the light on her desk too.

But as she prepared for bed and climbed under the covers, she knew sleep would be elusive.

And she'd be willing to bet it would be for Kayla too.

Because danger was in the air, as palpable—and chilling—as the ice crystals that had stung her cheeks the day she'd been attacked in the woods.

23

THIS WAS THE DAY.

In eighteen hours, all of the major players would be in custody—and if Jones cooperated and passed on what he knew, the head man would be next.

Zeke rinsed his mug, set it on the drying rack in his kitchen sink, and gave the condo a scan as he veered toward the foyer closet to retrieve his overcoat.

Nice digs.

But lonely.

If his prayers were answered, though, he wouldn't be spending his free time alone in the future. By tomorrow, the case should end—and the rest of his life could begin.

With Cate, God willing.

A buzz of adrenaline heightened his senses as he opened the closet door—the kind he always got on the cusp of a takedown.

But today the epinephrine rush had as much to do with anticipation—and nerves—over Cate's decision as it had to do with his case.

And that wasn't good.

After all the work that had gone into this investigation, it deserved his full attention until all the ends were tied up and the players booked.

So he'd finish out his Spanish-teacher gig for the next eight hours, keeping up the business-as-usual pretense—but the minute he left Ivy Hill this afternoon, Zeke Martinez would cease to exist and Special Agent Zeke Sloan would be back on duty.

It was going to be a long, intense day—and a long, intense night—that would require every bit of his concentration.

Assuming all went as planned, however, the results would be well worth the extended hours and unwavering single-minded focus.

Then he and Cate could spend the rest of their lives together.

He hoped.

As he reached for his coat, his cell began to vibrate.

He pulled it out and checked caller ID. His handler, with the promised status report.

After a quick greeting, the man got straight to business.

"The delivery occurred as scheduled last night, and all the pieces are in place on our end. We have surveillance on the top dealers, and we have two teams on Jones. We've also got two teams stationed at the back entrance to the school. The only loose end is the head guy."

"That's why we have to pull Jones in fast and see if we can get him to talk. You planning to bring in Hernandez too?"

"Yes. If he'll identify Jones as his supplier, that gives us more leverage. Like you've said, once we have grounds to book him, the threat of prison becomes more real. It's too bad Hernandez's brother-in-law can't make a positive ID."

"It was dark in the alley, and Jones was bundled up. I'm grateful he managed to get the license plate. Let's hope we can convince Hernandez to talk." He pulled his coat off the hanger. "I have to get to school—but I'll touch base as soon as I leave, see where you want me."

"If anything comes up before that, I'll let you know."

"Thanks." Zeke ended the call and started to put his coat on. Stopped to peer at the upper sleeve, near the underarm seam.

What was that faint, dark blotch on the wool?

His heart stammered as he identified the stain.

It was Cate's blood. From the night he'd carried her out of the woods after the attack.

Despite the thorough inspection and scrubbing he'd given the coat, he'd missed this spot.

He detoured to the kitchen in search of a cleaning solution that would remove the blemish.

But his step faltered as a sense of foreboding engulfed him.

Could this overlooked stain be an omen?

If he'd missed this, could he also have missed a piece of information that was vital to the case?

Blowing out an annoyed breath, he picked up his pace.

Ridiculous.

Believing in signs was silly and superstitious.

Yet hard as he tried to convince himself such thinking was pure folly, he couldn't shake the apprehension that paralyzed his lungs while he worked to remove Cate's blood.

Or stifle the stomach-churning fear that this day was going to turn deadly.

Four o'clock in the afternoon—and her tenure as a student at Ivy Hill was winding down . . . along with her undercover career.

Thank goodness.

Cate closed her trig text for the last time.

This type of detective work was definitely not for her. Give her a regular homicide investigation any day, where she could be herself—a dogged detective who didn't have to playact to get the job done.

Cate kept an eye on Kayla as the girl pulled on a pair of leggings in preparation for her date with the mystery man whose identity she still hadn't revealed.

"Did you tell Ms. Howard you're leaving the campus?" She shifted away from her desk.

"It's been taken care of."

Odd.

Only a student—or a legal guardian—could sign a girl out.

"How?"

"It's fine, Cate. I'm not going to get in trouble."

No, that wouldn't be like Kayla. She never did anything that could put her future at Ivy Hill at risk.

So who had authorized her to leave the premises?

The girl's cell chirped, and she pulled it out. Frowned at the screen. Put the phone to her ear. "Hey . . . That's okay . . . Sure. I guess . . . Yeah. See you there." She lowered the phone.

"What's going on?"

Kayla slipped the cell into her purse. "Slight change in plans. He got delayed. He's sending a cab for me."

Her friend didn't want to show his face on campus.

Alarm bells began to jangle in Cate's mind. There was a very bad vibe swirling around this whole scenario.

And her plans to get a glimpse of the guy when he picked up her roommate had just been blown to smithereens.

"I'm getting a weird feeling about this, Kayla."

She sank onto the side of her bed. "Me too."

"I don't think you should meet this person alone."

"I told him I would—and I've always trusted him."

"Do you want me to come along? The Starbucks is probably in a mall, and I could wait in a nearby store until you're finished." After she peeked in and got a look at the guy. Maybe took a photo with her cell. "He doesn't have to know you brought anyone."

The girl caught her lower lip between her teeth. "I promised him I'd keep this between us . . . but I *would* feel less nervous if a friend was close by. Are you sure you wouldn't mind?"

"Not at all."

"If you leave campus without authorization, though, you could get in trouble."

"I can get my dad to approve it." She pulled out her cell and held it up.

"What about the Spanish test tomorrow? You should study for that. I don't want to be the reason you get a bad grade. Mr. Martinez won't be happy."

"Trust me—it's not a problem."

"Well . . . if your dad is willing to call, I'd appreciate it."

"I'll text him while I run to the bathroom. When's the cab coming?"

"In twenty minutes."

"I'll be ready." She started toward the door.

"Wait."

She swiveled around.

"How will you get back here? I don't think I'll be taking a cab."

"But I can. I'll call one from Starbucks. It's no big deal. I have cash. Besides, after you talk to your friend, you may feel comfortable asking him to let me join you. Either way, I'm cool."

"That'll work."

Cate exited into the hall to call her handler.

He didn't answer until four rings in. "Sorry. It's crazy around here. What's up?"

She briefed him fast and ended with her requests. "I want you to call the school as my dad ASAP and spring me. Also, can you get a tail on us?" Overkill, perhaps . . . but better to be safe.

"In fifteen minutes?" He sounded frazzled. "We're working three homicide scenes, none of them close to you. Let me see if I can round anyone up. But call and give me the Starbucks location after you get there so we can keep tabs on you if the tail doesn't happen."

"Will do."

She pressed the end button and weighed the phone in her hand.

They were on the cusp of a solution to the Stephanie Laurent case. She could feel it.

Before she and Kayla got in that cab, she'd also send Zeke a quick text. By now, he'd have left the campus—and his Martinez persona—behind, and he didn't need any distractions.

But if Kayla's friend knew any details about Stephanie's case . . . and Stephanie had disappeared during a drug pickup . . . Zeke should be in the loop.

At this stage, all it would take was one pertinent fact to give them the breakthrough they'd both been hoping for.

And this could be it.

A number he'd hoped never to see again flashed on his cell screen, and Will stiffened in his seat behind the security desk at Ivy Hill.

Blast.

His contact had already said goodbye. Their association was supposed to be over.

And he or she never called during working hours—like tonight. They knew he was on duty . . . at their request.

Dread pooled in his gut.

This must be very, very important.

He pressed talk and put the phone to his ear. "Yes?"

"I need one more favor."

"I thought we were finished."

"We are. This will be our last contact. A cab will be arriving at the front gate momentarily. Kayla Harris will get into it. Don't stop her. She believes she's been cleared to leave school."

"Where is she going?"

"That isn't your concern."

He swiveled his chair toward the wall and lowered his voice. "I don't want anyone else hurt."

"She won't be."

"How can I be certain of that?"

"You'll have to trust me."

"That's asking a lot."

"Sign her out, Will."

The line went dead.

A few seconds later, the phone on the desk buzzed and he rolled forward to answer it, his mind still wrestling with this new development. "Security."

"Mr. Fischer?"

"Yes."

"This is Richard Sheppard, Cate Sheppard's father. I want to authorize an off-campus excursion for her this evening with a friend. Let me give you her date of birth and our security password." He recited them.

Will searched the database.

They both matched.

"I have it noted, Mr. Sheppard."

"Thanks for your help."

As they said their goodbyes, a cab rolled through the gate at the entrance to the property.

His pulse picked up as he watched the feed from the security camera.

What should he do?

Zeke Sloan had said to follow all the instructions his contact gave him—but neither of them had anticipated this particular instruction.

Better call him.

Cell in hand, he fished out the man's number and crossed to the window that offered an expansive view of the grounds and the circle drive.

The cab stopped in front of the dorm entrance, and Kayla emerged.

So did Cate Sheppard.

They were together.

Both girls were leaving campus for parts unknown?

His panic flared again, and he punched in Sloan's number.

If he stopped them, and their departure was somehow related to the DEA investigation, the whole takedown operation could be blown. The perpetrators could escape.

Sloan wouldn't want that.

The two girls got into the cab, and the vehicle rolled forward again.

Why wasn't Sloan answering?

The cab picked up speed as it passed the entrance to the main building, and Will squinted at the license plate. His vision wasn't as keen as it used to be, but he was able to decipher two of the numbers before the vehicle moved out of range.

Sloan's phone rolled to voicemail.

Of all times for the man to be incommunicado.

He left a message, along with the numbers he'd been able to make out on the license plate.

As the cab disappeared around a bend toward the entrance gate, he returned to his desk.

Hopefully the two girls inside weren't destined to vanish—as Stephanie and her boyfriend had.

But if that happened, the blame wouldn't rest with him this go-round. He'd followed the instructions of law enforcement to the letter.

This guilt trip would belong to Zeke Sloan.

Zeke toweled his hair dry after a fast shower, threw on his clothes, and headed for the kitchen to scarf down a frozen dinner. As long as he'd had to swing by the condo to change out of his Ivy Hill teacher garb, why not take advantage of the opportunity to clean up and chow down? Who knew when he'd have a few minutes to do either again?

He pulled the nuked dinner out of the microwave, peeled back the clear film, and dug a fork out of the drawer.

As he stabbed a bite of chicken, he glanced at his phone on the counter.

The message light was on.

He pulled out the power cord as he chewed and scanned the screen.

There was also a new text.

It figured.

The cell had been glued to his hip all day, but of course two people would try to contact him during the ten minutes he was unavailable.

If this was any indication of the volume of activity to come in the hours ahead, it would be prudent to throw an energy bar or two into his car to supplement this barely adequate dinner.

He speared another morsel of chicken and played back the voicemail, left at four-thirty.

The instant Will Fischer identified himself, he stopped chewing—and by the time the man got to the part about Cate leaving in a cab with Kayla, Zeke had lost his appetite.

This whole setup felt off.

Way off.

He jotted down the name of the cab company and the two digits from the license, shoved the nuked dinner aside, and moved on to the new text message.

It had come in at four twenty-five—and it was from Cate.

> Going w/Kayla 2 Starbucks 2 meet mystery man who knows something about Steph. Reason she was upset the other day. Will try 2 get an ID. My people in loop. Stay tuned.

He closed his eyes.

If her roommate's male friend had a connection to Stephanie's death and/or the DEA investigation, they could both be walking straight into danger.

This was very bad news.

The wiser plan would have been to have DEA agents—or County detectives—tail the cab and get photos of this guy . . . if they could have lined that up fast enough.

A long shot.

But that wouldn't deter Cate from going it alone. Not if she was convinced she was onto a hot lead that would evaporate if she didn't pursue it.

He punched in her number.

After five rings, the call rolled to voicemail.

He muttered a word that wasn't pretty.

She was either ignoring her calls or wasn't in a position to talk.

At least she'd alerted her people to her plan—and knowing County, they were on this.

They better be.

Because much as he wished he could direct his efforts to locating Cate and verifying she was safe, it was all hands on deck for the DEA sweep.

But he did have the partial license. That was a solid lead. They ought to be able to identify the cab without too much delay and determine which Starbucks had been the destination.

If Kayla and Cate weren't there, however, the tracking

process could slow—or stall. It all depended on whether any-one had noticed either of them.

He tapped in the office number to get someone on the cab ID ASAP.

All he could do for Cate beyond that was keep trying to call her . . . and hope the fears he'd dismissed earlier after being spooked by her blood on his coat didn't come to pass after all.

24

THIS WASN'T WHAT HE AND KAYLA had discussed.
Tyrone frowned and tightened his grip on the wheel as
two girls emerged from the cab at the strip mall.

Lucky he'd listened to his instincts and waited in his car
for his guest to arrive. That inspired decision bought him
breathing space to adjust his plan to accommodate two girls
instead of one.

But what a disappointment.

Who'd have thought Kayla would renege on her promise to
keep their discussion—and her worries—confidential?

You couldn't trust anyone anymore.

Cate gave Kayla a hug and continued down the sidewalk
to a clothing shop next door.

Kayla went into Starbucks.

Hmm.

Why had they separated?

Had Kayla kept her promise, after all? Brought her friend
along for moral support but told her nothing?

A moot point at this stage.

Both girls had to be dealt with. Since Kayla wasn't going
back to Ivy Hill tonight, neither could Cate.

He waited eight minutes, then took out one of his burner phones . . . just as Cate came out of the clothing shop.

She pulled up a hood that shadowed her face and walked to the edge of the window in Starbucks. Stopped to fiddle with her phone as she peeked inside—like she was spying on Kayla. Trying to see who she was meeting.

Some friend.

A few seconds later, she wandered back to the clothing store.

He tapped in Kayla's number.

She didn't answer until the third ring.

"Kayla, it's Reverend Wilson."

"Sorry. I didn't recognize the number."

"It's new. Be sure to save it in your contacts list."

"Okay. Where are you?"

"In the parking lot. I think I'm coming down with a cold and would rather not infect everyone in the place—but I didn't want to cancel our get-together. Why don't you grab whatever beverage you want and meet me out here? We'll keep the car windows cracked to let the germs escape, and I'll reimburse you for the drink."

"Would you rather meet another day?"

"No. I drove here from downtown to see you even though I'm feeling poorly. I don't want any misunderstanding between us. I'm in the aisle across from the shop, about eight cars down."

"All right. I'll get a hot chocolate and be out in a minute."

"The perfect drink on this cold day."

Tyrone ended the call, put the phone away, and felt around in the other pocket of his coat for the 9mm Smith & Wesson pistol he'd hoped never to need.

Too bad it had come to this.

But fate was fickle—and if it turned, you had to be prepared to take regrettable actions for the sake of self-preservation should the situation spiral out of control.

And with two frightened teenage girls in the mix, that was a very real possibility.

Cate paused beside a table of folded sweaters in the women's clothing store and consulted her watch.

Ten minutes had passed since she'd wandered over to Starbucks and spotted Kayla sitting alone in the coffee shop. Whoever she was meeting should have arrived by now.

But who knew how long they'd chat?

It couldn't hurt to take another quick peek.

She strolled toward the door . . . but stopped as her cell vibrated.

Kayla's number popped up on her screen.

Drat.

Were they finished already?

Had she missed the opportunity to catch a glimpse of her roommate's suspicious friend?

"Hey. Are you done?" She stopped by the door that led outside, where light snow was beginning to fall.

"Yes. We're getting ready to drive back. He said it's okay if you come with us." The girl's voice was a tad unsteady.

"What's up? You sound kind of shaky."

"We're outside, at his car, and it's freezing. You want to come? Taking a cab would be s-silly."

"Yeah. I'll be out in a minute." She slipped the phone back into her parka.

This was an unexpected development.

If Kayla's friend was willing to reveal himself to her, he may not have anything to hide.

Or he could be a smooth talker who'd been able to bamboozle the teen.

On the drive back, she could assess the guy and decide for herself whether he was on the level.

She pushed through the door, snuggling deeper into her down-filled coat as a blast of frigid air whooshed past.

Dang, it was cold today. The sooner she could get back to the toasty dorm, the happier she'd be.

And tomorrow night she'd be able to sleep in her own bed again.

Bliss.

She scanned the parking lot—and Kayla waved at her from beside a midsize car.

Tucking her chin down against the icy gusts, Cate crossed the pavement, her hair whipping around her face and obscuring her vision.

A few feet from her destination, she shoved the strands back and lifted her head. "The wind is blowing a gale to—"

Her step faltered as a familiar figure emerged from the car and stood beside Kayla.

Reverend Wilson?

What on earth . . . ?

"Keep walking, Cate." The man's mellow baritone floated across the dark air toward her, as relaxed as if they were having a chat over lattes. "We wouldn't want Kayla to get hurt, would we?"

He shifted slightly aside.

Far enough to display the pistol pressed snug against her roommate's side.

Dear God in heaven!

The *minister* was involved in Zeke's drug ring? He was the one who knew details about Stephanie's disappearance?

Yet as the pieces began to fall into place, it made perfect, awful sense.

He had the run of Ivy Hill. Knew the property and the players. He could also have contacts in the drug world through clients at his rehab center. Will Fischer may have confided in him about his financial difficulties—and Wilson could have passed that useful piece of information on to the head of the ring.

The minister wasn't anything like the image he presented to the world—or the man Kayla had thought he was.

No wonder the girl had been distraught and confused.

"Keep walking, Cate."

Legs stiff, mind racing, she lurched forward again.

Why would a respected man who presided at a popular church . . . who'd founded and ran a lauded rehab center in the heart of the city for addicts unable to afford expensive treatment centers . . . who'd received national recognition for his efforts to clean up the north side . . . be involved in anything nefarious?

She was as confused as Kayla.

"I don't understand." She stopped three feet from the duo.

"You don't have to. Go around to the driver's side. Get behind the wheel. One wrong move, you can say goodbye to your friend."

If only she had her Sig!

But it wouldn't have made much difference at this stage, anyway. Wilson would still have had the upper hand—and if he'd been involved in the other killings, he wouldn't hesitate to kill again. The parking lot of a popular mall wouldn't be an ideal location to shoot someone . . . in fact, it was a huge deterrent . . . but desperate people took desperate actions. And he had to be desperate to pull this stunt. If she balked, it was possible he'd snap.

Could she take that chance?

No.

She had to play along, buy herself as much time as possible to come up with a plan that put Kayla at as little risk as possible.

At least she'd passed on the Starbucks location to County

a few minutes ago—though it wasn't likely they had anyone here yet.

After she circled the car and slid behind the wheel, Wilson settled into the back seat, pulling Kayla in with him.

"Shut the door. Both of you."

Kayla did as he instructed.

So did Cate.

"You do have a driver's license, don't you, Cate?"

No sense lying. If he asked for her wallet, he'd find the one the department had prepared as part of her cover.

"Yes."

"Excellent. Give Kayla your phone."

No!

The phone was her lifeline. Without the GPS connection, no one would be able to find her.

"Your phone, Cate—in the interest of Kayla's health."

She had to let it go.

Trying to quell her panic, she retrieved it and extended her arm toward the back seat.

"Take it, Kayla. Then remove the batteries from both of your phones. While she does that, Cate, start the car."

"Where are we going?"

"Somewhere safe."

"For you . . . or for us?"

"You're quick on the uptake. I like that."

"You didn't answer my question."

"No, I didn't. Leave the mall and turn left. Let's go."

She glanced in the rearview mirror.

Kayla met her gaze.

The girl's eyes were filled with fear, shock—and apology.

"I'm sorry, Cate." Her voice broke.

"This isn't your fault." She put the car in gear. "And I'm glad you don't have to deal with this alone."

"You were right, Kayla—she's a true friend. I suppose it's

fitting you go through this experience together." The man leaned back. "Yes. I do believe this was meant to be. You can rely on each other."

"For what?" Cate flipped on the blinker, her fingers none too steady.

"For what's to come."

"Which is?"

"You'll see."

That's what she was afraid of.

"Why are you doing this?"

Silence.

She checked the rearview mirror again.

Wilson was looking back and forth between her and Kayla—his lips pressed together.

He was done talking.

Fine.

She had thinking and planning to do, and that would require every minute of the drive that was taking them who knew where.

At least he didn't know she was fully briefed on the drug investigation and was privy to everything happening behind the scenes with law enforcement on this critical day.

All he knew was that Kayla had overheard a confusing conversation—and pulled her friend into her attempts to resolve it.

The question was, what was Wilson's role in the ring?

If Jackson was the number two man, where was the minister in the hierarchy?

Unless . . .

Sweet mercy!

Was it possible *he* was the leader?

It seemed crazy—yet he had the perfect cover to run a drug ring. Who would ever suspect someone with his reputation and credentials?

The question was why.

"Toss the first battery onto the road, Kayla."

At the man's instruction, her roommate lowered her window and threw one out.

A block later, he repeated the instruction, keeping the gun aimed at Kayla. "Now let's sit back and enjoy our drive to the country."

They were leaving the city?

Cate looked at Kayla again in the rearview mirror.

The girl's eyes were wide and terror-filled.

She could relate.

Whatever the man had in store for them wasn't going to be pleasant.

She knew something he didn't, however.

He wasn't dealing with two naïve teenagers.

There was a cop-turned-detective in this car, and even without her Sig . . . even sporting painful injuries . . . she was more equipped to deal with him than he could ever suspect—if she could do so without endangering Kayla.

Unfortunately, that was a big if.

But unless Zeke and his crew or her own people figured out how to find them, it was going to be up to her to see that the two of them got out of this alive.

After relieving one of the surveillance agents assigned to Hernandez, Zeke parked a few doors down from Eduardo's house and hunkered down in his car. The agent stationed in back was more likely to spot activity if the man drove out the alley, but due to the high stakes, they were covering all the bases tonight.

He'd have put agents front and back too if he was running this takedown.

The gentle snow that had begun falling wasn't helping visibility, however.

He flicked on the wipers. At this rate, he'd have to clear the windshield every couple of minutes—not ideal if he wanted to stay under the radar.

Since no one was lingering outside on this cold night, however, his presence might not be noticed.

He pulled out his cell. If Hernandez stayed put, they wouldn't be moving in for the arrest for six hours. This was a perfect time to connect with Cate.

Keeping the phone below window level, he clicked on her name. Put the cell to his ear.

When the call went straight to voicemail, a tingle of alarm raced through him.

Her cell was turned off or not receiving a signal.

Where was she?

What was she doing?

Had she been in touch with her own people in the past hour?

Were there any hits yet on the partial license plate number he'd passed on to the office?

He wanted answers.

Keeping watch on Eduardo's front door, Zeke keyed in the number for his handler—who'd spoken with the County PD after Zeke's unexpected reunion with Cate. He ought to have a number or two he could pass on. It would expedite the process to talk with someone who was already aware of the overlapping investigations. Plus, County had been briefed on the takedown tonight and was providing backup personnel. At this stage, the two agencies were working in tandem.

His handler answered on the first ring, clearly distracted.

Join the club.

But the man did scroll through his calls from early January and pass on the number for Cate's sergeant.

Too bad it wasn't a name he recognized from his tenure with County.

"Any news on the cab?" He squinted at a shadowed movement behind the drawn shades in Eduardo's unit.

"Yeah. I was getting ready to call you. We identified the cab and the driver about ten minutes ago. You want to pass the info on to County, or shall we?"

"I'll do it. Cate's boss is my next call." He pulled out a notebook. "Ready." He jotted down the information as the man recited it. "Thanks."

Three seconds later, he punched in the sergeant's number. He too answered on the first ring.

After a brief introduction, Zeke got straight to the point. "Has anyone from County heard from Cate?"

"She called to give us the Starbucks location after they arrived. That was her last contact."

"As of five minutes ago, her phone is going straight to voicemail."

A beat of silence passed.

"I don't like that."

"Neither do I. I also have information on the cab and driver—not that you'll need it, since Cate called with her location. But here it is anyway." He passed it on.

"Thanks."

"Can someone keep me in the loop? Cate and I have been briefing each other on developments in our cases during our undercover assignments, and I'd like to stay current with her situation."

"Sure. We'll call if we have any news."

"Thanks."

Zeke pressed the end button and peered at Eduardo's house through the flakes of snow. Lights continued to shine from behind the shuttered windows, and at last report all three occupants were home—as they would likely be all evening.

Based on the conversation Eduardo had overheard, Hernandez appeared to have fallen from grace with the ring after his attempt on a federal agent's life. It was doubtful he'd go anywhere until the DEA knocked on the door in the early hours of the morning and took him in for questioning.

Zeke flipped up the collar of his coat as his breath formed a cloud of vapor in front of his face. Tried to tamp down his frustration.

Instead of sitting here idly while the hours to the take-down ticked by, he could be pitching in on the search for Cate. Helping track down people who may have seen her at Starbucks. Who could describe the man Kayla had met. Or who had overheard a telling snippet of conversation. And if Cate and Kayla had left, perhaps someone had spotted the vehicle and could provide a make and model . . . or part of the license plate.

He twisted the key in the ignition and cranked the heat up to take the chill off the car. In this weather, he'd have to do that every ten or fifteen minutes to avoid frostbite and hypothermia.

Despite the surge of warmth from the vents, though, he remained chilled to the core.

And only one thing was going to change that.

News that Cate was safe and unhurt.

Until then, all he could do was sit tight—and pray hard.

25

"TURN LEFT IN FIFTY YARDS, CATE."

As Wilson spoke from the back seat, Cate surveyed the rolling, wooded terrain. The ground and the skeletons of the bare trees were a ghostly, translucent white under a thin veneer of snow, but no structures were visible. Nor were there any clues to indicate their location.

And after the twisting route they'd followed for forty-five minutes, all she knew was that they were somewhere west of the city, past Defiance and Augusta. Beyond that vague sense of direction, she was lost.

"This is it."

Cate slowed and tried to detect any indication of a lane forking off the two-lane state road.

"Turn this side of the sign."

She shifted her attention higher and homed in on a small, rustic wooden placard difficult to read through the light snow sifting to the ground.

Camp Oasis.

Beside it, parallel gravel tracks led into the woods.

"What is this place?"

Silence.

"It's where Reverend Wilson has his retreats for teens and

people from the rehab center. But it's . . . it's closed in the winter."

Cate frowned as Kayla supplied the shaky answer.

Why would the man bring them here?

If this was their final destination, though, she'd have to go with the plan she'd developed during the drive to deal with a remote location where no one was available to come to their assistance.

Problem was, the odds of success were fifty-fifty at best.

But it was all she had—and if Wilson intended to kill them anyway, she wasn't going down without a fight.

She swung onto the track, inching along on the bumpy surface.

A couple hundred yards in, a log structure came into view.

"Keep going."

"I can't see the road."

"It winds between the trees. Follow the clearing."

She pressed on, passing a dozen small, rustic cottages set into the woods.

At last the lane widened into a turnaround.

They were at the end of the road.

Perhaps literally.

Her pulse picked up.

"All right, ladies. We've arrived. Cate, pass the keys back to me."

She shut off the engine, set the brake, and complied. "Now what?"

"Get out of the car and stand beside the door. We'll do the same on the other side. If you're thinking about making a break for it, you may want to reconsider. There's very little traffic on this road at night—especially in weather like this— and it will take you a long while to find help. You'll also leave Kayla at my mercy. If, on the other hand, you both cooperate, neither of you will die this evening."

The man could be telling the truth—but believing him required a huge leap of faith.

And given the presumed fate of Stephanie and her boyfriend, her trust level wasn't all that high.

But in any case, she couldn't leave Kayla behind.

What they had to do was work together to overpower the man, wrest the gun from his control, and secure him until they could call in reinforcements.

The challenge was how to accomplish that.

If they had a brief window—a single moment when Wilson's aim at Kayla wavered and they were all close together—they could bring him down with a tandem effort.

It was possible they'd get hurt in the attempt, but trusting the man's promise to spare them was foolish.

"You're trying my patience, Cate." A touch of irritation crept into his voice.

She fumbled for the handle and opened the door. Slid out into the blustery cold.

On the other side of the car, Kayla emerged first.

Cate leaned as close as she could over the roof, pointed from Kayla to herself, and spoke in a whisper. "Work together. Follow me."

The girl gave a jerky nod as Cate stepped back. Wilson got out, the pistol still aimed at Kayla's midsection.

Maintaining his grip on her arm, he motioned with his head toward the woods. "There's a path through the trees. Follow it."

After a brief hesitation, Cate started down the trail. A few steps in, she glanced over her shoulder.

Wilson hadn't moved.

She stopped.

"Keep going."

Expecting a bullet in the back any second, Cate walked on.

A shuffling sound came from behind her.

Wilson was following with Kayla.

The man was smart.

He was allowing enough distance between them to keep his two prisoners from working together to launch a physical attack.

This was going to be a challenge.

They tramped over the fresh, transparent layer of powder for a hundred yards before Wilson issued another order.

"Stop here."

Cate halted. Gave the area a sweep.

As far as she could see, they were in the middle of the woods, surrounded by nothing but trees and a few boulders and—

Wait.

There. Off to the side.

What was that cylindrical protrusion coming up from the ground several yards away?

"I see you've spotted our destination."

Cate stared at it through the swirling white flakes.

"Why did you bring us to the c-cistern?"

At Kayla's tremulous question, Cate's lungs locked and dread congealed in her stomach.

What better place to hide bodies than in an abandoned cistern on remote property?

Wilson hadn't lied. He wasn't going to kill them tonight. He was going to stash them below ground where no one would ever find them and walk away, leaving them to die on their own.

Panic clawed at her windpipe as she regarded the two-foot-wide access portal sticking up above the ground.

Death was bad.

But being locked into a confined space underground?

Almost worse for someone with claustrophobia.

"It's the perfect place for you ladies to strengthen your bond—and give me a few hours to catch my plane and escape."

"From what?" Kayla appeared to be totally confused.

"From prison, my dear."

"Did you . . . did you hurt Stephanie?"

"Not directly. I don't believe in harming innocent people. But she got in the way and had to be dealt with."

"Did you *tell* somebody to hurt her?"

"I'm not discussing that. Go over to—"

"No!" Kayla was angry now. "Not until you tell me what's going on. What did Stephanie ever do to you?"

"Nothing. I regret what happened to her—but she was in the wrong place at the wrong time."

"Like I was?"

His tone softened. "I never wanted to hurt you, Kayla."

"But you're going to, aren't you?" She choked out the question. "Just tell me why. Please. I trusted you. I thought you were a good person."

As Cate listened to the exchange, she tried to jump-start her numb brain.

No go.

All she knew was that if she went down into that hole in the ground, she could lose her sanity as well as her life.

"I *am* a good person. Haven't I spent my life doing everything I can for those who seek help?"

"Yes. That's why none of this makes any sense."

"It will. Eventually. Move over to the cistern."

"What if I don't? Are you going to shoot me?"

"Only if you leave me no choice."

He hauled her toward the opening.

As they drew closer, Cate fought down her panic. This would be their sole opportunity to overpower him. They had to go for it—and take their chances.

She locked gazes with Kayla. Despite the darkness, the other girl seemed to read her expression—and dipped her head.

Cate took a deep breath. Curled her fingers. Filled her lungs. "Now!"

She raced toward the twosome six feet away.

Kayla twisted in Wilson's grasp.

Cate dived for his legs.

They all went down in a heap of thrashing limbs, accompanied by grunts and groans—until a loud pop ricocheted through the trees, defiling the quiet night.

There was a scream.

Cate froze.

And everything went silent as death.

His phone began to vibrate, and Zeke pulled it out of the insulated jacket that didn't have sufficient padding to keep the bitter cold at bay despite periodic bursts of warmth from the heater.

Please, let this be news about Cate.

He skimmed the screen . . . and his spirits sank.

It was his counterpart behind Eduardo's house.

"Yeah?"

"Our man's on the move. Get ready to follow."

Zeke straightened up in his seat and turned on the engine. Could Hernandez be involved in tonight's pickup after all?

"Which direction is he going?"

"East out of the alley. I've got him. Stick close in case we have to switch off. Stay on the line."

"Affirmative." If the guy was traveling any distance, rotating cars in the front follow position would make it harder for him to verify he had a tail.

Zeke put the phone on speaker, set it on the seat beside him, and fell in behind his colleague, keeping a half block between them—and psyching himself up for a game of musical cars.

Didn't happen.

Three blocks later, Hernandez pulled into a low-end bar, parked, and wandered inside as if he had nothing more important to do on this Wednesday night than guzzle a few beers.

And maybe he didn't.

Maybe he'd come here to drown his sorrows after being ousted from the drug ring.

"I'll go in." His colleague emerged from his vehicle in the parking lot, cell pressed to his ear. "He knows you. We can't risk tipping him off to the tail. If he stays too long, we'll call for backup."

"That works. I'll sit tight." He ended the call, then tried Cate's number.

It rolled to voicemail without ringing.

Her phone was still out of commission.

Zeke drummed his fingers on the wheel.

Should he contact her boss again?

No.

The man had said he'd call with any news.

They were probably following up at Starbucks to see if anyone had noticed Cate or Kayla.

But who had paid for the cab?

That was an even more critical question.

Had County looked into it?

His finger hovered over the keypad—but instead of calling again, he fisted his hand.

Of course they had. That was basic procedure. Investigation 101. If they'd uncovered anything worthwhile, Cate's boss would have let him know.

He had to give them space to do their work. She was one of their own, and they'd pull out all the stops to find her. That's how County worked. He had to be patient.

And he would be—for thirty more minutes.

After that, all bets were off.

Wilson scrambled to his feet and backed off as Kayla groaned and curled into a ball on the icy ground, gripping her shoulder.

Ribs aching, Cate crawled over to her. "Kayla? Are you hurt?"

"M-my shoulder. He s-shot me." Disbelief and shock rippled through her words.

"I didn't intend to. If you both would have cooperated, this could have been avoided." Wilson sounded agitated. "How bad is it?"

"Kayla . . . let me see." Cate tugged the girl's hand away from her shoulder and unzipped the top of her coat. "I need light."

A few moments later, a beam illuminated Kayla.

Cate lifted the jacket and inspected her shoulder. There was blood on the upper sleeve of her white sparkly sweater, but the wound didn't appear to be gushing. Considering the location of the stain and the ragged rip in the sweater, the bullet had grazed her arm and kept going.

She checked the parka.

Yes.

There were entrance and exit holes very close together on the outside of the upper sleeve.

"Well?" Wilson edged closer.

"She's bleeding. We should get her to an ER."

"There are first aid supplies in the cistern, along with other provisions. You can help her."

"I'm not a doctor."

"You'll have to do the best you can until help arrives. I'll leave directions to your location after I'm gone."

"Gone where?"

"Far away, where no one will ever find me. You girls will be fine."

Maybe they would . . . maybe they wouldn't. Kayla was hurt and it was cold. Death was a very real possibility.

Would a heaping dose of guilt sway him?

"Do you really want more blood on your hands? What if I can't help Kayla?"

"I can't . . . I didn't mean to . . ." He sucked in a breath, and his tone hardened. "There's no choice. Help her up and go over there." He waved the gun toward the narrow opening. "If you don't, I'll have to finish this now."

Would he actually follow through on that threat?

Unknown.

He did seem upset about hurting Kayla—and he claimed to have stocked the cistern with supplies. Why do that if he wanted her to die?

But survival instincts were strong, and many people were willing to sacrifice their principles to save their neck.

Like Will Fischer had.

Besides, despite Wilson's claims to the contrary, he was no paragon of virtue if he'd had anything to do with eliminating Stephanie and her boyfriend. He may also have been the one who'd arranged to have her roughed up so Fischer would have an excuse to restrict access to the undeveloped parts of the campus.

A man like that was definitely capable of pulling the trigger and tossing their bodies into the cistern.

Delay, Cate—as long as you can. Another idea to gain control of the situation may come to you.

"How do we . . . do we know you left supplies?"

He tossed the small flashlight to her. "Take a look—and don't aim the light my direction. You do, I aim the gun at Kayla again."

Stomach churning at the thought of merely approaching the small opening, she forced herself to walk toward it.

Up close, it was apparent the man had, indeed, done advance preparation.

A rope ladder was attached to the edge of the protrusion and dangled down into the darkness.

Cate crept toward it. Bent down and swept the light around the interior.

The abandoned, bricked-in chamber was about ten feet in diameter and ten feet deep. It appeared to be very old.

And Wilson hadn't lied. A sleeping bag, two plastic sacks cinched at the top, and a lantern rested on the floor.

Since her ribs were aching from the tumble she'd taken and Kayla was bleeding, it was clear they weren't going to be able to overpower the man.

Plus, he continued to control the gun.

She could try blinding him with the flashlight despite his warning, but a quick peek confirmed he'd taken precautions against that possibility. He'd backed too far away for the small beam to have much impact on his vision.

They'd run out of time.

They were going to have to do what he said.

Bile rose in her throat as she scanned the inside of the cistern again. The space wasn't tiny. But it was confining. And suffocating. And dark.

Her chest tightened, her pulse slammed into overdrive, and she began to sweat.

"Climb down the ladder, Cate."

"I-I can't."

"Kayla's life is in your hands."

Oh, God!

She tried to draw in air, but her lungs wouldn't cooperate.

Why, oh why, had she let her sisters talk her into getting into that chest in the attic when they were kids? And why had the lid stuck on the stupid thing after Eve knocked it shut by mistake?

Whether that was the source of her claustrophobia, or it had simply activated a dormant condition, was irrelevant.

All that mattered was that ever since her dad had pried open the lid and pulled her out, frantic and screaming, confined spaces had brought on panic attacks.

"I don't . . . I don't like small spaces."

"It's not that small—and it won't be for long."

"Cate—please." Kayla's voice was racked with fear and pain. "I think we should do what he says. I don't want to die."

"Listen to your friend."

"We'll f-freeze down there."

"No, you won't. It's deep enough that the temperature is warmer than out here, especially near the floor." Wilson edged closer. "Are you going or not?" He swung the gun toward Kayla, who was huddled on the ground.

Do it, Cate. For Kayla. You can overcome your fear. You can. And once he leaves, you can try to come up with a plan to climb out.

Wilson aimed the gun at the ground next to Kayla.

Pulled the trigger.

At the loud pop, Kayla shrieked.

Message received.

Cate forced herself to step into the opening and onto the rope ladder. Rung by rung, she descended into the smothering darkness.

As her foot hit the floor, Wilson aimed his flashlight down. "Light the lantern."

Respiration shallow and rapid, Cate followed his instruction.

The illumination helped dispel the gloom, but not the sensation of walls closing in on her.

A few seconds later, Kayla descended the ladder.

Think about her, Cate. She's young and she's hurt. You have to be strong. Guide her through this. Care for her and keep her hopes up.

Repeating that mantra, Cate crossed to the ladder and helped Kayla down. Tremors rippled through the girl, and Cate drew her into a hug.

"We'll survive this. Your arm isn't too b-bad, and I can bandage it. Hang in, okay?"

"Help will come. You'll both be fine." Wilson's assurance echoed through the small chamber as he pulled up the rope ladder.

Half a minute later, he dragged the cover back over the opening to the cistern.

Deathly quiet descended.

Kayla continued to shake, and Cate clung to her.

Or was *she* the one trembling?

More likely they were both quaking.

Because Kayla had to know, as she did, that Wilson's promise to send someone to rescue them after he escaped could have been a lie. Once he left the camp behind, he might forget all about them.

And if that was the case, the odds were high they'd just been sealed into their tomb.

26

SHOOTING KAYLA hadn't been part of his plan.

And it was all Cate Sheppard's fault.

Tyrone inched along the rutted gravel road toward the Camp Oasis exit, knuckles bloodless on the steering wheel, teeth gritted.

If her roommate hadn't come along tonight, he could have convinced Kayla he meant her no harm—because it was the truth.

All she would have had to do was follow his instructions and wait in the cistern for help to arrive. Five minutes before takeoff—in a mere twelve hours—he'd have alerted the local sheriff to her location. By the time they got her out and she told her story, he'd be winging to his new life under his new identity.

She wasn't supposed to get hurt.

He banged the heel of his hand against the wheel as he stopped at the main road and surveyed the deserted pavement.

The situation with Stephanie and her boyfriend had been tragic. But leaving Kayla behind, bleeding and hurt, in the care of another teen who probably knew more about manicures than medicine?

Much worse.

Yet there wasn't anything he could do about it without risking incarceration—and the mere thought of being locked up with felons and murderers and drug dealers for the rest of his life sent a shiver through him.

He was better than that.

Far better.

He had never purposefully set out to harm innocent people, as those lowlifes had.

But it was hard to escape collateral damage in this business.

He pulled out onto the dark road, aimed his car toward town, stiffened his resolve—and silenced his conscience.

A man had to do what he had to do.

If a few innocent people had been hurt, that was a small price to pay for avenging two wrongs and helping multitudes.

He pressed on the accelerator and flipped on his wipers, leaving the camp—and his regrets—behind.

The medical supplies Wilson had left weren't adequate to treat a gunshot wound, superficial though it had turned out to be.

But she was doing the best she could.

Thank heaven the bleeding had been minimal.

Cate finished cleaning the wound as Kayla sat on the floor of the cistern, back against the wall and tucked into the sleeping bag, staring at the bricks ten feet away, eyes glazed.

The girl was in shock—part medical, part psychological.

She needed TLC, not a dose of angst from someone dealing with claustrophobia-induced brain freeze.

Fighting back another wave of panic, Cate gave herself a pep talk as she wound gauze around the girl's arm and secured the end with tape.

The walls may feel as if they're closing in on you, but they aren't. The cistern is as large as the bedroom in your apartment, and you never got claustrophobic there. This entombment is temporary. You'll find a way out, or someone will rescue you. Your irrational fear is nothing but a mind game, and you're in control of your mind. You have to be strong for Kayla's sake, if not—

"I don't understand anything that happened tonight."

As Kayla whispered the words, Cate draped the sleeping bag around the girl's bandaged arm, tried to regulate her breathing so she didn't hyperventilate, and debated how much to tell her.

She'd already been disillusioned by someone she trusted. Someone who wasn't what he'd pretended to be.

How would she react to the news that her new friend had also deceived her?

But the truth would come out eventually. Why delay the inevitable?

Cate rummaged around in one of the plastic bags and pulled out a bottle of water. Twisted off the top. Held it out to Kayla—but she was shaking so hard, the water sloshed out the top.

Kayla jerked away from the splashing liquid . . . regarded the quivering bottle . . . and drew a shuddering breath as the glassiness in her irises began to fade. "This is really s-scary, isn't it?"

"Yeah." She eased the water into Kayla's hand. "Take this before I spill the whole bottle."

The girl wrapped her fingers around the plastic. "You want to share the sleeping bag? You're shivering."

"No." Cate fumbled around in another bag and pulled out a blanket. "I'll wrap up in this." She draped it around herself and sat next to Kayla, back propped against the wall, heart pounding as she pulled her legs into a tuck and squeezed them close to her chest.

"Hey—what's wrong . . . beyond the obvious?" Kayla swigged the water and focused on her, fully alert now.

Cate clenched her hands until her nails dug into her palms. Her claustrophobia was a secret no one but her family was privy to.

Other than Zeke, who'd found out the hard way.

Who knew a ride in a crowded, glassed-in elevator would trigger a full-blown panic attack?

Smart man that he was, he'd realized there was a problem almost instantly and pressed the button for the next floor, where she shoved through the grumbling crowd and escaped as soon as the doors opened.

That had been one of her most mortifying moments.

But he hadn't made a big deal out of it. He'd simply said everyone had their foibles and moved on. And later, when she'd told him the story about the trunk in the attic, he'd listened with his usual empathy and pulled her into a hug after she finished.

One of the many reasons she'd fallen in love with him.

One of the many reasons she *still* loved him.

That was the truth of it.

Hard as she tried to pretend she'd insulated herself from his warmth, she—

"Cate?" Kayla touched her arm.

She forced herself to shift gears. There were more pressing issues to deal with at this juncture than romance.

Like their predicament—and her claustrophobia.

In view of the circumstances—and her roommate's perceptiveness—trying to keep her phobia a secret was foolish.

She swallowed. "I have claustrophobia."

"Oh, geez." Distress darkened Kayla's irises as she gave the small space a sweep. "This is the wrong place to be."

"Tell me about it."

"Are you going to freak out?"

"You mean more than I already have?"

"I've seen freaked. You don't look freaked. More like super anxious."

"You should see me *inside*. But I have it under control."

Sort of.

"Is there anything I can do to help?"

"Keep me distracted."

"Okay—let's talk about tonight. I can't figure out what's going on, can you? I mean, why would Reverend Wilson bring us here . . . at gunpoint? Why would he threaten to kill us? That's not the man I've known all these years."

"He's the same man, Kayla—but he's been leading two lives. You saw the public life." Cate took her hand. "The truth is, he's a drug dealer—or worse. He could be the head of the largest drug ring in St. Louis."

The girl's eyes popped. "No."

"Yes. It's true."

Kayla tugged her hand free and pulled the sleeping bag tighter around her. As if the thermal filling could insulate her from the truth. "How would you know that?"

Here it came.

"Because I came to Ivy Hill undercover to investigate Stephanie's disappearance—and Mr. Martinez was there undercover for the DEA to investigate a connection between the school and a Mexican drug cartel pipeline that feeds the St. Louis market. Our cases ended up intersecting."

Not a sound penetrated the stone walls of the cistern as Kayla gaped at her.

Ten seconds ticked by.

"You're a cop?"

"Detective."

"Oh, man." She lifted her chin and regarded the domed ceiling.

"There's more. Ivy Hill is being used as a drop-off and pickup site for drugs from Mexico. There's a pickup by the old barn tonight, and the DEA is planning a major takedown. The conversation you overheard Reverend Wilson having on the terrace was as suspicious as you thought it was."

"You're not a student."

Kayla was still processing that part of the deception.

"No."

"How old are you?"

Cate braced. "Thirty-three."

Kayla's jaw dropped. "Seriously?"

"Yeah."

"You're old enough to be my mom."

Ouch.

"Barely."

Kayla leaned her head back against the wall again. "So much for my new friend. I knew it was too good to be true."

"Hey. We can still be friends after this. Age shouldn't matter if people click."

"I was just part of your job assignment."

"Maybe at the beginning. Not anymore. I don't plan to lose touch with you after this is over." Kayla would need all the friends she could get, especially in the weeks ahead. And longer term, a friendship—and mentorship—could be gratifying for both of them.

"Yeah?"

"Yeah."

Kayla scrutinized her. Nodded. "Okay, then. But it may not be an issue if we don't get out of here. I'd like to believe Reverend Wilson will tell someone where we are, but I'm not counting on that."

"Me neither." Cate examined the ceiling. "I think we have to come up with a plan to escape on our own."

"You don't happen to be a rock climber, do you?"

"Sadly, no. I do have decent upper body strength thanks to my workouts, but I was never into rock climbing. How about you?"

"Nope. Besides, even if we could find a toehold in the bricks, that sloping ceiling would work against us. The opening is in the center. We couldn't reach it."

She had a point.

Cate scanned the walls and ceiling.

They were solid brick, with no protrusions to offer a leg up or to cling to. Other than some disintegrating mortar on a section of bricks near the bottom, the surface was smooth and—

Wait.

Disintegrating mortar.

Cate gauged the distance from the floor to the cover at the top of the access tube.

It appeared to be about ten or eleven feet to the apex, as Wilson had said.

Her pulse picked up as an idea began to percolate in her mind.

Kayla was an inch or two shorter than her five foot seven, giving them a combined height of around eleven feet.

If they added another few inches to that, this could work.

"I have an idea."

"Tell me." Kayla angled toward her.

"If we could pry out a few of the bricks and build a small platform, one of us could climb on the other's shoulders and try to push off the cap. Then that person could lever herself up and out through the opening."

Kayla didn't appear convinced. "My arm is hurting bad. I don't think I could be the one on top. I'd never be able to pull myself out. And your ribs are bruised. I don't know if you could, either."

That made two of them.

But what other choice did they have?

"I'm open to suggestions."

The girl sighed. "I don't have any. I guess we could give your idea a try."

"Let's see if we can find anything in the supplies to loosen the mortar."

"I have this." Kayla felt around in her jacket and pulled out a pocketknife. "I forgot all about it until it jabbed me in the side while I was coming down the rope ladder."

"You carry a pocketknife?"

"Yeah. My brother got it in Scouts, and he asked me to take care of it while he's in the army. I always keep it with me."

"That will help." Cate scooted over to the bags, handed one to Kayla, and began to root through the other one.

"You really think this could work?"

At Kayla's question, Cate paused in her search. "I have no idea. I'm not an acrobat—but I *was* on a cheer squad in high school. We did pyramid formations at a few games, and I've stood on a guy's shoulders. I'm hoping that skill is like riding a bicycle—assuming we get that far. If it's not, my idea will be toast." She went back to digging through the bag.

Kayla did too.

Less than half a minute later, the girl held up a pair of tweezers. "These were in the first aid kit."

Screwdrivers or a hammer and chisel would be of more use—but there was no possibility Wilson had left those kinds of items in their stash.

"Set them aside, but let's see if we can find anything else." She went back to rummaging through the other bag.

In the end, they came up with only one other makeshift tool—the metal loop that served as a handle for the battery-powered lantern.

Kayla ran her fingers over the bricks beside her. "Trying to pry these loose with what we have is going to be tough."

Or impossible.

But Cate left that unsaid.

Giving up wasn't her style, and if this was all they had to work with, they'd have to make do.

Unless . . .

She gave the distance to the cap another visual measurement. "I wonder if I could reach the top without a platform?"

Kayla tipped her head back. "It's too high. You'll lose eight or ten inches standing on my shoulders."

"Why don't we give it a dry run? See if I can reach up and push the cover aside a bit, at least." And let in fresh air to mitigate the lethal CO_2 levels that would begin building up fast with two people breathing the air—and expelling carbon dioxide—if the cistern was sealed tight.

"I'm game—but you're going to have to walk me through how to do this."

"It's not that hard." Cate pushed herself to her feet, trying to ignore the twinge in her ribs. They were healing, but the process was slow and this maneuver wasn't going to help them.

Especially if she fell.

But thinking too much about that would spook her—and what choice did they have?

Kayla stood too.

"Here's how it works." Cate pulled off her boots and shed her excess garments, positioned Kayla under the opening in the center of the cistern, and dug deep in her memory for the how-to of the acrobatic stunt. "I'm going to stand behind you. You spread your legs apart, kind of squat down, and lift your hands shoulder height. Try it."

Kayla complied, wincing as she raised her wounded arm. "Ouch."

Cate caught her lower lip between her teeth. The maneuver could be dangerous even for able-bodied, trained acrobats.

They were neither.

"Are you certain you're up to trying this?" Adults could often suck it up and muscle through pain in an emergency, but that was asking a lot of a seventeen-year-old.

"Yeah." Kayla straightened her spine, her mouth set in a resolute line. "What next?"

Cate hesitated—but only for an instant. If the tools and techniques at your disposal were limited, you worked with what you had.

"I'll take your hands and climb up on your thighs. Once you feel steady, I'll put my feet on your shoulders one by one, still holding hands. When I lift my second leg, you straighten up as best you can. After we stabilize, I'll let go of your hands and you grab the back of my calves, down near my ankles. Coming down, I'll take your hands, bend my knees, and jump forward."

"Let's give it a shot."

As Kayla got into position, Cate moved behind her. Grasped her hands. Stepped up onto her thighs.

So far, so good.

Now came the tricky part.

Cate lifted one leg to Kayla's shoulder. Filled her lungs. Pulled herself up and stepped onto Kayla's other shoulder.

The girl wobbled as she tried to rise from the squat position.

"You're doing great, Kayla. Give yourself a few seconds to adjust to the weight."

"You . . . you aren't as light . . . as you look."

"Sorry."

Cate looked up. She was directly under the opening. "I'm going to let go of your hands. Stay as steady as you can. I'll balance myself."

Or try to.

If she failed, a painful tumble was in her very near future.

"I'll do my best."

She could feel the girl bracing beneath her as Kayla grasped the back of her legs.

With slow, careful, deliberate movements, Cate raised her

hands. Placed them flat against the cistern cover, elbows bent. It was closer than she'd expected, giving her more leverage than she'd dared hope for.

Yes!

"I can reach the cover. Hold steady. I'm going to try and shove it off."

She pushed.

Nothing.

Tried again.

Nada.

What was it made of, lead?

"Is it . . . moving?" Kayla's question was choppy, and she was beginning to waver again.

"Not yet."

"I don't . . . I'm not sure I can hold you much longer."

"I'm about done."

She pushed as hard as she could—and while it didn't come off, the cap did slide several inches to the right.

A few snowflakes swirled into the opening—along with cold, fresh air.

But her hard shove threw them both off-balance. Kayla wavered, and Cate lost her balance.

She groped for something—anything—to latch on to in the narrow opening that extended above the ground.

Her fingers found a couple of deep crevices . . . chipped bricks perhaps, and she dug in.

It provided sufficient stability for both of them to regain their balance—even if it did destroy her fancy glitter-polish manicure.

"You have to come down, Cate." There was a note of desperation in Kayla's voice.

"I am. Give me your hands." With one last, longing look at the opening, she latched on to Kayla's outstretched fingers, bent her knees, and jumped to the floor.

The girl was shaking, and she sank down to the bricks. "If we get out of this mess, I'm adding a workout to my schedule. My legs are like rubber."

"I'm shaky too." Cate dropped down beside her and pointed up. "But we made progress."

Kayla followed the direction of her finger. "You got the top halfway off!"

"Not quite—but close. It weighs a ton."

"If we try this again, could you get it off and pull yourself out?"

"No. Not without another few inches of height. I have to be high enough to get my elbows out of the opening and support myself under my arms. I don't have the strength to pull myself straight up. In fact, even if I get my elbows out, I may need a boost. But after I've locked in my elbows, you can hold the rolled-up sleeping bag under my feet and I'll use that to push off. That should do it."

It had to.

Or they could be stuck here until the spring thaw.

"That's assuming we can build a platform." Kayla gave the bricks a dubious once-over. "Or two small platforms, one for each foot—but they won't be very steady."

Cate couldn't dispute that.

But one of them had to stay optimistic.

"It should only take me a few seconds to push the cover off and get my elbows out. Now that we've done the maneuver once, it will be faster next time. Let's get to work on the bricks."

Kayla picked up the pocketknife. "Where do we start?"

"Over there." Cate motioned toward a row of bricks near the bottom that had lost a fair amount of mortar. "They should be the easiest ones to loosen and remove."

They crossed to the bricks and set to work.

Whether they would be able to dislodge an adequate number to build a small platform was questionable.

But if nothing else, the job would help stave off the smothering panic she was barely keeping at bay in this confined, subterranean space that was the stuff of her worst nightmares.

27

HERNANDEZ HAD MADE A NIGHT OF IT at the bar. Zeke checked his watch, a cloud of vapor forming in front of his face in the cold car.

Eleven-ten.

The man was obviously not part of the Ivy Hill pickup crew.

His phone began to vibrate, and his pulse accelerated.

Please let this be news about Cate.

But his brief surge of hope nose-dived when he skimmed the screen. It was his surveillance partner.

He put the phone to his ear. "What's up?"

"I just got the word to move in on our subject. The brass agrees he's not part of tonight's operation. A city patrol officer should be here any minute for backup, and two more from our team are en route to handle transport. You ready to do this?"

"Yeah." Anything was better than twiddling his thumbs and pestering County for updates on Cate every thirty minutes.

As a police cruiser pulled into the parking lot, he stashed his phone and plunged into the swirling snow, which had morphed from a light sifting of powder to a full-blown blizzard over the past three hours. One that showed no signs of abating.

Not a terrific night for a drug bust.

His colleague met him outside the door, and the patrol officer joined them. "He's at the corner table in back. Last count, he's had half a dozen beers."

"Has he eaten anything?"

"A few pretzels."

"He ought to be feeling the buzz. Maybe it will loosen his tongue."

"Or make him belligerent."

"Also a possibility."

"You want me to take the lead—or would you like to do the honors?"

Zeke pulled out his creds. "Arresting the man who roughed up a County detective and tried to kill me would be a pleasure."

"Have at it." The other agent motioned for him to go first.

"You want me to come in or wait out here?" The patrol officer surveyed the lot as he spoke.

"Give us five minutes, then step inside." Zeke entered and wove through the tables toward the solitary man in the corner, his colleague following a few paces behind.

A hush fell over the bar, as if the other patrons sensed trouble, and a few edged toward the exit.

The only person who appeared oblivious to the sudden tension in the air was Hernandez. He remained slouched in his seat, angled away from the bar, and fixated on the half-filled pilsner glass in front of him.

Zeke stopped at the table and flipped open his creds. "Good evening, Mr. Hernandez."

The man stared at the badge and ID card Zeke extended. Stiffened.

"We meet again—this time not in a parking garage." Zeke stowed his ID.

Hernandez glared at him. "I don't know what you're talking about."

318

"That's not what the evidence suggests." He recited the charges and read the man his rights. "Stand up, turn around, spread your feet, and put your left hand behind your back."

Hernandez scanned the bar, as if seeking an escape route.

The other agent edged closer, into the man's line of sight.

A muscle in Hernandez's cheek twitched—but he remained sitting. "You don't have grounds to haul me in."

"We can debate that later. Don't add resisting arrest to the charges."

"I want a lawyer."

"You're welcome to call one—or a public defender will be assigned to you. Follow the instructions I gave you. Now. Don't make me repeat them."

All noise in the bar ceased, and the man's gaze flicked toward the door.

The police officer must have come inside.

Slowly Hernandez complied, and after a pat-down, Zeke cuffed him.

His colleague pulled out his cell to take a call, and after more listening than talking slid it back on his belt.

"Jones was picked up at the school ten minutes ago. It was a one-man show. He is *not* a happy camper."

"I'll bet." Zeke directed his next comment to Hernandez. "We also have your friend Jackson Jones in custody."

The man's face went blank.

Either he was an excellent actor or the name was unfamiliar to him.

"I don't know a Jackson Jones."

"He may go by a different name on the street." Zeke pulled out his cell and scrolled through his photos for one of the surveillance shots of Jones. Held it out.

Hernandez's breath hitched—but he otherwise remained cool. "I don't know him."

That was a lie.

But they'd have plenty of time to talk about it in the hours ahead.

The agents assigned to handle transport entered and strode toward them. Zeke handed the man over and fell in beside his surveillance partner as they followed the trio out. "What's next for us?"

"I'm done. The boss said you should call in after the arrest."

"Meaning I'm *not* done."

"Considering your involvement in this case, I have a feeling your night is just beginning." The other man grinned and lifted a hand as they parted in the parking lot.

Wonderful.

Much as he wanted to be part of the questioning that could ferret out the name of the ringleader, Cate's MIA status was turning his stomach into a blender.

Where was she?

Did County have any news?

He slid behind the wheel of the rolling icebox that was his car, cranked up the heater, put the defroster on full blast—and pulled out his phone.

Yes, he'd call his St. Louis boss for his next assignment.

But first, he was getting an update on Cate.

———

"I think that's about the best we're going to be able to do, Kayla." Cate surveyed the two small platforms they'd built, three bricks high, one for each foot. They would boost her another six or seven inches, which ought to allow her to get her arms through the opening and lock her elbows around the sides.

Assuming the bricks didn't wobble and send them both tumbling first.

But they'd cleaned off as much mortar as they could and butted them close for stability. All they could do was give their plan a try—and hope the bricks stayed in place.

Kayla examined their handiwork, faint furrows creasing her forehead. "You think this will work?"

"I'm counting on it. I didn't ruin my manicure to fail." Cate called up a smile. No point in sharing her doubts with the girl.

"Yeah." Kayla held out her hands too. "What a mess."

Her roommate's fingers were scratched and rubbed raw—as were her own.

Small price to pay if it bought them their freedom, however.

"Our hands will heal—and I'll treat us both to a professional manicure after they do."

"Really?"

"I promise." She crossed her heart.

"Then let's get you out of here." Kayla stood.

Cate shrugged out of her jacket and boots again. Picked up the rope they'd fashioned of tied-together blanket strips. Knotted it at her waist and wound it around.

"How's your shoulder?" She tucked the end of the makeshift rope into her waistband.

"It hurts—but it could have been a lot worse." Kayla rummaged around in one of the bags and pulled out two energy bars. Slid them into the pocket of Cate's jacket. "You may be glad to have these, depending on how long it takes you to find help."

"Thanks. You ready?"

"I guess." Kayla leaned forward and gave her a gentle hug. "I'd squeeze harder, but I don't want to hurt your ribs."

Cate patted her back. "You'll be fine while I'm gone. Stay warm. Drink water. Eat energy bars. I'll get help here as fast as I can."

"I know. But it's gonna be awful lonely while you're gone."

"At least you don't have claustrophobia. If I was left here by myself, I'd be a basket case." She eased back. "We made a great team."

"Yeah." The girl's eyes began to shimmer. "No matter what happens, I liked being your roommate."

"The feeling is mutual." She squeezed the girl's uninjured arm. "Okay—let's do this. As quick and smooth as we can."

Kayla stepped up onto the two small platforms. Rocked back and forth. "They're steadier than I expected."

"That's a plus." She positioned herself behind the girl. "Remember, after I'm locked into position up there, hold the sleeping bag under my feet and push as hard as you can. I'll push too. That ought to boost me high enough to wiggle out."

"Got it. I'll pass up your coat and boots after you drop the rope, once you're out." Kayla spread her feet and squatted while Cate sent a silent plea heavenward for assistance—and fortitude.

They'd need all the help they could get to make this work.

She took Kayla's hands and positioned one foot on the girl's thigh. Swung the other one up.

Kayla remained steady.

"On three. One . . . two . . . three."

Cate followed the exact sequence she'd used on their first run-through.

The extra few inches did the trick. The instant her palms connected with the covering, she shoved sideways with all the force she could muster.

After a brief resistance, the cap slid off.

Kayla wavered, but Cate kept moving.

She pushed her arms through the opening, locked her elbows over the edge, and clenched her fingers around the rim.

"Cate . . . I'm slipping!"

"That's okay. I'm solid!" She yelled as loud as she could. "Get the sleeping bag."

The support beneath her feet vanished, and she sucked in a breath as the muscles in her shoulders and back stretched and the weight dragged on her ribs.

Seconds later, Kayla thrust the sleeping bag against her feet, forcing her knees to flex.

She straightened them and pushed. Tried to lift a leg up into the opening.

The space was too narrow to accommodate her upper body *and* a leg.

What to do?

She'd have to flop her upper body over the edge of the tube and wiggle out while grasping at anything on the ground that could provide leverage.

But her ribs weren't going to like that.

"Cate?"

At Kayla's alarmed call, she mashed her lips together and launched her upper body up, out, and over, her bruised ribs screaming in protest as they scraped along the rim.

Dang, dang, dang, dang, dang!

Bad as the pain had been the night of the attack, the pressure against her midsection as her upper body dangled over the edge was excruciating.

But the only way to alleviate the agony was to complete the escape.

She bent her knees and drew her legs up, searching with her toes for the crevices that had given her a handhold on their first attempt. Found one of them. In the darkness, she felt around the ground outside the tube. Her fingers connected with a large, solid rock, and she wrapped them around the frozen surface.

Pushing with her toe, pulling with her fingers, she managed to wriggle out of the opening inch by painful inch.

Once free of the tube, she collapsed in a heap on the snow-covered ground, gasping and shaking as silent tears coursed down her cheeks and black spots peppered her vision.

"Cate? Are you all right?"

Kayla's voice was hollow and far away.

Gritting her teeth, she crawled back to the opening. "I'm out." Not an answer, but why complain about her own discomfort when Kayla was suffering from a gunshot wound?

"Are you going to send the rope down?"

"Yeah."

She unwound it from her waist and lowered it into the opening.

As she waited for Kayla to tie a boot or her jacket to the end, she huddled into a tuck and scanned the landscape as an icy blast of wind slammed into her.

There was a blizzard out here!

How could the meteorologists have gotten the weather so wrong? What had happened to their prediction of a light snow that left a minor dusting of powder?

Already there were four or five inches on the ground.

Kayla tugged on the rope, and she pulled it up.

Her parka was attached.

She untied it and sent the rope back down, leaving the end attached to her waist.

Her boots were next, and she hauled them up in rapid succession.

Once she had all her gear, she put everything on.

An improvement, but not sufficient protection in this type of storm for any extended outdoor activity.

And who knew how long it would take to find help?

Much as they'd accomplished, they weren't out of the woods yet—literally or figuratively.

"Cate?"

She leaned over the opening to find Kayla looking up at her, anxiety written in every taut line of her face.

"We did it, Kayla!" She mustered as much enthusiasm as she could. "Sit tight until help comes."

"Be careful."

"I will. See you soon."

She backed away from the opening and turned toward the path that had led them to the cistern, now covered in snow.

Getting back to the main road wouldn't be an issue. Once

there, all she had to do was walk along the edge until she came to a house or could flag down a passing car.

Wilson, however, had said few cars traveled that road at night, let alone in weather like this. And he'd claimed there were no houses nearby.

But he could have lied.

She started forward, grimacing with every step as pain shot through her midsection.

Just do it, Cate. You've already accomplished far more than you expected to. Getting out of that cistern is huge. If you can survive hours being locked into a ten-by-ten underground room, you can survive this cold. You didn't go through all that trauma to freeze to death.

That was all true.

Yet as she trudged through the snow amid the swirling flakes, it was impossible to ignore the reality of her situation. She *could* freeze to death unless someone else was out and about on this awful night or happened to live nearby.

But she couldn't fail Kayla—or let Wilson escape to parts unknown. He had to pay the price for his role in the attack on her, the demise of Stephanie and her boyfriend, and all the lives he'd ruined through the drug ring.

And he would.

All she had to do was push on through the snow and find help.

Soon.

Before the frigid weather finished the job Wilson had begun on this dangerously cold winter night.

28

RAZOR HADN'T CALLED to verify the pickup—and that spelled trouble.

Wilson squinted at his watch. Twelve-thirty. His right-hand man should have been in touch an hour ago.

And *he* should be in bed, trying to catch a few hours of sleep before his alarm went off at three-thirty so he could get to the airport well in advance of his six-thirty flight—the first leg of his escape to freedom.

But thanks to the unexpected blizzard, the airport had closed and all flights had been canceled through six o'clock. His own flight was iffy at this stage, pending developments in the weather and the speed with which runways could be cleared. It was possible it too would be canceled and he'd have to take a later one.

Meaning Kayla and her roommate were going to be stuck in that cistern far longer than planned.

Perhaps too long.

What to do?

He began to pace in his kitchen.

If Razor had been arrested, he could be pressured to reveal the name of his boss, despite his promise to keep it secret. Everyone had their breaking point.

That meant he had two choices—find somewhere in town to hole up under his new identity until the storm passed and he could reschedule his flight, or go to the airport now and join the throng waiting to board a plane the minute the runways were cleared.

With the snow beginning to diminish, it took him no more than a few seconds to come to a decision.

Airport.

Here in St. Louis, he was Reverend Tyrone Wilson—celebrated do-gooder and secret drug lord.

But the instant he boarded that plane and left his old life behind, he became wealthy and reclusive Marcus Alexander. The new credentials in his pocket, courtesy of his less-than-savory contacts, would mask his true identity for the rest of his life.

The question was how to get to the airport.

He paused at the window and surveyed the darkness.

Taking his own car wouldn't be wise. If the police had put out a BOLO alert on him, someone could spot his license.

A cab would be safer.

He pulled out one of his burner phones and called the same cab company he'd used yesterday afternoon for Kayla's trip to Starbucks. Fished out the credit card number Essie Brown had supplied to make an offering for the funeral service for her sister.

It took fifteen rings for a harried-sounding dispatcher to answer the phone and give him the bad news.

The wait for a cab at this late hour and in this inclement weather was running five to six hours.

Too long.

He'd have to take his own car and hope for the best. If he dirtied up his license plates, the cops wouldn't be able to ID the car—and in this weather, a muddy plate wouldn't raise suspicions.

Besides, it was rare for a storm in St. Louis to shut everything down for more than a few hours. His flight could end up departing on schedule.

Armed with that plan, he crossed to the luggage piled near the door. It wouldn't take him long to load the car and change into his traveling clothes. In less than an hour he'd be at the airport.

As for Razor—if the man was in trouble, there was nothing he could do to help him. If he wasn't, the instant he verified that the pickup was complete, he'd get a text directing him to the location where all the information necessary to run the operation was stashed. That text and two phone calls—to his Mexican supplier to alert them to the change in command, and to the local police to tell them where Kayla and her roommate were—would be his last chores before boarding.

Then he'd ditch his burner phones and be done with this life of subterfuge.

And all he'd have to worry about after tonight was whether he was getting too much exposure to the tropical sun.

Her feet were numb.

So were her nose and cheeks, despite the scarf she'd wrapped horizontally around the hood covering her head.

She'd also lost sensation in the tips of her fingers.

Cate fought back a wave of panic.

The swirling snow had abated somewhat, but the blustery wind curtailed her speed, and progress along the road was slow. If this kept up, hypothermia could pose a real danger.

How long had she been walking, anyway?

Impossible to tell without exposing her wrist to the elements to see her watch, and doing that would hasten the loss of body temperature.

In any case, the passage of time was inconsequential. Bottom line, she had to keep going until a car came by or she spotted a house through the trees.

The latter was unlikely at this late hour, though—unless the residents had security lighting. Few people stayed up past midnight.

She shivered as another blast of cold air swept past.

After everything that had happened over the past seven hours—and after managing to escape from that cistern—wouldn't it be ironic if she died of hypothermia?

Her sisters and her father would be devastated.

So would Zeke.

At the little nudge from her subconscious, she sighed—and acknowledged the truth.

Maybe the depth of his feelings scared her, but he still loved her, heart and soul.

And despite all that had transpired between them . . . despite their long separation . . . despite the protective wall she'd tried to build around her heart . . . she still loved him too.

Her vision misted, and she stumbled. Choked out a sob. Plodded on.

Only fear had kept her from admitting her feelings.

But a woman who'd survived hours in an underground cistern despite a bone-deep terror of small spaces ought to be able to overcome the fear of another heartbreak.

A fear that was likely groundless, after all the evidence she'd seen over the past month.

So if God blessed her with a second chance at life tonight, how could she refuse to give the only man she'd ever trusted with her heart a second chance at love?

"How's it going with Jones?" As he entered the room arrayed with video monitors, Zeke checked the feed from the DEA interview room where the man was being questioned. He was sitting with his arms locked tight against his chest, staring at the wall, ignoring the questions being fired at him.

One of the agents watching the screen responded. "He's not talking."

"I have information that may encourage him to be more forthcoming. Hernandez gave me a few tidbits."

"We saw. Have at it."

Zeke left the room with the monitors, walked a few yards down the hall, and knocked on a closed door.

The agent opened it a few moments later, and Zeke told him the same story.

"You're welcome to him. I could use another caffeine infusion anyway."

Zeke entered the room. Took a seat at the small conference table. "I understand you're not cooperating."

Jones ignored him.

"Your choice—but it will go easier for you if you talk to us." Zeke leaned back and folded his arms. "Hernandez is down the hall."

The man's left eye twitched slightly, but he didn't respond.

"He was happy to spill his guts after we showed him your photo and told him you were in custody."

"I don't know a Hernandez."

"He didn't know a Jones, either. Said your name on the street is Razor—and that you're the number two man in the biggest drug ring in town. He also told us he was being groomed for your job . . . until he decided to settle a few scores for his friends in Mexico and tried to take me out. We have him on first-degree attempted murder—and you're on a slippery slope too. Aside from your drug activities, what do you know about Stephanie Laurent and her boyfriend?"

Jones glared at him. "Like I told the last guy—I want a lawyer."

"You'll get one. But it's the middle of the night and we're in the midst of a blizzard. It could take a while."

"I'll wait."

"Suit yourself." Zeke rose. "But let me leave you with this thought. We want the main man—and anyone who helps us identify and locate him will be giving us valuable information. Cooperation can have a positive influence on a judge." His phone began to vibrate, and he moved to the door. "Don't put your neck on the line for someone who's letting you take the fall."

He stepped into the hall, clicked the door shut behind him, and pulled out his cell.

An unfamiliar number appeared on the screen.

But the 636 area code meant it was from an outlying area.

An Ivy Hill number, perhaps?

Who would be calling from there at this hour?

He put the phone to his ear and continued down the hall. "Sloan."

"Zeke—it's Cate."

He jolted to a stop, heart lurching.

Thank you, God!

"Where are you? What happened? Are you hurt? I've been calling County every half hour, but—"

"Whoa. I'm fine."

She didn't sound fine.

She sounded shaky and weak.

"I'm not buying that."

"Let me rephrase. I *will* be fine. You need to listen."

"Where are you?"

A muted conversation took place offline.

"In the vicinity of Cappeln."

"I have no idea where that is."

"Neither do I." More muffled conversation. "Somewhere southwest of New Melle. Zeke—listen to me. You have to find Reverend Wilson. I think he could be the leader of the drug ring."

Zeke blinked.

The beloved and lauded minister? The kind and caring chaplain at Ivy Hill?

He tried to wrap his mind around that notion, but it wouldn't compute.

"Are you certain?"

"If he's not the leader, he's in neck-deep."

"Okay." Brain buzzing, he ducked into an empty interview room. "Tell me what you know—and what happened tonight." He pulled out a notebook.

Twice while she told him her tale of terror he had to coax his lungs to keep working.

As she wrapped up, her voice was wobbling. Strong as she was, she was barely holding herself together. Spending hours in a small, subterranean space would freak out even people who didn't have claustrophobia—and plodding through a blizzard was a recipe for hypothermia.

All he wanted to do was pull her into his arms and hold her forever.

Not an impulse he could follow through on at the moment— but all bets were off after tonight.

"You need medical attention."

"I'll be fine."

"Cate, you—"

"The people who answered my knock here gave me blankets and are making me hot chocolate while the sheriff goes to get Kayla and I wait for my ride from County. Where are you?"

"At the office, but—"

"Get Wilson, Zeke. That has to be your top priority."

Workwise, yes.

Nowhere close on the personal front.

"He's not flying anywhere tonight. The airport's shut down. We'll dispatch agents to his house ASAP. Also to the airport, in case he's hanging out there. Me included—if my boss agrees."

"I don't have my cell anymore, but I'll borrow the phone from the officer who picks me up and call you once I'm back in town."

"Go to an ER."

"I'm warming up fine on my own."

Since she was lucid, didn't appear to be suffering from memory loss, or have slurred speech, it was unlikely her hypothermia was in the danger range.

"What about frostbite?"

"I was covered up. My toes may have a touch, but I've got my feet propped in front of a heater while I wait for my ride. Stop worrying about me and go get Wilson."

He rubbed the back of his neck with an unsteady hand. The time for restraint was over. From now on, he was putting his feelings out on the table—come what may.

"Worry goes with the territory when you love someone." His voice hoarsened as he finished.

"Zeke, I . . . I'm not in a position to respond to that."

"Understood. But I want you to know that the past seven hours have been the worst of my life. Worse than the raid in Mexico where I took two bullets."

"They were bad hours for me too." Her tone was warmer. More intimate. "But also enlightening. We have a lot to discuss after this wraps up."

"That could be in the next few hours, if you're right about Wilson."

"The sooner the better."

"Amen to that."

"I'll call you after I'm back in town."

The line went dead, and Zeke stood.

He'd be counting the hours until he saw Cate.

But in the meantime, they had a drug dealer to find and an arrest to make.

Yes!

Thanks to the diminishing storm, the status of his flight had changed from delayed to on time.

In five hours, he'd be in the air.

Tyrone let out a slow breath and strolled back toward his gate from the large monitor in the concourse. A wise choice to go directly to the airport rather than find a hotel to wait out the blizzard.

He cast a longing glance at a shuttered Starbucks as he passed. An espresso would help keep him alert during the remainder of the night, but the shop wouldn't be open for hours.

He'd have to find another way to stay awake and—

"Good morning, Reverend Wilson."

At the familiar voice from Ivy Hill, he swung around—and found himself face-to-face with Zeke Martinez.

No!

This couldn't be happening!

How had the federal agent located him?

How had he even known to *look* for him?

Only two people were aware he was flying tonight—and they were both in the cistern.

Unless . . .

Had they picked up Razor—and had the man identified him as the head of the ring?

If so, could the Feds have gone to his house, seen signs of departure, and concluded he was trying to leave town?

Questions swirled through his brain as he struggled to maintain his composure.

None of this made sense.

But Martinez was waiting for a response.

He had to decide how to play this.

Act dumb until you see what they know. It's possible he's here on another assignment and happened to run into you.

A long shot—but he had nothing to lose by keeping up the act until the man revealed his hand.

"Good morning." Somehow he managed to come across as nonchalant. "What a surprise to see you here."

"I'll bet. But I'm not surprised to see you."

Uh-oh.

"What do you mean?" He feigned puzzlement despite the pounding in his chest.

"I think we both know." Zeke pulled out a pair of handcuffs as a second man who'd been standing nearby moved closer.

Another agent.

They knew.

Invisible fingers squeezed his windpipe.

This couldn't be happening. Not after all these years. Not when he was so close to leaving his old life behind.

"What are you talking about?" But he already knew the answer.

"Let's not play games, Wilson." Martinez's features hardened as he went into a you're-under-arrest-and-here-are-your-rights spiel.

The words barely registered as passersby walked a wide circle around them, sending curious glances their direction.

It was a surreal scenario.

But it became all too real as Martinez slipped the cuffs on his wrists and they locked into place.

The symbolism—and finality—of that simple action shook him to the core.

Because he wasn't being arrested on mere supposition.

Somehow . . . some way . . . the truth about what he'd been doing had been discovered.

And his dream of a carefree retirement under sunny, tropical skies had just evaporated as quickly as a morning mist on the Mississippi River.

29

ZEKE MET CATE IN THE FOYER when she arrived at the DEA offices downtown a little after 3:00 a.m., courtesy of a lift from a County patrol officer.

After one comprehensive sweep, the best he could say about her was that she was still on her feet.

But based on her pallor, the unsteadiness in her bruised and scratched fingers, and the stiff posture that suggested every movement hurt, she shouldn't be.

She ought to be at an urgent care center, an ER—or home in bed.

The hug he longed to give her would have to be deferred yet again unless he wanted to risk hurting her more.

Instead, he bent down and brushed his lips over hers.

She didn't back off.

In fact, she leaned into the kiss.

And when he held out his hand, she twined her fingers with his.

Silent, charged seconds passed as they stood in the post-midnight, unnatural quiet of a space that teemed with activity during daylight hours.

"You shouldn't have come. You look dead on your feet."

She offered him a smile that seemed forced. "I can sleep

later. I wanted to be here for Wilson's interview. I'm still trying to come to grips with the fact that he could be the mastermind. Have you talked with him yet?"

"No. We had processing to do first. We're about ready to begin, though. I've got a spot saved for you in the monitoring room."

"Thanks for letting me sit in."

"An easy sell. We wouldn't have him if it hadn't been for you. Would you like water or a Diet Sprite first?"

"No thanks. The people at the house I found gave me three cups of hot chocolate."

"Are you hungry? I could raid the vending machines."

"I have energy bars." She patted her pocket. "But I'm more hungry for answers."

"Then let's see if we can get some." He walked toward the door that led from the foyer to the interview rooms at the back of the building—but didn't relinquish her hand. "How's Kayla?"

"Being treated as we speak at the ER. I talked with her a few minutes ago. She'll be fine—physically anyway. Bring me up to speed on what's been happening here."

He'd rather take her home—but Cate was a force to be reckoned with when she was close to solving a case, and he was as convinced as she was that someone in this building was responsible for the fate of Stephanie and her boyfriend . . . or knew who'd killed them.

As they walked toward the monitoring room, he briefed her.

After he finished, she cocked her head. "So Hernandez appears to have spilled everything he knows, but Jones hasn't given you anything worthwhile yet."

"That sums it up—but I'm hoping the status quo is about to change. After I drop you at the monitoring room, I'm going to revisit Jones and give him the news we have Wilson in custody—and that he was arrested at the airport en route to Belize. I suspect that will surprise him."

"It could also loosen his lips."

"That thought did occur to me." He opened a door and introduced her to the agents gathered in the small room. After escorting her to a cushioned seat that offered a view of the video screens, he picked up a manila file folder. "Let's hope Jones talks. If he does, I doubt Wilson will be far behind."

She lifted her hand and crossed her battered, bruised fingers. "My luck's been great tonight. Maybe I can pass it along to you."

He leaned down so she alone could hear his next comment. "It's always my lucky day if I'm with you."

And then he left—before he could follow up on the very unprofessional urge to give her another kiss in front of his colleagues.

But that would come later, unless he was misinterpreting the signals she was sending him.

For now, though, they had a compelling question to answer.

Assuming Wilson was not only involved in the St. Louis drug ring but perhaps held the leadership position, why would a man of his stature and reputation moonlight in such a violent and abhorrent business?

Cate leaned closer to the video screen as Zeke entered the interview room, set the folder on the table, and sat. He propped an ankle on a knee, keeping his posture open and casual as he sipped from a disposable cup.

"Would you like coffee?" He lifted his brew.

Jones eyed him warily. "What is this, the good cop routine?"

"I thought you might want to fortify yourself for the news I have to deliver." Zeke extracted a printout of Wilson's mug shot from the folder and laid it on the table in front of the man. "Your friend's latest picture. Taken less than half an hour ago. He's sitting in a room like this, three doors down."

Jones didn't respond.

"Here's where the coffee may have come in handy." Zeke set his cup on the table. "We picked him up at the airport. He was heading for Belize under a new identity. Apparently he realized we were closing in and decided to leave—and let you take the fall tonight."

Jones's nostrils flared. "I don't believe that."

Zeke opened the file again. Removed a passport. Flipped to the photo page and held it in front of Jones.

The man's Adam's apple bobbed.

Cate scanned the monitoring room. Everyone was riveted to the screen.

Understandable.

Getting Jones to abandon the man who'd betrayed him would give them huge leverage with Wilson—and all the grounds required for prosecution with or without Wilson's cooperation.

And Zeke was doing a masterful job of persuasion. He'd always been an impressive interrogator, but his skills had gotten even sharper over the years.

"The way I see it, loyalty to a man like that is misplaced." Zeke closed the passport, keeping his tone conversational. "He was going to let you go to prison while he enjoyed the good life on a tropical beach."

Jones didn't speak, but he fidgeted in his chair.

Zeke was getting to him.

He pulled several other pieces of paper from the folder and laid them on the table. "In case you want more proof about your friend's plans. His airline ticket and boarding passes."

Jones skimmed them. Swallowed again. "Those are fake. You're just trying to get me to talk."

"Let me disprove that theory." Zeke's thumbs worked on his cell, and he held it up. "My colleague took this at the airport as I arrested him."

Jones muttered a word that burned Cate's ears.

"He wouldn't do that to me."

There was a collective exhale in the monitoring room.

With that one sentence, Jones had admitted to their collaboration. Zeke had cracked the man's protective shell.

Now all he had to do was wedge it open.

"The evidence proves otherwise." Zeke folded his hands on the table and moved in for the kill. "Do yourself a favor and answer this question. Was he your boss?"

Several beats of silence ticked by.

Cate squeezed the arms of her chair.

Please, Lord, let him talk. Help Zeke solve his case . . . and help me solve mine too.

Jones raked his fingers through his hair, and his shoulders slumped. "Yeah."

Two of the agents in the room high-fived each other.

"Let me clarify that." Zeke remained calm and in total control. "You were the number two man in the St. Louis operation. That would indicate Tyrone Wilson was in charge of the organization. Is that correct?"

"Yeah."

The DEA had what it needed—but Zeke wasn't finished.

"Explain to me why a man like Wilson, who was loved and respected, would run a drug ring."

"I don't know. I never asked. He never told."

"How did *you* get involved?"

"I came through his rehab center. He got me off drugs. Helped me find a job. He saved my life. I stayed in touch. When he recruited me after he started his operation, I signed on. The money was huge, and he was always fair to me."

"Until now."

The man's face hardened, but he remained silent.

"Tell me what you know about Stephanie Laurent and her boyfriend."

Cate's pulse picked up. That wasn't a DEA investigation, but Zeke was taking advantage of Jones's sudden willingness to talk—for her benefit.

The man was having none of it, however.

A hood dropped over his eyes. "I don't know what you're talking about."

"I think you do. You were on pickup duty tonight. That suggests you were likely on pickup duty in October too—the night they disappeared."

"I'm done talking. I want a lawyer."

Meaning he was willing to dish the dirt on Wilson's nefarious activities but wasn't going to implicate himself in a murder.

"Fine." Zeke rose. "We'll continue this conversation later."

He crossed to the door, exited, and returned to the monitoring room.

"Nice work." One of his colleagues slapped him on the back.

"Thanks." His gaze sought hers. "Sorry I couldn't get him to admit his involvement in Stephanie's disappearance."

"I didn't expect him to—but Wilson may do the honors."

"He's next on the list." Zeke checked another monitor, which showed the man sitting alone in one of the interview rooms. "Are you up to coming in if that seems like a prudent strategy at any point?"

"Absolutely."

That was a lie.

Every breath hurt, and if her adrenaline hadn't been flowing at warp speed for the past few hours, she'd have folded long ago.

But she could hold it together for another thirty minutes.

Maybe.

Zeke's skeptical appraisal indicated he wasn't convinced about her stamina either—but he didn't argue.

Smart man.

After all the cases they'd worked together, he knew better than to try to rein her in this close to the finish line.

"I'll signal to the camera if I want you to join us."

She nodded.

He took a final swig of his coffee, set the empty cup on a cabinet, and left the room.

As he disappeared from view, Cate swung back to the monitor displaying the image of Wilson.

This was the moment of truth.

Would he tell them what they wanted to know—or clam up until an attorney was present?

Sad to say, the odds were in favor of the latter. The man was sophisticated enough to understand the importance of letting legal counsel speak for him in a situation like this.

On the other hand, Wilson wasn't the usual suspect in a drug case. Nor were his motives likely typical. As a result, it was possible he'd be willing to talk about why he'd done what he'd done. Explain his justification. Try to create sympathy.

Hard to say how he'd play this.

But if anyone could convince him to talk, it was Zeke.

———

Zeke paused outside the room where Wilson sat. Took a calming breath.

Much hinged on the results of this interview. He had to watch the man's nuances, give him whatever rope was necessary to hang himself—and pray he'd provide the answers that would wrap up both the DEA case and Cate's investigation.

Bracing for a battle of wits, he pushed through the door.

Wilson watched him approach, though he appeared to be a bit dazed.

That could work to his advantage.

Zeke took a chair at a right angle to him at the table. "I just finished talking to your friend, Razor."

Wilson blinked—but his face remained expressionless.

"As you might expect, he wasn't happy to hear you were getting ready to leave the country—and let him go to prison. To paraphrase a line from an old play, hell hath no fury like a minion scorned. He confirmed you were his boss."

At that news, Wilson's posture sagged, and resignation dragged down his features. "So much for Belize."

"Tell me why a man in your position would choose to run a drug ring."

Wilson traced a hairline crack in the table with his index finger.

Five seconds ticked by.

Ten.

Twenty.

Zeke tamped down his frustration.

They were at a dead end. Wilson wasn't going to—

"I can sum it up in three words—LaTasha and Xavier."

Yes!

That was tantamount to a confession—but as long as Wilson was willing to talk, it was best to keep the dialogue going as long as possible. Every piece of information he revealed could prove valuable.

Zeke ran the names through his mind. Came up blank. "You'll have to explain that."

"My wife and son."

"Go on."

The man rested his hands on the table, one atop the other, and lowered his chin. "Xavier was in the Marines. Twelve years ago, he was killed in the Middle East—not defending his country, but by one of the guys in his unit who got high on heroin and went berserk. He shot Xavier, wounded three others, and turned the gun on himself. Two years later, my wife was murdered in our neighborhood market after a guy who came in to rob it decided to open fire. He was high too."

Zeke let out a slow breath.

No matter what the man sitting across from him had done, it was hard not to feel empathy for all he'd gone through.

"I'm sorry."

"Everyone was. But being sorry doesn't fix the problem. We have to help people get off drugs."

Zeke frowned at the disconnect. "If you believe that, why were you distributing them?"

The man lifted his head. "I can't force people to stop using. All I can do is help the ones who want to kick the habit. And I devoted my life to doing that after LaTasha and Xavier died."

"You also ran a drug ring." Zeke struggled to connect the dots. "That's inconsistent."

"No, it isn't." A glow began to glimmer deep in his dark irises. "I've done everything I can to convince people not to use drugs, from preaching on Sunday to antidrug campaigns to community outreach. I built a rehab center where addicts can come free of charge to learn to live without drugs."

"But . . . you sell drugs." Hard as he tried, Zeke couldn't make sense of this.

"For legitimate reasons. If people choose to use, they should be part of the solution." He leaned forward, his eyes alight with a chilling fervor. "All of the large, anonymous donations that help keep the center running are from my drug profits. The users who wreak havoc on our society are helping fund my efforts to bring order to our neighborhoods, banish drugs. That's only fitting."

The convoluted logic boggled Zeke's mind.

But telling that to Wilson could shut down the conversation.

"What about all the money you took to fund your retirement in a cushy tropical setting?"

The man's features hardened. "After what they did to my wife and son, the users owed me. But"—he lifted his hands, palms up—"I'm not a greedy man. The operation was never about getting rich, and my retirement was going to be comfortable, not cushy. The business was created to offer a second chance—to me, and to those who'd repented. It was about atonement and restitution. The logic is clear."

Only to a twisted mind.

"What about the people who got hurt? Who died? Like Stephanie Laurent and her boyfriend?"

A spasm of pain contorted Wilson's features. "I never wanted anyone innocent to get hurt. That wasn't part of my plan."

"But they did."

"Yes."

"Did you kill Stephanie?"

"No."

"You know who did, though."

"Yes."

"Did you order the kill?"

"No—but Razor recognized the risk when the girl and her boyfriend stumbled onto a pickup and he . . . he did what he had to do."

So the man sitting in the interview room down the hall was the killer after all.

"What happened to the two of them?"

"I don't know. I never asked him."

But the DEA—or the County PD—would ask that question . . . and many more.

Zeke stood. "We're done for tonight. In the morning—"

"Wait." Wilson looked up at him, anxiety tightening his features. "There's something else. I left two students from

Ivy Hill in a cistern last night. Someone has to get them out. I was going to alert the authorities before I got on the plane."

At least part of the man's conscience was in working order.

"That won't be necessary." Zeke twisted toward the video camera and motioned.

Wilson's forehead puckered. "You don't understand. I only left enough supplies for one girl for a few hours. If they stay there too long, they—"

The lock on the door clicked, and a moment later Cate walked in.

"Meet St. Louis County detective Cate Reilly." Zeke moved beside her.

The man did a double take. "Neither of you were who you pretended to be?" He sighed and shook his head. "So much subterfuge in the world."

That was rich, coming from him—but he seemed unaware of the irony.

"In case you're wondering, Kayla is fine." Cate listed slightly, as if she was having difficulty remaining upright, and Zeke absorbed her weight.

"I'm glad to hear that. She's a fine young woman with tremendous potential. Would you tell her I'm sorry—about everything?"

Instead of responding, Zeke opened the door, guided Cate out—and wrapped her in his arms in the deserted hallway. "I'm taking you home."

"Please."

He helped her to a chair in an empty office, finished his business as fast as he could, and had her in his car and barreling west on I-64 within fifteen minutes.

"There are still so many unanswered questions." She leaned against the headrest, her profile shadowed as he pushed the speed limit to the max to get her back to her apartment ASAP. "Like—how did Wilson make his Mexican connections?"

"We'll get to all those questions—but in terms of connections, think about this. Given his work with addicts, some of whom were probably dealers as well, it wouldn't have been difficult for him to gather information about local leadership . . . and cartel contacts. Based on the cover that kept him off law enforcement's radar, the cartel would have been happy to shift power to him over time."

"I guess that fits—even if I'm having difficulty understanding his rationale for getting involved in the whole sordid enterprise."

"Join the club."

She yawned. "Do you mind if I . . . if I let myself drift off?" Her words slurred.

"Not at all."

Two minutes later, he glanced over.

Her eyes were closed, her breathing even.

She was already asleep.

So he'd see her home, tuck her into bed, spend the night on her couch—and first thing tomorrow, resolve another question that hadn't yet been answered.

Namely, where the two of them went from here.

30

A S HER PERSONAL CELL began to vibrate on the nightstand beside her, Cate groaned, groped for it— and forced her eyelids open.

It took her a few seconds to focus on the name on the screen.

Sarge.

She put it to her ear and slowly eased her legs over the side of the bed, wincing as her ribs protested. "Morning."

Or . . . was it?

Hard to tell with her room-darkening shades.

She squinted at her watch.

Nine-twelve.

It was either morning, or she'd slept almost sixteen hours.

Judging by her bleary vision and utter fatigue, it was morning—and she'd had a mere four hours of shut-eye.

"Did I wake you?"

"Uh . . . yeah."

"Sorry. I know you had a long night. How are you?"

"I'll be fine after I log five or six more hours of sleep."

"Take a few days off too. That's an order. I also called to let you know we have Noah Evans in custody, along with all his electronics."

"Okay." She sniffed. Was that coffee?

"I'll let you get back to sleep. Take it easy. And good work."

"Thanks. But I'm done with undercover. We agreed on that, remember?"

"You have my word."

They said their goodbyes, and she inhaled again.

Definitely coffee.

An aroma too hard to resist.

Phone in hand, she stood and examined her attire. Since she had no recollection of changing her clothes last night after arriving home, it wasn't surprising she was still wearing her leggings and the sweater she'd donned for her excursion with Kayla.

A shower and fresh duds jumped to the top of her priority list.

After coffee.

But who was brewing java in her kitchen?

She shoved back her hair and padded in her stockinged feet down the short hall.

Zeke was sitting at her table, mug in one hand, cell pressed to his ear.

The instant he saw her he cut the call short, set his coffee down, and erased the distance between them in three long strides. "Why are you up?"

"The office called."

He blew out a breath. "Couldn't they have waited a few hours?"

"Sarge wanted to let me know they picked up Evans. Why did you come back?"

"I didn't."

"Huh?" Fatigue must be numbing her brain.

"I never left."

"You mean . . . you stayed all night?"

"What was left of it. I racked out on your couch."

"It's a love seat, not a couch. Much too short for you."

"I made do. We have a lot to talk about, and I didn't want to waste a minute commuting back here after you woke up—which I expected to be hours from now. This can wait if you want to grab a few more z's."

The intensity in his eyes suggested otherwise—and much as she needed more sleep, knowing that he was waiting nearby wouldn't be conducive to slumber. Better to talk first—after she had a huge infusion of caffeine.

"Any coffee left?" She peeked past him.

"I finished the first pot an hour ago, before I ran out to get us breakfast." He motioned toward a carton of eggs and a box of bagels on the counter. "I just brewed a fresh one."

"You must be wired."

"Not from caffeine."

Electricity arced between them.

"Um . . . let me get a cup and—"

The cell in her hand began to vibrate again, and she skimmed the screen.

"Do you have to take that?"

"I think I should. It's Eve. I'm guessing she heard about last night's excitement at the radio station while she did her drive-time program and suspects I may be in the thick of it."

"Why would she jump to that conclusion?"

"She saw us together at the hotel, I told her we ran into each other because of our jobs, you're with the DEA—and Eve's analytical skills are formidable."

"I'll keep that in mind for future reference. Go ahead and take the call while I pour your coffee."

She put the phone to her ear. "Hi, Eve. I—"

"Thank heaven you answered! I've been worried sick! The station's buzzing about the Ivy Hill drug bust, and after finding you and your DEA buddy together at the hotel, I had a feeling you were in the middle of it. I tried to get the scoop from my inside source, but Brent's tied up with a homicide and unavailable. *Are* you involved?"

"I *was*—past tense. My undercover gigs are officially over. In fact, I've earned myself a few days off." Zeke handed her a mug, and she mouthed a thank-you.

Instead of moving away, however, he moved *in*. Close enough to let his lips graze her temple and send her pulse into overdrive.

"Why? You never take days off. Did you get hurt again?"

She tuned in to Eve's question. "No. I'm fine." Better than fine.

"You want me to come over? I could swing by Nathaniel Reid Bakery and get us two of those fabulous breakfast sandwiches—and maybe an almond croissant to split."

"That's, uh, tempting." She cleared her throat and resisted the urge to fan herself as Zeke invaded her personal space in the most delicious way. "But can I have a raincheck?"

"Why? You never keep much food at your place under normal circumstances, and you haven't lived there for a month. Your cupboard has to be bare."

"Not quite."

"How is that possible?"

"Um . . ." Hard as she tried to fabricate a story, her mind wasn't cooperating, thanks to the trail of fire Zeke's mouth was branding across her forehead.

"Wait." Another pause, and Cate could almost hear the gears grinding in Eve's brain. "Is Zeke there?"

Cate glanced at him. "Uh—"

He leaned closer and spoke into the phone. "Yes, he is."

A chuckle came over the line. "In that case, I'm happy to issue a raincheck. But you should call Grace. She—" The ding-dong of the doorbell echoed through the apartment. "Uh-oh. Too late. I was going to warn you she's been texting me like crazy since I told her about the Ivy Hill bust. She's in town for a meeting, and I bet she decided to swing by and see if you happened to be home."

"Thanks for the warning." Cate started toward the door, leaving Zeke to follow close on her heels.

"You want my advice? Let Zeke answer the door. She'll disappear faster than she does whenever I mention working on a DIY project."

"I'll consider that."

"Call me with details soon. On the case too."

"Ha-ha."

Cate continued toward the door as Eve chuckled and ended the call. "I think this is Grace. Eve said she's been frantic too."

"You want me to answer it? That should put a damper on a long cross-examination."

"No, I'll handle it. She'll want to see me."

Cate verified the identity of her visitor through the peep-hole and opened the door. As she pulled it back, Zeke drew close and rested his hand on her shoulder in a proprietary gesture impossible to miss.

Grace opened her mouth to speak . . . saw Zeke . . . snapped it closed.

"Morning." Amusement tickled his deep baritone greeting.

"Uh . . . good morning." Grace looked at Cate. "I've, uh, been texting with Eve since dawn. She thought you might be in trouble."

"I was . . . but all's well now."

"Yeah . . . I can see that." Grinning, Grace took a step back. "Why don't you give me a call when you have a free minute?"

"I'll do that. I appreciate you stopping by. If you talk to Eve, will you reassure her I'm in one piece?"

"Oh, I'll definitely reassure her. You guys enjoy your day."

"That's the plan." Zeke ran his hand down Cate's arm.

Grace beat a hasty retreat.

"Sorry about that." Cate closed the door.

"Don't apologize. Having people who care about you is a blessing." He moved beside her, draped his arm around her shoulders, and led her into the living room. "Let's sit on the aptly named love seat."

She faltered. "I need a shower first."

"It can wait. I can't. My patience is gone." He urged her forward. "I'll scramble eggs while you clean up if you give me ten minutes first. I'll toast your bagel too."

"What a deal."

"Is that a yes?"

"It is."

She let him guide her to the love seat, trying to regulate her erratic pulse—but it was hard not to be nervous when you were preparing to leap off a cliff.

This time around, though, every instinct in her body told her Zeke would be waiting to catch her.

He sat and tugged her down with him.

She angled his direction, giving him her full attention.

For some reason, her rapt concentration seemed to discombobulate him.

He shifted his position. Ran a hand over the bad-boy stubble on his chin. Swallowed.

Interesting.

For a man who'd conducted two critical interviews with absolute calm and total control mere hours ago, he appeared to be very nervous.

For whatever reason, his discomfiture helped calm her.

"So . . ." He took her hand and lightly stroked a finger over a purpling bruise. "It's Thursday, and the cases are winding down. Which means we can concentrate on us at long last. I know you have concerns about my staying power . . . and I realize I have to prove myself all over again to you . . . but I hope you'll give me—"

"Take the job in St. Louis, Zeke."

His face went blank. "What?"

"Take the job."

Several seconds passed as he absorbed the implications of her comment.

"You mean . . ." As his surprise dissipated and his brain kicked in, a slow smile chased away the tension in his features. "You mean you're willing to give us another go?"

"Yes. Hard as I tried to convince myself otherwise, I never got over you. I also never expected us to have a second chance. But I'm not going to pass up what feels like a God-sent opportunity."

He touched her cheek, his fingertips quivering against her skin, and his eyes began to shimmer. "I can't begin to tell you how grateful—and happy—I am."

"You could show me instead."

"With pleasure."

He cupped her cheek with one hand and slowly . . . oh, so slowly . . . lowered his lips to hers.

The kiss lasted a minute . . . an hour . . . a day. Hard to say. Time stopped as Zeke demonstrated how much he loved and cherished her.

All she knew in terms of duration was that it was over too soon.

As he at last backed off, she had to clutch his arm to steady herself. "Wow. That was . . . it was even more spectacular than I remembered."

"I'll second that—and it was well worth waiting for. As the rest will be well worth waiting for if and when the time is right."

He was telling her he wouldn't push for a repeat of the night she'd ignored her conscience and let herself be swept away. That he respected—and agreed with—the moral principles she'd always followed until she'd unwisely let her passions override them.

"Thank you for that."

"If that kiss is any indication, though, I think we're going to have to agree to keep each other in check going forward." One side of his mouth rose.

"I'll do my part—even if I don't want to."

"And I'll do mine." He fingered the lock of red hair she couldn't wait to restore to normal. "Do you think you'll be up for dinner tonight?"

"If I sleep most of the afternoon."

"I don't see why you can't. I may catch up on shut-eye too after I run back to the office for a couple of hours. If we go, dress up. I plan to launch this courtship in style."

"Where are you taking me—Tony's?" Like that would happen. A meal at St. Louis's legendary fine dining establishment would put too big a dent in a detective's—or DEA agent's—budget.

"You got it."

She stared at him. "Are you kidding? That'll cost a week's pay."

"Not quite—but even if it did, it would be a small price to pay for the memories we'll make."

"Count me in."

"Why don't I get those eggs going while you shower?" He stood and held out his hand. "I'm starving."

She placed her fingers in his, and he drew her to her feet—but he didn't let go as she turned toward the hall.

Angling back, she raised her eyebrows. "I thought you were hungry?"

"I am—but I want an appetizer first." He leaned close to claim another kiss.

She didn't protest.

And as the world once more faded away . . . as Cate melted into his embrace . . . she gave thanks.

For despite all the close calls they'd had . . . despite almost losing each other forever . . . God had granted them tomorrow.

And if they chose, they could spend it together.

Cate laid her hands against the familiar broad chest where she'd found such comfort—and love—in the past. Felt the steady, rapid beat of Zeke's heart beneath her fingertips.

A heart he was offering to her.

She wouldn't make a rash or hasty decision this go-round. She was older now, and wiser. Also more cautious.

But if she were a betting woman, she'd wager far more money than Zeke was going to leave on the table at Tony's tonight that by next summer or fall, *together* would be the perfect description for all their tomorrows.

EPILOGUE

'D SAY THIS IS THE PICTURE of wedded bliss." Cate held out her cell to show him the photo Eve had texted her.

Zeke obliged by leaning closer . . . but looking at someone else's honeymoon photos couldn't hold his interest after daydreams about going on his own honeymoon had been dominating his thoughts for days.

Assuming the lady said yes when he popped the question, of course.

The very next item on his agenda.

He examined the photo of Eve and Brent, who were sitting on the ground, their backs against a weathered stone wall, heads tipped toward each other for the selfie, the remnants of a picnic strewn around them. "Wedded bliss sums it up."

"I'd venture to say they're loving Tuscany." Cate scanned the message, then set her phone aside.

"Romantic honeymoon destination."

"I suppose—although I'd be happy camping right here."
She swept a hand around the scene spread before them from
their own picnic spot in Cuivre River State Park, quiet on this
warm midweek May day. "The location is less important than
the companion."

"I agree . . . but a honeymoon does seem worthy of a memo-
rable destination."

"That was Eve and Brent's take too. I must admit, after
drooling over all the photos she's sent, Italy fits the bill." She
leaned back on her palms, lifting her face to the blue sky. "It
was a beautiful wedding, wasn't it?"

"Very."

"Eve made a gorgeous bride."

"True—but the maid of honor stole the show."

Cate flashed him a smile. "You're prejudiced."

"Guilty as charged."

As her lips drooped, he mentally kicked himself. Bad term
to use. It would only remind her of the news she'd received
yesterday.

Her next comment confirmed that his word choice had been
poor.

"That makes me think about our Ivy Hill cases—and all the
sad outcomes." She ran her fingers across the tender spring
grass beside her. "I'm glad Stephanie's body was found,
though. It provides closure, if not comfort, for her family. I
hope her boyfriend turns up eventually too."

"Whether the river gives him up or not, we know what
happened—and we have more than adequate evidence to put
Jones away for life."

"Wilson too." She shook her head. "I can't believe he's still
convinced his drug dealings were justified. It's obvious something warped inside him after he lost the two people he loved
most."

"People can also be masters at deluding themselves."

"I know. Like Noah Evans insisting he was helping the girls he supplied with marijuana. As if." She snorted. "At least he wasn't selling it to them—and he *was* little league compared to Wilson. But the fact he was beginning to source his drugs on the dark web to avoid the risk of in-person deals could have led him deeper into that shady world if he hadn't been caught. As it is, he earned himself a police record and derailed his career."

Zeke plucked another grape from the bunch the gourmet food shop had included in the lunch he'd ordered. "Ivy Hill took a huge hit in the press from all the nefarious activities taking place on the premises."

"True . . . but people have short memories—and nothing that happened was the school's fault."

"Plus, all the players are getting their due . . . including Will Fischer."

"Yeah." She took a grape too and popped it in her mouth. "I'm sorry he got caught up in this, but it goes to show how addictions can tempt otherwise good people to veer off the straight and narrow." She shooed away a fly. "On the positive side, Eduardo and his wife had a happy ending."

The perfect segue.

It was time to get this conversation back on a pleasant— and more personal—track.

"I agree." He took her hand and examined her fingers. "Pretty nails."

"Thanks. A rare indulgence. I got the manicure for the wedding and took Kayla along." The breeze ruffled some stray wisps of hair that had escaped from her ponytail, and she brushed them back. "I'm glad she's doing well. I was afraid being disillusioned by Wilson would have a long-term negative impact. But it didn't affect her academics—and I have no doubt she'll get the full ride to Cornell she's aiming for. With her smarts and drive, she'll make a terrific engineer."

"I think it's great how you two have bonded. And speaking of bonding . . ." He angled a bit more her direction. He was done being sidetracked. "These past almost-five months have been the best of my life—thanks to you."

Her features softened, and the corners of her mouth bowed up. "Are you going to get mushy on me?"

"I think a man is entitled to a little mush when he's about to ask a woman to marry him, don't you?"

Her breath hitched—and his stomach clenched. He'd promised not to rush her, to let her set the pace . . . and he thought he had. In light of all the signals she'd been giving him, she'd seemed ready for this.

But perhaps he'd misread the cues.

Better backtrack.

Calling up a grin, he lightened his tone. "Unless his timing is off—in which case he'll can the mush, dive into the chocolate dessert waiting in the basket, and curb his impatience until the lady gives him a more definitive green light down the road. What say you, fair maiden?"

Before she could respond, a Frisbee skidded across the grass and came to rest against the picnic basket.

"Sorry about that." A teen bounded over. "My dog was supposed to catch it, but the wind took it off course and he got distracted by a squirrel." He motioned toward a black lab.

"No worries." Cate snagged the neon orange disc, rose, and handed it back.

The young man jogged away, but Cate remained standing.

Uh-oh.

Zeke braced.

Maybe this day wasn't going to end as he'd hoped after all.

Cate filled her lungs. Exhaled. But hard as she tried to put the brakes on her galloping pulse, it refused to be corralled.

Zeke was going to ask her to marry him!

Sooner than she'd expected, yes—but what difference would another few weeks make, other than to delay the inevitable?

Because she'd known since January that the two of them were going to end up together.

Prudence and caution had dictated the pace of their courtship, but she was as anxious as he was for the main act to begin.

And now that her mind was adjusting to the idea of an accelerated proposal, she was liking the idea more and more.

She pivoted back to Zeke and dropped down beside him.

He looked worried, despite his lighthearted comment moments ago.

She'd have to fix that. Pronto.

"Anxious as I am to sample that dessert you brought, I think we should save it for after."

"After what?" Hope flared in his eyes.

"After your speech. You do have a speech prepared, don't you?" She gave him a teasing elbow nudge. "A fair maiden deserves no less."

He exhaled. "You know you about gave me a heart attack, right?"

"Why don't I give you my heart instead?" She softened her tone and ran a finger along the strong line of his jaw.

He caught her hand in his. "Stop that or I'll be too distracted to get through my speech."

"So you *did* prepare one."

"Long ago." He withdrew his wallet from the pocket of his jeans, lifted a flap behind the bills, and pulled a crumpled sheet of paper from the hidden compartment.

She leaned closer. "What's that?"

"The proposal script I wrote eight years ago."

Wow.

Here was hard proof that he had, indeed, been planning to ask her to marry him the weekend after she'd somehow lost her moral compass in the euphoria of love—as he'd told her in January.

"I've been carrying it around with me ever since."

Double wow.

"Would you like to hear it?"

Not trusting her voice, she nodded.

He didn't unfold the worn, frayed-around-the-edges sheet that had yellowed through the years.

Instead, he set it between them, took both her hands, and spoke from memory.

"For most of my life, I didn't think I deserved to be loved—especially by someone like you. But over these past months—now years—I've come to realize that whether I deserve it or not, I want to spend the rest of my life with you. You've been the greatest blessing I've ever received, and your love has given me hope. It's made me believe that with you by my side, my tomorrows can be better than my yesterdays."

He paused. Swallowed. "I'm not the prince you deserve, but you'll never find anyone who loves you more. And I guarantee that every day, for as long as I live, you'll come first in my thoughts—and in my heart. I love you, Cate Reilly. I always have, and I always will. Would you do me the honor of being my wife?"

Her vision misted, and despite her aversion to mush she felt as if she'd dissolved into a pile of sticky-sweet syrup.

She sniffed and tried to regain control of her emotions. "Is there . . . is there a ring to go with your speech?"

He released one of her hands, pulled a small box out of another pocket, and flipped open the top to reveal a large, emerald-cut diamond in a platinum setting flanked by two smaller emerald-cut diamonds.

His hands were shaky as he held it out for her to see.

Her heart melted.

"The ring is new. Eight years ago, I was going to have you pick the ring out yourself after I proposed, but I was passing a jewelry store a few weeks ago and saw this in the window. The strong, bold, confident design reminded me of you—but if you don't like it, we can exchange it for one you prefer."

In answer, she simply lifted the fourth finger of her left hand.

"Is that a yes?" He worked the ring free of the box, never breaking eye contact.

"Yes." Her answer came out in a whisper, but it was the best she could do.

He slipped the ring on.

It was a perfect fit.

As he was a perfect fit for her.

He leaned toward her—but in her peripheral vision she caught sight of a familiar orange disc whizzing close by.

Too close.

Zeke changed direction and snatched it as it skimmed the side of her head.

Seconds later, sixty pounds of black fur leaped up and grabbed it from his hand.

In the melee, Cate dived for the precious piece of paper lying between them.

"I'm so sorry again." The teen ran over, contrition written all over his face. "Flo's hard to control while she's in hot pursuit."

"I know the feeling." Zeke waggled his eyebrows at her behind the kid's back.

"But we're out of here. I'm taking her down to the beach for the rest of this game. Come on, Flo."

The dog bounded after him, mouth clamped around the Frisbee.

"Talk about bad timing." Zeke sent the duo a disgruntled scowl.

A chuckle bubbled up inside Cate. "A sure cure for mush, though."

"I kind of like mush." Zeke settled back down on the blanket. "Where were we?"

"I was salvaging this." She held up the tattered, time-worn script.

"Are you keeping it?"

"Forever."

"I thought you weren't the mushy type?"

"This isn't mush. It's love."

"Is there a difference?"

"Oh yeah." She tucked the sheet into the pocket of her shirt and rested her hands on his broad shoulders. "Now that the canine crew has left . . ."

He scooted closer to her, until their crossed legs were knee-to-knee, and draped his arms around her neck. "Are you ready to indulge your sweet tooth?"

"Are you thinking of that chocolate dessert?"

"No. Something much sweeter."

"Show me."

"My pleasure. But one question first. How long are you going to make me wait to tie the knot?"

"Depends on how big of a wedding you want."

"Can we elope?"

She gave a soft laugh. "My sisters would never forgive me. But I don't need anything elaborate. A simple ceremony, an elegant dinner with close family and friends . . . does that work for you?"

"How long would it take to put together?"

"Two months?"

"Sold. And you know what? That would be the perfect time for a honeymoon in Provence. The lavender fields will be in bloom—and the balmy temperatures should appeal to your warm-weather gene. Unless you prefer to come here."

"Now that you've dangled Provence in front of me, this pales by comparison."

"Shall I begin planning our honeymoon?"

"By all means—after we finish one important piece of business." She tugged him close. "The engagement isn't official without the kiss."

"Then let's take care of that formality immediately."

"Is the coast clear?"

He gave the area a sweep. "Yep."

"I'm all yours, Zeke Sloan."

"I like the sound of that."

And without further ado, he sealed the deal with a kiss that sent her heart soaring—and offered a tantalizing taste of all the sweetness to come in their years as man and wife.

Loved this book from Irene
Hannon? Read on for a sneak
peek of the next installment in
the HOPE HARBOR SERIES,

Sea Glass Cottage

COMING SPRING 2022

ASKING FOR HELP from a man who hated you was hard.

Really hard.

But she was out of options.

Jack Colby was her last resort.

Despite the cool Oregon breeze tripping along Dockside Drive, a bead of sweat trickled down Christi Reece's temple as Jack completed his purchase at the stand on the wharf. Prying one white-knuckled hand off the steering wheel, she inhaled a lungful of the briny Hope Harbor air and swiped away the external evidence of her nervousness. Thankfully she alone was privy to the pretzel twist in her stomach and the erratic lurch of her heart.

A savory aroma wafted toward her from the white truck that had been Jack's destination on this sunny end-of-April afternoon, setting off a rumble in her stomach. But eating was low priority—even if her last meal hours ago had consisted of a stale bagel and gas station coffee.

The man she'd driven thirty-plus hours to see lingered to exchange a few words with the cook, who adjusted the baseball cap over his long gray ponytail as the two shared a laugh.

Still smiling, Jack picked up the brown bag containing his order and strolled her direction.

Unless time had softened his heart, however, he wouldn't be smiling for long.

Pulse pounding, Christi fumbled with the handle on the older-model Nissan that had carried her more than two thousand miles. Pushed the door open. Swung her shaky legs to the pavement, praying they wouldn't fold.

Jack gave her a casual glance as she slid from behind the wheel and stood. The kind you bestowed on a stranger who happened to catch your momentary attention.

No hint of recognition flickered in his eyes.

A twinge of disappointment nipped at her—but that was foolish. Eleven years had passed. Her once-long hair had been cropped to shoulder length, and she didn't lighten the dark blond hue anymore. Oversized sunglasses hid most of her face. And life had taken a toll. The frothy twenty-year-old college coed he'd known—and loved—was long gone.

Jack's pace slowed, as if he'd realized there was more to this encounter than chance.

Her cue to move forward.

Squeezing her fingers into tight fists, she approached him. Unlike her, he'd benefited from the passage of time. The handsome twenty-three-year-old who'd brightened that carefree summer had filled out. Matured. Acquired an intriguing aura of worldliness that enhanced the considerable appeal she'd once found difficult to resist.

Christi stopped a few feet away and tried to fill her uncooperative lungs. "Hello, Jack." The greeting came out a bit husky, thanks to the tail end of the cold she'd been fighting for the past week.

His smile evaporated, and twin crevices creased his brow. "I'm sorry . . . have we met?"

Still no glimmer of recognition.

"It's been a while." She drew a shaky breath and removed her sunglasses. "Christi Reece."

———————

As the name of the woman who'd once stolen his heart—then trampled on it—reverberated in the quiet, peaceful air of the town he now called home, Jack's lungs locked.

Christi Reece, here?

Impossible.

Yet as he scrutinized her, reality smacked him in the face. Her hair was shorter and not as blond . . . and a decade of living had snuffed some of the youthful glow from her complexion, added a smudge of shadow beneath her lush lower lashes. But the brilliant cornflower blue of her eyes remained undimmed, and those full lips that had caressed his with eager abandon looked as soft as ever despite a slight droop at the corners.

It was her, even if her voice was deeper than he remembered.

His stomach bottomed out, and he swallowed past the sudden bitter taste in his mouth.

Why, after all these years, had she invaded his turf? Tainted the new life he'd created far from his Midwest roots? Resurrected the memories he'd banished of the day his world had crumbled?

He gritted his teeth, his appetite vanishing despite the savory aroma of Charley's tacos wafting up from the bag clenched in his fingers.

"What are you doing here?" The question came out harsher and more resentful than he intended . . . but so be it. The sentiment was spot-on.

She tucked a lank strand of hair behind one ear. "I came to see you. To t-talk to you."

He frowned at the subtle stammer. Christi Reece, nervous?

Major disconnect.

With her wealth and privileged upbringing, she'd always possessed an overabundance of confidence and composure. What was going on?

But curiosity wasn't sufficient motive to extend this conversation or probe for particulars.

"I have nothing to say to you." He pulled out his shades, slid them on, and prepared to make a fast exit.

As if sensing his intent, she took a step closer, palms extended in a placating gesture. "Look, I know I hurt you. I know what I did was wrong. Worse than wrong. It was unconscionable. Not a day has gone by that I haven't regretted my behavior. If I could fix the damage, I would."

He steeled himself against the trace of tears in her voice. "What happened between us is ancient history. If you came here for closure, consider it done." He turned on his heel and walked away.

"Wait! Please!"

Please?

He faltered midstride.

That word hadn't been in her vocabulary eleven years ago. Christi Reece had known how to cajole and sweet-talk her way into getting whatever she wanted, but she'd never resorted to pleading.

Keep walking, Colby. You know she's a master manipulator. Don't be fooled again.

He resumed his retreat.

"Jack . . . please. I need help, and I-I don't have anywhere else to t-turn."

He hesitated again—and bit back a term that would have shocked his mother.

How could this woman who'd used him and hurt him still have the power to get under his skin?

But he'd always been a sucker for people in trouble—especially desperate ones.

And Christi sounded desperate.

Bracing, he slowly angled back.

Big mistake.

She'd followed him, stopping touching distance away. A brimming tear was poised to spill down her cheek.

A knot formed in his gut, and he took a quick step back. Didn't help.

Seeing this once-poised, self-assured woman reduced to tears activated a potent—and unwanted—protective instinct.

"What kind of help?" He shifted into the intimidating, wide-legged stance that served him well as a cop, shoring up his resolve to keep his distance.

"I need money. A loan. I'll pay it back as fast as I can. With interest."

Silence fell between them as he tried to process her request. Failed. Why would a woman from her wealthy background need money?

"You'll have to explain that to me."

"I just did. I need money."

"Why don't you ask your father?"

Her throat worked. "He died six years ago."

Hard as he tried to quash it, a brief surge of sympathy swept over him. Losing her father would have been tough. Hard-nosed and snooty as the man had been, he'd doted on Christi. They'd been as tight as father and daughter could be. As she'd told him during that golden summer, it had been the two of them against the world after her mother died when she was ten.

Good as David Reece's intentions may have been, however, giving his daughter everything she wanted had been a mistake. All he'd done was create a spoiled little rich girl—and a spoiled *big* rich girl.

Water under the bridge now. What was done was done.

But in light of her father's generosity to his only offspring, why was she having money problems? As his sole heir, she should have inherited his estate.

"Are you telling me your father didn't leave you well-fixed?"

She moistened her lips. "His businesses weren't as successful near the end."

He cocked his head. "As I recall, you had a penchant for designer clothes, first-class trips to Europe, and high-end resorts. Did you squander the inheritance?"

A shaft of pain darted through her eyes, and she dropped her gaze. Picked at a piece of lint on her jacket. "No."

"Then why do you need money?"

"Like I said, he didn't leave me as much as you may think."

"But he left you what he had."

"Yes."

"What happened to the money?"

"It's a long story."

And not one she intended to share.

Message received.

He switched gears. "Why come to me—of all people?" He at least deserved an answer to *that* question.

She watched two seagulls flutter down and snuggle up together ten feet away. "Because you cared for me, once."

He wasn't going to fall for the hint of wistfulness in her inflection that suggested she'd harbored feelings for him too, back then. He knew better.

"Like I said, that's ancient history. Over and forgotten." He used his most dismissive tone.

She searched his face, her voice soft . . . but certain . . . as she responded. "If that were true, you wouldn't still be angry with me."

Checkmate.

AUTHOR'S NOTE

WRITING A NOVEL is a massive—and daunting—undertaking. And the process doesn't get easier even after 60+ books. That's why I'm so grateful to all those who share their time, expertise, and experience to help me get the facts and the tone correct.

As has been the case with so many of my suspense books, I relied heavily on FBI veteran and retired police chief Tom Becker, who is always willing to answer my often-complicated law enforcement questions. With his dual background at both the national and local levels, he has been a trusted resource for many years, and I'm deeply grateful for his kind and gracious assistance.

I'd also like to thank Sharri Black, Margarita Flores, and Charles K. Poole for their invaluable insights and suggestions. This book is better because of you.

Heartfelt thanks as well to all those who've supported and encouraged me throughout my career—especially my husband, Tom; my mom and dad, Dorothy and James Hannon; the readers who buy my books; and the talented, professional team at Revell, including Dwight Baker, Kristin Kornoelje, Jennifer Leep, Michele Misiak, and Karen Steele.

Looking ahead, in April 2022 I'll revisit my charming Oregon seaside town of Hope Harbor, where hearts heal . . . and love blooms. You'll find an excerpt from *Sea Glass Cottage* at the end of *Labyrinth of Lies*. And next October, watch for book 3 in the Triple Threat series, when forensic pathologist Grace Reilly enlists the help of a local sheriff after noticing a curious pattern in the autopsies of some elderly residents—and finds herself in the line of fire.

Until next time, be well—and keep reading!

Irene Hannon is the bestselling, award-winning author of more than sixty contemporary romance and romantic suspense novels. She is also a three-time winner of the RITA award—the "Oscar" of romance fiction—from Romance Writers of America and is a member of that organization's elite Hall of Fame.

Her many other awards include National Readers' Choice, Daphne du Maurier, Retailers' Choice, Booksellers' Best, Carol, and Reviewers' Choice from RT *Book Reviews* magazine, which also honored her with a Career Achievement award for her entire body of work. In addition, she is a two-time Christy award finalist.

Millions of her books have been sold worldwide, and her novels have been translated into multiple languages.

Irene, who holds a BA in psychology and an MA in journalism, juggled two careers for many years until she gave up her executive corporate communications position with a Fortune 500 company to write full-time. She is happy to say she has no regrets.

A trained vocalist, Irene has sung the leading role in numerous community musical theater productions and is also a soloist at her church. She and her husband enjoy traveling, long hikes, Saturday mornings at their favorite coffee shop, and spending time with family. They make their home in Missouri.

To learn more about Irene and her books, visit www.irene hannon.com. She posts on Twitter and Instagram, but is most active on Facebook—where she loves to chat with readers.

Hate Mail Was One Thing.
This Was Quite Another...

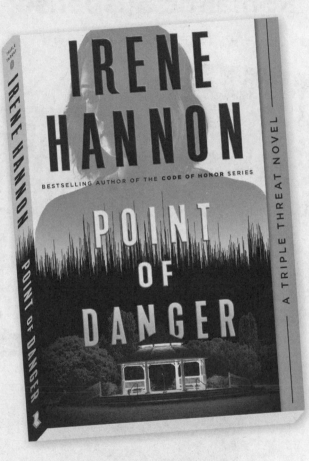

Radio show host Eve Reilly is used to backlash for her on-air commentary. But when angry online posts escalate to menacing harassment, it will be up to Detective Brent Lange to track down a dangerous foe who wants to silence the fearless woman now stealing his heart.

Don't miss Irene Hannon's bestselling
HEROES OF QUANTICO series

"I found someone who writes romantic suspense
better than I do."—Dee Henderson

DANGER LURKS AROUND
EVERY CORNER

Her lifelong dream is in sight,
but does a new–*and better*–future
await in *Hope Harbor*?

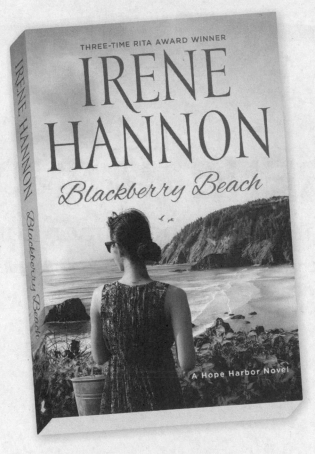

Katherine Parker is on the cusp of achieving the kind of career success
she's always dreamed of. But a visit to Hope Harbor for some much-
needed R&R—and an unexpected partnership with a handsome local
coffee shop owner—may cause her to rethink her ambitions
and open her heart to a new dream.

 Revell
a division of Baker Publishing Group
www.RevellBooks.com

Available wherever books and ebooks are sold.